THE ELIXY OF LIVES

Joseph Orbi

The Lives of Felix V ©2013 by Joseph Orbi
The Lives of Felix V - Rpt. of Peter's Choice (1998)

ISBN: 978-0-9661619-9-1

Printed in the U.S.A.

Red Crest Tower
Crans-sur-Sierre
(213) 533-0774
info@redcresttower.com

*I had most need of blessing, and
'Amen' stuck in my throat.*
— *Macbeth*

THE APPARITION

1

Louie the Fox scurried down the narrow and muddy country road flanked by cow-less pastures, hopscotching to avoid the huge potholes on a stifling hot and wet afternoon when even the toads and the crickets refused to wave hello.

Half-hour after leaving Father O'Malley hitting tennis balls against the wall, the Fox tucked the black duffel bag in his parka to keep it from the pelting rain, wiped his nose with his sleeve and swatted a persistent swarm of mosquitoes that, untroubled by the downpour, had chased after him all the way from church.

An odd and sorry-looking specimen typical of the impoverished back roads of Louisiana, Louie was thin, old, twitchy and poor, though not as old, thin and twitchy as he was poor. He also looked more like a gerbil but was dubbed "the Fox," which implied cunning and vigilance, after getting caught stealing chickens from Bernie's ranch.

Arriving dripping wet at the run-down white trailer that in some ways resembled a one-eyed Moby Dick thanks to an over-sized hailstone that smashed through the glass, ending a puddle in the living room, the Fox kicked open the rusty gate, scrambled across the yard, pushed in the door, and said: "Ray, where the fuck are you?"

"Sunbathing," replied a voice hidden in the corner of the small, bleak and shabby room where the ceiling fan missed a blade, an old blanket covered the sofa bed, three plastic chairs and two shade-less, bulb-less lamps stood for furniture over a pale-green industrial carpet, and a family portrait accompanied Elvis and a velvet Blessed Mary on the walls.

A gas stove and a small fridge in the rear made up the kitchen, while the bathroom had been strategically placed between two small bedrooms with nothing but mattresses on the floor.

Ray looked sick and pale. He wore a pair of soiled dungarees, was barefoot, unshaven, with long oily hair and dark circles framing his bleary eyes.

"You look like shit," observed Louie. He immediately pulled the Walkman, a blender, a juicer and an eight-millimeter movie projector with a spool of film from the bag and spread them out on the floor. "I would've come earlier but Father O'Malley made me sweep and mop the rectory before letting me go. Well, fuck his tennis balls. Now, Ray, my man, pay attention," added the Fox. He plugged the juicer and the projector to the wall to show their workings while he detailed the cost of each item. "I'll let you have it all for ten bucks. What do you say, eh?"

"I say you're a thief," said Ray.

"Yeah, I know that, you know that, even the cops know that—though not well enough, eh?" The Fox made a quick showing of his few teeth. "Hey, buddy, what can I say, I am what I am, we are what we are, you are what you are—but, what's a feller to do? I'm splitting—leaving this fucking town for good and need cash."

Ray grabbed Louie by the neck, pulled him up, and said: "Let us here suppose I had a few bucks. You think I'd spend it on stolen shit? You're an asshole!"

"Easy there Bud!" cried out the Fox, before Ray let go. He put his hand to his chest, and with a look meant to convey sincerity but that ended up as an unvarnished display of fear, cried out: "What the fuck! What's the matter with you? Oh, you're gonna turn against me, I know you are, I see it in your eyes! After everything I've done for you, I mean—!"

"You're a fucking fruitcake, Louie, you're brain dead."

The Fox reached into his parka and pulled out a wet, limp cigarette, and said: "This ain't right, that's all I gotta say! It ain't right!"

"Get the fuck out."

"You know what your problem is?" said the Fox. "These walls, your old lady and the kids—hey, man—it's like death! I know, I been there, Ray."

Ray stared at Louie and for a thousandth of a second felt sorry for him. In that thousandth of a second Ray saw, not Louie looking up, scared, with saliva dribbling from his mouth, but himself. Ray, however, was not Louie. Louie was an oddball who was shunned by everyone. Ray had a family and friends who loved him, so he seized the ranting Fox by the throat, dragged him outside, gave him one last shove, and said: "Don't come back."

"Mother-fucker shit!" yelled the Fox, tripping and falling face-first in the mud. "Didn't you say you wanted a blender to give to the wife? Well? You know what, you're an ungrateful fuck!" Louie picked himself up and stormed out the gate, when he remembered the bag. "Ray!"

The Fox waited in vain.

Surprised, angry, frightened by the unfriendly welcome and unwilling to risk a beating, Louie the Fox decided to return at a later date for his belongings. "Fucking-a, fucking ungrateful shit!" he muttered, hunching his shoulders and beginning the long march to town.

By then, Ray Miltedew was in his rocking chair when he too realized that the Fox had left his spoils behind. He ran outside, and yelled: "Hey, shit-head!" but the Fox was nowhere in sight.

Ray slammed the door and felt an uncontrollable urge to bang his head against the wall, which he did, until blood oozed from his forehead. "Goddamn it!" What if Harriet came home and found the stolen church property on the floor? "First a loser, now a thief?" Ray dropped to his knees. "Why me!" The gods, it seemed, had singled him out. As a husband, father and provider he was a failure. Yes, his kids loved him and so did Harriet, but that made everything much worse. The worthless feeling had turned to shame, and of course shame is only the beginning, followed by resentment that is inevitably layered by intense anger towards those you love most. Unbearable.

Ray gasped and lashed out, kicking everything on the floor, punching the walls and, before too long, turning the inside of his home to rubble. The thunder claps muted his tearful pleas for mercy, cries that saw him stumble, grab an electric cord, wrap it tightly around his neck, pull up a chair, rope the ceiling fan and hang himself. Or try to, anyway.

Human nature being what it is, Mr. Miltedew changed his mind, thrashed out in midair for what seemed a long time, unable to free himself from a cord determined to end his life until the cheap, old fan gave out under his weight and landed on his head with a terrible, painful thud.

Three hours later, after lying in total darkness with a great lump on his head Ray dreamt he heard the voices of his sweet children calling him, imagined his mother-in-law's Corolla pulling up to the house, heard Teddy and Alice cry out: "Bye, Grandma!" and granny ordering them inside: "Don't you get wet, now!"

"Yeah, okay!" cried Teddy.

"Okay!" echoed Alice.

Ray thought his children climbed up the steps as they did every day.

He guessed that Teddy and Alice were tired. That Teddy led his younger sister to the door. That they carried their backpacks and that, although poor, the children were unburdened by a sense of shame because most of their friends lived under similar circumstances. That Teddy opened the door. That he made sure it was safe for Alice to enter. That he turned on the light. That . . .

"Daddy!" This was Teddy.

"Daddy!" This was Alice.

"Why don't you turn on the—?" began Alice when a daz-zling, brilliant kaleidoscopic universe made up of billions of twinkling stars, as lively as if the Creator had just finished setting them against the immensity of eternal black, flashed above their heads, buffeting creation and beating down the bleak and gloom to infinity.

Teddy and Alice Miltedew, of course, stared in wonder when the Blessed Mother, the Virgin Mary, the mother of Jesus Christ, dressed in crimson robes embroidered by celestial nymphs with silver and gold thread, appeared wearing a crown studded with sparkling galaxies, and holding a silver diamond encrusted scepter and an incandescent sphere of emeralds, rubies and sapphires.

"Hallelujah!" screamed Teddy and Alice when a lofty choir of a million angels sang praise to the Son of God. Suddenly, the terror and the confusion of everlasting, all-encompassing love struck the little Miltedews. A veritable river of tears streamed down their cheeks and the children dropped to their knees, crossed themselves over and over, clasped their hands in fervent prayer, looked at each other one last time, lifted their terrified gaze at the blazing Mary, and fainted.

Legacy of Madness

2

In 1941, long before little Teddy and sweet Alice met the Blessed Virgin Mary, Hitler, they said, was not a happy man. A British-backed coup had toppled the pro-German government in Belgrade, forcing the Fuhrer to blitz the Yugoslavian capital and postpone Operation Barbarossa.

While bombs rained down on the hapless state, a black Mercedes-Benz with Red Cross markings on the doors and Vatican diplomatic plates left Banja Luka at dawn, and arrived a few hours later at a massive gate identified by an Ustaša checkerboard flag, and a sign that read: "Work Service of the Ustaša Defense Assembly Camp III."

The journey had posed a challenge for thirty-eight year old Father Krunoslav Draganović. War often alters the topography of the land and does away with guideposts, which made a map a necessity. Yet, he refused to bring one along for fear it would betray his mission if, by chance, he ran into partisans.

Tall and strong-built, with dark brown hair cut fastidiously close, and clear eyes that revealed his determined faith, Draganović, in spite of his cassock, looked more like an athlete than a servant of Christ.

Even before he turned off the engine, two sentries armed with Maricić carbines and wearing military fatigues and wool caps approached from both sides and subjected the driver and his vehicle to a thorough inspection, despite the religious garbs, the Red Crosses and the diplomatic plates.

Moments later, the guards ordered the priest to drive along two electrified fences that encircled a vast complex of barracks east of the Jasenovac plain, on the banks of the river Sava. Under the surveillance of watchtowers manned by heavy machine guns, Draganović stopped in front of a low flat building with a loud-speaker on the roof. He knocked on the door when a loud cheer and boisterous laughter caught his attention. "Filipović?" he said stepping inside.

The room had a cot, three metal chairs, a wood-stove, a bucket in place of a sink and lavatory and two small windows that looked south and provided a clear view of the embankment.

"Father Draganović," said the camp Commandant, turning from the window, "you're early." The friar dressed, not as a Franciscan, but in full Ustaša uniform that included a pistol and a wooden mallet stuck in his belt. Plain-looking and of dark complexion, Brother Miroslav Filipović was of average height, with wide shoulders, a broad square forehead, black eyes, a pencil-thin mustache and slicked combed-back hair.

"What is going on?" asked Draganović, joining Filipović at the window.

Known as Brother Satan, the Commandant pointed to a group of guards outside that had lined up the prisoners in four rows extending two hundred meters at the river's edge; thousands of emaciated men, women and children on their knees, with their hands tied behind their backs. "Oh, it's a bit of fun," he said. "The boys bet who can do more prisoners in a day. Life here is—well it's dull—and the last thing I need is a couple of hundred armed Croat peasants getting bored. Besides, it's good for morale. Nothing but Serbian trash, Jews and Gypsies."

"Charming," remarked Draganović wryly. He noticed that the guards were cutting throats and bludgeoning prisoners to death. "Why not shoot them?"

"Can't do that, no. The rules are quite specific: they must be killed in medieval fashion, with a knife or a hammer," explained Filipović, pointing out a stumpy fellow moving with incredible speed from one prisoner to the next. "His name is Braciko and he's way ahead of the rest. He has a special knife you see, and so far he's done over a thousand three hundred and sixty—what, in a couple of hours? He's tricky, though. He likes children—I guess because their throats are easier on the blade. Still, it's unbelievable, I have never seen anything like it in my life."

"War," sighed Father Draganović.

"It's a strain," joined Filipović. "Talking of strain, you must be exhausted. Would you like some coffee?"

"Coffee? You don't mean that Turkish mud that tastes like—?"

"No, no, Father. It's Puerto Rican coffee. It is delicious."

"It's just that—well, I don't have much time."

"You're always in a hurry," added Filipović. "There they are—the two fellows I told you about. They're keeping score, see? You'll get along, I'm sure. They're hard working and conscientious, exactly what you need," he added, before calling the friars over the PA system that, of course, made them lose count of the bodies falling in the river.

The brothers quickly handed over their notebooks to the guards and made their way to the Commandant.

Brother Silov Petronović joined the order as a boy and was in his early twenties. He was short, stout, with black eyes, red eyebrows and pale skin. His tonsured scalp combined with premature baldness made it difficult to judge whether his lack of hair was due to that unattractive Catholic hairstyle, his unusually excited disposition, or both. Unlike Brother Satan, Silov the friar always dressed in his Franciscan habit but liked to carry a Walther-P38 tucked in his belt.

His colleague, Brother Borna Radonić, was taller, older, thinner and far more restrained. He had thick, black curly hair, green eyes and a small nose. Unlike Petronović, Borna procrastinated about everything and thought that initiative in a human being was a curse.

"Braciko, he's the one to beat," observed Petronović.

"Silov—Borna, this is Father Draganović, from Banja Luka. He's come for you," said Brother Satan.

"Come—for us?" asked Petronović.

Explained Draganović: "We need help with our new laws of conversion; we are overwhelmed."

The friars looked at each other, then at the priest, and smiled. They had been at the camp in Jasenovac for nine months, time full of misgivings and hard work.

"I beg your pardon," said Draganović to Filipović, "what is Puerto Rican coffee?"

"Oh, you're not the only one with connections at the Holy See," smiled Filipović, brewing the coffee. "I get a pound every two months. Don't we, Silov? So you know, Father, the Vatican buys most of the coffee grown in—"

"But—what is Puerto Rican?" insisted Draganović.

Filipović shrugged, and said: "From Puerto Rico? I'm not sure but I think it is an island in the tropics."

Father Draganović could only imagine the worthy tropical paradise that grew the Catholic coffee. Although he would have loved nothing more than having some right then, it occurred to him that the hut had no running water, and the coffee was, in all likelihood, brewed with that taken from the Sava, the same river whose waters ran red. "I do not want coffee."

"It's very good," volunteered Radonić. "Really."

"No coffee? Why? Oh, I see—" said Brother Satan noticing the look of disappointment in the priest. "No need to worry, Father. We have our own well, uncontaminated, fresh water, I assure you."

"But the smell, it's different," added Draganović.

"That's not the coffee," said Borna of the sweet, acrid stench that blew from outside, one that could never be mistaken for anything other than what it was.

Brother Satan darted an apprehensive look at the friars, and replied: "It's the pottery shed. It smells funny, I know, but you get used to it." He failed to mention that the pottery shed served to reduce the population at the camp by burning alive between fifteen and twenty prisoners at a time.

"In that case, I will have coffee after all. Then we really have to be on our way," said Father Draganović.

Brother Satan served the black Puerto Rican brew in tin cups and apologized for not having sugar or any niceties to enjoy with the coffee, but no doubt Draganović would understand.

A louder than usual roar came from the riverbank, and before too long, the survivors of the contest were being dragged back to their barracks. At the same time a group of guards carried their champion on their shoulders. Petar Braciko was a happy man, brandishing his deadly and victorious instrument for all to see.

"I take it you two know how to drive?" said the priest to the friars.

"I do," said Petronović.

"I don't," joined Radonić.

"Filipović, you were right. The coffee, simply delicious. Thank you," said Draganović, before turning to the friars. "Let's go. Oh—take that off."

"Why?" Petronović had gotten used to his Walther.

"Friars are not supposed to carry weapons, now are they?" insisted Draganović, putting down his cup and walking outside.

Brothers Silov shrugged and handed his pistol to Filipović, before he and Borna joined Father Draganović in the car. The priest asked them to sit in the back because both men smelled like raw onions.

"God be with you!" called out Brother Satan, from the door, a cup of Puerto Rican coffee in one hand, while he waved with the other.

Father Draganović expected to arrive in Banja Luka in a few hours, where he would meet Ante Pavelić, the Poglavnik. At least, those were his plans.

To avoid an ambush he turned off the main road at Bosanska Dubica and the detour led him to Mrakovica. He had driven almost two hours up a mountain pass when, at the other end of a particularly difficult turn, a roadblock appeared, forcing Draganović to slam on the brakes and downshift to avoid a collision.

The car had not come to a complete stop when a group of men dragged the occupants outside. A thin and gaunt-looking fellow, sporting a large scar on the side of his forehead walked up to Draganović, and said: "And what do we have here?" The man looked from one face to the other, always ending on Father Draganović. "Missing your flock, Father? And where is your Christ leading you on this lovely day?"

"My name is Father Krunoslav Draganović," said the priest, impassively. "I am the Vatican attaché to the Red Cross in Yugoslavia. These are Brothers Silov and Borna. They are my aides. You will find my papers in order."

"What about them? No papers?" said the partisan.

"They are mendicant friars, my son. They never carry papers."

"I am not your son, priest, and you are a spy."

Draganović observed that had they been spies, they traveled in the most conspicuous disguise of all. The partisan countered that if not spies, the priest and the friars were couriers for the Ustaša. "Find anything?" he asked. By then his men had pulled the seats inside out and slashed the rich interior with their bayonets.

"Too clean," said one fellow holding a piece of leather in his hand.

"I really don't know what you're looking for," ventured Radonić, accentuating each syllable with contempt.

"For a reason to shoot you," returned the partisan leader. "Move it."

The insurgents led Father Draganović and the friars into the woods, emerging an hour later at a once proud summer villa with a few faded tiles still left on the roof, a pockmarked façade, boarded up windows and a lawn that became a graveyard for military hardware rusting in the sun.

The priest vehemently protested, quoting several protocols of the Geneva Convention the partisans had allegedly violated. He also complained about the uncharitable treatment that found three members of the Catholic clergy stripped naked and tied down in a dimly lit barren room splattered with blood.

A much bigger soldier in an olive green uniform, a full beard and a fresh scar on his right cheek, entered and watched his comrades force Silov and Borna to the concrete floor, leaving Draganović standing against the wall.

With a lumbering gait, the man approached Father Draganović, looked him in the eye, and said: "What was your business in Jasenovac?"

Defiantly, and realizing they would be murdered, the priest stared back, and replied: "I am a man of God on a fact-finding—" As God would have it, the soldier did not allow him to continue. Instead, he punched the priest in the face, slammed his head against the wall and crushed his cheekbone. Father Draganović instantly felt the urge to lie down, but a second blow to the groin changed his mind and he bent over spewing black bile.

Radonić screamed, and damned the insurgents to hell with such vehement vitriol that one guard pulled a large knife and ordered him to stand. He refused. That's when, to his horror, he saw his flaccid member stretched forcibly to an impossible length and, to the amusement of the comrades in the room, felt the cold, steel edge of the blade, which brought to mind the rumors of partisans castrating their prisoners, and forcing them to bite off each other's testicles.

That particular piece of business, of course, was no longer a concern for Father Draganović. He had already lost most of his teeth, and his head had become a swollen, oozing blob. With the priest unable to remain on his feet and slowly wandering into the soothing void of near death, his tormentor prodded him with a kick to the ribs, and a shower of piss, behavior that roused the most curious response from those watching the friars, who quickly set themselves upon Brothers Silov and Borna, raping them with their long guns, and forcing them to fellate each other.

And there they were: the Croatian priest on the floor in a pool of blood and piddle, and the Franciscans bleeding and gagging on semen, when another member of the communist resistance walked in. His name was Milan.

"Seen them before?" asked the man relieving himself on Father Draganović.

Milan had gained considerable weight and facial hair since Brothers Borna and Silov saw him last. He pointed at Draganović, and said: "Him, no. Those two, yes!"

Silov and Borna remembered him as well for the young man belonged to a very small number of prisoners ever to escape the death camp at Jasenovac.

"That one," said Milan, pointing at Silov, "he pinned down my little brother while Filipović beat him with a hammer!" If they had not told Milan that the trio was condemned to hang, he would have killed them on the spot. "Please," he begged, "let me have them! Please!" And just as he reached for his knife, his chest exploded, as a thousand rounds pierced the walls and two mortar shells blew the side of the building, killing everyone standing in the room.

Minutes later, the Ustaša patrol appeared. "Looks like we got them all," observed an officer, turning over the bodies.

"Help! In the name of God, help us!" screamed Brother Borna, crawling out from under his tormentors.

3

Holding a dainty cup in his hand, Ante Pavelić walked from the serving table by the windows to the ostentatious blue-satin upholstered sofa at the far end of the office of the President of the Independent Nation of Croatia, where Abbot Josip Ramiro Marcone nibbled on Viennese pastries. Pavelić was an average looking middle-aged man with a long face, short black hair, a wide nose, floppy ears and lips that almost never cracked a smile.

Dressed in a black shirt, khakis and polished boots, he complemented the fascist look with a shiny holster that housed the nickel-plated Walther PP-K General Edmund Blaise-Horstenau gave him for his birthday. "Well, I am pleased that the Holy Father approves our policy of conversion," he said.

The lumpy old monk, who wore a Benedictine cassock, brought a napkin to his lips, sipped one last taste of tea, and asked: "Is it true you are meeting with the Führer?"

"Yes, I am," answered Pavelić with the required gravitas.

Marcone smiled, had a little trouble getting out of the sofa, nodded to the President and was led out by the Ustaša escort without finding out if the newly established leader of Croatia was more loyal to Hitler and Mussolini, who put him in power, or to his Church, the source of his inspiration. Pius XII, however, liked the Poglavnik, as Pavelić was known, considered the Croat leader an admirable Catholic and appreciated his passionate defense of the faith in a Central Europe threatened by Orthodox Christianity and Bolshevism.

Pavelić returned to his desk and spent a few minutes pondering how to further the interests of the new state. He glanced at a secret communiqué from Minister Artuković that showed a number and nothing else: 425,534. It could have meant almost anything: the young nation's deficit, the money spent bribing foreign dignitaries, the cost of a new bridge, the number of guns bought from Italy, or the loan received from the Holy See. Few would have guessed that 425,534 represented Croatia's success eliminating its ethnic minorities.

The Poglavnik sighed and looked at his watch, picked up his calendar, flipped the page and clicked the intercom. "Where is Draganović?"

"N-not here, Excellency," replied a timid voice at the other end.

"I can see that. Where is he?" asked the President. "Well?" Pause. "Get in here!"

Nikola, the Poglavnik's personal assistant struggled with the enormous doors, stepped inside, stood in ballet position number one for a second, then walked the full twenty meters and stood gasping for air, across the desk from the Poglavnik.

Where Adolf Hitler chose his adjutants among a cadre of distinguished officers, Nikola was a thin, nervous little man with tired, teary eyes and the stench of stale nicotine.

"I'll ask you again. Where is Draganović?" said Pavelić.

"He went to Jasenovac," answered Nikola.

"Speak up, man!"

"He left early this morning for Jasenovac!"

"Wasn't he supposed to be back by now?" asked the Poglavnik. Nikola shrugged.

"You're useless. Let me know the moment he gets back. Open the windows and take those with you," ordered Pavelić pointing to the tea tray and left over pastries. "Go! You're stinking up the place."

Nikola bowed, carried out the orders and quietly went away.

Pavelić pushed back his chair, stood up straight and proud,

placed both hands on the desk and admired his newly inaugurated office designed to emulate, in style if not quite in size, what Albert Speer did for the Reich Chancellery, with marble walls, deep window reveals, hard-edged moldings and inlaid ceilings.

He then stepped by the window and looked out on the tree-lined avenue and the ornate park across the street, when the door to his personal quarters opened and his wife and children entered.

"Papa!" called out Katarina, running to her father.

Pavelić got down on one knee and received her with open arms.

The little girl wore a green dress adorned with white lace and satin, white silk stockings and a pair of shiny black shoes with blue and gold velvet buckles. She was a beautiful child with long light brown hair and brown eyes.

"She wanted to show you her new dress," said Marija, prompting her daughter to model for her father. Madame Pavelić was as tall as her husband, elegant, with dark brown hair neatly coifed, dark brown eyes and a face that, if not beautiful, was pleasant enough.

"Are you sure you're not a princess?" said the Poglavnik kissing his daughter and beaming with delight.

"I am. I am!" answered Kati with a giggle when her father got off the floor to greet his nine-year-old son, Damir.

Dressed in a navy-blue sailor suit with short trousers, black long stockings and matching high-top shoes, Didi, as his sister called him, was a quiet boy who preferred to speak Italian, the language learned living in Italy. He was slender and tall for his age, had blond hair, big hazel eyes and a meditative, inquisitive nature.

After shaking hands, Ante picked him up and dispensed as many kisses and hugs on his son as he did to his daughter.

"Papa," said Damir, "why can't we go to the park?"

"We talked about this already, didn't we?" said the Poglavnik, placing his son on the desk and kissing the boy on the forehead.

"Didi," he added, "I am President of the country. Many people admire me but some don't, and they would rather I went away. They will also do anything to hurt me and those I love the most, and that's your mama, your sister and you."

"That's not fair. We haven't done anything!" cried Didi.

Pavelić understood that it was hard on his children to keep to their apartments and the indoor courtyard of the Ministry, and that they could only befriend children whose parents were trustworthy members of the government. It was an unnatural arrangement, particularly for Damir, and Ante hoped someday to make it up to the boy. "I'll tell you what, do you want to go to the country with me?" said his father.

"Yes!"

Twenty minutes later, Dr. Ante Pavelić and his son Damir, escorted by a fleet of Ustaša troop carriers the size of a small army, sped out of Banja Luka on the way to Glina, a Serbian village nestled halfway between the capital and Zagreb, running over anything or anyone that dared venture in its path, including seven chickens, a dog, two cats and almost seven-year-old Amela.

The little girl had decided to cross the road when the armed convoy appeared out of nowhere. Had it not been for her older sister risking her own life running after Amela, and dragging her to safety, the lead truck would have struck the child and kept on going.

Kneeling in the back seat of the car, Damir looked out the rear window and caught a quick glance of the sisters holding each other, trembling in a cloud of dirt and soot left behind by the motorcade.

A short distance away, Archbishop Aloysius Stepinac, Member of Parliament of the Independent Nation of Croatia and Vicar to the Army of the Ustaša, entered Glina at the head of a procession that included four priests and a hundred Croatian soldiers as loudspeakers on military trucks called the Serbian folks to step forward and convert. Of course, for the villagers it was alarming to see Croatian troops march into their Serbian town, and more so when the archbishop ordered the construction of an altar on the steps of the Christian Orthodox church, where he planned to hold mass employing the symbol of the Ustaša government: a cross formed by a gun, a dagger and a grenade.

A thin and unremarkable looking man with a taut face, an inflexible gaze and a bald crown, Stepinac's powerful voice and outstretched hands urged the mostly old, feeble and very young villagers to partake of a Eucharist improvised from Serbian peasant bread and wine.

While administering the sacred rite to a toothless grandmother expecting the Host to drop in her mouth, the archbishop pronounced a sincere: "In nomine Patris, et Filii, et Spiritus Sancti, amen!", set an example for the former Orthodox Christians before him by crossing himself in the Catholic direction, threw his gaze beyond the crowd, and from a distance, caught an indiscreet ray of light that had bounced off one of the Poglavnik's medals.

The presidential motorcade had arrived at the outskirts of town and Pavelić and his son, surrounded by bodyguards, ventured on foot to witness the conversions, as the archbishop leaped from the platform, left his assistants to fend for themselves, shoved, pushed and dug his way through the crowd of peasants, and surfaced next to—

"Dr. Pavelić, Dr. Pavelić! This is an honor! What brings you here?"

"I could not stay away, I wanted to see this, had to see it for myself," replied the Poglavnik. "It's amazing."

"We are only doing our duty, Your Grace," said the archbishop, when his eyes drifted from the President of Croatia to the child at his side.

"Excellency, this is my son, Damir," said Pavelić.

"Hello young man," said Stepinac, smiling and putting out his hand.

In return, Didi presented his customary curious frown and was ready to kiss the prelate's ring when His Excellency pulled back the hand, tenderly patted Didi on the side of the face and made the mistake of looking the boy in the eye.

The experience disoriented the archbishop who felt he was being judged. His Excellency immediately refocused on the child's father, seized the President by the arm, led him to inspect the many people who, up until a few minutes before, had been loyal Orthodox Christians, and said: "Glina is smaller than your average town, but we've been places where we converted twenty thousand in one afternoon."

Conversion. Didi did not understand what it meant, but he sensed that it was a good thing because his father seemed pleased.

"And what do we have here?" asked Pavelić when a group of soldiers appeared with a shepherd and his son in custody.

"We were not hiding," pleaded the shepherd, who explained that he had gone to look after his animals.

His son was about the same age as Damir, but that's where the comparison ended. Didi was possibly the most privileged child in the country. The other dressed in rags, his head was shaved, he trembled from fear, was hungry, filthy and barefoot. He also held a svirala, something that caught Damir's attention.

"Papa," said Didi, tugging at his father, "what is that in his hand? A toy? Can I play with him?"

"That's a flute, son. And no, you can't play with him," answered Pavelić, before turning to the shepherd boy. "What is your name?"

Confused, the child expected his father to tell him what to do, but the terrified man had been forced to his knees and was unable to say much. His son, then, fixed his eyes on Damir, who thought he looked as scared as the girl he had seen earlier by the side of the road.

"Hello? Look at me. Did you hear what I said?" asked the Poglavnik when the boy hesitated. "What is your name?"

"A-le-xander," softly stammered the child at last.

"Alexander?" continued Pavelić. "Your name is Alexander?"

The boy nodded without daring to look up at his interrogator.

"I bet they call you Saša, eh? Is that what your papa calls you? Of course he does, of course he does." The Poglavnik exchanged smiles with Stepinac before he asked the frightened child to cross himself. "Do you know how to make the sign of the cross? Come, boy, cross yourself," directed the Poglavnik.

Saša sighed, then slowly began the ritual learned as a toddler from his grandmother. First, he tapped his forehead and was going to touch his right shoulder when Pavelić pulled out his gun and shot him in the head.

Only those nearby realized what had happened because the report from the small-caliber PP-K went mostly unnoticed. The svirala, of course, fell to the ground and rolled a little ways while the old shepherd threw himself on his dead son and quietly cradled the body, not daring to look up at the man who murdered his son.

Conscientious of his duty, Archbishop Stepinac immediately administered the last rites although he felt it was for naught because the young shepherd had not been converted to the true faith before he was killed and was, therefore, destined for hell.

As Pavelić holstered his pistol, Didi, well, he stepped away from his father.

"Stupid peasant," muttered Pavelić, quickly making his way back to the car, leaving Stepinac and the soldiers to tie up the loose ends. "Damir?" he called when his son did not follow. "What's the matter? Why are you crying? Give me your hand," said the Poglavnik, while in the background, a soldier stabbed the old shepherd in the eye, and another crushed the dead boy's skull with his boot.

Damir refused his father's hand.

"Get in the car," said the Poglavnik.

Damir did as told, but sat huddled in the corner, away from his father.

"Look, those people are the enemy." Pavelić pointed to the village. "I dare say, if they were in power, if they ruled the army, they would have us murdered. They are not Catholics like us, that's why the archbishop came all the way here, to convert them. Only when we are rid of the Orthodox, the Jews and those filthy Gypsies, only then will we be proud of our Croatia, then, and only then can we have a nation pure and strong. Do you understand what I'm saying? The Holy Father has given his personal blessing. He urged me to bring the true religion of Christ to these people. It has to be done," continued the Poglavnik.

Didi shut his eyes, frightened because he suddenly realized that he was sitting across a stranger. That fellow was not the father who read to him at night before the fireplace; who played with Didi and his sister on the floor, tickled them silly and made them laugh. He was certainly not the one who told him bedtime stories and he was definitely not the papa who walked into his room in the mornings to help him get dressed. That man whom Didi now recalled with such longing, that man who used to reassure his young son with loving words and hugs, that man existed no more. In one clear summer afternoon, a Serbian peasant lost his son and Damir lost his father.

"You're just a child. Some day you will understand and be proud of what I did here, today."

Yes, Damir was a child, but his father's prophecy remained forever unfulfilled.

4

As quickly as it arrived, the Poglavnik's motorcade bolted
from the pastoral setting of the Serbian village on the
way back to Banja Luka when, fifteen minutes from Glina, the
troop-carrier in the lead barely missed crashing into a car that
had broken down in the middle of the road.

The President's personal bodyguards immediately took up
defensive positions to protect the Poglavnik and his son from a
possible ambush while a group of soldiers rushed the offending
vehicle. They were ready to shoot its passengers but discovered
that the three men inside were already half dead, with one of
them lying unconscious in the back seat, his face a bloated mass
of bloody black and blue.

Pavelić waited until the soldiers had secured the area, then
left Damir in the car and, pistol in hand, went to investigate for
himself. "Who are they?" he asked a lieutenant.

"I don't know, Excellency. They are in bad shape. That one
doesn't have much left," replied the officer, pointing to Father
Draganović.

Pavelić stepped back, saw the red cross on the passenger side
door, and said: "Get him out of there. Let me see his face! Father
Draganović?"

"Yes, yes, it's Draganović! Draganović!" screamed Brother
Borna.

"Get some water! Help them! Now!" ordered the Poglavnik,
as the friars described their ordeal at the hands of the partisans.
"It's an outrage!" complained Pavelić, not because of what had

31

happened to the priest and his companions, but because it meant the insurgents were operating close to Banja Luka. "Get my son," he ordered one of the bodyguards.

The child quickly appeared behind a wall of dark, armed men. "You know that man," said Pavelić to Damir. "That is Father Draganović. He has been at the house many times, remember? Look what those animals did to him! Look what they did to a priest, Damir, to a man of Christ. Look!"

Damir stared absent-mindedly from Draganović to the friars, feeling sorry for them, while his father arranged for their immediate transfer to the hospital in Banja Luka.

With the wounded clergy provided for, Pavelić ordered a return to Glina. This time his Ustaša soldiers made their way into the center of town, where they found Stepinac and his entourage moving out.

The news about Father Draganović appalled the archbishop, but the Poglavnik was not going to accept the treatment of the priest as an unfortunate, unavoidable consequence of war. Those who mocked the authority of the Catholic state by assaulting the clergy would pay with their lives.

He ordered his troops to seize the more than two hundred and sixty old men, women and children unlucky enough to have answered the call to convert, and lead every single one at gunpoint to the Orthodox church.

"Run, run! Get away!" screamed Damir from his window, before he dropped to the floor, shut his eyes tight and covered his ears, sobbing uncontrollably because there was nothing he could do to stop the screaming outside.

His conduct did not amuse his father, who had returned to the car in the company of Archbishop Stepinac. The Poglavnik could not understand how a simple outing to the country had mushroomed into an irritating imbroglio.

Inside the Orthodox church, the good people of Glina were thinking more or less the same thing, for in the choking madness of the moment, a sturdy old peasant woman who never ceased to look on the bright side of things, stood in the center aisle, underneath an enormous chandelier hanging from the dark, vaulted ceiling, and decided that Catholic rituals were very odd. First, you convert and swear loyalty to the pope, then your sins are cleansed in your own blood.

As a hundred saints and an Orthodox Christ and Mary watched from their gold perch above the mass of screaming women, children and old men, elite Ustaša troops stormed in and, employing only knives and mallets, slowly and meticulously slaughtered the new Catholics in the small town of Glina.

The car had barely stopped at the Ministry when Damir jumped out, dashed past the security men, ran up the stairs, flung open the door to his mother's room and threw himself in her arms.

"What is the matter? Why are you crying?" asked Marija.

"That boy is an embarrassment," yelled Ante from across the hall, pointing at his son. "In front of the archbishop, no less! I am ashamed of him!"

The outburst shocked his wife. She could not remember the last time her husband raised his voice at her.

"Acting like a whimpering buffoon? I will not tolerate it!" concluded the Poglavnik, with arms akimbo, his head thrown back and his jaw thrust forward like a regular Croatian Duce, before disappearing into the secret halls of the Ministry.

"Didi, what happened? Tell me, my darling," urged his mother, stroking back his hair. "What is that in your hand?"

"Saša. Saša—" repeated Didi over and over, never letting go of the shepherd's flute.

Next morning Damir did not leave his bed and refused to eat anything all day. The same thing happened next day, and the one after that until his mother became so concerned that she summoned a team of doctors from Switzerland who prescribed a number of remedies that proved unsuccessful.

With Saša's flute under his pillow, Damir spent the days drifting in and out of consciousness and ate just enough to stay alive. The child, who was not stout to begin with, became emaciated to the point that Dr. Hansmann, a psychologist from Bern, advised Marija to prepare herself for the worst. In his opinion, Damir suffered from depression and was willing himself to die.

Angry and frightened for her son, Marija refused to accept the medical opinion, threw the doctor out, then burst in on her husband and demanded to know why Damir had come home so troubled after venturing to the countryside with his father.

Weighing each word, Ante described how, on their way to meet Archbishop Stepinac, Damir witnessed the Ustaša executing several insurgents in Glina.

Marija stared at him in disbelief. "Why did you allow it?" she screamed. "He's a little boy!"

"We're at war!" the Poglavnik shot back, indignant. "Let me tell you what happened to Father Draganović—!"

"I don't care about anything but Didi! Don't you realize your son is dying!" she yelled before storming out.

Of course he did. And he was as concerned as she was, even though the boy refused to have anything to do with him and would turn away the moment he walked in the bedroom; indifference that confounded and hurt his feelings. Still, Ante spent hours at his son's bedside; like the time when rain rattled the windowpanes and the warm breeze from the garden flirted with the feather-like curtains, the Poglavnik buried his face in his hands and pleaded with his Lord Jesus, even begged forgiveness for his misdeeds in case they caused the divine wrath now bearing down on Didi.

Late that same evening, after everyone in the family had gone to bed, Damir heard someone calling his name.

"Damir!"

It sounded like the voice of a child.

"Damir! Damir!"

It took a few minutes for Didi to push aside the seemingly impenetrable mist of his subconscious and opened his eyes. The fireplace was still lively but a strange and exquisite fragrance now filled the room.

"Damir!"

He slowly turned and lay on his back.

"Damir!"

Thinking perhaps that there was someone hiding under his bed, Didi leaned over the side but only saw his slippers.

"Damir! Damir!"

Feeling weak and lightheaded, he summoned his strength, cast aside the plump goose feather comforter and silk sheets, left his bed and propped himself on the windowsill . . .

"Damir!"

. . . when a gust blew open the French windows and he saw stars like sparklers dancing against the black sky on New Year's Eve.

"Damir!"

Below, a magnificent blaze of colors and a collection of flowers the likes of which he could not believe: thousands upon thousands of cowslips, marigolds, red and yellow and white roses, assorted colored tulips, daisies and forget-me-nots, each brighter and taller than the next, all blooming spectacularly that late autumn night with hundreds of yellow birds and blue butterflies chasing each other about the garden as if it were spring.

"Damir, Damir, Damir, come play! Come play, Damir, come play!"

"You woke me up!" said the boy to the flowers. "And you know I can't go out. I'm not well. Besides, it's the middle of the night!"

"Damir, Damir, Damir, come play! Come play, Damir, come play!"

"I can't, I really can't," said Damir.

That's when he saw a boy standing in the middle of the garden, dressed in a shiny holiday suit with white, long sleeves, a woolen shirt, an embroidered vest with beautiful intricate patterns of silver and gold silk, a fine pair of sturdy woolen pants held in place by the traditional colorful sash, and for shoes, a brand-new pair of yellow opanci.

"Damir," called out Saša, "you have my flute!"

"Your—" startled, Didi lost his balance and fell backwards.

"Damir!" insisted Saša, "I want my flute!"

"Yes, of course!" said Damir getting to his feet and helping Saša climb in through the window. "I—I was just keeping it for you."

"Wow! Look at this place!" exclaimed the shepherd boy. "You must be rich!"

Damir quickly pulled the svirala from under his pillow, gave it to Saša, and said: "I thought you were dead." He noticed that the young shepherd had bright brown eyes and an abundance of curly light hair that fell just above his brow.

"You won't let me die," answered Saša, smiling and sticking the flute in his vest pocket. He then picked up a kite and a ball, followed by climbing on the rocking horse before throwing himself on the bed. "This is—heaven!"

"Is it?" asked Damir, surprised. "Does that mean—are you saying I'm dead?"

"What?" said Saša, jumping from bed. "Oh no!" He laughed. "No, no. I'm saying this room is fantastic, you have every toy I ever heard of. My goodness!"

"So I'm not in heaven?"

"Well, you're as close to heaven on earth as you'll get, is what I'm saying." Saša tossed Didi a big blue ball supposed to represent planet earth. "Catch!," then picked up a picture book, lay down on the bed and two minutes later, was fast asleep.

Marija returned to look in on Damir at six in the morning and was alarmed when she found the windows wide open and toys scattered throughout the floor. Because she thought Damir did not have the strength to leave his bed, let alone to make a mess of his room, she stepped out in the hall and called the servants. "Who did this? Who!?"

"Mama, shhh! You're making too much noise!" said Didi from his bed. "You'll wake him up!"

Marija dismissed the maids that had hurried upstairs, and went to Damir. "What is the matter, darling?"

"Shhh!"

"What's wrong?"

"Shhh!"

"What—what is it?" asked Marija.

"Saša! He stayed up all night looking at pictures. He's very tired," Damir nodded to his right, where Saša slept with his face under the picture book.

"Saša?" again from his mother.

Damir nodded and smiled.

Marija remembered that Dr. Hansmann had predicted hallucinations before the inevitable end. "Oh, my poor, poor child!" she said, trying to take the boy in her arms.

"Mama, please stop!" Damir left his bed and with unusual vitality for someone so ill, led her to the door. "Do you think I can have breakfast? I'm very hungry and I'm sure if he ever gets out of bed—" Damir meant Saša. He grinned, shrugged and gave his mother a look as if to say: "I can't ask him to leave, now, can I?"

Marija remained outside her son's bedroom for a moment before she regained her composure. It seemed Damir had acquired an imaginary friend called Saša. She thought she had heard the name before but could not remember when or where.

"Ham, eggs, toast, strawberries and a big glass of milk!" said Damir popping his head out the door and giving his mother a start. "Make that ham, eggs, toast, strawberries and milk for two. Can we send for goats' cheese? Isn't that what they eat in the country? I mean, I don't know—" he added, before going back in his room and closing the door.

When Katarina heard her brother was hungry, she threw modesty aside, barged in his room without so much as knocking on the door and found him sitting on the bed, half dressed and tying his shoes. "Didi!" she yelled, "you're not sick anymore!"

"Don't make so much noise!" returned Damir. "Can't you see he's resting? Now, really!"

"What—what do you mean?" asked Kati.

"Saša. You'll wake him up," answered Damir.

At that moment, the shepherd tossed aside the picture book, opened his eyes, yawned and stretched out.

"I sent for breakfast. Ham, eggs—"

"Oh, I love ham and eggs," interjected Kati.

"I'm talking to Saša. Saša, this is my sister, Katarina."

Saša waved and said: "Hello."

"He—he said hello," said Damir to his sister, after a pause.

"He did?"

Damir suddenly realized that perhaps no one else could see his friend. "Can she see you?" he asked Saša.

"I hope so," answered the shepherd boy, jumping out of bed.

"Why is he making faces at me?" asked Kati.

"Showing off," answered her brother, relieved.

Marija, the cook and the maid were halfway upstairs with Damir's breakfast when they heard the children laughing.

"Mama!" cried out Katarina, when her mother walked in the room. Marija found her children playing marbles on the floor, "Damir is not going to die, he's not going to die!"

"Of course he's not," joined Saša. "He has to play with me!"

Kati and Damir giggled, confounding their mother.

Marija took Kati by the hand and led her outside. "You need to dress for breakfast. Come."

"Hurry," called Didi. "We're hungry!"

It was a miracle, but Marija was still fearful because it was possible Damir could relapse. That morning, however, he was hungry!

The arrival of the imaginary Serbian boy in the Pavelić household unsettled the servants for a number of reasons. They objected in particular to his ethnicity but, more to the point, at the extra responsibility of caring for three children, one of them invisible. Everyone decided, however, to humor Damir's fascination, that is, except his father, who assumed the boy had lost his mind.

Almost a month to the day after Saša first appeared under Damir's window, the shepherd boy sat quietly in a corner of the room. "What's the matter?" asked Didi. "Are you all right? Are you sick?"

"No, I'm sad," answered Saša.

"Why? What's wrong?" asked his friend.

"I have to leave. I don't want to, but I must."

"Leave?" asked Damir, concerned. "W-why? Why are you leaving? What happened?"

"It's just how it is. I won't be here when you wake up."

"Please—"

"And you cannot come with me, Didi. You have to stay and take care of your mama and your sister," said Saša.

Damir looked out his window and saw the beautiful colorful garden that every night joined the boys in song and play, had turned gray and cold and the moon became dull and terribly sad.

"Are—are—" It was almost impossible for Damir to get out the words. "Are you going to heaven? Are you?"

"I don't know," said Saša. "And here—" he added, giving his friend the svirala. "Keep it for me, will you."

"Does that—does that mean you're coming back?"

Saša nodded.

"When? Where?" asked Damir.

"Oh, I don't know. One of these days, I guess," answered Saša with a shrug, while outside, the flowers began to sing: "*Saša, Saša, Saša, come to play!*"

5

The Führer stood on the arriving platform rubbing his hands and talking to no one in particular. "He's late. Isn't he? Of course, he is. I don't understand why he's coming here. I don't like the man. Have you noticed he never smiles?"

Reich Marshall Göring offered his own assessment of the Poglavnik as the locomotive with the Croatian delegation sounded its whistle on its approach to Berchtesgaden: "Glum, that's what he is, simply glum."

"Serbs and Croats, they are the same to me," added Hitler, which made his Foreign Minister smile. Von Ribbentrop knew that the Führer, as the ditty went, "had a little list," and the Croats were at the very top.

Inside the waiting room of the station the German swastika and the Croatian checkerboard were displayed side by side behind a long table catered with assorted drinks, coffee, tea and fruit tarts.

An enormous clock that, to the chagrin of the Station Master, always ran late, overlooked the spacious lounge, with rows of tall windows allowing the bright Bavarian sun to shine on the proceedings.

"Mr. President, wonderful to see you—again," declared Herr Hitler, greeting Ante Pavelić with a quick snap of his right arm.

Eager to ingratiate himself with the Führer, the Poglavnik followed suit raising his arm a little too high while photographers recorded the meeting between the German leader and the President of the newly established Independent Nation of Croatia.

Inside the station the smiles turned to frowns, nods and delicately worded phrases indicating mutual understanding, if not agreement.

"My dear Dr. Pavelić," said Hitler, leaning forward in his chair, "I think your government should establish a fifty-year policy of national intolerance, as we did."

The Poglavnik avoided the tray of strudel placed before him, and said: "But we have. What's more, you will be hard-pressed to find a Jew anywhere in Croatia."

Hitler looked from von Ribbentrop to Göring, then back at Pavelić, and added: "Well done! But, I must warn you, Jews are like cockroaches. They hide in the most unusual places, adapt to the harshest environments and disguise themselves as something they are not. Isn't it true, Reich Marshall?"

Göring, who had trouble keeping his eyes open, quickly nodded, and said: "Indeed, yes. Jews—they're natural actors."

Hitler found the Reich Marshall's observation amusing and waited to see if Pavelić thought the same.

He was not disappointed. The Poglavnik broke into a laugh and observed that although his nation had accomplished many things in a short time, they had to remain vigilant for Slavs and Jews.

The Foreign Minister clapped, Hitler grinned, but Marshall Göring yawned, and countered: "I beg your pardon, Mr. President. I was under the impression that Croats share the identical ethnic—complexities of Slavs. Am I mistaken?"

It should be noted that Pavelić did not flinch. He looked directly at Göring, sipped his tea, then replied: "Yes, I'm afraid you are. Croats are descendants of the Ostrogoths, who as you know, have been traced to a distinct third century German tribe known as the Greuthungi. Around the fifth century the Ostrogoths reluctantly joined Attila the Hun. In 455 the Goths left the Huns and settled on Roman soil, in what is today Croatia. Later, in 485, a struggle developed between the Eastern Empire and the Goths, each trying to secure the Balkans for themselves, with the difference that we—I mean the Goths—fought for Rome and that's why we are Roman Catholics. I must say, there are many Serbs that are not Slavs but are descendants of the Goths. Unfortunately, they converted to the Eastern Church, but their blood remains Gothic in every way."

"That is most illuminating, Dr. Pavelić, quite extraordinary," joined Hitler. "Live and learn, I say, live and learn. So tell me, how else can we help your country?"

"We need guaranteed autonomy—full independence," replied the emboldened Poglavnik. "Mussolini, you see, threatened to take back Dalmatia because Germany and Croatia established commercial ties, which I feel is in our national interest. It would be unfortunate if il Duce did something rash."

The Führer nodded, pushed back his chair, thanked those at the table then walked outside with Pavelić to meet the German press. "Don't worry about Mussolini," he said almost under his breath. "He shouts, bangs the table with his fist, but will not do anything. I promise."

A moment later, with Pavelić ready to board his train, Hitler turned to an open microphone, and announced: "It is with joy and satisfaction that Germany embraces the new state of Croatia and its people after they so valiantly helped the Axis powers demolish the artificial nation of Yugoslavia."

For his part, the Poglavnik, feeling quite satisfied with the outcome of his meeting with Hitler, graciously presented the Führer with a flag from the Seven Years' War and a chess set that once belonged to Frederick the Great. In less than two hours the Croatian leader had put the overbearing Reich Marshall in his place, but more to the point, he had obtained a commitment from Hitler himself that Italy would respect Croatia's sovereignty.

Unfortunately, no one bothered telling Mussolini, who, notwithstanding Pavelić's exalted sense of confidence, sent two divisions to occupy Dalmatia, then called for the dissolution of the Independent Nation of Croatia, convinced its government was infiltrated by German agents.

As a result, Pavelić and the Ustaša split, his cabinet was forced to resigned and before anyone knew what happened, the partisans took over much of Croatia, and the great Poglavnik was compelled to, once more, direct his political affairs from exile.

6

Father Draganović spent four months in the care of the Sisters of Providence under the exacting supervision of Archbishop Stepinac. Two surgeons flown in from Budapest rearranged his jaw and shattered nose in a surgery so painful that it compared with the beating he suffered at the hands of the partisans. Nevertheless, the day the communists launched their first attack on Banja Luka, the archbishop helped the priest to a wheelchair, placed him carefully in the back seat of a gray Citroën and sent him to his family's farm in the mountains above Travnik.

Friars Silov and Borna did not fare as well. They spent less than two days in a hospital, armed themselves, and became couriers for the Ustaša for a time, a risky undertaking that, if caught by the partisans, would have gotten them shot on the spot.

The war in Europe ended shortly after. Destitute, the pair roamed the countryside in search of a monastery that would take them in, joining hundreds of thousands of despairing and displaced emaciated men, women and children on the road ... Serbs, Croats and Muslims ... who lost everything in the war, and now marched to the peculiar syncopation of Tito's drumbeat.

Unfortunately for the friars, troops from the new Federal People's Republic of Yugoslavia now occupied most monasteries and convents, and every soldier was their mortal enemy.

Hungry, despondent and feeling as miserable as anyone without food for days had a right to feel, Silov suggested the one place undoubtedly still under the control of their brethren.

"Toranjmost," said he. "I was there once and I know I can find my way back."

"Are you crazy?" said Borna, alarmed.

The monastery of Toranjmost was not far from Komar in the heart of Bosnia-Herzegovina. It was a four-level, four-teenth-century impossibility set atop an extremely inhospitable, exceedingly high and unduly jagged ridge that was always blanketed with a dark, ominous mist.

Cut off from the rest of the world by a dense forest of hidden crevasses and thickets of poisonous thorns, the charming mountain spot was accessible only by crawling on your belly across a decayed wooden plank with a flimsy rope railing above a vertiginous five-hundred meter drop, while turbulent winds were certain to knock off the side any brave soul that challenged the twenty-five-meter crossing.

Now, if traveling to Toranjmost during the day was ill-advised, getting there at night was suicidal; precisely what Silov and Borna set out to do, not in order to challenge fate, of course, but because hunger impaired their thinking.

Shortly after sundown, a fearful Borna grabbed Silov's frock and together plunged into the thick, dank forest, beginning an exhausting and perilous climb in total darkness while swarms of mosquitos, leeches, voracious ants, ticks and every other imaginable creepy-crawly feasted on them.

Finally, after three and a half hours of the most tortuous and frightening hike of their lives, the brothers reached the edge of a precipice and found the narrow span that led to the abbey. Struggling against the violent gusts that shot upwards from the abyss, the two immediately lay down on their stomachs on the makeshift bridge and inched their way forward.

As improbable as it seemed, they would have made it across had it not been for two powerful searchlights, barks, snarls and growls followed by machine-gun fire that only missed them because the rulers of the universe intended to enjoy their suffering just a bit longer.

Startled and completely disoriented, Silov and Borna scrambled to their feet, ran hysterically in the opposite direction and no sooner reached the other side, fell in a sinkhole twenty meters deep, escaping death only because the entire population of the monastery, their rotting flesh, dismembered joints, hair, teeth and eyeballs, cushioned their fall.

Terrified, the Franciscan brothers remained gasping for breath in the mass grave for almost one hour, then crawled out, wandered in the dark until daylight, hobbled down the mountain, found a solitary dirt road and stretched out exhausted on their backs under a heavy downpour that, at least, allowed them to scrub the filthy stench and bits of putrefied body parts from their persons.

"This is not fair!" screamed brother Borna, retching bile, his left knee bleeding from a wound that cut deep into the bone.

"Get a hold of yourself," scolded Silov, nursing a head-wound. Yes, they were not the best of times, but if found by the army they would be shot. Sure they were starving, but they had to keep faith and God would look after them.

"God?" sobbed Borna.

"He's testing us," joined Silov.

"Is He now?" yelled Borna. "Fuck God! I hate God! God is nothing more than a cruel joke! We—we have been forsaken!"

"So what do we do about it? We have spent our lives learning scriptures, doing other people's dirty work and have nothing to show for it," said Silov. "Crap, I even lost my sandals in the fall. I'm barefoot. Let's go."

"Where are we going?" asked Borna.

"I don't know—to find something to eat."

Borna raised himself with difficulty. "It hurts."

Silov examined his friend's damaged knee. "You'll be fine. Do try to walk a little faster. I don't want to risk running into anymore reds." And he was off.

Half the morning had already gone by when the brothers ran into a man; a tall, thin Muhammadan driving an empty horse-drawn wagon, with a large black dog sitting attentively at his side.

Borna stayed back but Silov carefully approached the cart as it passed by, and said: "Bless you, brother. Do you—can you spare anything to eat?"

The only answer he got was a show of teeth from the dog and a slow growl that left no doubt what would happen if Silov got any closer.

Two hours later they met three shifty-eyed deserters from one army or another who did not waste time knocking them to the ground and threatening to cut their throats if the brothers did not hand over everything.

Overwhelmed by fear and the midday sun, brothers Borna and Silov passed out and the robbers realized that they would probably die on their own before sundown.

"What—what happened?" asked Silov, regaining consciousness minutes later, then helping his friend do the same. "Borna—come, wake up!"

"Are they gone?" asked Borna, weakly.

"I guess," answered Silov, getting to his feet. "What is that?" He pointed to a dot in the distance that turned into a hunched-over Muslim woman in black, helped by a walking stick marred by deep gashes, and a red and green bag over her shoulder.

"Old woman," called out Silov.

She stopped, turned ever so slowly and in a croaking, powerful voice, yelled back: "Old? And how do you know I am old?"

"You are bent and walk with a stick," returned the friar.

"And you're ugly and smell like dog shit!"

"Leave her be," said Borna to his partner.

"Mother!" Silov called out with contempt.

"I'm not your mother! I spit on your mother!" yelled the woman raising the cover and spitting on the ground.

"And I spit on you, you Muslim whore!" answered Silov. "What do you have there, money, jewels, eh, witch?"

"Swine!" she screamed. "You murdered my children! The wrath of the Prophet will avenge the martyrs!"

"The Prophet is a sheep-fucker, you filthy-tongue, fornicating she-devil!" answered Silov.

The back and forth between the old woman and Silov the friar lasted a couple of minutes, while Borna, too weak to join, sat by quietly, hoping to die.

Suddenly, the woman dropped her stick, clenched her chest, howled and collapsed.

"What happened?" asked Borna, after a pause.

"I—how should I know?" said Silov, staring at the heap of black fluttering robes in the middle of the country road. Moving with the grace of a scavenger rat, he carefully approached the body and looked for anything worth taking, and said: "Borna."

"What?"

"What are we going to do now?" asked Silov.

A baby, not more than six months old, wearing loose diapers and a colorful paisley shawl to protect him from the cold, smiled back at them. Beside the baby, the brothers found bread, cheese and milk.

With tears rolling down their faces, Silov and Borna thanked the heavens and divided the food, not paying much attention to the child, who remained by the dead old woman.

"What are we going to do with her?" asked Borna.

"She's dead, isn't she?" asked Silov. "We can't do a damn thing, even if we wanted to, and I can tell you she can rot in hell."

"Don't you think we should pull her off the road?" again from Borna.

"No!"

Having gained a little strength, Borna walked over and picked up the baby. "It's a boy."

"Good. Put him down. Someone will come along—" began Silov.

"We can't leave him here!" protested Borna. "He'll die for sure."

"So?" said Silov removing the woman's veil. "I told you she was old."

"We have to find his kin," added Borna.

"You are not Saint Christopher! Besides, even if you were that burdened saint you would never bear a Muslim devil on your back!" said an angry Silov.

"I'm not leaving him here, and that's it," replied Borna.

"Fine! We drop him off at the next town. Except that you don't know what town or where, and it will be you who carries him because I—me, Silov Petronović—is going to—to Rome!"

"No money, no jewels—only some food and a sniveling, fiendish Muhammadan whelp!" protested Silov.

"You know what I was thinking?" asked Borna.

"I don't care! Do you hear me, I don't give a damn! As if we didn't have enough to worry about!" Brother Silov walked over to his friend. "Christ is weeping this day, Borna; he can see you carrying that little demon! Look at you, just look at you! How Christ weeps this day! You're a disgrace, a traitor to the faith!" he yelled, then turned, walked backwards and pointed at the baby. "Remember those people are worse than Serbs; at least Serbs believe in Christ who died on the cross!"

7

"He's much maligned," said the pope, with a slight emphasis on much. He held a Chesterfield loosely between his lips and walked two steps in front of Archbishop Giovanni Montini, Pro-Secretary of State for humanitarian affairs and Abbot Marcone, who had left Croatia just days before Ante Pavelić became another fallen star.

Rows of towering Roman cypress and lush ivy hid the tall surrounding walls, providing privacy and shade for the midday stroll around the small pond of granite tiles shaped like water lilies; the centerpiece of the peaceful garden behind Castel Gandolfo, the pope's summer residence overlooking Lake Albano.

Pope Pius XII was a small man in his sixties with a nose that was a bit too wide, lips that were bit too full and a demeanor that was a bit too stern.

He had become pope in 1939, at the outset of Hitler's invasion of Poland, claimed neutrality for the Holy See, but kept the Vatican indirectly involved in the war through an intricate network of emissaries and spies. "Dr. Pavelić was a bastion against Orthodoxy. He did everything we asked for." The pontiff put out the last of his cigarette on a modern standing ashtray placed inconspicuously behind the Madonna of the Water Lilies. "Does he know our plans?"

"No, Holiness. We—we thought the information might be better received if it came from you," said His Excellency Marcone.

"You said he escaped to Austria?" asked the pope, looking at Montini.

The archbishop flipped through his notes. He was a mousy little fellow about forty-five years old, with an olive complexion, a small, plain face with large circles under his brown eyes and a stamina that was legendary. "Dr. Pavelić fled to British-held territory at Maribor at the end of the war and, in a move arranged by Father Draganović, relocated to the Institute of Saint Jerome when the Americans ordered his arrest.

"And his family?" asked the pope.

"Hiding—in Yugoslavia, Holiness. Father Draganović is looking out for them."

"Our brother Draganović is certainly keeping busy," observed Pius XII.

"Unfortunately," added Montini, "the situation with Dr. Pavelić has become difficult. Tito demands his extradition and of course, there are reports of atrocities perpetrated by the Croatian government during the war."

"Stop! Enough about reports," said the pope. "Communist propaganda, that's what I call your reports! First Orthodoxy, now Bolshevism. Where will it end?" Annoyed, Pius XII reached for another Chesterfield and his Zippo. "Reports of death camps in Poland, reports of millions murdered by Stalin; reports of hundreds of thousands slaughtered by Tito! Let's not talk any more about reports and get this man safely out of Europe so he can rebuild his life."

The iron gate creaked and Father Gratale entered the garden, approached the Holy Father, and simply said: "He has arrived."

Neither the pope, the archbishop nor the abbot acknowledged the old priest. They knew who "had arrived," and he arrived in secret.

"Mr. President, wonderful to see you—again," said Pius XII softly, putting out his hand.

Ante Pavelić quickly kissed the pious ring of Pius XII, although the smell of nicotine and the unbecoming yellow stain on the pontiff's ring finger made him queasy.

The exiled leader looked like an international financier and not a deposed tyrant. Dressed in a conservative dark gray suit tailored by the house of Personeni, in Bergamo, he accompanied the pope around the water lilies, while Montini and Marcone trailed a few steps behind.

"My son, you know how grateful we are for your struggle in Croatia, a struggle that even if set back for the time, will continue until communism is dead," expressed the pope after one lap around the pond. "Unfortunately, we have been placed in a most awkward situation. It is outrageous, but the present government of Yugoslavia demands your arrest. The Reds in your country suspect we are helping you in some way, as well we should." The pope stopped for a moment and looked straight at Pavelić. "We will continue to do so, of course, but may I suggest we help you somewhere else?" The Holy Father, Pavelić, the archbishop and the abbot had now completed the second lap.

"Somewhere else?" asked Pavelić, with a frown.

"Argentina," offered the pope.

"Argentina!"

"You will be well received. We have many friends there. Why, Perón himself inquired as to your willingness to—" and Pius XII sighed, "—advise him on matters of state security; on how to combat communism."

The statement from the pope meant one of two things: Either Perón ignored Pavelić's record as a failed dictator, why seek advice from a man who could not keep insurgents out of his own backyard, or the Argentinean ruler was doing the Holy See a favor that sooner or later would have to be repaid.

"President Perón is a very good Catholic," joined Marcone.

"We will get you safely out of Italy and your family out of Yugoslavia. His Excellency has the details," and the pope gestured to Montini. Having finished the third lap around the pond, Pius XII took a rosary from his pocket, gave it to Pavelić and wished him a safe trip to South America.

The Poglavnik offered his obeisance and watched the Holy Father returned inside with Marcone.

"Mr. President, you can't stay in Rome," said Montini. "There's an army of assassins looking for you. Besides, it is not fair to compromise the Holy See."

"What of my family?"

"I have no doubt you will soon be together again." Montini led Pavelić out of the garden to the gleaming black Mercedes-Benz waiting at the front of the building. He stood aside as the chauffeur, a young swarthy Croat called Rostas, opened the back door so Pavelić could join Father Draganović in the back seat.

"Everything all right, Mr. President?" asked Father Draganović.

Pavelić shook his head in disbelief. "Did you know about Argentina?"

Pius XII watched from his second-story window as the car vanished around a corner. "He's much maligned, much maligned," said the pope reaching for another Chesterfield.

8

While the Poglavnik suffered the indignities of an Atlantic storm on his way to the Pampas, Marija and the children were forced to flee their hideout on the outskirts of Zagreb, and head for the mountains above Travnik in the middle of the night. They looked surprisingly well, although they had spent the last four years hiding in cellars and relying on complete strangers for protection. Unfortunately, they had become fair game for government agents, mercenaries and anyone else seeking retribution for the crimes attributed to the short-lived dictatorship of Ante Pavelić.

The trip to Travnik was perilous and so full of unknowns that Nikola, the Poglavnik's former assistant, was ordered not to stop for anything or anyone, and to drive straight through along the uneven, narrow mountain roads made more treacherous by the constant heavy rain.

"Nikola!" yelled Marija, striking the back of the front seat with her shoe when the Citroën skidded on a tight turn, piling the Pavelićs to one side. "Do you have to drive so fast!?"

"Yes!" returned Nikola. His patience had run out about the same time as his cigarettes.

"Mama—"began Katarina.

"Soon, we'll be there soon," said Marija, softly.

"Where is Father?" asked Damir, not out of concern, but because he was curious. They had not seen the Poglavnik in more than six months.

"I don't know," answered his mother.

Another ten minutes went by before Damir continued. "Is he alive?"

Marija looked at her son, and said: "Yes, of course he is."

Damir looked out into the dismal, sopping night as the rain buffeted the speeding car and the dark shadows and silhouettes of the countryside raced by. The boy often found himself thinking of Ante Pavelić, the Poglavnik, the murderer; his father. He wished to wake up one morning and be told that he had been switched at birth, that he was the son of a peasant, a teacher, a scientist, a baker, a musician; anyone but Ante Pavelić.

And there they were: Marija with her eyes closed, praying for a safe journey; Katarina silent fearing that any sound might wake up some horrible monster lurking outside; Damir looking out the window, pondering the many turns their lives had taken since the end of the war, when the car hit something that almost forced it off the road.

"God have mercy!" screamed Marija.

"Mama!" cried Katarina.

Nikola slammed on the brakes and stopped less than a meter from a tree.

"What happened?" yelled a hysterical Marija.

"I don't know! I didn't see anything! It—it must have been a deer!" screamed back the secretary, getting out with a lantern to inspect the damage.

Brother Silov and Brother Borna's mangled, twisted and bloody remains laid scattered a few meters from where the car stopped. By gravitational coincidence Borna landed in an upright, sitting position with legs crossed, his head propped to one side and with his face incongruously distorted, as if to say: "Where in hell did you learn to drive!?"

"Oh crap!" muttered a trembling Nikola under his breath. "I murdered two men!"

The rain had turned into an annoying drizzle and the air was saturated with a dense mist.

"It was an accident," said Damir who, against his mother's pleas, went to see for himself. It never occurred to him that he had seen the same two fellows, in slightly better shape, on another country road, years before. "What was that? Listen—"

"What? Oh, my God! Reds! We'll be shot!"

"Shhh!" Damir thought he heard the faint cry of a baby. "It's Saša!" he quickly added, finding the infant in a wet thicket, under a shawl.

"Who?" blurted the terrified secretary.

"What do you have there?" asked Marija, when Didi returned with the child in his arms.

"A baby!" cried Katarina.

"A what? Oh, God have mercy! Damir, where is his mama? Nikola, my God, don't tell me you ran over his mama! Nikola, where is—"

"There is no mama," interrupted Damir.

"Are you saying that child was by himself? Nikola, what happened? Answer me!"

"There is nothing to do, Mama, they're dead," said Damir, examining the baby for injuries.

"Who's dead?" asked Katarina.

"The men!" yelled Nikola, getting in the car, backing up and stepping on the gas.

"Men! You hit a man—more than one? How many? Keep your eyes on the road, damn you!"

"Stop screaming! You're frightening Saša."

"What? 'Saša!' Don't start that again, Damir! Nikola, go back!"

"It's too dangerous. Besides, there is nothing we can do. They're dead," explained Didi.

"Damir, you simply can't keep that baby!" insisted Marija.

"Saša stays with me."

"That is not Saša!"

"Yes, he is!"

"Nikola, go back—go back at once!" ordered Marija. "We have to find out—"

"There's nothing! They had no papers or anything! I looked!" answered Nikola.

"We have to ask—find out where that baby comes from!" insisted Marija.

"It's Saša. He's back and I will not let anyone take him from me."

"That is not Saša! That baby has a family somewhere, we have to—" screamed Marija, though she could have been talking to the late Brother Borna, for all the good it did.

"He's beautiful." Katarina fed the baby a piece of cheese, then gave him some juice. "He's hungry."

"Oh, dear Lord, he does not look well," said Marija, feeling for the tell-tale signs of fever. "He has a temperature. Any bruises, broken bones? Take off that dirty thing. Here—" Marija covered the baby with a blanket they had brought along.

Thankfully, the baby only showed a light bump on his forehead.

Damir took out the svirala and softly played a folk tune he had learned on his own, a song shepherd boys played when they laid down under the stars.

"He likes you," said Katarina, when the baby put his hand on Didi's face.

"Here," whispered Damir, giving the baby the flute, "or did you think I'd forget?"

The car reached the outskirts of Travnik at one in the morning, coming upon Mount Vlašić from the west.

"Look!" Nikola pointed to the shadowy outline of the town half a kilometer below. At that hour no sign of life was apparent; the citizens of Travnik were resting, getting ready for whatever the next day might bring.

"Drive on, please," said Marija.

Nikola had been told to drive east along the north side of town, crossing a mountain road that cut north to south, and to continue until he came upon a woodcutter's cart blocking the way. "Ah, there it is!" The secretary then turned left and headed up the mountain, taking another half hour before the car could go no further. "And now, are we supposed to—"

Suddenly, from behind a tree about five meters away a powerful light blinded everyone in the car for a moment as a well-armed man in a dark-green rubber cape threw open the door, and pushed Nikola to the side.

"Who are you?" said Marija, firmly.

"You are two hours late," said the man at the wheel, as the car bounced up and down and sideways.

"W-we had a little—a little trouble on the way," said a relieved Nikola.

Ana Draganović had been waiting in the parlor reading her prayer book and toying with her rosary when she heard the car pull up.

Time, that unkind undoer of youth, had treated Ana Draganović with a certain gentleness. Her eyes were large, brown and serious. She was in her late sixties, but except for the white hair, always combed straight back, with a tight knot that held every strand firmly in place, she could have passed for a woman ten years younger. Hard work around the farm had kept Father Draganović's mother strong and fit. "Come, come! Inside, all of you—wait, who's that? No one said anything about a baby. Kruno, what is this baby doing here?"

Father Draganović stood in the middle of the room, drinking coffee. He was in a pair of work pants and a peasant shirt. "Rostas?"

Rostas shrugged and shook his head.

Draganović set down his cup and turned to Marija. "Welcome. I am glad you made it safely."

"Oh, Father, oh, Father!" Marija swooned, forcing the priest to take hold of her while Ana slipped a chair underneath. "We are being hunted like savages!"

Father Draganović looked at Damir, then shifted his eyes to the baby. "Who is that?"

"His name is Aleksandar but he's called Saša," answered the boy.

"Aleksandar?"

"Oh, God, oh, God!" cried the secretary, getting up and down on his tiptoes. "Father, I have sinned!"

"Stop that, please, it's very annoying," said Father Draganović to Nikola.

"Do you have a cigarette, Father?"

"No."

"Oh!" sobbed the secretary, burying his face in his hands.

"Kruno, you didn't tell me about a baby," whispered Ana to her son.

"Don't let it worry you, mother," said the priest, before pressing the family for an explanation.

"We—had an accident," explained Damir, and slowly filled in the blanks.

"What makes you think his name is Aleksandar?"

Damir looked at Father Draganović, and simply said: "It is."

"The poor thing was wrapped in a filthy rag," added Marija.

"Where is it—the rag, I mean?" asked the priest.

"In the car."

"You will tell me about it later, won't you?" said Draganović to Damir.

The boy did not answer. He turned his attention to Saša and left the priest assume what he liked.

"Father, where's my husband?"

Father Draganović sat next to Marija and took her hand.

"How is he?"

Father Draganović would not say.

"When was the last time you saw my husband?"

Father Draganović could not say.

"Is he still in the country?"

Father Draganović did not say. In fact, he did not answer any of her questions.

"Oh, God!" cried Marija. Katarina knelt beside her mother, took her other hand and kissed it.

"Madame," said Draganović finally, "you and your children are safe. This place is isolated, no one ever comes up here. If they do, however, you are not to tell anyone who you are. There's an old man who's been with us for some time, a shepherd. He sleeps in the barn, does odd jobs and looks after the animals. As far as he's concerned you are cousins from Banja Luka and your last name is Draganović, do you understand? Please, it is for everyone's safety. I cannot stress the point enough."

"They will be careful, won't you my darlings?" said Marija, looking at her children.

"I am sure you are very tired," said Father Draganović, helping Marija from the chair. "Get some rest. We will talk later."

"But the baby, Kruno, what are we going to do with the baby?" Ana pointed emphatically at Saša.

"I will take care of him," said Didi.

Ana appealed to her son.

"You heard Damir, Mother," said the priest. "He will take care of the kid."

"How can he? He's just a boy!" protested Ana. "Oh, come with me then, come, come," she added with a sigh of resignation.

Damir cradled the baby and followed Ana up the stairs to the second floor. Old as she was, she skipped two steps at a time and showed Damir to the end of the hall, to a door so small it belonged in a doll's house.

"He looks about six or seven months," said Ana.

"Oh, no, he's really about my age," explained Damir.

Ana frowned, looking mystified. "He'll cry all night, pee and poo-poo. Don't say I didn't warn you." She mumbled something under her breath about boys not knowing a thing about babies. "Watch your head." She touched the ceiling with her hand. "When Kruno—Father Draganović was about your age he sat by the window and read for hours and hours and hours. He liked it up here; I do not know why, so do not ask me. Maybe he felt closer to God, up in this room. He also banged his head on the ceiling a lot." Ana started to walk away. "Oh—I have a crib; it was Kruno's, has to be in the cellar. I'll bring it up, yes, and—old diapers, even baby clothes. I never throw anything away. You never know, you just never know."

Ana flew down the stairs before Damir could say thank you, leaving him and the baby in the small attic room they would call their own.

The triangular niche had a latched casement window that opened to a grand view of the mountain and beyond.

The rain had stopped and the wind nudged the thunderclouds away, revealing the stars and the biggest, fullest moon Damir had ever seen. "Saša, look!" said Damir, releasing the latch and gently pushing the window with his elbow. "The moon—it's smiling again!"

9

Draganović's two-story, four bedroom, one bathroom (with Italian fixtures) farmhouse reflected provincial prosperity. Made of brick, mortar and capped with a thatched roof, the house stood against an immense cliff overlooking a swooping valley that Ivo Draganović cleared of trees and wolves so his animals could graze in peace.

There was no electricity, of course, and indoor lighting took the form of candles and oil lamps, but a wood boiler outside provided hot water for the bathroom and steam for the radiators in the main rooms.

A short distance from the side door, a large barn housed dozens of chickens, two cows, many pigs, even more goats and sheep, several generations of rabbits, one veteran sheepdog, a family of cats, an old horse and an even older shepherd named Pero Bojić.

As usual, he was up at daybreak, stretched his limbs and blinked twenty-five times because, he thought, it helped his eyesight. Then, the shepherd donned a pair of crusty pants and shirt, put on the only boots he owned, dragged himself to a washstand on the other side of the barn, scrubbed his face with a wet rag, grabbed his walking stick that was as bent and full of knobs as its master, put on his hat and went outside to feed the chickens.

After spending a lifetime watching out and being watched by wolves, it didn't take Pero very long to feel the presence of someone he did not know.

"Hello," called the shepherd, without bothering to look up.

"Hello." Damir wondered if the old man was talking to him.

"Who is that you're holding, your brother?" said Pero.

"No."

"Your sister?"

"No."

"Your uncle?"

Damir laughed.

"Why do you laugh? I had a baby for an uncle."

"He is my friend," said Damir.

"What is his name, this friend of yours?" asked Pero, spreading chicken feed.

"Aleksandar," answered Damir.

"Me—I am Pero. And you?"

"Damir."

"I bet you want to come down and help feed the pigs."

"The pigs?"

"You can bring Aleksandar. He can feed the pigs too," added Pero, then returned to the barn, leaving Damir to ponder whether or not to help feed the pigs.

The boy shut the window, put Saša on the bed and tried to change his diapers when Ana came into the room followed by Marija and Katarina. "Do not tell him your real name," warned Ana.

"I only said—"

"You said enough. Pero is a good man, but he's Serb. Remember, you are cousins from Banja Luka."

Katarina laughed. "What are you doing?"

"What does it look like I'm doing?"

"You will be a good papa some day," Ana said to Damir.

"Did he give you trouble last night?" asked his mother.

Damir shook his head. He had spent half the night staring at the ceiling and the rest of the time watched the baby sleep in the old crib. Between one and the other a shepherd boy was murdered by the Ustaša; between one and the other was Saša. "I think he's hungry."

"Come downstairs." Ana turned and left the room with her customary, lively step, expecting her guests to follow. She had slept only a few hours because she wanted to make sure that Marija and the children felt welcome. She understood that it was much harder for the Pavelićs to depend on the Draganovićs than it was for the Draganovićs to show compassion for the Pavelićs.

"Madame, we are so very grateful to you and Father Draganović," said Marija, walking in the kitchen.

"It's our Christian duty, my dear," replied Ana.

"Where's Nikola?" asked Katarina.

"He went with my son—to town I think. They'll be back tonight. Now, please, sit down, " added Ana before a bountiful breakfast table. "Eat."

The first couple of months at the farm were very trying for the cousins from Banja Luka. As a precaution, Father Draganović insisted they change their elegant wardrobe for clothes more in line with life at the farm, and suggested they find something to keep them busy.

Ana undertook the herculean task of teaching the Pavelić women a few basic household duties, like how to prepare a meal, make a bed, sweep and dust; routines as unfamiliar to them as taking a cat for a walk on the moon.

Nikola helped with odd jobs that did not require physical exertion, but Damir did little other than look after the baby.

His mother and sister continued to pamper him as before, and Ana, impressed with his tender nature, favored him above the others.

Only Father Draganović regarded Damir with polite disinterest. The priest believed that the boy's devotion to a stranger, a child found under extremely mysterious and troubling circumstances, reflected an obstinate temperament that further complicated his family's predicament.

Although accurate in some ways, the priest's opinion did not keep Damir from caring for Saša, who, in the space of seven months went from a thin, frail baby, to a healthy, rugged and playful little fellow.

He learned to walk and talk faster than anyone thought possible and sputtered long sentences driving everybody to distraction. "Maja" was Marija. "Ina" stood for Katarina. "Nana" meant Ana. "Ola" implied Nikola, "Tata" represented Father Draganović, and "Pu" indicated the old shepherd. The only name Saša never confused with anything else was Damir, who every so often he called Didi.

By then it was impossible to pick him up against his will. When Kati tried feeding him, cradling him as she did just a few months earlier, Saša would sit up, point and demand in incomprehensible gibberish whatever he felt like having at the time. Then he would fidget, kick and cry unless he was let go, sometimes in diapers, sometimes naked, and allowed to run loose.

"This Aleksandar is a real pain in the ass," complained Pero, more than once.

"Saša, did you hear that?" Damir laughed, hugging and kissing the baby. "You're a pain in the ass!"

Having learned that he could get from point A to point B much faster if he ran, Saša acquired the nerve-racking tendency of crashing against doors to get in. When, for some reason, the doors did not yield, the child bounced off and landed on his rear.

One day, in a fine display of confidence, he bolted down the slope outside the front door, tripped and tumbled past a group of grazing sheep that were astonished to see him rolling by. A large black rock finally stopped his descent and, fortunately, only his pride needed mending.

Later that afternoon, Saša took advantage that Damir was busy arguing with his mother, who scolded him for acquiring the manners and language of a peasant and for shaving his head to simulate the traditional rural remedy for fighting lice (something that was visually effective though unnecessary), and dressed in sagging diapers, the baby ran off to chase chickens, the rabbits and the cat.

The feline, a large striped warrior used to fending off wolves, turned on Saša, and, well, the baby never went after the cat again. Instead, he grabbed a piglet, made his way to a fat indolent sheep, and tried to ride the astonished creature. The animal panicked, baaed loudly, bucked and called her sisters to stampede.

"They're out!" yelled Pero, pounding the ground with his stick, cursing aloud and calling the dog to chase after the animals who made their wobbly way down the hill.

Damir found Saša in the pigpen, trying to hold the baby pig while a large, fat sow jabbed him with her snout.

The cries, the oinks and the baas brought everyone out of the house. Marija and Ana shrieked; Nikola rushed to help the shepherd, fell, banged his head and had to be attended to by Ana.

"Tell me what to do!" yelled Kati, being as unacquainted with irate pigs as her brother.

"I don't know! Pull her off!" yelled Didi.

While Saša refused to surrender the pig, Katarina laughed and lost her footing when she yanked the sow's tail and slipped under the animal as Didi, holding Saša upside down, stumbled and fell backwards.

It was a few minutes before the three made it out of the pigpen covered in mud and other less agreeable stuff.

Kati rushed Saša to the well, took off his diapers and ordered him not to move, not to twitch, not to breathe while pouring bucket after bucket of water on his head.

"Didn't I tell you?" said Pero when the animals were back safe in the barn. "That Aleksandar is a pain in the ass!"

10

With Marija and her children safely under his mother's care, Father Draganović spent less and less time at the farm, while traveling from one refugee camp to another as director of the Pontifical Commission for Assistance, an organization that was supposed to help repatriate refugees in postwar Yugoslavia, but was in fact, a cover for securing false Red Cross identification papers and passports for war criminals trying to escape from Europe.

Every couple of weeks, the priest, like a long, lost relative, would resurface, his car parked in the space between the house and the barn, as if he had never been away.

One such time, after supper, everyone gathered in the main parlor and watched Damir parade Saša, who dressed in a new outfit Kati made for him. "What a handsome boy!" said Ana, while the rest clapped and cheered.

Unexpectedly, Saša walked to Father Draganović and beckoned the priest to pick him up.

"Ah!" said Marija and Ana, at the same time.

Draganović took Saša in his arms, and said: "Damir, don't you think it would be a good idea to have this child baptized?"

"Wonderful idea, Father!" interjected Marija.

"Oh, yes, very much so," agreed Ana.

"I-t-it s-should have been d-done m-months ago," joined Nikola.

"Of course not," said Damir. "It's not a good idea at all."

"What are you saying?" asked Marija. "Why not?"

"He has to be baptized," insisted Ana. "He just has to!"

"What if he's already baptized?" suggested Katarina, since the child had been six or seven months when found.

"There is no way of knowing one way or another," added Ana, "and we lose nothing doing it again."

"Saša cannot be baptized," insisted Damir.

"Why not?" Ana darted confused looks from one end of the room to the other. "What's wrong with having the baby—"

"No!"

"Damir, you are being rude," said Marija.

Father Draganović handed the baby back to Damir, and said: "Our young friend must have a good reason for not wanting the baby baptized. Unfortunately, we don't know what that is because he is not sharing it with us. That said, I know Damir to be responsible and honest, and there is no doubt how much he loves the child."

"Well, yes, that is all true," admitted Ana.

"So, let us respect his wishes," added the priest. "In the end, it will be up to Damir whether the little one attains salvation or not and I'm sure he will do what is right."

The evening went on without further talk of baptisms or anything else, except one or two trivial references to sheep, the approaching winter and some passing allusions to life in Zagreb, Belgrade, Rome and Berlin.

As the cold mountain winds howled, Ana brought out her knitting implements, Marija perused a fashion magazine Father Draganović had brought for her, Nikola fantasized about American cigarettes, the priest tended the fire, and Damir and Kati played chess.

Saša sat next to Ana for a few minutes, then wandered around, lay down next to Damir and Kati, and promptly fell asleep.

"Well, well," said Kati.

"Half hour later than y-yesterday!" observed Nikola with a cough.

"I better put him to bed," said Damir, picking up the baby.

As the evening wore on, Ana, Katarina and Nikola retired one after the other, leaving Marija and Father Draganović by themselves. "More coffee, Madame?" offered Father Draganović.

"Oh, yes, thank you. You know, Father, I never drank coffee until I came here. Tea, I drank tea. But your coffee is positively delicious."

"It's very special; it's grown in a tropical island and I bring it from Rome."

"Interesting." Marija did not really care about the immense distance the coffee had traveled before ending up in her cup, instead, she wanted to ask Father Draganović . . .

"Yes, it is," interrupted the priest. "And it began in the mid-1840s, when a Puerto Rican bishop ingratiated himself to Pius VII with a kilo of coffee from Puerto Rico."

"Puerto what?"

"It's an American island-colony in the Caribbean. Anyway, the coffee caused a sensation and when the bishop complained that his island did not have a relic, Pius VII offered to exchange any of the saints resting in the catacombs, for a yearly supply of coffee."

"A saint?" Marija frowned.

"For coffee."

"Trading coffee for a saint, isn't that sacrilegious, Father?"

"Depends."

"On what?"

"The prominence of the saint and the quality of the coffee."

Marija smiled politely, and said: "Father, when are we going home? It's been almost two years!"

"Madame Pavelić, please understand that we are doing everything possible to reunite you and the children with your husband."

"And we are very grateful to you—and your mother—for everything you've done for us, Father, but I think it is time we got on with our lives. The children have to—need to be in school—"

"I must tell you that Damir worries me," said the priest. "It must pain him to be separated from his father because I am sure he idolizes the Poglavnik, as he should. What I don't understand is Damir's infatuation with the baby. Is he thinking of taking Saša when you leave here?"

Marija did not answer right away. She had not considered the baby's future once she and her children left the mountain. "A few years ago, Didi fell gravely ill. He was nine at the time and the doctors all said he would die. Then, one morning, after being bedridden for months to the point where he had withered down to nothing, he woke up and said he had a new friend— imaginary of course; a Serbian shepherd boy called Saša. Almost immediately, Didi regained his appetite and in a few weeks, was healthy again."

Listening to Marija tell the story, Father Draganović could not help reflect that Saša was the nickname for those called Aleksandar, a name also identified with Serbian kings, the last of which Pavelić's henchmen assassinated in 1934. It never occurred to the priest, however, that he and the young shepherd boy Saša shared a very special bond, thanks to Ante Pavelić's messianic panache for granting and taking life.

11

Although he was not free to do as he liked, for example roam the countryside, go hiking and maybe explore the caves Pero swore were hidden in the hills, the time spent on the farm gave Damir an inner peace he never knew before.

He loved going out with the shepherd at sunrise to take out the herd, then spend the day wrapped in a blanket on a grassy slope, watching Saša running after the dog who drove the sheep, and listening to Pero reflect on just about everything, from sheep to salvation, hell, women and the crucifixion.

"If you were on a boat and the boat smashed against the rocks and you almost drowned," began the shepherd, covered in a thick quilt a lady friend had made for him years back, and sipping raki from a tarnished tin flask, "you would think twice about getting on a boat again, right? Or say you were burnt in a fire, you'd hesitate going near a flame, yes?"

Damir listened intently, and although he had no idea what Pero was talking about, he knew that the man would make his point sooner or later.

"Well—" added Pero, "—can you imagine the look on Jesus' face the day he comes back and finds crosses everywhere?"

Damir thought he was unqualified to offer an opinion, so he shrugged and picked his teeth with a straw.

"Didi! Didi!" called Saša, chasing after the sheep. "Come here—come here, Damir!"

"Let those poor animals be!" returned Damir.

The baby ignored the warning, laughed and grabbed a goat by the tail.

"That boy's not afraid of anything," said Pero matter-of-factly.

"Never been," returned Damir.

Pero thought for a moment. "Never?"

"Never," confirmed Didi.

"You had sheep in Banja Luka?"

Instead of answering Pero, Damir munched on bread and chocolate, and said: "Were you in the war?"

"All my life. I don't remember a day when someone wasn't shooting at someone else."

"But, did you fight in the war?"

"Why should I fight in the war?" answered Pero.

"Don't you have enemies?" asked Damir.

"Wolves," returned Pero. "Other than that—"he added, taking out his pipe and letting his mind drift back sixty years, when he worked for Ivo Draganović, a man that called for the extermination of anyone who was not a Croat, and twenty minutes later, offered to buy drinks for everybody in the kafana; vodka for the Serb, wine for the Jew, and juice for the Muhammadan.

He also remembered the times that he and his Croat master drank and winked at the ladies together, and the many, many nights when he carried home a drunken Ivo stinking of cheap perfume. "I don't have enemies, do you?"

Again, Damir avoided the question. He sat quietly for a moment, then threw off his blankets and chased after Saša, tackling him to the ground, and tickling him until the baby screamed with laughter.

Pero aimed his pipe at Saša and extemporized:

"Such a little pain in the ass,
And what a strange friend he has,
A boy with big eyes,
Little hair, and no lice."

Damir grinned, rubbed his head and wiped Saša's runny nose.
Pero threw a blanket on Saša. "Where's his papa?"

"He's an orphan," explained Damir.

"Ah—" Pero smoked for two minutes. "And you, are you orphaned too?"

Damir frowned, blushed and looked away.

Pero stuck his nose in the brandy flask. "I have known the Draganovićs for a long time. Longer, I think, than I would have liked to. He was a good kid."

"He is a good kid," corrected Damir.

"I meant Krunoslav the priest, not your Aleksandar," said the old man. "Your Father Draganović was ten or eleven when I showed him the caves. Once the little shit tried to find them on his own and got lost. Ha! Ana was furious. She hit me, can you believe that? She whacked me with a broom and kicked me out of the house," added Pero, laughing and looking at the sky. "I remember everything," and he tapped his forehead. "It's all in here."

"What do you think, you think God exists?" asked Damir, after Saša took off his mittens, stuck his thumb in his mouth, lay down beside him, and fell asleep.

"What kind of a question is that coming from a Catholic boy like you? God—exist? Of course!" answered Pero, with a chuckle.

"How do you know? How do you know there is a God?" insisted Didi.

"Because—" and Pero swept his right arm, taking in the landscape as far as the eye could see, "—he is all around; in the trees, grass, clouds, sheep—in this child." Pero pointed at Saša. "He is in you, and even in me."

"So—God is not in heaven?"

"Heaven is here," and Pero poked Damir in the chest, then, lit his pipe and puffed away, pleased that he was able to share some of his wisdom with the boy.

"Inside? But I thought—"

"Yes, and hell is too—in you, in me, heaven, hell!"

Damir frowned.

"You don't think God's got a looooong white beard, sits on a throne and rules the universe like a granddad, now—do you?" said Pero.

Damir had never thought about the white beard.

"God is—let's see," and the shepherd rubbed his forehead, "God is All."

"All? But, if God is All, He is good and He is evil!"

"Well, to have one," Pero pointed his finger to the west, "you must have the other." Then he pointed to the east. "The other side of right, is wrong, like daylight is to night, like hot is to cold and ugly to beautiful."

"Opposites!" said Damir with a smile.

"And from that eternal struggle of opposites, life is born," added Pero.

"Then half the people in the world are evil," said Damir.

Pero shook his head. "No, no. Everyone in the world is a little of both. However, human beings by nature choose good over evil—as they prefer beauty to ugliness. For instance, what if all the people in the world saw two pictures: one, a picture of a crystalline mountain stream surrounded by a lush forest of evergreens covered with glistening, pure snow under a perfectly blue sky, while the other picture is that of a dead rat rotting in a sewer, stuffed with stinking bile, garbage and shit? Which picture would the people prefer? I say the nice picture—the one that is obviously beautiful, don't you think?" said Pero.

"Yet, there is always someone who likes rats," observed Damir.

"But that's because they are stupid and ignorant. Ignorance blinds men so they can't tell the difference between beauty and ugliness, between right and wrong—good and evil," followed Pero.

Damir sat up, and said in a loud whisper: "So, then, how's a person punished when they've sinned and died. If they don't go to hell, where do they go?"

"Here," sighed Pero.

"Here?" Damir's brows got closer and closer.

"I believe that when someone's been evil, they have to make up for it when they are reborn," explained the shepherd.

"Reborn?" It was the first time Damir had heard someone talk about what he always felt was much more than a possibility.

"It depends how much harm, pain and suffering they caused back when they were before," finished the shepherd with unusual logic.

"What if it's a lot, a real lot?" asked Damir, raising his voice a little.

"One might be born blind, deaf, retarded, poor, miserable, stupid, sick, armless, fingerless, without a nose—you name it! That way, they're destined to stay out of trouble next time around. It's one way to pay what's due, to gain a balance, harmony between the soul and God the All," speculated Pero, the shepherd.

"What else can happen to a man that's evil?" Damir did not have any trouble imagining the fate waiting his father.

Pero pondered, then laughed so hard he bounced up and down. "He spends his life working for the Draganovićs!"

"You must have been very wicked!" roared Damir, making such a ruckus that Saša woke up, crying. Damir picked him up, hugged and tickled him until he shrieked with laughter. "How did you learn all that?" Damir was in awe of the shepherd's grasp of mountain metaphysics.

"I am old," smiled Pero.

Damir had a thousand more questions that needed answers, and in time, he would bring them before Pero the shepherd, the wisest man he had ever met.

"And—how old are you, Damir from Banja Luka?" asked Pero.

"Seventeen," replied Didi.

"Tell me something, Damir from Banja Luka, do you have a girl waiting for you there? Did you break her heart when you left?"

Damir rolled his eyes and shook his head, pretending he was bored. It was not the question that confounded Damir as much as the concept of being in love. "Have you ever been married?" he asked the shepherd.

"Married?" said Pero, then broke into verse:

*"Marriage was invented by the Devil himself
For torturing the humans on their way to hell."*

The moon showed half its face over the range when it was time to return to the farm. Saša ran around like a sheepdog's assistant, and at one point, followed the dog into the woods. The dog, wise creature that he was, ran back to Pero; Saša did not.

"Go get him—wolves, you know," said the shepherd.

"They're no match for Saša," said Didi.

The baby had hid behind a tree, waiting for Damir. "Come on, you!"

Didi picked up the little troublemaker, stopped, put down the baby, pulled out his pocketknife and carved his name on the bark of a tree. Then, holding Saša's hand, said: "Your turn," helping him scratch Saša next to Damir.

It was half past seven when they got back to the farm, and while Pero took care of the animals, Damir and Saša hoped they were in time for supper.

Katarina had labored in the kitchen all afternoon, determined to impress the household with a dish of rabbit with tomatoes, onions, garlic and potatoes, seasoned with generous amounts of paprika.

While everyone enjoyed the meal, the baby ran around telling of the mischief he did that day when a sudden, urgent pounding at the front door brought the good time to a halt.

"Father Draganović!" called Rostas from outside. He was armed and arrived on horseback. "Militia! Six, or seven of them—in two cars. They will be here in less than fifteen minutes!"

"Get Pero," ordered the priest. "And hide in the woods. I will signal from upstairs when they're gone." The priest hurried to the dining room and announced to the party that they were—

"Leaving? What is happening, what is it?" asked Marija.

"Soldiers are on the way. You have to get out of here now. There's no time to take anything. Damir, the baby stays."

"No!" Damir grabbed Saša and held him tight.

"Listen! Pero is going to take you where no one will find you. But, it's a d"angerous hike, especially in this kind of weather. You can't afford to be held back and that's exactly what will happen if you take the baby. It would mean the end for everybody. Now, put him down and go!"

"Damir, my darling, think of your sister!" Marija held Katarina, who was very scared.

Saša sensed something was wrong and he darted frightened looks left and right. Damir tried to calm him down, but the baby began to cry.

"Damir!" Marija was losing patience.

"I'm not leaving Saša!" Damir backed up against the wall.

Father Draganović raised his voice slightly. "If you take him, you will be caught, if you stay you will be caught. Either way you will certainly never see him again!"

The boy glared at the priest. He hugged and kissed Saša before slowly handing him over to Father Draganović.

"Damir! Damir!" cried Saša, reaching out.

"I'll be back, Saša, I swear I'll come back for you, you'll see!" said Damir, tears streaming down his face.

Ana gathered jackets, sweaters, blankets and two oil-lamps for the Pavelićs.

"Nikola, you too."

The little man had remained in a corner looking around not knowing what to do and wishing someone would tell him. "I-I-will not s-s-stay for a-anything!" he stammered, then hopped nervously around the table, before rushing out the door.

Pero was already waiting outside with a lantern in one hand and his club in the other.

"Take them to the caves," ordered Father Draganović, holding the baby in his arms. "Stay there until I come for you."

The old man never asked why the cousins from Banja Luka had to go hide in the mountains; he wanted to, but never did.

As they walked in the dark, down the mountain and into the adjacent plain, it took less than a minute for the group to vanish in the almost impenetrable mist. With luck, Pero would find his way through the score of hidden paths and forgotten ravines and reach the hideout in an hour.

12

The police and soldiers arrived in two nondescript automobiles which almost did not make it up the mountain. Comrade Durković was first getting out of the lead car, followed by a small, fat red fellow wearing a long, brown leather coat.

Durković was an ordinary pale-looking man of thirty-five. He had a widow's peak, brown eyes, gray teeth, hunched shoulders and a tired look. "I am sorry to disturb you," said Durković. "I need to ask you a few questions. Do you mind? Are you busy? Would you like for us to come back some other time, perhaps?"

Father Draganović received the men at the door, and said: "You could have sent word you were coming—maybe come during the day? It's not as dangerous driving up the mountain when you can actually see the road."

"You're right, of course," said Durković. "I'll consider that—next time."

Draganović led the men into the parlor. "And what brings you to these parts?"

"I was told that you are good friends with Aloysius Stepinac? Is my information correct?"

"I know His Excellency," answered the priest.

Durković darted a quick look at Ana, who sat in a corner whispering soothing nothings to Saša, praying the baby did not call out for Damir. "And, please tell me," he said to the priest, "when was the last time you saw Stepinac?"

"A few months ago," said Draganović.

"Before he was arrested?" interposed the small, red man in the brown coat.

"Obviously," answered Draganović.

"Would you mind if we look around?" asked Comrade Durković.

"Of course I do," returned Father Draganović, annoyed.

"It won't take long," said the comrade, signaling his men to search the house. "You don't mind if I smoke, do you?" he added, taking out a pack of cigarettes and sitting down in the chair usually occupied by Nikola.

Ana heard the men going through the upstairs and a short time later saw them go in the cellar.

"Nice place you have here, Madame," said Durković. "The upkeep must be expensive."

"The farm has been in my family for generations," answered the priest, instead.

"I don't know what you mean by 'generations,'" returned the policeman. "Records show that your father built the house in nineteen hundred and seven."

"Excuse me," said Ana at last. "We do not bother anyone. I am an old woman and my son is a man of God. What is it you want from us?"

"Is that your grandson, Madame?" Comrade Durković knew that Ana was, as she said, an old woman. He also was aware that her son was a priest and an only son. Who then, was the child in her arms?

"My great nephew," said Ana softly.

Comrade Durković smiled. "Of course."

"Perhaps if you said what you're looking for," suggested Father Draganović.

Durković beckoned the fat little red man to hand the priest a copy of an official document from the Foreign Ministry of the Independent State of Croatia, in Zagreb. It read:

Confirmation of Receipt. Hereby the receipt of the archives of the Foreign Ministry of the Independent State of Croatia is confirmed, specifically:

1. A chest covered with tin and marked with AB-I, sealed with two locks,
2. A wooden chest marked with AB-II, sealed with two locks,
3. Three wooden chests marked with PAV-I-III, sealed with one lock,
4. A wooden chest marked with OL-I, sealed with two locks,
5. A wooden chest marked with OL-II sealed with one lock,
6. A small wooden chest covered with tin and marked RZ, sealed with one lock.

For all of the locks the keys are simultaneously transferred, one for each lock.

Zagreb 6 May 1945
On orders of the Poglavnik to transfer 8 chests.

Received a total of 8 chests
A. Stepinac
Archbishop

Draganović glanced at the paper, shrugged and gave it back. "What is it?"

"Why, it is a receipt—signed by your friend Stepinac for the war booty hoarded by the Ustaša."

"I don't understand how it concerns us," returned Draganović, apathetically.

Comrade Durković pointed his nicotine-stained finger at the priest, and said: "Not us, sir, you. Your relationship with Stepinac is documented. This house is almost inaccessible, a perfect place to hide the spoils of defeat."

"You are wasting your time," said Father Draganović, softly.

"I'm afraid we have to look anyway," returned the comrade, smiling.

The search went on for almost an hour. Draganović remained standing in the middle of the room. Ana put Saša to bed and Comrade Durković and the fat little red man smoked one pack of cigarettes between them.

"Nothing," said one of the soldiers climbing out of the cellar. "But—"

"What?" Durković flipped his cigarette butt into the fireplace.

"Well, down there—I don't know, it's too neat."

"Explain," ordered his superior.

The soldier was a tall dark-haired man about twenty-three years old, with a bushy mustache, black eyes and a long nose that he put to good use. "My mother's cellar is full of dust, cobwebs and junk. This place here, well—there's none of that. It looks like someone's been sleeping down there."

"Any visitors, lately?" asked Durković.

"Pero, our shepherd, we allow him inside when it gets too cold," replied the priest.

"And where is Pero now?" asked the comrade.

"I don't know. I called him before sundown but he did not answer. He's probably in town getting drunk. Pero is a good man but has always been morally reprehensible," offered the priest.

Comrade Durković stared at Father Draganović for a moment, then turned to his men. "Let's go."

The soldiers and the fat little red man casually filed out of the house, got in their cars and waited.

"Thank you for your cooperation," said the comrade before going outside. "Good night."

Draganović waited five minutes, then recalled Rostas with a very loud whistle.

"Do you think they'll be back?" asked Ana, upset.

"Yes, not tonight, but they'll be back."

"What are we going to do?" asked Ana.

Just then, Rostas tapped on the kitchen window. He held the shotgun ready in case it was a trap.

"Take the baby home with you," ordered the priest.

"Rostas—take the baby?" said Ana. "Why? Kruno, you can't, you just can't!"

"Mother, please don't interfere!"

"You promised Damir!"

"It has to be done."

"He's going to be heartbroken. Saša adores him!" said Ana, crying.

"Look," said her son, gently, "Damir cannot have a say. He must believe the militia took the baby." The priest had decided that the Pavelićs were to leave immediately from the mountain and taking Saša would have put everybody at risk. He also could not allow Damir to challenge his decisions. "Once they are safely out of the country, then—maybe. If nobody claims the kid, I'll wrap him up in a Sunday suit and send him to—wherever. Right now, I don't have time for to deal with adolescents' whims or tantrums."

Pero had not been in the cave in ten years, when he sought shelter from a mid-afternoon blizzard. Back then, it had taken him forty-five minutes to remember how to get there and another five to find the opening, so he figured that now, at eighty-three and on a moonless foggy night, the hour and a half it took them to reach the cave was, by any measure, reasonable.

The cave was big. It spread six meters wide and four meters high, with a long underground passage that burrowed deep into the mountain.

Right away, the shepherd built a small fire, then watched the frightened mother and her children sit quietly, wrapped in whatever they brought with them.

The long, difficult climb affected Nikola most of all, and Damir sat brooding because he had left Saša with the priest.

"Where are you going?" asked Marija, when the boy took a lamp and began making his way deeper inside the cave.

"For a walk," he answered, holding back his anger.

"Stay where you are, it's dangerous. Heaven knows what's in—"

"To you everything is dangerous," shot back Damir. "I've never been able to do anything—never had friends or could play outside because to you it was always dangerous! I'm sick and tired of dangerous!"

It was his first adolescent outburst and it unnerved his mother and earned a rebuke from Nikola.

"Bonk!" yelled Damir.

Pero looked from one player to another, chewing his unlit pipe.

"Don't you ever, ever use that tone of voice with me!" warned his mother. "Sit down! You're not going anywhere! All I need is for you to get lost in this—in this—Sit down!"

"I am not going to sit down! I'm tired of sitting down, tired of not having a life, tired of—"

"Stop it!" screamed Marija.

"You are lucky your papa's not here," blurted Nikola. "The Po—"

"Nikola!" yelled Marija.

The secretary caught himself just in time and fell as silent as the stalactite perched over his head, which, had Marija controlled matter with her mind, would have dropped and cut him in half.

"Damir, please!" pled his sister.

"Bonk!" said Didi, disappearing into the bowels of the mountain.

He walked for a few minutes, dazzled by the strangeness around him and found that the cave got narrower and narrower as he made his way inside.

He pressed on, the light from the lamp producing strange forms on the craggy walls, when the trail split. To the left was a rivulet that trickled from an unseen tributary and led to a grotto guarded by a huge rock; the depository for several sealed tin and wooden chests with different markings.

"What the—" awestruck and confused, Damir could not decide whether to return to the group and tell them of his discovery, or try to find out what was inside the boxes.

"There you are," said Pero, coming up from behind. "Get back. Your mother's very upset."

"Shit! Don't do that! You scared me half to death!" yelled Damir, before pulling the old man by the arm. "Look at this! What do you make of it? Do you think it's a treasure? Maybe pirates?" Damir's voice cracked with excitement.

Pero shone his light on the chest and brushed away the dust with his hand.

"Wait till Saša hears about this! Open it, go ahead!"

"With what?" said Pero. "Hold on," before he found a hard smooth rock that had been in the same place for a millennium.

"Do you think we'll get in trouble?" asked Damir.

"People my age don't get in trouble," returned Pero, raising the rock and smashing the lock on the chest marked PAV-I.

Slowly, the shepherd lifted the top and revealed. . .

"Oh, it's gold, all right, but—but these nuggets—" Pero picked one up, looked at it carefully then showed it to Damir. "Looks like a tooth, a gold tooth."

A piece of letterhead from the Foreign Ministry of the Independent State of Croatia was half buried alongside the contents. It read: *From the Work Service of the Ustaša Defense Assembly Camp III—on orders from the Poglavnik.*

"What does it say?" asked Pero.

Damir felt his body go numb. True, he did not understand about the Defense Assembly Camp III.

"What's the matter? Read the rest, come!" insisted the shepherd.

"I—I can't," said Damir, shaking.

"Don't be silly—" said Pero, then put up his hand. "Wait.

Did you say Ustaša Defense Assembly?" Pero stepped back from the box. "Jasenovac! It's the gold teeth, yes, from the victims of Jasenovac! The Poglavnik, the Ustaša—of course!"

Damir burst into tears. "My father."

"What do you mean?"

"My father did this."

"Your—father? I don't—"

"Ante Pavelić is my father." Damir wiped the tears with his hand.

Pero's blood shot down to his feet and his brain was unable to command the body. Only his eyes gave sign that Pero was alive, eyes that stared at the boy, eyes that could not believe for one moment the child he thought to be the most compassionate, caring, giving and loving of all the people he had ever met could be the son of the murderer Ante Pavelić.

"Pero, you asked me once if I was an orphan. I am, we all are, we have been made orphans by Ante Pavelić." And Damir told of his trip to Glina when he was a young boy, where, for the first time he met the Serbian shepherd boy named Saša. "Oh God, I am so sorry!"

If Damir was the Poglavnik's son, then Marija and Katarina were his wife and daughter. And Nikola? A bodyguard? A servant? Slowly, overcome with sadness and pity, Pero held out his hand and said: "You are not responsible for this. Come, let's leave this place."

"Who else knows about this cave?" asked Damir, as they slowly walked back to join the others.

"No one," said Pero. "Except for—"

"Where have you been?" asked Father Draganović. He had just arrived when Damir and the shepherd appeared from the tunnel.

"I—I took a walk—went to explore the cave," Damir was not going to let the priest in on his secret.

"Pero?" Draganović looked hard at the old man.

Pero nodded toward Damir. "Like he said."

"Is everything all right, Father? Are we going back to the farm?" asked Marija, getting her things together.

"Everything is not all right. The police have taken an interest in the farm—it's not safe for you. Damir, I am afraid I have bad news. They—"

"Where is Saša?"

"They took him."

"You're lying! What have you done with Saša?" screamed Damir.

"Madame," said Father Draganović to Marija, "control your son."

"Why did they take him?" asked Kati, crying.

Pero wondered the same thing, but kept quiet.

The priest never answered their questions.

Outraged, Nikola denounced the abuse of the authorities.

Marija took her son in her arms. "I am so terribly sorry!" Saša had become one of them and they all loved him.

Damir fell on his knees and wept for the infant he found on a wet, dismal night; wept for the baby he nurtured back to health; wept for the Serbian shepherd boy who shared his dreams, his hopes and his nightmares; wept for the little friend who years back returned to save him from death; wept for the child who was all joy, laughter and love; wept for Saša who, once again, was lost.

THE TENOR & HIS DAUGHTER

13

"**P**ress? What press! What is going on?" said el Jefe (as he was called), pacing up and down the living room and pulling on the telephone wire. Someone should have warned him about the famous opera singer aboard the Afortunato, especially when *La Prensa*, the largest daily in the country had sent reporters, photographers and a newsreel crew to greet the star.

"Listen carefully, make sure no one takes their picture! Do you understand?" He slowly put down the telephone and realized that the simple life he had enjoyed as a respected political expatriate was a thing of the past. He always held that the decision to bring Marija, Damir and Katarina to Argentina had been a mistake because they could just as well have gone to Switzerland, but the priest Draganović did not give them a choice.

—*Dávilas arrive Buenos Aires on the third. Stop. KD. Stop.*

As a result, the Poglavnik was forced out of the small, comfortable apartment inside the military base where he spent the first two years in exile plotting his political resurrection, and into a spacious two-story Spanish colonial hidden behind a tall, massive wall and no-nonsense iron gate in the Buenos Aires suburb of Caseros.

Bought at great expense from a disgraced admiral after his falling-out with Perón, the impressive pale-yellow three bedroom, two bathroom dwelling set on 6600 square meters, featured a sweeping gravel driveway, a red-tile roof, French doors, and windows encased in wrought iron grills. Its kitchen was very modern and spacious, and the library of floor-to-ceiling bookshelves packed with leather bound tomes dealing with the philosophy of the high seas, included a phonograph with a magnificent collection of classical records, sumptuous leather chairs, an exquisite variety of cut glass decanters of brandy, cognac and whiskey and an exaggerated number of hunting trophies.

A second floor balcony opened to a less-than-grand view of the front lawn and its neglected rose garden and large ombú, while, to the side, a two-car garage and a small bungalow preserved strict architectural harmony, with the latter serving as living quarters for a short but corpulent Argentinian called Rubén, Pavelić's all-in-one manservant, driver and bodyguard.

In any event, while Ante Pavelić made last minute arrangements for the arrival of his family, far offshore, his daughter Kati jumped up and down with joy, tugged her brother's sleeve, pointed to a brown strip in the distance, and said: "We're here!"

Not really. The Afortunato was not scheduled to dock for another six hours. Still, after their terrifying escape from Travnik to Mostar, from Mostar to Baška Voda, then across the Adriatic on a ferry to Pescara before driving all night to Naples where they finally boarded the Afortunato, the promise of a new life, friends and school was enough to make Kati as anxious as a child on Christmas morn.

The ship commissioned as Titano di Mare, was re-christened Afortunato after the war because it had carried troops and supplies for the Mussolini government hundreds of times without ever coming under fire. It had three enormous stacks, two huge masts, and was five decks tall, with the first class compartments at the very top and the measure of comfort and service diminishing the nearer passengers got to the sea.

Travel to South America was a lark for the Dávilas, Spaniards from Mallorca. Even so, the tension and the tantrums increased day by day because they did not know what to expect from the land of che and tango.

Father Draganović had warned them against fraternizing with the other passengers, to stay clear of homesick Spanish nationals with a yen for conversation, and especially, to avoid Yugoslavian assassins traveling on business.

Marija felt sorry for Damir and Katarina because she knew that it was very difficult for them to remain sequestered in their cabins most of the time, with nothing to do but read and play cards, venturing outside for walks only after dark.

Damir, in particular, brooded, refused to talk unless it was absolutely necessary and showed signs of succumbing once more to the sadness that almost killed him as a small boy because he could not forgive himself for abandoning Saša.

Twelve days after the Dávilas went to sea, during a rather misty twilight and following a leisurely hour-long walk going back and forth and up and down the ship dressed in a pair of green corduroys that were too short, a light brown shirt that was too tight, tall rubber boots and a black rubber cape that flapped like the wings of an anxious bat trying to overcome the ocean spray, Damir found himself in the lower deck, separated from the deep by the hull, surrounded by hordes of sweating, stinking Bohemian Gypsies with their screaming filthy children, old men smoking, young men flirting, young women teasing and crones praying they survive the ocean crossing.

One of these sat surrounded by burning incense and candles in a makeshift tent of glitter and satin, beckoned Damir with a promise to reveal his future.

Of course he ignored the hag. The stench of incense and the formidable heat and humidity made the boy nauseous, but her words: "You have lost someone very dear more than once and I have much to tell you," caught his attention.

"Are you—are you a Gypsy?" he asked.

"Do you have anything against Gypsies? That is not a question. Sit." And in a croaking monotone voice and Italian that was as disjointed as her features, the old woman pointed a crooked finger to an empty spot in front of her, and added: "Let me look at you," then described, not his fortune but his past.

With Damir sitting cross-legged, she took his hand, peeked into his soul and detailed his melancholy with magical accuracy, begging Damir to cast aside the sadness, the anger and the futility of killing himself. "You have known evil intimately, yet you are compassionate and just," she said. "Such contradictions are never resolved without suffering. You have been blessed by two. You'll be blessed by three. Now go. You are wasting time! Climb and find the sovereign that will comfort and cheer your coming days."

It took Damir a moment to shake off the sensation that his strange encounter had been a hallucination, at which point he found himself one deck above, where political refugees with money left over were privileged to travel to another country.

"*Climb!*"

He did, and continued until he reached the top deck, where he looked around, took a deep breath, grabbed the railing, felt the sticky wet salt from the sea on the polished, wooden railing, closed his eyes and fell . . .

"*Find the sovereign!*"

. . . falling by second class and the porthole to his mother's cabin, where he caught a glimpse of Katarina waving back; by the political refugees with money left over; by the Gypsy incense and sweaty peasants; dropping from the first deck into the void until he hit the water and quickly sank in the perfect cold, wet blackness of the sea.

That is when, from nowhere, Damir thought he heard God singing.

Oh sure, he had heard music before in the streets of Florence, Zagreb and even in Banja Luka. In fact, just before they sought sanctuary in Travnik, the family had stayed a week with people whose youngest son played jazz records from America. Still, having grown up in a home where music was as alien as a book on Serbian folklore, Damir had never heard the kind of music that now overpowered every one of his senses, as he gasped for air and tears welled up in his eyes. "What is happening?" he whispered, before answering his own question: "Love." Not the love of temporal infatuation or lust, but love as the worship of life.

Choked with emotion, Damir opened his eyes, shook off the vision of death and followed the glorious melody to a stateroom just as the tenor reached for one of those high notes that makes legends of fat little men.

"*Scusi.*"

The singing stopped. Didi was shaken from his reverie by another, equally beautiful sound. This time it was a girl's voice speaking to him in Italian, a girl about his age, quite adorable, with the softest yellow hair and large sparkling blue eyes that seemed to laugh aloud even when she did not. She was dressed in a delicate flowing white gown adorned with ruffles and pink trim that matched her soft, rose-colored cheeks.

"Isabella—" crooned the little man from inside.

"I'm coming, Papa!" answered the girl before turning to Damir. "Well? What are you doing? What is your name?"

Given his state of mind, Damir did not remember his real or assumed Spanish name. Instead, he wiped away the tears, stared at Isabella for the longest time, then summoned courage to point to the wide throat in the red ascot, and ask: "Who is that?"

"That is the greatest tenor since Caruso," said Isabella. "The magnificent Beniamino Gigli, my papa."

Didi searched for words while grasping the contradictions of that impossible night when Isabella led him inside. "Papa," she said, "this boy will not give me his name but I think it's because he's so taken by your 'Nessun Dorma'." Isabella stopped, took a short breath and added, "as well he should." She then let go of Damir, walked to the Great Gigli, and added: "Isn't he gorgeous, Papa? I think I am in love with him."

Damir's brows made such a deep furrow and his eyes opened to such a degree that Gigli was forced to interject: "Don't worry, it's my fault. It's what I get for singing Puccini, Verdi and Bellini day and night." And just as he began to ease the boy's mind somewhat, the tenor turned to his daughter, and said: "You will make a lovely couple."

"Are you going to tell me your name?" insisted Isabella.

"Errr—Damir."

"Da-mir," she said, in a musical cadence. "I am Isabella, and this talented lady at the piano is Elvira Pucci, my father's accompanist and personal assistant."

"Where are you from?" asked Beniamino.

"Cr—Spain."

"Crspain? Is that in Spain? I have been to almost every corner of that country, that fine, fine country," said the tenor.

"He speaks perfect Italian," observed Isabella.

Too perfect for a Spaniard, thought Gigli, smiling.

Didi confessed that he had lived in Florence where he learned to speak the language of Boccaccio, Dante and—Isabella.

For his part, Gigli conceded that his repertoire included works in various languages that he sang around the world; French in Paris, German in Berlin and Spanish in Madrid, meaning that he could converse with Damir in Castilian.

That possibility, together with Isabella's adoring look, compelled Didi to flee the stateroom, run as fast as possible down three slippery flights of stairs, burst in his mother's cabin, turn off the lights, lock the door, pull the porthole's curtains together and sit gasping for air on the bed.

"What's wrong?" asked Marija, then Kati; frightened because cabins in second class did not have telephones to call for help.

A light tap-tap-tap made them hold their breath. Katarina grabbed the lamp from the night table and was ready to defend her mother and brother when they heard another light rap at the door followed by the sweetest nightingale calling: "Da-mir—"

"Who is that?" Kati asked, in the dark.

"Da-mir, are you in there?"

"Maybe this is not his cabin."

"I saw him go inside, Papa!"

Marija had heard enough. She turned on the lights and when Damir tried to turn them off again, slapped his hand away, opened the door and found a beautiful girl and a chubby, well-dressed fellow getting wet in the drizzle. "Yes?"

"Buona sera, Signora. My name is Isabella Gigli. This is my father, the great Beniamino Gigli. Where is Da-mir?"

"I think—" Marija turned and saw Didi leaning against the back wall, waving her off. "Oh, there you are! There's a young lady asking about you."

Madame Dávila begged the visitors inside, then introduced her daughter.

The Great Gigli bowed and apologized that it had not been his intention to show up unannounced but that he was forced to chase after his daughter—his impulsive daughter—who thought she had offended young Damir because he had left their room suddenly and without explanation.

No sooner did he stop talking that Isabella spent the next ten minutes telling Madame Dávila that she was too young to have a son Damir's age, and marveled at Katarina's complexion, before stating her intentions to marry their son and brother as soon as he was willing, which caused Didi to swallow hard, Madame Dávila to cough, Kati to scratch her head and Gigli to explain—again—that his daughter was an incorrigible romantic thanks to Puccini, Verdi and Bellini.

The encounter between the Giglis and the Dávilas was brief but Marija was delighted and she smiled politely, unable to express her joy seeing that Damir's demeanor changed suddenly from depressed and lonely, to one of calm introspection as he tried to make sense of the beautiful and charming signorina.

"Why don't you join us for dinner?" said Isabella.

"Signorina, Maestro, you do us great honor," said Madame Dávila, "but, really, we cannot impose—"

"Yes, we can!" joined Kati.

"There! It's decided," said Beniamino.

Marija smiled and said nothing else.

A moment later, as the Great Gigli and his daughter returned hand in hand to their cabin, he advised Isabella not to talk or try to talk to the Dávilas in Spanish, and counseled against asking probing questions, like: "What does your papa do?"

"You don't think they are who they say they are?" asked Isabella, innocently.

"Well, how's one to know unless told otherwise, right?" returned her father, with a chuckle.

Isabella, Katarina and Damir became inseparable for the rest of the trip, and Damir was granted the privilege of watching the Great Gigli at work from a corner of the stateroom.

He was still tormented by guilt, but now had another thing to worry about: Isabella Gigli.

He could not understand why she made a fuss over him and her boldness made him wary and anxious.

The morning Kati spotted land in the horizon, Gigli invited the Dávilas to lunch, then, offered them a rare treat when he asked his daughter to sing.

Isabella hesitated but her father insisted, so, accompanied by Elvira at the piano, the girl smiled and set her eyes on Damir.

"Vissi d'arte, vissi d'amore—"

The voice was a silver thread, each delicious musical passage kept aloft by the most delicate nuance. It was clear, vibrant and dynamic, expressing the passion and anguish of the betrayed as the pianissimo faded and the lament claimed a love that could not be denied, not even by death.

"Bravo! Bravo!" Gigli rushed to kiss his daughter, with Marija and Katarina joining the tenor with "Magnificent! Fantastic!"

Only Damir remained seated, staring at Isabella in open-mouthed reverence, when a knock at the door interrupted the special moment.

It was the chief officer of the Afortunato, who, in the company of two men dressed in long dark leather coats, hats and sunglasses, requested to speak to Madame Dávila.

Marija joined the men on deck, returned a few minutes later and thanked her host because it was time to say good-bye.

Beniamino bowed as Isabella hugged and kissed Kati, then waited for Damir, who did the only thing his nerves would allow: he offered his obeisance and brought her hand to his lips.

"Oh, please!" cried out Kati. "Give her a kiss! She won't bite you."

In formal greetings and farewells, the kiss is nothing more than a mechanical convention and lips are excluded. Didi's first attempt was an uncomfortable brush of the cheek because he had trouble breathing. Then, he did something that surprised even Isabella; he gave her a hug.

Isabella gently took his face and returned the courtesy. "Da-mir," she said in the same musical way she first pronounced his name, then pressed a piece of paper in his hand where she had written down the telephone number and the address to the Alvear Palace Hotel.

"Stop it, you're going to make me cry," said Gigli to his daughter. "I'm sure Damir and Katarina will call you as soon as they can."

The good-byes, the kisses and embraces were over quickly and the Dávilas were escorted back to their room where they gathered their belongings, before joining the men on a small motorboat that took them ashore.

Perhaps the Dávilas were members of a royal family traveling incognito, remarked Isabella, as they waved good-bye from the deck of the Afortunato.

"That possibility," answered Beniamino, "is quite remote."

14

It was dark when the motorboat with the Dávilas docked a distance away from the crowd waiting for the Great Gigli.

Rubén crammed the luggage in the trunk, and in passing Italian, said: "Welcome to Buenos Aires, señora. El Jefe is waiting at the house."

"Who—did you say was waiting?" asked Marija.

"*Il Capo*," explained Rubén.

"Who is that?" asked Didi.

"Your father—I think?" Rubén was as tall as Katarina. That meant he was tall for a girl, but short for a thirty-four-year-old man. He opened the back door for Marija, got behind the wheel of the big, black American automobile, stepped on the gas and raced toward Caseros. "This is the Avenida 9 de julio, named for our day of independence. It is the longest and widest city boulevard in the whole world, more so than Park Avenue, in New York."

"You are taking us home, yes?" asked Marija.

"We will be there in about fifteen minutes. Your first time in Argentina, Madame?"

"Yes," returned Marija.

"It's a great, beautiful and vast country," announced the bodyguard with patriotic fervor.

"Excuse me, sir—" interrupted Marija.

"Please, call me Rubén."

"Rubén—thank you. As you probably know, we have had a very long and tiring two weeks on a boat. I do not mean to be rude but I am not in the mood for conversation. Please, get us wherever you are taking us, to meet whoever—"

"Your husband. You're going to—"

"Drive, please—quietly!"

"As you wish, señora," said Rubén. If someone had asked him at that moment to name the worst sin in the universe, he would have removed his hat, scratched his scarred cheek and without another moment's thought said: "Ingratitude." Ingratitude after he had been friendly when he did not have to be, after he was helpful when it was not expected of him, even when, unbeknown to his passengers, he drove out of the way to enchant the new arrivals with the marvels of the most magnificent city in the world. To be ungrateful was worse than to be unfaithful and el Jefe was obviously married to a stuck-up, ungrateful German bitch. Her loss to be sure. Pendeja!

"I think we should go to the opera," said Damir in Serbo-Croatian.

It was past nine o'clock in the evening when Ante turned on the perimeter lights from the study, flipped the switch that opened the gate, then saw the Pontiac drive up to the front of the house.

"Where is my husband?" asked Marija, leaving the car and straightening her skirt.

Rubén dropped his hat on the driver's seat and quietly walked in the house through a side door, expecting Marija, Damir and Katarina to follow.

"Ah, there you are," said Ante, pretending he had been looking at an atlas when his family walked in the room. "Rubén, please take the luggage upstairs." An optimist would have expected his wife and children to rush into an effusive embrace followed by kisses and tears of joy after being away from each other for so long, but it did not happen.

Pavelić looked carefully at his wife and children, thought Marija had put on weight, was surprised at how tall his son had grown and how beautiful his daughter had become.

They, on the other hand, thought Ante looked old, tired and indifferent.

"Are you hungry?" he asked, leading the family into the kitchen, where he emptied the contents of the refrigerator on the kitchen table.

The family sat around the small table and mostly avoided the ham, boiled potatoes, and the leftover bottle of white wine.

"Is he going to be here long?" asked Marija.

Pavelić had been looking in the pantry for more things to offer his family. "Are you talking about—Rubén?" he said, turning around.

"How much does he know?" asked Marija.

"He knows we are not Italian. Frankly, he cannot tell a Hungarian from a Bulgarian, an Albanian from a Rumanian or a Greek from a Croat, so it does not matter what we say in Croatian or if we call each other by our real names when he's around. That, however, does not take away that he can be very useful, like the dogs, two Dobermans out back."

After an hour, the briefing that began in the kitchen moved to the living room. The family watched each other's reactions as Ante explained what life would be like in Argentina. First, they would be called Bianchi, not Dávila. "It's a common family name," he said. Second, to go along with Bianchi, Marija would be called María, Damir Miguel, and Katarina Sara.

"Sara! That's ghastly!" protested Katarina.

"It's a biblical name," explained her father, matter-of-factly.

The names had already been recorded with immigration authorities and identification papers had been issued.

Finally, they had to understand that contact with Croatian or Yugoslavian nationals was out of the question, whether in person, by telephone and most definitely by post.

"Does that mean I cannot write to Father Draganović?" Damir had intended to bombard the priest with letters asking about Saša.

"Especially to Father Draganović," Ante replied quickly.

"But—"

"Didi, the point is that nobody back home must know where we are. It's that simple," joined Marija.

"You are no longer little children. The time you spent at the farm was not so you learnt to be farmers or sheep-herders. The Yugoslavian government has Father Draganović under surveillance and any attempt to get in touch with the priest would be intercepted by the secret police and we would all be in great, I repeat, great danger," added Ante, looking at his son.

Damir sank in his chair.

"Are we allowed to have friends?" asked Katarina.

"Friends?" Ante looked at his wife. "What friends?"

"What Kati is trying to say—" began Marija.

"Sara," interposed Ante, "her name is Sara."

"—friends in school, around the neighborhood—" continued his wife.

"Why? It would put everyone at risk," replied Ante.

Damir left his chair, looked at his mother, pointed to his father, threw his arms in the air, and said: "Nothing's changed!"

"Why don't you take your sister and—check out the bedrooms?" said Marija to her children.

Didi stormed out the library. Kati hesitated but soon followed up the stairs.

Marija shut the door behind them, turned to her husband, and said: "We are not going back to the old ways. I refuse to have my children live in fear, and if that's what you have in mind, say it now and we'll go back to Europe. They've suffered enough!"

"That is not your decision. You are my wife, they are my children and you will do as I say."

"No!" said Marija, shaking her head. She had married a man who became an embarrassment to his people. Even his Church wanted nothing to do with him. Unfortunately, for her, Damir and Kati, they were in a country as alien as another planet and had become irrelevant, a nuisance.

"What is the matter with you?" returned Ante. "You obviously forgot who I am!"

"I'm afraid that is impossible," Marija shot back.

"This will not do," said Ante, almost to himself and looking impassively at his wife. "Let me tell you something, generals—they're as capricious as popes and our stay in this country depends on their self-interest, their profit and on our discretion. As far as returning to Europe is concerned, it would be suicide."

"We will go to America, then," said Marija.

Damir sat on the bed in a room devoid of charm, thinking of Saša, then stepped to the window, looked at the Argentinian moon—one, he thought, that spoke Spanish and did not share his secrets—and wished he could turn back the clock and wake up in Travnik.

That is when he saw two silent, vigilant and deadly shadows patrolling the grounds.

Welcome to Argentina.

Next morning, the newly baptized Bianchis woke up to the stunning brilliance of a perfect Argentine sunrise, that as every Argentinean will tell you, out glows every other in the world, so much so that the Sol de mayo (the sun of May) has center stage in the Argentinean flag, symbol of that nation's independence from Spain in July of 1816. (The fact that the sun of May is bursting through clouds in July does not seem to bother Argentinians.)

Daniel Bianchi left the house at seven, allowing for his wife and children to familiarize themselves with their new surroundings as they began another period of adjustment.

Didi was up long before anyone else, since the absence of crashing waves had prevented him from getting a good night's sleep. He had thought of waiting until he was called to breakfast but decided otherwise when he heard his father summon the bodyguard, and moments later, drive away.

Dressed only in a pair of trousers, the boy walked out of his room and down the cold marble steps. He stopped at the kitchen, did not find anything worth munching in the icebox, continued through to the dining room, made his way to the living room, and from there arrived at the library.

There was a time when Damir would not have dared enter Ante Pavelić's private study, the Poglavnik's sanctum sanctorum, but a brown square box on a small table next to a floor lamp caught his eye from the door.

Slowly, cautiously, as if the room had been booby-trapped, the boy lifted the cover of the phonograph, tilted the bulky metallic arm, held it for a second and put it back in place. He gently spun the turntable and noticed the record albums stacked on top of each other all the way to the ceiling, classified by genre, and in alphabetical order.

Upstairs, Kati thought she was dreaming when she heard the thunderous rendition of Pagliacci:

"Ridi pagliaccio!"

Disoriented, she leaped from the bed in her nightshirt, dashed out the room, and crashed into her mother in the hall.

"Gigli!" beamed the boy proudly, showing his mother and sister the cover of the 78 RPM disc with Beniamino's picture, he had found in the collection.

"Get out!" yelled Marija.

"Have you gone mad?" screamed his sister, still dazed.

"I said get out!" again from Marija. "Now!"

In took more than threats to get Damir out of the room and he argued, stomped, pouted, reasoned and whined so his mother would allow him to stay and listen to music.

"Under no circumstance," she said, firmly. "You have no right or business being in here!"

"Would you ask him for me, please—if I can listen to music when he's not home?"

Marija grabbed her son by the arm, pulled him outside, and said: "Ask him yourself."

"I don't want to talk to him!"

"Have it your way, then." Marija shut the door to the library and returned upstairs with Katarina, leaving Damir standing in the hall, barefooted, shirtless, bewildered and angry.

He finally marched off to his room and did not come out until his father returned home at two that afternoon.

No sooner was Ante behind his desk that there was a knock at the door.

"Who is it?"

"Sir, I need to talk to you," said Didi, talking to his father for the first time—in a manner of speaking—in three years.

"Yes, Damir? What do you need?" returned Ante. He could not imagine why the boy wanted to talk to him. Did Damir want to go back to Croatia, maybe move out, get a job, live on his own and not go to school? He was old enough—how old was he, anyway? Damir was already taller than his father. What did he have in mind?

"I would like to listen to music."

"What was that?"

"I said, sir, I would like to listen to music," repeated the boy.

"Music?"

"Yes, sir."

"Where? What music? Explain yourself, please." In the seven months Ante had lived in the house he never noticed the brown box until his son pointed it out. "What is that?"

"A phonograph. I would like your permission to listen to records," added Didi, ready to argue his case.

"Yes, of course," said the Poglavnik without hesitation. "Certainly you can listen to music, if that's what you want."

"It is, sir, with your permission, sir," added Damir.

"Fine," said Ante, relieved his son's request was reasonable.

"Thank you," said Didi, starting to walk out when . . .

"Wait."

"Sir?" The boy did not turn, but closed his eyes, his hopes dashed; convinced that in the brief moment it took him to walk to the door, his father had changed his mind.

"I have a better idea. I'll be leaving in a few minutes—why don't you take that machine and the records to your room?"

This time Damir did turn around. "To my room, sir?"

"Well, that way you can listen to music anytime. I don't care much for music these days."

Damir nodded, quickly closed the door, let his broad smile and pounding heart lead him to the kitchen, fixed himself something to eat, finished his meal in five minutes and waited for his father to leave the house.

It took Didi the rest of the day to haul the twenty-odd thousand records from the study to his bedroom, and he spent the rest of the week doing nothing but listening to opera. Sometimes he sat by the window and followed the music with the accompanying libretto; even sang along, something his sister discouraged.

Little by little, Didi created a world for himself where only operatic highs and lows were heard, sounds that for very brief moments made him forget who he was, where he was, why he was there, his love for a child in a distant land and the confusion provoked by a delicate name embossed on a perfumed piece of stationery.

"Mother—" Damir had waited until Marija sat down in the kitchen for a cup of tea, one afternoon. He made sure Kati was present because she could help explain that it was a matter of honor to call Isabella.

"Honor?"

"I told her I would call her, Mama," said Kati, "and we can't say we're going to do something and not follow through. It's not right."

"Not at all," seconded her brother.

Marija remembered how kind the Giglis were to her children.

"Mother!" insisted Damir.

It suddenly dawned on Marija that Damir was not calling her "Mama," and wondered when the change took place. She liked it better when he called her "Mama."There was a sweetness about the word, an innocence that was lost in the way he said . . .

"Mother!"

"I'm sorry. I was distracted."

"Did you hear what I said?" asked Kati.

"As I remember, I never heard either of you tell Isabella you were going to call her," said Marija with an expression too serious to be sincere.

Kati looked at her brother but addressed her mother. "Of course we—"

"I heard Isabella tell you to call her. I saw Isabella give Damir the note with the telephone and the rest, but, you tell her you were going to call? No, sir, I did not hear that. I'm quite positive I did not."

"Well—" Damir was fishing not only for words but for a reason to call Isabella. "I have to assume that she gave me her telephone number so I would call her. Don't you think?"

"Ah, that is something else altogether," observed Marija, when Rubén entered the kitchen with a newspaper in his hand.

"El Jefe wants to talk to you, señora," he said, then turned around and left.

Marija finished her tea, and said: "I'll ask your father."

"Mother—"

"Yes, Damir?"

"It's a matter of honor," said the boy seriously. Then, looked at his sister and waited for his mother to leave the kitchen before cracking a smile.

Marija found Ante writing in a small notebook while the bodyguard sat close by reading the newspaper—all about a soccer game between Córdoba and Rosario. "Marija—" said the Poglavnik without looking up; he continued to write for a moment, then turned to the bodyguard. "Rubén, will you please—" The little man folded the newspaper, placed it under his arm and left the room. "We should employ a servant." Ante did not feel it was appropriate for the wife of the Poglavnik to be sweeping, dusting and cleaning like a housemaid.

"I did that and more at the farm," said his wife.

"This is not a farm. Do you have any objections to a servant?"

Marija had no objections. The only problem was that she did not speak Spanish and could not, therefore, interview the candidates herself. Ante had anticipated that and already had an applicant in mind. It was a woman recommended by a friend at the Foreign Ministry, someone with excellent references. She was hardworking, a wonderful cook, humble and of a quiet disposition. "And she speaks some Italian."

"No one related to your friend outside, I hope?" said Marija, referring to the bodyguard. "The last thing we need is a little female brute making soup."

"No," said Ante softly.

"And she's not kin to any other thug that works for you?"

Ante stared at his wife for a moment, then he almost laughed. "You are more insolent than ever, Marija," he said before returning to his writing. "I'll have the woman come by. You can talk to her. As I said, she speaks Italian. You can make up your mind yes or no. One more thing—" Again, Ante stopped his note-taking and this time put down his pen alongside the notebook and leaned back in his chair. "The children look like peasants." Ante did not mean that his son and daughter's refined features had become crude or that his heirs had been transformed into country bumpkins by the mountains of Travnik. What he meant was that Damir and Kati's dress was unacceptable.

"It's been years since I bought them new clothes."

"We're living in a cosmopolitan, fashion-conscious and sophisticated city," said Ante. He took an envelope from the desk and handed it to his wife. "Money for clothes. Let me know if it's not enough. Rubén will take you shopping when you are ready." Ante assumed the discussion was over. It was not.

"Damir needs a haircut and both children need to see a doctor and go to the dentist. It has been too long, far too long," said Marija.

"Yes, of course—very important. I'll get a few names of doctors and dentists. As far as a haircut, well, I have a man who comes to the house to cut my hair. How about Friday—at noon? Anything else?"

"We need a gardener. The front of the house looks like a jungle and jungles breed vermin."

Ante made a note to that effect.

"And the children want to call on a friend."

"Say again?" asked Pavelić, looking up at his wife.

"The children want to call on a friend," repeated Marija.

"Friend? What friend? Who? Where did they make the acquaintance of this friend? How long have they known this friend and what do you mean they want to call on the friend?"

Marija told her husband about Beniamino Gigli and his daughter, Isabella.

"Gigli!" thought Ante. "He is a singer," he said softly, which, as Marija knew only too well, meant the Poglavnik was upset.

"An opera singer," she explained.

Ante did not care for the distinction. The singer was followed everywhere by photographers and the press.

"His daughter was quite taken by your son," said Marija, smiling.

Ante pushed back his chair, walked around his desk and made his way to the window. He drew open the curtains, allowed a flood of light into the room and pointed out the dangers to the family if he allowed Damir and Katarina to call on their "friend." Why not bring down the protective fence surrounding the house? Why not dismiss the bodyguard, get rid of the dogs and have their pictures displayed on one of the many billboards around the city? On the other hand, why go through all that trouble when all they had to do was go to the opera, have their picture taken with Beniamino Gigli and be murdered by the end of the week!

The lecture lasted fifteen minutes and only when he talked of being murdered did Ante's voice became nearly inaudible.

"What kind of fool do you think I am? No one is going to take pictures of my children," returned Marija, indignant, "but I'm also not going to allow Damir and Katarina to become reclusive paranoids. They need to enjoy what's left of their youth!"

"Why not choose someone less inclined to get themselves on the cover of every magazine and newspaper in the world? Why not the daughter of a mason? Why not the children of a bookkeeper? Why not the son of a clerk? Why did it have to be a singer, and why did it have to be Gigli!" said Ante.

The point was irrelevant, replied his wife, because it was Isabella who chose Damir and Katarina was going along for the ride.

The Poglavnik stood at the window for the longest time, his eyes staring out into space. He was debating ten alternatives at once. Since he did not like any of them, he chose number eleven. "Do as you please," he said, and left the room.

15

In Buenos Aires, Beniamino Gigli and his daughter Isabella were guests of the Alvear Palace Hotel, the most elegant and exclusive lodging establishment in Argentina. With a classic collection of works of art and enormous sparkling chandeliers that suggested a French chateau in the center of the Recoleta, the hotel pampered its distinguished clientele with unparalleled service and comfort.

Isabella, however, was oblivious to the amenities. "Papa, do you think he lost the telephone number?"

"No, I don't, dear," answered the tenor putting on his overcoat while Elvira called for the car. "And if he did, I'm sure his sister or his mother would remember the name of the most famous hotel in the country and look it up in the directory."

"But what if he does not have a directory or a telephone, Papa?" Isabella walked to the window and looked up at the Argentinean sky, which had lost some of its haughtiness.

"Then it does not matter whether he has lost the number or not."

"But Papa!" cried Isabella.

Beniamino handed the briefcase to his assistant and asked that she wait in the lobby because he needed a few minutes alone with his daughter.

"What is it? Why are you so—" began Beniamino.

"He needs me, Papa. Damir needs me!" said Isabella, holding back the tears.

"Unfortunately—and I hate to say this—but it is possible you may never see Damir again."

"Why!? Oh, Papa, don't say that, please don't!" Isabella threw herself on the sofa and wept.

"Maybe it's not that he does not want to see you, but that he can't. You don't know anything about that boy—or his family. What kind of name is Damir, anyway? Not Spanish, and neither is—what was his mother called?" Beniamino tapped his forehead.

"Marija," said Isabella between sniffles.

"Right. If they are Spanish, I'm a goat. Heaven knows why they came to Argentina. I hope there's nothing to it and they're just—eccentric, but, remember how his mother did not allow him or his sister to meet anyone else on the boat? I hope he's not related to Bormann—or any such thing. That would be very unpleasant."

"Bormann?" asked Isabella, wiping off her tears.

"Martin Bormann, Hitler's secretary. He disappeared after the war."

Not too far away, but far enough in other ways that proximity was irrelevant, Damir indeed wanted to call, but would not, Marija said it had nothing to do with her and refused, whereas Katarina was more than happy to dial the Alvear Palace hotel.

"Alvear Palace, buenas tardes," answered the operator.

"Isabella Gigli," said Katarina to the operator.

"Gigli? Un momento, por favor," returned the operator, and Katarina was able to understand everything she said—well, all except *por favor,* because *un momento* meant the same in Spanish as it did in Italian.

"Lo siento, pero no contestan. ¿Quiere dejar un mensaje?"

Katarina looked at her mother and shrugged. It was as far as she could go with the hotel operator.

"Scusi, ma non—"

"Ah, parla Italiano?" Nothing like an operator at a first class international hotel.

"Si, si—Italiano!"

"Non ce risposta da la habitazione de la signorina Gigli. Vuole lasciare un messagio?"

"Si, grazie. Communicarli a la signorina Gigli che la ha chiamato Kati e Damir. La chiameró piú tarde." Kati and Damir would call later because their mother did not allow them to leave the telephone number to the house.

"She's with her father," explained Marija. "Just keep trying."

They did. Katarina called five times between four and six in the afternoon and still Isabella had not returned to the hotel. By then it was too late.

Two hours after they placed their first call, Supi, an affectionate nickname for Supencio Martínez del Arrollo, a wisp of a fellow, looked at the guest book, stroke his thin, matinee idol mustache and focused on Suite 315, when two men dressed in long black leather coats, black hats tilted to the right and dark glasses, approached his green marble station.

"Psst!"

The quintessential hotel whip turned slowly, raised his left eyebrow, stared at the men who, in his opinion, looked terribly out of place, and in a voice that sounded like an upper-class Englishman . . . though he spoke Spanish . . . vsaid: "May I help you?"

"You're the front desk manager," said one fellow, showing his badge.

"That is correct," conceded Supi.

"Gigli," said his partner, in two syllabic bursts.

"What about him?" asked Supi.

"Gets a lot of calls?"

"Of course—many. Is there something wrong, gentlemen?"

A slip of paper with several names crossed the green marble

top. "No calls to Gigli or his group from anyone on that list, under any circumstance, or else—"

"Of course, gentlemen," said Supi, glancing at the foreign names. "I'll take care of it, at once," he added, ringing for a bellboy. "Needless to say that the Alvear Palace is more than willing to help in—"

"Yes, Mr. Supi?" said a short thin lad, about thirteen years old, with red hair and a face full of freckles who suddenly appeared at attention.

"Ah, there you are, Mr. Ferrín. Please put out your chest a little more if you can; otherwise, it is excellent," declared the manager, when he realized the two men had vanished in the crowd. "Breathe, Mr. Ferrín, please take in air or you will collapse and wouldn't that be a pretty sight. Go ask doña Inés to give you any and all messages she may be holding for the Gigli group. Please—bring them to me at once, sir."

Young Ferrín was gone and back in a flash with a fistful of jottings. "Thank you, Mr. Ferrín, back to your post, thank you," said Supi, waving the boy away and glancing at the notes. "My, my—this Kati has been busy. There must be a dozen—I wonder how the name's pronounced. What is Kati? Is it a man or woman? I guess we will never know."

Katarina tried calling the hotel another six or seven times, until eleven o'clock that night. "Try again tomorrow," said Marija to her son and daughter, kissing them goodnight.

Next morning Damir was up at five, woke up his sister at seven and by seven-fifteen were calling the hotel.

"Who may I say is calling? One moment, please. I'm sorry. Line's busy. Would you care to leave a message?"

"Who may I say is calling? One moment, please. I'm sorry. No answer. Would you care to leave a message?"

"It's Damir and Kati. Two names. Damir, D-a-m-i-r; Kati, K-a-t-i. We'll call later."

"Do you think—" Damir began but could not finish the thought. The possibility of Isabella not wanting to talk to them was so painful he could not even put it into words.

"One way to find out," said Katarina reading his mind.

"How?"

"I'll tell them I'm someone else," answered Kati with a smile.

Except that if Isabella was really trying to avoid them, getting through by lying might make things worse. Isabella's anger at the deception would be even bitterer than her disinterest. "No, it's not right," concluded Damir. "Besides, they know your voice by now."

"Then you call and tell them you're her uncle."

"Uncle!"

Bewildered, Damir and Katarina returned upstairs to ponder their predicament. They thought it was inconceivable that Isabella's friendliness might have been a pretense. Impossible!

Unfortunately—or fortunately, depending on the point of view—because of their sheltered life, Damir and Kati had never experienced duplicity as expressed in hypocrisy. Evil, yes, but evil was not hypocrisy, and although most evil people are hypocrites, it is also true that there are many evil people who are perfectly sincere. Most likely, Isabella simply had a change of heart because, in the end, she determined that Damir and Kati had nothing to offer, and much to hide. Who could blame her? Everyone has the right to a change of heart, even if they break someone else's along the way.

Later that morning, after being told for the eleventh time that the Giglis had gone out and would not return any time soon, Damir and his sister . . . under protest . . . accompanied their mother on their first trip ever to buy clothes at a fashionable emporium in the heart of Buenos Aires, not far from the Teatro Colón.

Why not, suggested Katarina, drop by the Alvear Palace hotel and look up Isabella?

"People like us do not 'drop by' on people like the Giglis," said her mother. "Remember that Maestro Gigli is not here on a holiday. He is working on the show."

"Opera," corrected Damir, thinking of Isabella.

It was six o'clock already when they arrived at the house and Damir and Kati picked up where they had left off, calling the hotel without success until they retired for the night, at eleven-thirty.

While everyone slept, Damir spent the time sitting by the window, listening to "Vissi d'arte" playing softly in the dark. He ran out of patience around two o'clock in the morning, tiptoed downstairs and called the hotel.

"Alvear Palace, good evening," said the operator in a very tired voice.

"Buona sera," said Damir to let the operator know he spoke Italian, not Spanish.

"Buona sera."

"Isabella Gigli," continued Damir.

"Gigli. Ehh—" the operator hesitated. *"It is very late. Is she expecting your call?"* asked the operator.

"She asked me to call her," returned Damir, telling the truth—

"Who may I say is calling?" the operator followed the check-list.

—except that in order to find out if Isabella was a fraud or the loveliest creature he had ever seen, he would have to lie: "Eduardo."

The operator took one last precaution, put Damir on hold and rang señorita Gigli.

"Yes?" answered a startled and dazed Isabella. She had cried herself to sleep, thinking of Damir, wondering if she had frightened him off, if he did not like her or perhaps, like her father suggested, he was someone else.

"I'm sorry to disturb you at this hour, Señorita," said the operator, "but Eduardo is on the line."

"Eduardo? I don't—" Isabella almost shut Damir out of her

life forever, but her instincts took over and the memory of a lost boy forced her to sit up in bed and tell the operator to put the call through.

"Go ahead, sir," said the operator.

"Hello? This is—"

"Isabella!" Damir barely got the words out.

"It's you! Where are you? Why didn't you call? I've been waiting—"

"But we did! We've been calling for two days! Called and called—left you all kinds of messages!"

"Oh, dear, sweet Damir—!"

Click.

Long pause. "Damir?" said Isabella as the line went dead. Why did he give a different name? And where are all the messages he said they left?

"Isabella!" Across town, Damir stood in the dark, holding the receiver. Although he was relieved to get through to Isabella, he was even more pleased that she had been waiting for his call, and he re-dialed. "We got cut-off," he said to the operator.

The woman, who sounded like she had been crying, then put him on hold and hung up.

Confused and angry, Didi called a third time and demanded to be put through to Isabella Gigli.

"*I am sorry, but it's not allowed. I have orders,*" admitted the operator. She assumed that Maestro Gigli was trying to keep his daughter away from an unworthy suitor because no sooner she disconnected the young man that Isabella Gigli called the switchboard and insisted on an explanation. "*I apologize, Señorita, but, like I told your—friend. I have my orders.*"

It was a situation that confounded Damir. No sooner did he hang up the phone, that he crept upstairs and into his sister's room, shone the lamp in her face and in an urgent tone of voice, said: "Wake up!"

"Where am I?" said Katarina sitting abruptly in bed, looking around.

"Listen! I talked to Isabella!" said Damir.

Katarina rubbed her eyes. "What time is it?"

"Late! Wake up! I'm telling you—I got through to Isabella!" Damir shook his sister just a bit.

"You did? When?"

Quietly, Damir and Kati walked downstairs, and sat across each other in the kitchen, whispering in the dark.

"Maybe they're not to put calls through after a certain time," remarked Kati.

"She said she had orders!" returned her brother.

"From who? Beniamino? Maybe he doesn't want her having anything to do with us," she said.

"Why?" asked Didi, softly.

"Who knows?" Kati shrugged.

"He liked us," said Didi. "I mean, he said so—on the ship."

"People change their minds," argued his sister.

"What's this?" Ante groped for the light switch with one hand while he held a gun in the other; the same small black pistol used to murder the shepherd boy.

Damir froze for an instant. He did not see the hand holding the gun, or the man attached to the hand. He fixed his eyes on the weapon, was barely conscious of his sister or the room they were in, and instinctively pounced on his father. "Kati, run, get away! He'll murder you, get away!" he screamed, beating Ante to the ground, lucky the gun did not go off by accident.

Marija and Rubén arrived on the scene about the same time and tried to pull Damir away.

"Murderer!" yelled Damir.

"What have you done? Villain!" screamed Marija, throwing herself on her husband.

"Mama," screamed Kati, grabbing at her mother. "It's not Papa's fault! He did not do anything! Nothing!"

Ante gave Marija a violent shove and struggled to his feet. "Are you insane? Fool! I heard a noise and—!"

"Killer! Murderer!" shrieked Damir one last time, then collapsed.

As songbirds skipped from treetop to treetop praising another spectacular morning in Buenos Aires, Supi enjoyed his coffee and toast in the relative peace of his small office, surrounded by pictures of dead kinfolk and two watercolors depicting the majesty of the pampas, when the phone rang.

"Please, come at once to 8111," said the voice at the other end.

"Oh, what is wrong now?" thought Supi. He put down his coffee, looked at his watch and confirmed it was exactly eight o'clock. Then, he straightened his tie, made sure the flower on his lapel was as fragrant as when it was plucked, cheerfully stepped into the elevator that would take him to the top floor, and ran head-first into a disaster.

The opera star stood by his daughter, who sat on the leather sofa. Next to them was the Great Gigli's assistant, and in the center of the room—standing alone, agitated and sober for once—Manolo Ortiz, the hotel General Manager.

"Supencio," said Ortiz, removing his tortoise-shell glasses and wiping off the sweat on his forehead, "Maestro Gigli has a complaint."

Complaints at the hotel ranged from getting a glass of tepid orange juice to having pigeon droppings on your window and the front desk manager knew that Ortiz, sooner or later, would get around to the complaint.

"My daughter tells me that last night the hotel operator disconnected a telephone call from a friend, saying she was following orders! Whose orders? I want to know who dares to have my calls intercepted!" demanded the Great Gigli in a voice better suited for an operatic stage.

"I have informed Maestro Gigli," added Ortiz, feeling light-headed, "that it is the policy of the Alvear Palace to jealously safeguard the privacy of our guests and anyone caught intercepting calls will be dismissed at once."

Ignorance is bliss, thought Supi, when the Great Gigli raged for five minutes, until he ran out of breath and had gained considerable color.

"Don Manolo," said Supi at last, "may I have a word with you—in private?"

"In private!?" bellowed Gigli, approaching Supi. "Let's see how the Minister of Culture and the Artistic Director of Teatro Colón—who are on the way here, by the way—will break the news to President and Madame Perón that I, Beniamino Gigli, will never sing in Argentina because you, sir, want to talk in private! This is an outrage!"

"Maestro, I am sure it is nothing but a misunderstanding. Please bear with me a moment." Ortiz then turned to the front desk manager. "Supencio, anything you have to say, you can say in front of Maestro Gigli, and I suggest you do it now!"

"Very well," sighed Supi, calmly taking out his watch and confirming it was nearly eight-ten in the morning. "Yes, as much as I loathe and repudiate the practice, your calls are being monitored and some are intercepted."

"But—on whose orders?" inquired the General Manager.

"This is infamy!" roared the great Beniamino.

Someone else (like Ortiz), some spineless creature would have dropped on their knees, kissed the tenor's velvet slipper and begged for mercy. Not Supencio Martínez del Arrollo. He glanced at his watch, noticed it was eight-twelve, then accurately described the visit to the hotel by members of a security branch of the government.

"And why was I not informed of this?" asked the General Manager, very red in the face.

"I was preparing a memorandum when you rang just now," explained the Front Desk Manager.

"It was I who should have been told at once!" screamed the Great Gigli. "Did you, for a moment, consider the consequences of your shameful enterprise?"

"Shameful? Tsk, tsk, Maestro," Supi grimaced as if the stench of folly permeated the suite. "I think a better word might be judicious. I do not, never have, never will involve myself in other peoples' affairs. I do not, never have and never will care who anyone," by his emphasis on the pronoun Supi apprised those in the room that the guidelines applied to all members of the human race, regardless of fame or notoriety, "who anyone consorts with, talks about, or is connected to. However, sir, when two properly identified detectives—I assume the two men were detectives in one way or another—request that I do my duty, my patriotic duty, and exercise my limited authority as Front Desk Manager of the most prestigious hostelry in the world to intercept a few telephone calls—an action, that as I said before, I feel nothing but contempt for, sir, but that, as it might be related to national security was deemed absolutely necessary for reasons no one has shared with me—then, sir, I am afraid that Supencio Martínez del Arrollo has no choice but to nod, assent and comply." Supi's exposition, which lasted, by his own estimate, forty-five seconds, befuddled every one present. Taking advantage of their temporary inability to speak, he added: "Perhaps, Maestro, if I told you the names of the people I was told not to put through it might help elucidate our differences, yes? They are foreign names, you understand. One sounded like kitty, although I'm sure cats had nothing to do with anything. You must forgive me but I never heard names like these before. The other was Didi something or other, and the last was Marica or Mariachi," concluded Supi with a flourish of his right hand.

"Oh, Papa!"

"For your information, sir, Damir and Kati are two children my daughter befriended on the way to Argentina. Are you telling me that in your country children cannot talk to other children?"

At that moment, while Beniamino comforted his daughter, the doors to the suite flung open and don Anastasio Gómez, Minister of Culture of Argentina and don Fulgencio de Jesús, Artistic Director of Teatro Colón, entered panic-stricken.

"Finalmente!" cried Beniamino Gigli.

"Maestro! What is going on?" asked the Minister.

"Nothing! Not even opera!" With that Beniamino fulminated against Argentina, the Alvear Palace Hotel and its den of spies, especially the front desk manager, who did not look at his watch again until he left the room.

The Minister and the Artistic Director took turns trying to convince the Great Gigli not to cancel his engagement. "It would be a scandal," exclaimed the white-haired Minister. "A national disgrace," added the thin, balding Artistic Director. "The President and the First Lady are expected opening night!" added the Minister. "Maestro, we have a contract!"

"Indeed, with a clause that, as you know, allows me to cancel if I get sick," said the tenor with a sudden fit the likes of which had not been witnessed in Buenos Aires since the influenza of 1918. "Call del Monaco! He'll sing for you. He's not Gigli, but then again, who is?"

"Pray he changes his mind because if not, I will have you shot! Get out! And no more hanky-panky with the phones!" said the Minister to the hotel managers, who retreated, bowed, turned and fled.

"This is all very strange," whispered aside Beniamino to his daughter.

16

Damir looked out for the open beam where he bumped his head more than once. Nothing had changed in the room except the crib was gone. He guessed Ana took it back to the cellar.

He missed the baby so much. "I will never forget you," he said. "I love you, Saša!"

He stepped to the window and saw the moon's beautiful glow upon Mount Vlašić, and many more stars than he remembered.

And where was the shepherd? "Pero, where are you? It's me, Damir!" He wanted to tell the old man all about Argentina and Isabella but the barn was empty; no Pero, no cot, no dog, even the washbowl was gone.

That's when he heard the lamentations.

A woman Damir had never seen before sat crying in a chair next to the bed where Ana, dressed in black, lay with an almost translucent veil on her face, holding her beloved rosary to her bosom.

Two rows of candles on the dresser table bathed the room in sepia, their billowing smoke escaping out the partially opened windows.

On the floor, at the foot of the bed, a little boy about six years old that Damir guessed belonged to the woman in the chair, had fallen asleep, his head resting on a seat cushion.

Damir felt a deep sense of loss. Ana had always been loving and kind.

And the priest? He entered his mother's room, looking older and tired, said a prayer, then gently picked up the child, carried him upstairs to the attic, removed his sandals, and tucked him in bed.

"It's not possible!" whispered Damir, when the boy pulled the svirala from under his pillow.

Three days after his relapse into the depression that almost killed him as a child, Damir wandered into the uncharted plains of the spirit, lacked the will even to rise from bed, and refused to eat. Two doctors—an internist and a psychiatrist—recommended that he be placed in a psychiatric hospital, and Marija concurred, though not before she reached out in a last desperate attempt to rescue her son from a psychosis no one seemed to understand.

"Maestro, thank you so much for coming. I know you are very busy. Isabella, my dear—" Marija greeted the Giglis, before stepping aside. "May I introduce my husband?"

Beniamino turned to Pavelić, paused, offered his obeisance, and said: "Sir! This—is an unexpected pleasure."

"Oh, please, where is Damir? May I see him, please?"

"Will you excuse us," said Marija, leading Isabella out of the library, leaving the Great Gigli and the Poglavnik to become acquainted.

"Allow me," said Pavelić, helping Beniamino with his overcoat and hat. "I understand you sing."

Halfway up the stairs, Marija stopped, looked at Isabella, and said: "I am not going to lie to you. Damir is willing himself to die for reasons you may find out in time. If his condition does not improve, he will have to be committed to save his life."

"Oh, thank God!" said Kati, when Isabella entered the room.

She greeted her friend with tears, hugs and kisses. "Here, take my chair."

"Damir," said the voice in his dream. "Damir," it said again. The music and the voice were almost one. "It's me. Isabella. Oh, please, please get well!" she said, holding his hand to her face.

"Didi, my sweet," said Marija. "Isabella has come to see you. Won't you say hello? What is it?"

"Saša," he whispered.

Isabella looked up at Marija. "Who is Saša?"

"You want to tell Isabella about the baby?" said Marija, wiping his forehead with a wet towel.

"He's—not a baby anymore," he said, slowly opening his eyes, looking at Isabella, and smiling. "Where is the Great Gigli?"

"Downstairs, talking to your papa."

Indeed.

"Yes," replied Beniamino, when Pavelić offered him a chair. "That is what I do, I sing. And you, sir? I don't think Madame Dávila—"

"Bianchi," corrected Ante. "You mean my wife? Yes, the name is Bianchi, not—that other name." Pavelić leaned back and looked intently at the Great Gigli. It occurred to him that the man sitting on the other side of the room was perhaps not a singer at all, but an assassin from Belgrade who had made contact with Marija and the children aboard the Afortunato, preyed on their lack of caution, and by way of a complicated and melodramatic ruse wormed himself into their confidence in order to kidnap Ante's family, assassinate the Poglavnik, or both.

"Oh, well," joined Beniamino. "What's in a name? That which we call a rose by any other name would smell as sweet," quoted the Great Gigli.

Pavelić was not impressed. He did not think he looked or smelled like a rose.

"I have to tell you something," said the tenor, smiling. "You have heard of Benito Mussolini, I'm sure."

Pavelić put his hand in his jacket pocket and looked slightly bored.

The Great Gigli continued: "Sometime around 1933, il Duce held a lavish dinner party at Villa Torlonia. I was there. I was his favorite tenor, or so he said. I admit that, back then, I agreed with his vision for Italy and Europe. Anyway, halfway through the evening, I noticed a very moody, very serious man in the company of other moody, serious fellows who mostly kept to themselves. Impressed with this man's no-nonsense demeanor, I asked Pietro Mascagni—who you may or may not have heard of—wrote *Cavalleria Rusticana*—"

Ante shook his head.

"It's not important," Gigli went on. "What's important is that I pointed out the man to my friend Pietro, and he said: 'Oh, that's Dr. Ante Pavelić, the leader of the Croatian resistance.' Of course, after that, every time I read the Poglavnik's name in the paper, I say to myself 'I know that man.' Small world, is it not?"

It is worth mentioning that Pavelić did not set in motion an elaborate fabrication to deny who he was. He simply let go of the pistol in his pocket, and said: "So, you've come to Buenos Aires to sing?"

"Though I said I would not," replied Beniamino.

"But—will you?"

"Yes."

"What made you change your mind?"

"You did." And the tenor smiled but did not offer further explanation.

"I want to thank you for everything you've done for Marija and the children," said Pavelić, after a pause. "I am grateful."

Beniamino indicated that Damir and Katarina's company was its own reward.

"However," continued Ante, "there are a few things I must explain. You are here because my wife feels that having your daughter visit Damir may relieve whatever ails him. Personally, I am against my family associating with you or your daughter.

Please understand that my feelings have nothing to do with personal likes and dislikes. You are a charming man. But, as I have tried explaining to my wife, you lead a very public life, whereas we enjoy our privacy. That cannot and will not change. Therefore, please keep whatever thoughts you have as to who is what and what is who to yourself. I find speculation distasteful, irrelevant and unnecessary."

Beniamino nodded, got up, walked to one end of the room, turned around, stopped as if waiting for a conductor to snap the baton, and said: "What I do, sir, I do for the sake of my daughter. I will say to you that there is very little I would not do for Isabella, except make her unhappy." Beniamino then described the day Isabella was born, and how his wife Edda, a woman he cherished, had lived long enough to call out her name. Edda, explained the tenor, died because she had invested the baby with so much beauty, effervescence of spirit, intelligence, and such a determined, yet thoughtful and generous disposition that she had none to keep for herself.

But, growing up without her mama presented problems of its own and Isabella spent the first years of her life under the loving care of her grandparents, playing and prancing in the topiary garden in Gigli's Roman manor where golden butterflies twiddled "The Dance of the Hours," bees buzzed *William Tell*, bunnies whispered nursery rhymes, nightingales sang lullabies, two Persian cats . . . a white and a Russian Blue . . . constantly hummed from *Aida*, Pucho the Pekingese spent its mornings tooting *Turandot* and a pair of crows, determined to add a little variety, harmonized to *The Magic Flute*. "Even Isabella's pony," remembered the tenor, "galloped to the stirring measures of the 'Light Cavalry Overture.' I have tried to make her life a fairy tale without goblins or stepmothers, evil or otherwise." Beniamino was about to sit down when he thought of something else. "I share with my daughter the adventure, the exhilaration, the satisfaction and the many privileges of my fame. But, it's not going to last forever. I have about five years left. Fifteen years from now, nobody will remember my name. But, I do not care. By then, Isabella will speak at least six languages, will have met some of the most important people of our time, will have gone down the Amazon and up the Nile, enjoyed breakfast in New York and supper in Canton."

"Lucky girl," said Pavelić, amused with the tenor's intensity.

"In many ways she is, in many ways she's not, because she cannot enjoy being with other children, and children need other children. I am certain that is one reason why she has become so fond of Damir and Kati and I do not believe, sir, that their friendship can be anything but a healthy experience for all three. Still, I am sensitive to your predicament and willing to oblige. If you feel that it is too—how shall I say—compromising for Isabella, Damir and Kati to be together during our stay in Buenos Aires, so be it. If you do not, you will find me just as accommodating." Beniamino stopped and this time imitated Pavelić in his delivery. "God knows I am a very busy man who does not need ghosts intercepting my telephone calls."

Later, as the Giglis made their way back to the Alvear Palace Hotel, Isabella turned to her father with eyes full of smiles, smiles because she was helping Damir recover from something she still did not understand but knew was terrible enough, and said: "Well, is Didi's papa Martin Bormann?"

Beniamino shook his head, looked at his daughter, and said: "Worse."

17

Marija's instincts proved correct. Isabella's company and enthusiasm forced Damir to slowly peel off the stupefying gloom and melancholia during walks around the neighborhood and visits to the Teatro Colón to watch the Great Gigli in rehearsals for *Turandot*.

Damir, of course, had never been to a theater before, let alone to a legendary opera house. Opening night was a couple of days away and, as with every theatrical production since the first cave man decided to get up in front of his tribe and scream, everything was running behind schedule and artistic sensitivities were unmercifully cast aside and crushed.

Arriving at the stage door, Isabella took Didi's hand, led him through a series of narrow and dimly lit corridors until they reached the Salón Dorado, with its impressive massive columns, chandeliers and ornate decorations. Then, they entered the two-thousand seat theater, where, on any given night, the ruling classes sat looking like music loving penguins.

"It is magnificent," exclaimed Damir, following Isabella to the empty stage. He looked out into the seats, then up at the high ceiling crisscrossed with catwalks, thousands of ropes, curtains and counterweights. "Huge!"

"Opera is the greatest show in the world," said Isabella. "It is more spectacular than a circus and many times it becomes just that. Can you imagine a flock of witches crossing the stage on their brooms or the absurdity of having immense women who are, for the most part, three times the size of the set, feigning starvation while twittering like songbirds on a sofa that is half their size?" It was enough to make the young, the very proper Isabella laugh aloud.

Backstage, they witnessed a hundred people running up and down with varied expressions of sadness, exuberance, doubt, exasperation, desperation, outrage, anger and finally—horror.

At the end of one corridor, the dimmest, shyest table lamp tried in vain to cheer the universe, and counter the thunderous reverberations heard from the tiny room.

A very short, thin woman covered with measuring tapes, ribbons, needles and pins, shot out of the cubicle and because it happened so fast, the young couple did not see if she had left of her own volition or had been expelled by force. Her two assistants were also covered with an assortment of tailoring accessories and flew out of the room with equal speed and violence. One of them, a frail little fellow, was in tears as he stood outside the door picking up trousers, coats, belts, buckles and shoes thrown in his face. "You should not be designing costumes, sir, you should be growing figs! Get out of my sight and never, never, come near me again! Fool!" The poor man grabbed his armload of fabrics and leather and fled with a face that had "panic" tagged on its nose.

The Great Gigli then aimed his frustrations at the Stage Director, tearing the libretto in the man's face. "I will stand where I will stand! Who do you think you are telling me where to stand on that stage? I want you to know, sir, that Puccini wrote the part for me and he never, ever dared suggest where I should stand! I will stand where I damn please and you will not tell me where to stand! Get out!"

The Stage Director, an extremely dignified man who towered over Gigli by at least one-and-a-half meters, and who, dressed in layers of gold rings, bracelets, silk handkerchiefs and large glasses, carried himself with great panache, grew very red, very emotional and very offended, flipped a handkerchief over his right shoulder, bowed to Gigli and quickly left the dressing-room.

Waiting in the hall when the disgraced man rushed by as "moron" rang in the air like a piercing midnight bell, Damir hesitated following Isabella to meet her father, but to his surprise, Beniamino turned without a frown or ill-humor, embraced the disconcerted and anxious young man, and said: "Damir, my boy, how are you feeling? Isabella, my sweet, how is he doing? Come, let's go to lunch."

Thought Damir: "People in opera are bizarre."

Half-hour later, the Great Gigli, Isabella and Damir arrived at Armánd's, a small, intimate and discreetly lit restaurant not far from the Teatro Colón, where no one was allowed to approach the singer for autographs or conversation, and those that did, were politely asked to leave.

"Bonjour, Armánd," said the Great Gigli as two waiters helped him with his coat and his fedora.

A terribly affected man whose French was worse than his hairpiece, Armánd, of course, was as Argentinean as a bowl of chimichurri, with a thin head, fish eyes, small ears, a Chaplinesque mustache, and tails. "Bonjour, bonjour, Maestro!" said Armánd with an exaggerated bow. "Your secretary just phoned. It seems you forgot your lunch with the President and the First Lady. She's on her way to pick you up—not Evita—I meant your secretary," added Armánd, laughing, before he whipped around, snapped his fingers, and called: "Pepe! Bring back the Maestro's coat and hat! *Tout suite!*"

"Oh, dear—that's right!" said Beniamino to Isabella. "Damir, you will forgive me, won't you?" he added, patting Didi on the cheek. "Armánd—"

"Oui, Maestro?"

"Only the best for my daughter and her friend," said the Great Gigli, rushing out.

And there it was; whether by accident or design Damir and Isabella had their first candlelight lunch with their conversation revolving around opera and the Giglis, which to Damir was one and the same.

After the veal Florentine, the grilled trout fillet, the wine selected by Armánd himself, and several samples from the dessert tray, Isabella and Damir walked out of the restaurant and strolled through the neighborhood, ending in a small park of narrow winding paths, ornate iron lamps and wide wooden benches where old men sat to read the newspapers, mothers nursed their babies and lovers cuddled under the mid-afternoon winter sun.

Talk of opera led to talk of music in general, Argentina, music in Argentina, and the tango.

"The what?" Damir had never heard of the tango.

"Tango is a dance from Argentina. It's known all over the world."

"Do you dance the tango?" inquired Damir.

Isabella thought for a moment. "A little. It is very involved."

"Why?"

"Because," she answered, smiling, "you should only tango with someone you love."

"I need to ask you something," said Damir, with a frown. "Why—do you like me?"

"Who said I like you?" returned Isabella.

"You don't—you don't like me?"

"No," she added. "I love you."

"How can you say that?" asked Didi, concerned. "We just met. You don't know anything about me—don't know who I am, where I come from, nothing."

Love, as romantics, philosophers and cynics agree, is nothing short of a confounding miracle that can be both creator and destroyer at the same time. It is a divine spark that sends every particle in the body into a condition of extraordinary happiness or inexplicable despair. It blurs the vision with tears of joy or melancholy; at times endows a person with superhuman strength, or leaves him weak, suffering from headaches and mood swings of depression and elation, aggravated by eating and sleeping disorders. Of course, there is no formula for falling in love. It appears when one least expects it and blows away and dies just as capriciously. It is as impossible to fall in love wittingly as it is not to fall in love when you do and Isabella had fallen victim to that disconcerting of all human indiscretions.

"Your name is Damir Pavelić. You are the son of the exiled president of Croatia, Ante Pavelić. I know because Papa told me he met your father in 1933, at a reception for Mussolini. What else?"

"What was Beniamino doing there?"

"Like many others then, he admired Mussolini," said Isabella.

"Beniamino Gigli is a fascist?"

"Beniamino Gigli was a fascist."

"Do you know what a fascist is?"

"No," answered the girl. "I know what Papa tells me and what he tells me is that, in those days, Mussolini was a great leader that most people in Italy liked very much. Then, one day, he was not liked anymore and those that were fascist in Italy became something else. I don't understand anything about it but I still love you."

Damir looked away for a moment, took a deep breath and said: "I know very little of Mussolini, I know too much about my father and when I tell you the things he has done, you will not want to see me anymore."

"That is not possible," said Isabella firmly.

Damir's voice acquired an urgency, like a signal calling those nearby to flee from danger. "Isabella, my father is a monster, a mass murderer responsible for the deaths of hundreds of thousands of people."

"I love you," was all she said.

Damir told her about Jasenovac, about Glina and Saša.

"I still love you."

"You don't care—?" said Damir, alarmed.

"Of course I do," she answered, "and it makes me sick. I know you can never forget the nightmares, but you must understand that none of it—nothing—was your fault."

"I have his blood—his evil in every cell of my body!"

"No. Evil is not in you nature," said Isabella kissing Damir on the cheek.

Damir looked intently upon the girl. Saša, he thought, would have loved Isabella.

⊕

The next couple of days found Damir, his mother and sister getting ready for the most wonderful and exciting evening of their lives, Beniamino Gigli's opening night of *Turandot*, when Juana Fritz, or the Fritz, as she became known, appeared on the scene, as if dropped by parachute.

Katarina heard the bell, looked out the door and saw a woman she did not know standing by the gate, waving from under a newspaper. "Si?"

"Juana! Juana Fritz!"

"It's the maid," said Marija, walking up to her daughter. "Where are the dogs?"

"In the back."

"Let her in," said Marija.

Juana was in her mid-forties, tall, thin, with thighs like saddlebags and a neck and head resembling an ostrich, and yet, she was not so much ugly as curious to look at. It is true that her nose, black eyes, mouth and ears were too small to be in proportion with the rest of her features, but the Fritz had a disarming wide-eyed smile, an honest face and an indomitable spirit that Marija felt was necessary in dealing with her family.

"Señora Bianchi?" The Fritz folded the wet newspaper that had protected her from the drizzle and placed it carefully in her large purse.

"Hello. Please, come in. My husband said you'd be calling." Marija liked the Fritz at once and after a short interview offered the woman a tryout period of one month.

The day of the gala, it was the Fritz who bounced from downstairs to upstairs, helping Marija dress in an elegant and exquisite black silk evening gown, pearls and a mink stole, then crossed the hall to assist Kati with her gorgeous blue velvet dress and silver slippers.

And Damir? He kept to his room all day, nervous that he would look silly in his brand new, tailored made tuxedo.

It was not until 5:30 in the afternoon, with Marija and Kati ready to leave, while the Fritz tended to last minute details of their dress and Rubén waited to drive them to the opera house that Damir took one last look in the mirror, sighed and went to meet his mother and sister.

Marija and Kati had been arguing about some silly thing when they saw their son and brother coming down the stairs.

"*¡Qué bello!*" said the Fritz, smiling. "He looks like a young Gary Cooper."

"Who's Gary Cooper?" asked Kati.

The Bianchis arrived at the theater fifteen minutes before curtain. Isabella was splendid in a charming green silk gown with gray trim that made her blue eyes sparkle more than usual and a fabulous emerald tiara that kept her golden hair perfectly in place. She greeted Marija, Kati and Damir at the stage door with her usual hugs and kisses. "Madame, that's a fabulous gown. Kati! Where did you get that dress? It is dazzling." Isabella turned to Marija, "we must keep an eye on Kati tonight. There are dozens of handsome boys here, especially the son of the Venezuelan ambassador. I'll be sure to introduce him to you." Isabella winked at Katarina. "Of course," she continued, "he comes up short, next to Damir." And Isabella gave Didi a kiss that made him turn very red.

"Will you sit with us?" inquired Marija.

"Some of the time. You will forgive me, won't you? Papa likes to have me in the wings when he sings."

"Of course, darling, don't worry about us."

"Look at this place!" exclaimed Katarina as she walked through the magnificent opera house. "Isabella, is Evita—"

"Not yet," answered Isabella, showing them to their box, not far from the President's. "She should be arriving any moment now."

As soon as Marija, Damir and Katarina were seated, Isabella excused herself and rushed backstage.

An usher arrived with the program for that evening's performance of *Turandot* and some of the future events planned at the opera house.

"He looks thin," remarked Katarina when she saw Beniamino's picture on the cover.

"And tall," added Marija.

"So, Didi, what is this thing about?" Katarina made herself comfortable, expecting to sleep through the performance.

"This thing is an opera called *Turandot*," replied Damir with as much condescension as he could pack into an lifted brow and a sigh.

His sister was not going to make it easy for him. "Well, is it fun?"

Damir rolled his eyes, looked at his mother as if to say: "She is such a child."

Turandot, he explained, was the last Puccini opera—the composer being the greatest of opera composers, ever—according to him. It was the story of a Chinese princess called Turandot who has a vendetta against all males, especially those that want to marry her.

"Why?" interrupted Katarina.

"Never mind why, she does, that's all," said Damir in his most patronizing tone.

So Turandot gives every man of royal blood who wants to marry her . . .

"Why of royal blood?" interposed Kati again.

"Because she's a princess! She's not going to marry just anyone. As I was saying, she gives her suitors three riddles, and if they don't answer all three correctly, they are executed."

"Good for her!"

"Now comes Calaf—that is the role that Gigli will sing. He is a prince but no one knows it. After an exchange with his father, who was lost and was suddenly found, Calaf sees Turandot and falls in love with her."

"Why was his father lost?" Katarina was curious.

"It's not important," shot back an impatient Damir. "Calaf then begs the chance to answer the riddles so he can marry the princess."

"That's dumb," observed Damir's sister.

"Kati," intervened Marija, "enough."

"Anyway," continued Damir, "Calaf answers correctly all three questions. Still, Turandot refuses to marry him. She tries to have the whole thing called off but her father, the emperor, does not allow it. Calaf replies that he does not want to marry the princess Turandot if she does not want to marry him, so, if she can guess his name, he is willing to give up his life. Immediately Turandot orders everyone in Peking to find out the name of the stranger so she can have him executed. When that fails, Calaf takes Turandot in his arms and gives her a kiss. Then, he tells her his name, putting his life in her hands. Turandot is so taken by the kiss that she falls in love with Calaf and tells her subjects that his name is *Amore*."

"That's it?"

Damir sighed, and was about to open his program when there was a great commotion in the audience just as Isabella returned to the box.

"*Perón! Perón! Perón! Perón!*"

"Kati, look!" Isabella pointed to Juan Perón, dressed in a very becoming Italian suit, and his wife Evita, who matched her husband's elegance with a lovely Dior gown and a diamond necklace that must have cost many shirts from the backs of their supporters.

"*Perón! Perón! Perón!*"

"Didi, are you all right?"

He was not. As a little boy, he had witnessed similar mani-
festations, except that instead of *"Perón!"* the crowds cried out
"Pavelić!" Fascism was very much alive in Argentina.

"I'm sorry," whispered Isabella. She gave Damir a kiss, and left.

While Perón and Evita waved to the crowd, Damir returned
to the program. He read about the future productions at the
Teatro Colón and *Maria Stuarda* caught his eye. It was an opera
by Donizetti and one of the characters was Elizabetta, that is,
Queen Elizabeth of England.

Suddenly, the house went dark and the conductor walked
out to the accompaniment of *"Bravo!"* The man bowed once to
the Presidential Box, once to each side of the house, turned, and
the Teatro Colón exploded in a fantasy of music.

Damir almost fell from his chair. It was real music, certainly
not the kind he was used to cranking out of a phonograph.

Then, Beniamino Gigli walked on stage and the audience
went wild. They were not calling out *"Perón,"* they screamed:
"Gigli! Gigli! Gigli!"

Tears streamed down Damir's face as he sat quietly listening
to the crowd: *"Gigli! Gigli! Gigli!"*

An hour later, the first curtain call was pandemonium when
the great tenor stepped forward to take his bow: *"Bravo Gigli!"*

A few minutes after that, during the first intermission,
Isabella rejoined her guests. This time she brought along a little
girl with a tray of refreshments.

"You like it so far?"

"It's great!" said Kati.

Marija laughed, and Damir rolled his eyes and shook his
head. Isabella kept them company a few minutes until the first
bell announced that the second act was about to begin. Then she
dashed off to her father.

It is the great talent of the human mind to take one thought
and connect it to another by logical or sometimes illogical associa-
tion. When Damir returned to the program he stared at the name
Elizabetta. The boy had studied enough European history to know

that Elizabeth of England had been a great queen. But why did that fact hold his interest? Elizabetta. Isabella. No. The two names were different, no doubt about it. Elizabeth, or Elizabetta, as was written in the program, was Queen of England; it was also the name of the empress of Austria and the czarina of Russia.

Damir put aside the program when the lights went down and was caught in the heavenly music vibrating in the air. The second act ended like the first, with *"Gigli! Gigli! Gigli! Gigli!"* except that, as Beniamino walked in front of the curtain, the audience tossed flowers at his feet. "Just wait," Damir warned his mother and sister. "You haven't seen anything yet."

"What do you mean?" asked Kati.

"Wait," was the only thing Damir said.

"Isabella has not come up this time," observed Katarina.

"She must be busy helping her father," suggested Marija.

Damir read the program. Yes, he thought Elizabetta and Isabella were two different names. Isabella, of course, was the name of Isabella d'Este, an Italian noblewoman of the Renaissance, famous as a patron of the arts. And then, there was Queen Isabella the Catholic, who made it possible for Columbus to travel to the New World.

Just then, the third act of *Turandot* began. Damir dropped the program on the floor as the house became quiet, so quiet you could hear people shuffling in their seats. The silence was solemn and absolute as the Great Gigli began: "Nessun Dorma."

Damir edged so far forward, he might have fallen off. He closed his eyes, and suddenly every moment, every sight, every smell of that night aboard the Afortunato hit him like a tidal wave. He remembered how he almost killed himself had it not been for that voice.

"Vincero! Vincero!"

The house sat stunned. Not a sound was heard after the great aria. Then suddenly, there was an outpouring of enthusiasm so extraordinary that it was heard outside the Teatro Colón. *"Bravo! Gigli!"*

The ovation lasted ten minutes and the great tenor was forced to sing an encore of the most inspiring aria in opera.

Damir, however, remained in his seat, wiping the tears with his sleeve, when he stopped paying attention to the music and stared into space. He searched on the floor for the program, and, with the help of a little stray beam of light from the hall, read the name *Carmen*. The opera by Bizet was going to be presented at the Teatro Colón as part of the next season. It was all about a Gypsy . . .

Damir shot up, as if his seat been electrified.

"Didi!" Marija whispered loudly and grabbed his arm to make her son sit back down. He would not.

"What's the matter with you!?" asked Katarina.

Damir rushed out of the box as the opera began its climactic finish and his mother and sister were unable to stop him; becoming targets of several nasty stares from their neighbors.

Rubén chased after him, waving off the other security men as Didi flew down the stairs, into the main house and out a side door he knew led backstage.

"Find the sovereign that will give you comfort and cheer your days."

Damir went to Beniamino's dressing room but did not find Isabella. She was on stage, in the wings, watching her father. "Isabella!" he called out.

Fortunately, the music was so loud the audience did not hear Damir scream. He rushed past several members of the chorus, past the stage hands and the Stage Manager, looking everywhere for Isabella.

"What are you doing here? Get out!" Elvira tried to keep Didi from distracting the singers on stage.

But Damir did not notice Elvira, the singers, or even the Great Gigli raising his arms and voice, because he at last caught sight of—"Isabella!"

"Damir!"

They faced each other. Didi was out of breath and Isabella looked at him with concern.

"*So il tuo nome!*" sang Turandot. "I know your name!"

"*Amore!*"

THE BISHOP

18

"**P**apa!" screamed the little boy. His father tried to hold onto him, only to have a soldier whack him in the face with the butt of the rifle. The same Ustaša then landed a violent kick on the shepherd's son, making the boy fall, lacerating his knees and elbows. And yet, he never let go of the svirala.

"Do as they say, do as they tell you! Don't make them angry!" pleaded his father, almost hysterical, a trace of foam dribbling from his mouth.

"What's your name, asshole?" yelled the soldier.

Terrified, the shepherd did not answer right away and it took a hard slap in the face before he screamed: "Ivan! Please! We weren't doing anything! We're poor people. We don't hurt anyone! I beg you! Don't hurt my boy!"

"Shut your face, sheep fucker! Get moving, go!"

Ronnoco woke up with a start and sat up in bed, soaked in perspiration. The alarm clock flashed a red, bold "six" and he felt a headache coming.

He staggered to the bathroom, ran the hot water and let steam fill the apartment. He then took off his undershorts, and stepped inside the acrylic doors, allowing the soothing warmth relax his body and soften the stubble.

"*Excellency!*"

"What?" he yelled.

"*Serafio is on the phone!*"

"Serafio? What time is it?" called out Ronnoco.

"Six thirty-five!"

"I'll be there by eight," he said, after a pause.

Outside, Sister Angelina opened the windows, before neatly laying out the bishop's dress on the bed: a black cassock with purple buttons, matching zucchetto and sash, a silver chain and cross, underwear, socks, and black shoes.

At sixty-two, the nun from Calabria was typical of women caring for the comfort of high-ranking church officials. They were plain, full of piety, and in her case, possessing a quick mind and a wit ready to lash out at anything improper.

"You look awful," she said, looking up from the newspaper when Ronnoco walked into the kitchen.

He placed his briefcase by the door, sipped his espresso, took a bite of toast and shrugged.

"Will you be home for supper, Excellency?"

"I don't know. I'll let you know by twelve," answered Ronnoco, finishing his grapefruit juice.

He arrived at his office at the end of a long, dark corridor in back of the Government Palace in Vatican City, at seven forty-five.

Secured with heavy cast iron doors and a Zeffir combination lock, the large room had white walls, tall windows dressed with yellow curtains, and a large portrait of Saint Jerome that concealed a safe.

Ronnoco placed his briefcase on the ornate wooden desk, turned on his laptop, reviewed his e-mail, logged out, opened the safe behind Saint Jerome, and pulled out a large envelope stamped "Secret."

"Good morning, Excellency," said Father d'Stesi, making his way in the room.

"You're early," returned Ronnoco.

"Yes, I am," said d'Stesi. He was small, thin and thirty years old, with wavy, dark brown hair and a large nose. Like his predecessor, the secretary not only answered to the Guardian of Saint Jerome, but boasted a fastidious mind that complemented Ronnoco's often distracted nature. "Remember you're supposed to meet the Four Horsemen—at two."

The Four Horsemen, as Bishop Ronnoco called them, were Pope Leo's closest advisors, after Bishop Ronnoco, of course.

"We'll see."

Across the Vatican, His Holiness Leo XIV paced back and forth in his private study on the third floor of the Apostolic Palace. He forced himself to concentrate on the correspondence laid on his desk by his secretary. Of the thousands upon thousands of letters received by the Vatican each day addressed to the pope, only a trickle were actually read by the pontiff, and they had to be very special, very unusual, or of incredible urgency. Most of the letters addressed to the Holy Father were handled by ten clerical workers, who opened, read and distribute them to those experts within the bureaucracy of the Vatican that could best reply, if indeed a reply was necessary. For instance, if a letter requested an audience with the pope, it was automatically routed to Cardinal Tomaso, who, depending on the individual making the request, would then forward his recommendation to the pontiff. Otherwise, the cardinal's assistant would answer with a polite and usually brief turndown. The most common petition was for a papal blessing. For that, the letters were automatically forwarded to Father Luciano Tenebroso, who would answer back in a form letter indicating the letter was being studied, and upon a decision, would then be passed along to His Holiness— which meant that the sender could make up his own mind about whether he had been blessed by the pope or not.

That morning, a letter did make it to the pope's attention. It was from America and talked about an apparition.

Apparition. Leo stared at the word. He suffered the chief ailment of the Vatican . . . grand antiquity . . . with every other bone and joint corroded by arthritis. Ten years into his tenure as Vicar of Rome, he had undergone heart surgery for clogged arteries and wore a pacemaker. Glaucoma had also been of concern, but although he suffered a slight blindness in his right eye, his vision of a greater, more powerful Church forced him to wake up every day and battle the impossible. Every one of his sixteen years on the papal throne had been excruciatingly difficult. Then again, he had expected nothing else. Leo XIV was the first non-Italian pontiff in the Roman Church in almost 500 years.

His rooms were spacious but modest, if modest can be applied to anything in the Holy See. The walls were of an off-white color, the ceilings were high, and the delicate cream-colored curtains fluttered back and forth in the gentle summer breeze. A plush white and yellow rug covered the parquet floors, large vases with plants and flowers filled the corners, and Renaissance images of the Madonna and Child hung on the walls in elegant, but plain gold frames.

"His Eminence Carelli is waiting outside, Holiness," announced Brother Serafio.

"Carelli? What is he doing here? What does he want?" asked the pontiff impatiently.

"He obviously would like to talk to you," replied the sixty-two year old Franciscan. "He was here yesterday, and the day before that."

"Well, I don't want to talk to him. Tell him to go away. I don't want to see anyone now but Felix."

"As you wish, Holiness." Serafio turned and left.

Antonio Cardinal Carelli occupied two chairs in the narrow antechamber outside the pope's door because a single chair would have collapsed under the eminent load. The "Humpback of the See" (as his detractors called him) was reading the Italian edition of TIME when the pope's secretary announced: "His Holiness is not receiving at this time."

Stung by the papal indifference, the cardinal did not look up from the page, but in stealthy silence, folded the magazine and started to glide away, looking more like a hovercraft than a prince of the church.

Brother Serafio, who by then was sitting behind his desk, said: "Ah, ah—the magazine, please."

The cardinal did not break stride but slowly banked to the left, retraced his steps and gently reinstalled the publication in its berth.

"Good morning, Brother Carelli," greeted Ronnoco, walking quickly past the cardinal. Carelli acknowledged the bishop with a slight and aloof nod before turning the corner.

"Good morning, Excellency," sang Brother Serafio.

"Good morning," answered Ronnoco without stopping.

"Shall I—" Brother Serafio was about to ask if he should announce the bishop, but by then, Ronnoco was inside with Pope Leo and all Serafio could do, was raise his bald eyebrows, pucker his lips and get busy.

"I see Serafio has a new toy." Ronnoco meant the computer on the friar's desk. He shut the door and walked to the pope.

Leo got up, embraced and kissed the bishop, and said: "Yes, we've made it to the twentieth century."

Bishop Ronnoco and Pope Leo XIV met almost every day, usually early in the mornings when His Excellency briefed the pontiff on any number of issues having to do with the Holy See and its archdioceses around the world: from progress by a secret federation of Catholic states in Europe established by pontifical mandate to block the spread of Islamic fundamentalism in the continent and the Eastern Church's supremacy in the Balkans and in Russia, to handling a brother, be it a lowly priest or a cardinal, whose indiscretions had mired the Church in scandal.

The topic to discuss that day, however, was the dissent and divisiveness among the eight hundred million Catholics worldwide because of the Catholic Church's stand on issues of morality, abortion, contraception and divorce.

In order to best confront and deal with the problem, the pope, at the urging of Bishop Ronnoco, ordered a secret study hoping to have a better understanding of the attitudes and the reasoning of his increasingly rebellious flock. There was nothing the study did not cover, no question it did not ask, and no answer that was not carefully noted; nothing like it had ever been done before and the voluminous task, with its impressive two hundred thousand respondents, took over two years to complete.

"One question," said the pope. "Are we in trouble?"

Ronnoco placed a chair in front of the ornate, mahogany desk, opened his briefcase and pulled out the secret memorandum he had prepared. "The numbers speak for themselves."

"We don't want to read anything; you tell us what's going on." Leo pushed away the memo.

The bishop shrugged, retrieved the paper and returned to his chair. "The bottom line is that there has been a 25 percent drop in church attendance in the last fifteen years. That translates into a twenty-five percent loss in revenues from collections. However, that does not reflect the total loss in contributions; that number is approximately 35 percent, since those who have remained in the Church are giving 10 percent less than they were before. The situation is not improving; in fact, it's getting worse and threatens many archdioceses, especially those in developing countries.

"We did not reach this critical stage overnight. This trend is part of a phenomenon that goes back almost thirty years, to the advent of mass communication—especially television—and the fostering of democratic principles around the globe. It is interesting to note that it is precisely this odd mix of democracy and mass media that has affected the way Catholics think of their Church, which had been very important in their lives, for centuries. Children went to catholic schools and their parents belonged to men's and women's societies connected to the church. If people had problems, they discussed them with their priest. Catholics felt secure that they could depend on the Church. Today, you will agree, things are different.

"Many Catholics today refuse to follow Church teachings. Some are against Church actions and are demanding changes in our policies. A significant number also believes that the Holy See is an inflexible monolith unable to confront the many problems of a modern society. Sixty-four percent of Catholics around the world disagree with the Church on abortion, convinced that ending a pregnancy is, sometimes, justified and not morally reprehensible. Seventy-six percent think that ending a bad marriage is better than not, and 48 percent disagree with our stand on homosexuality."

"Not good, not good," said Leo, under his breath.

"One of the problems—and I don't think this will surprise you—is that we don't have enough priests. Since 1985, the number of priests has dropped by 13 percent, and many Catholics say that since only priests are permitted to lead the holiest ceremonies, that lack of leadership denies church goers the unique experience of being Catholic. As it stands now, 10 percent of our churches do not have their own priest but depend on visits from those from other parishes with ordinary church members—mostly women—running things for their congregation, including dispensing advice and running parochial schools."

"Enough!"

"Don't you want to hear the good news?"

"Good news?" said the pope in a loud, angry voice.

"Eighty-five percent of respondents like you."

"But they question every decision we make. How dare they doubt the wisdom of the Holy See? It is shocking."

"We are not dealing with illiterate peasants anymore. People today have a degree of sophistication that is bound to make them question everything. If it makes you feel any better, I don't believe the problems described are exclusive to the Catholic Church. I am sure Protestants, Muslims and Jews are also experiencing a change in attitude among their followers.

"In conclusion, we must become relevant. We need leaders and that comes down to the urgent need to train and recruit more priests. Only then can we address the other problems faced by the Church. I have a list of recommendations for you to consider."

"How many people know about the study?" asked the pope, looking worried.

"You and me."

"What about the people who did the research?"

"This project was designed in four parts to make it impossible for anyone to know what was going on at any given time, and it was further disguised with sections of the questionnaire having nothing to do with what we were trying to find out. Once I was given a hard copy of the findings, I ordered the data and all the material related to the study destroyed." Ronnoco smiled. "Satisfied?"

The pope leaned forward in his chair. "You cannot tell anyone about this," he said.

"Not even the Four Horsemen?"

"Especially them. Before you know it, they'll tell the others and soon they will be having meetings and issuing proclamations without ever getting a thing done. They're just a bunch of old farts afraid of their shadows." Leo pushed back his chair and walked around his desk. "Dear God, how did we ever get into this mess?"

"Look, there is no doubt we have made mistakes, but I also think this crisis was, in some ways, inevitable," said Ronnoco.

"Why?"

"We have lost the magic, the mysticism that made us unique among the world religions. We have embraced communications, technology and progress thinking that it was to our benefit, when in fact, they have promoted incredulity and dissent. Somewhere along the way we forgot that the Catholic Church is founded on faith and the supernatural. Sure, the taking of the Eucharist is intended to make a holy union between man and the Lord Christ, but—did you know that 95 percent of Catholics believe that transubstantiation is symbolic?" Transubstantiation was the

Catholic rite performed by a priest in which the bread and wine used in the Eucharist are in fact changed into the body and blood of Christ.

Leo looked dumbfounded. "Ninety-five percent?"

"And the other 5 percent have no idea what the word means," concluded Ronnoco.

Leo stared into space for what seemed a very long time. "You are right. Yes, you are!" he said. "Take a look at this." The pope showed Ronnoco the letter from America describing the apparition by the Holy Virgin in a small town in the United States. The event had caused a sensation and thousands upon thousands of pilgrims had invaded the small community. "This is what they want, what they are waiting for."

"A miracle?" asked Ronnoco, returning the letter to the pope.

Leo nodded. "It is amazing," the pope said with a chuckle. "We forgot the one element that made all this possible." The pope opened his arms to embrace the Holy See. "Can't you see? Miracles justify their faith."

"And I thought I was cynical," said Ronnoco, also smiling.

"Cynical? We are not being cynical. We are truthful. Think back, Felix. We are the holy guardians of a trunk-full of miracles. That is our heritage."

Ronnoco conceded as much.

"We have been too busy looking at the future, when we should have kept our finger in the past. Oh, we need a miracle, Felix, one that will fire the imagination, one that will fix the attention of the world on the Roman Catholic Church, a miracle that will convince the skeptics that we hold the key to everlasting glory."

Ronnoco pointed out the canonical procedures set up to establish the validity of reports of apparitions, revelations, and the myriad of other such phenomena, most of which were due to feeble minds, charlatans and fraud.

"Unless we say the miracle happened," said Leo. "Our word is the law of the Catholic Church. If we say those children saw the Mother of our Blessed Savior, they saw the Mother of our Blessed Savior."

"And what could Mary have possibly said to those kids?" asked Ronnoco, playing along.

Leo returned the smile. "Your guess is as good as ours."

"But we don't have to guess, do we?" said Ronnoco. "The Blessed Mother of Christ was—is upset. She feels abandoned. She wept and made a pronouncement, a pronouncement that will make every Christian tremble, and hail Mary with unmistakable joy."

"And what is that?" asked the pope, like a little boy waiting for his surprise.

Ronnoco smiled. "I'm not sure—" He got up and headed for the door.

"Where are you going?" asked the pope.

"Back to my office. I need to think how the Church is going to respond to these findings."

"With a miracle!"

Ronnoco let go of the door handle and walked back to the pope. "Are you serious?"

"When have you known us not to be serious?"

"Tata, I was kidding just now."

"We were not," said Leo.

"But it's silly—absurd."

"It's not absurd. It's outrageous, that's why it's perfect."

"You'll never make it work," said Ronnoco, concerned.

"We have no intention of making anything work. We leave that to you."

"Me?"

"You." Leo stood face-to-face with Ronnoco. "We'll take care of the bureaucrats. They are a nuisance that can be easily circumvented or—ignored. But you—you, my boy, will be the ringmaster, the miracle-worker. We want magic! Go, find out what happened to those children. Get rid of the loose ends and make the apparition—the Blessed Mother's, not yours—true. Leave as soon as possible. We have no time to lose."

For a second, Ronnoco pondered the problem, his problem, actually. He had always been a zealous defender of the Church and he viewed his mentor as the embodiment of justice . . . Catholic justice, of course, with its all-encompassing love for mankind. In all that time, Felix had never questioned the motives of the pope because the logic behind the policies was always clear and correct. But to fake a miracle, an apparition . . .

"You will make it happen," said Leo.

19

Yes, it was inconvenient to cut a hole in the ceiling to install a glass-bubble sunroof above the exact spot where the Blessed Mother appeared in all Her glory to little Teddy and Alice Miltedew. Ray felt, and with good reason, that since they asked for a two-fifty donation for two minutes in the shrine, the pilgrims would better appreciate the effect of the apparition if blinded by the sun. Additionally, he built a water font under the opening where, for a dollar, the faithful might enjoy a cool sip. Of course, for two dollars they could take home a light-blue vial with an ounce of water that was not necessarily holy but had been blessed by the lucky children who, for a brief, splendid moment had met with the Mother of God.

Ray and Harriet added other improvements to their humble trailer including a brand-new porch and a fence around two empty lots they rented from the parish to provide extra parking at three dollars an hour, per vehicle.

For their part, little Teddy and Alice Miltedew made impromptu appearances to share their innocence with visitors; beautiful moments that were faithfully recorded for an upcoming documentary their father planned to sell at Wal-Mart and Amazon.com.

Several photographs of the children were also available, including the best seller that showed them dressed in sparkling white satin, kneeling and facing each other, their hands clasped in prayer as they looked up to the heavens, while holding a figurine of the Blessed Mother between them. Then there was the picture with the pastoral motif that showed Teddy and Alice sleeping under a tree as a group of lovely forest creatures, a flock of angels and the blessed Mary looked after them.

Fame, although an imposition, turned out quite profitable for the Miltedews and they did not complain. America is, after all, the land of opportunity and when IT descends from heaven, and well, it would have been downright unpatriotic not to seize it, tie it up in colored ribbons and share it with others.

Harriet never imagined that things would turn out the way they did the night she found her children and husband huddled in a corner, praying feverishly, expressing their love for Mary. It was, Ray observed, an honest-to-goodness humdinger, and they pondered a full day before sharing their experience with Father O'Malley.

Like many of his brethren stuck in small parishes, the good father had little to do, so he spent his time practicing his tennis strokes against the inside walls of the church, and gossiping with his parishioners, including Mrs. Lindgren who then made a point of calling everyone she knew to let them know that the Mother of Christ had dropped by the Miltedews. A brief mention on the local news gave way to the wire services and it was not long before CNN picked up the intriguing "human interest" story.

Except for the few atheists in town, everyone, it seemed, was curious about the children. And why not? They were white, innocent and beautiful. They were also a pair, which made it unlikely that both imagined the same thing. Of course, there was always the chance that Teddy and his sweet sister Alice suffered from Catholic hallucinations induced by ingesting too much host and cheap wine. And so, to avoid the slightest hint of collusion or impropriety, Father O'Malley referred all inquiries about the "apparition" to Bishop Cuyas in New Orleans, who in turn stated: "The matter is under investigation."

In truth, although a seal of approval from the Church would have helped the sale of the book and its accompanying single entitled "Angels in the Bayou," it was a great time for the parish, especially for the 7-11, the town's one motel and the diner, not to mention Harry's gas station and several local entrepreneurs selling oysters and crayfish side by side with figurines of the blessed children and Mary in roadside stands not far from where the miracle took place.

After years of being unemployed, Ray now managed the shrine, Harriet kept the books and dealt with the press, while the children. . . well, no one asked Teddy or Alice if they liked being the focus of so much attention. . . were always polite, never without a smile and forever mum because, if true that they had been visited by the Blessed Mother, it was also true that they did not remember what happened after they fainted. Therefore, to avoid being made uncomfortable by silly questions from the faithful, their parents decided not to allow them to talk about their sacred and personal encounter with Mary.

Of the children, Teddy was the most affected by the situation because he missed going hunting with his father. As his mother explained, killing wild but defenseless animals was inconsistent with one who was good friends with the Virgin Mother. Also, "Blessy Teddy," as his classmates called him, was unmercifully bullied in school, even having a fat Protestant boy sit on him during recess, an incident that forced Harriet to confront Father O'Malley.

"I won't stand by and watch my Teddy be tortured by these evil, violent Baptists and Jews, Father!" said Harriet one day, after Teddy came home with a bloody lip. "Enough is enough. I want Teddy to attend Saint Luke's."

Father O'Malley had been helping the altar boy move the pews against the wall so he could practice his backhand. Short and in his mid-fifties, O'Malley was thin, about five and a half feet tall, with gray eyes and sharp features. "I sympathize with you, Mrs. Miltedew," said the priest, "but I have nothing to do with Saint Luke's."

"Surely you have influence with the headmaster. Teddy is special," added Harriet. "How many boys do you know that have gazed upon the Mother of Christ?"

"You should take it up with Father Zaragai, directly," said O'Malley removing the cover off his racquet. "That would do two things. It would eliminate a go-between—in this case, me—and it would expedite matters considerably by making the headmaster aware of your predicament."

Harriet looked away for a second. Though not wanting to sound arrogant or inconsiderate, she said: "I feel strongly about this. I won't allow Teddy getting hurt. I mean, think of it, the Blessed Mother comes all the way to La Place, picks out my Teddy among a hundred million children, for what, so he gets beat up in school? I don't think so, Father, I really don't. I'll write to the pope, if I have to."

"Why, Mrs. Miltedew, that is an excellent idea! Why didn't I think of that? It's brilliant. That's exactly what you have to do," joined the priest, bouncing a ball a few times. "You see, once the Holy Father receives your note, he'll give it to one of his many aides who do nothing all day but look after such—unusual requests—and before you can say one Hail Mary, little Teddy will be at Saint Luke's. You must have been inspired, Mrs. Miltedew, honestly."

Needless to say that Harriet never intended to write to the pope, but after Father O'Malley's enthusiastic response, what did she have to lose?

Four months later, one Tuesday morning about eight, the parish priest from La Place received a telephone call from the Vatican and things were never the same again.

"Excellency!" called out Father O'Malley, waving at the only priest leaving the customs building.

"Father O'Malley," said Ronnoco.

"Let me help you with that, please," said O'Malley, putting the luggage in the trunk.

"Thank you," returned the bishop.

"Welcome to the US of A," said the priest leading His Excellency to a green Buick that was two years short of becoming a classic, parked outside the terminal. "First time in New Orleans?"

"Yes," replied Ronnoco.

"Then, let me warn you. There's great food, great music, but foul weather. If you feel the first two are important and are not inconvenienced by 95 percent humidity on top of equally high temperatures, you'll enjoy your stay, I'm sure. If not, you'll agree with me that the bayou state should be returned to the French," said the priest, stepping on the gas.

The conversation driving north on Route 10 was mostly one sided with O'Malley giving the bishop a history of the unassuming, irrelevant and ignored small church that had become part of the cause célèbre of the apparition, and the bishop from Rome nodding in return every now and then. "You speak very good English," said O'Malley after talking straight for ten minutes without getting a response from the bishop.

"So do you," returned Ronnoco, dryly.

The car finally reached the gate and a dirt road covered with a black layer of winged creatures that were unmercifully crushed and crunched by the Buick. "What is that?" asked the bishop.

"Locust," answered Father O'Malley.

"How—Ten Commandments," observed Ronnoco.

O'Malley parked under a large tarpaulin at the back of the church. The wooden structure with slanted roof and prominent bell tower was more than a hundred years old. It was white on the outside, brown on the inside and stood between several cypress trees covered with swamp moss that kept it forever in a sultry shade.

Behind the building was a churchyard that had long since stopped taking guests and a gravel path leading to the rectory that had none of the grace or southern charm of its neighbor and was built in the best tradition of utilitarian modesty.

Father O'Malley took the bishop's suitcase from the trunk and led the way inside. "Quickly—mosquitoes—they love priestly blood."

Ronnoco found himself in a dreary hallway decorated with fake wood paneling. O'Malley's office was to the right and was furnished with a wooden desk, two chairs, a couple of floor lamps, beige curtains, a small closet, a medium-sized couch, a pink marble coffee table with an embedded ashtray, an air conditioner and a small refrigerator next to the desk.

"Do you want to see your room?"

"Not right now." Ronnoco opened his briefcase, pulled out the letter from the Holy Father and gave it to O'Malley. "I am taking over the parish," he added.

The priest glanced at the papal mandate, and said: "Good luck."

"Where is the file regarding the Miltedews?"

"File? What do you mean?" asked the priest.

"I mean any note, memo, letter, record of baptism or birth—any document you have that mentions the children visited by the Blessed Mother," explained Ronnoco.

"Oh, that—yes, well—there's not much. I'm not their doctor, you know. Besides, it's all a crock of shit."

"I want to see what you have, and Father, do both of us a favor and keep your opinions to yourself."

"My apologies, Excellency," said the priest, before gathering the church records, including reports to the archdiocese, bank statements, account logs, letters (personal and parochial), memoranda, the list of past and present employees, and everything else that had been written down and filed going back more than ten years. Then he separated the documents in two sets, those that mentioned the Miltedews, and those that did not, handed the lot to the bishop, and went outside to put a sign on the door:

"Church closed until further notice. Any questions, contact the archdiocese."

It took the bishop from Rome most of the afternoon to read through Father O'Malley's file cabinet and two items caught his eye: the dismissal of the janitor, a man called Louie Peps, for stealing, and the complaint filed with the police listing the items taken and never recovered.

"Do you have a metal bucket?" asked the bishop.

"You mean—"

"The kind used to mop floors," added Ronnoco.

"There might be one somewhere," answered O'Malley.

"Get it, please."

Minutes later, as Bishop Ronnoco and Father O'Malley watched the entire contents of the Miltedew papers on fire, the priest said: "Anything else you'd like to set ablaze, Excellency?"

"Yes," answered Ronnoco, not saying what. "Now, Father, let's go meet the blessed children."

The priest and the bishop drove into the bayou, crossed the railroad tracks, turned right onto a two-lane street, cut across two large open fields and ran into the bumper-to-bumper traffic making its resolute way to "Mary's Haven — All are Welcome."

"Hello, Harriet," said Father O'Malley, stepping up to the porch.

"Father! And what brings you here, today?" said Harriet.

"This is Bishop Felix Ronnoco, from Rome. He's here to talk to you and Ray," said Father O'Malley, moving aside and allowing Ronnoco to come forward.

"Bishop? From Rome? Oh my," said Harriet waiting for the prelate to put out his hand so she could kiss the ring.

It didn't happen. "Mrs. Miltedew," said Ronnoco, "is there a place where we can talk in private?"

It was hard to tell whether Harriet was happy to be visited by a high-ranking Church official, whether she was worried for the same reason, or whether she did not care. "Well, dear me, this is a surprise. Is it very important? We're rather busy. Have you come to see the kids? They're at my mother's."

"Harriet," interjected Father O'Malley, "I think you should pay attention to His Excellency."

Instead of paying attention, Harriet invited the priest and the bishop inside the refurbished trailer, then called her husband.

Mr. Miltedew had been looking after a husband and wife who had traveled all the way from Arkansas to visit the shrine. "A bishop from Rome wants to talk to us? What about?" asked Ray.

He found the bishop and Father O'Malley perusing some of the items for sale.

"Please, take one—on the house," said Ray putting out his hand.

Ronnoco placed the CD back in its place and waited for O'Malley to intervene.

"Ray, this is Bishop Ronnoco. He needs to talk to you and—to your wife," said the priest. "I suggest you close shop for now."

The look from Father O'Malley warned Mr. Miltedew that trouble had just landed in his living room. He quickly consulted with Mrs. Miltedew, then together ushered everybody out because of an unforeseen visit by a bishop from Rome.

Ten minutes later, the Miltedews sat across Father O'Malley and the bishop, after the latter turned down some homemade lemonade.

"You say you're from Rome, Italy?" asked Ray from his favorite chair.

"I have come to tell you," began His Excellency, "that the Holy Father has taken an interest in the apparition and has sent me to find out what happened. If, as you say, the children were indeed visited by Mary, the Church will legitimize the event at once, not a hundred years from now. First, however, you must stop all exploitation of the event."

"But, Excellency—" Ray protested.

"I'm not finished," said Ronnoco, putting up his hand. "You are also forbidden to talk to anyone about the apparition."

"B-b-but why?" joined Harriet.

"That is not for you to question," said Ronnoco. "If you don't do as I say, I will hold a press conference and tell the world that you're just a group of charlatans and that the apparition never happened."

Harriet was slightly out of sorts. "Excuse me, Excellency, but my children saw the Virgin!"

"That, Mrs. Miltedew, is beside the point," said Ronnoco, heading for the door. "Please bring the children to the rectory tomorrow morning, at nine. I will first talk to them one at a time, and then meet with you and Mr. Miltedew. Let's go, Father O'Malley."

"He's not a bishop, that's what I think," said Harriet as she and her husband watched the green Buick drive away.

"Well, he's got me fooled," said Ray.

Next morning, as instructed, Ray and Harriet arrived with Teddy and Alice in tow. Father O'Malley led Teddy into the office while his family waited in the kitchen.

"Teddy Miltedew, Excellency," announced the priest in a formal voice, then closed the door.

Teddy was easygoing, friendly and talkative, and looked very handsome in his shiny communion suit that his mother made him wear.

"They tell me you and your little sister saw the Mother of Christ," began Ronnoco. "Tell me about it."

The boy described his encounter with the Virgin in words that were as sincere as they were innocent.

"Were you scared?"

"Lots!"

"And what did the Blessed Mother tell you?"

Teddy sat very straight, his hands resting on his knees. "Nothing."

"Nothing?"

"Nope. I passed out."

Ronnoco took the boy's hands, and said: "Teddy, you did not pass out. The Blessed Mother wanted you to fall asleep so the little angels could hold you in their arms and bring you to her. Then, she whispered in your ear."

"Really?"

"Yes, Teddy—really," said Ronnoco softly.

The look of wonder in Teddy gave way to a curious wrinkle of the brow. "And what did She say?"

Next it was Alice's turn, and she talked endlessly about everything, particularly about her older brother. It was Teddy this and Teddy that and Teddy likes this and Teddy likes that and Mommy says that Teddy is this and Daddy says that Teddy is that—and when she finally got around to talking about the apparition, she confirmed her brother's account.

"Were you scared?"

"Oh, yeah, lots!"

"What did the Blessed Mother say to you?"

Alice shrugged. "Nothing."

"Nothing?"

"Nope. I fainted!" said little Alice candidly.

"Oh," said Ronnoco, laughing.

Harriet was far more anxious than her children, but Ronnoco was particularly friendly that morning and did his best to put her at ease. "Mrs. Miltedew, I am not here to judge. I am interested in what happened, that is all."

"What happened is this," began Harriet. She had come home late one night and found her children and husband praying and crying because, they said, they had seen the Virgin. Harriet believed her husband, but more than that, she believed the babies. It was simply not possible for the little ones to make up the story and... "Excellency, we never ask for money. It is very important that you know that! We accept donations that help us keep the shrine, that's it. We're poor people, Excellency, and don't have money to—"

"I understand, Mrs. Miltedew, I do." Later, perhaps, he would take time and explain the ethical implications of her family's enterprise. But as Ronnoco wanted to finish quickly with Harriet, he allowed her to talk about the generous people of the community, about the letters and calls from all over the world asking for Teddy and Alice to hold special prayers for those in need, about the gifts and letters people... total strangers... sent with money for the kids. At first, she thought of returning everything.

"Why didn't you?" interjected Ronnoco.

Because being poor and in need, Ray decided that it was in the children's best interest to make their lives more comfortable so they could carry out the mission chosen for them by the Mother of Christ.

"And what mission is that?" asked the bishop.

"I don't know," answered Harriet. "Do you? I hope someone can tell me. What does it mean? Why pick on my children? Why us?"

Fifteen minutes later, Father O'Malley summoned Mr. Miltedew.

"Please, sit." Ronnoco pointed to a very uncomfortable-looking wooden stool he had brought in from the kitchen for the interview. "Now, Ray, may I call you Ray?"

"Yes, of course, of course."

"Tell me what happened—in your own words." Ronnoco walked back and forth, tossing questions at Ray like crumbs at a flock of pigeons.

Mr. Miltedew related that on the night of the apparition he had not been feeling well and was depressed because he had been out of work for so long. He was waiting for his children to come home but fell asleep on the couch. When he woke up, Teddy and Alice were unconscious on the floor.

As was his style, Bishop Ronnoco did not waste time with chitchat. He stood in front of Ray and asked: "Do you know a man called Louie Peps?"

"I—I don't remember."

"I think I should explain the rules of the game."

Ray looked up and caught the bishop's uncompromising stare.

"I ask questions and you do not lie to me. If you do, you'll wish you'd died and gone to hell. Now—" and Ronnoco waited to see the reaction of his threat on Mr. Miltedew. "Harriet told me you know Mr. Peps. That he used to come to your house often. As a matter of fact, your wife said this Mr. Peps was at your house the night of the miracle. Is that true? Did Louie Peps drop by your house before the apparition? Well?"

Ray nodded.

"That's better, that's better." Ronnoco paused long enough to walk behind Ray. "Of course, that brings us to another matter. You know that Mr. Peps used to work here, at the church?"

Ray nodded again.

"And you know he was dismissed for stealing?"

"Yes."

"Do you have any idea what he stole from Father O'Malley?"

Ray shook his head.

"Come, come, Ray, you were doing so well. You know what I'm getting at, don't you?" continued the bishop. "You may not remember everything but you remember the movie projector, the one Father O'Malley used to show movies on Friday nights, mostly silly pictures produced by the archdiocese to help teach and indoctrinate? Let's try and make some sense of what happened, shall we? And please, feel free to correct me at any time. What I think happened, Ray, is this. Louie, as your wife calls Mr. Peps, stole the projector from the church, took it to your house, sold it or gave it to you—it really does not matter which—and you used the machine in a desperate attempt to get out of the awful situation you were in. How long were you unemployed?"

"Two—two years," replied Ray, his lips quivering.

"Two years. You just had to do something to get out of the hole, out of the rut, as you Americans call it. And what did you do? You waited for your children to get home, and the moment they walked through the door, you played one of Father O'Malley's short films on the Virgin. In their innocence, Teddy and Alice thought they were in the presence of the Holy Mother of Jesus Christ! But they were not, right Ray? It was just a silly movie, one that you used in a stupid plan to fleece the simple and trusting men and women who want to believe, who have to believe in a miracle in order for their faith to have meaning. You have made fools of everybody. You made fools of your children, made fools of all the people you have been taking money from, and you have made a fool of your wife. I wonder what Harriet will say when I tell her what really happened. It'll break her heart, Ray, that's what it will do, she'll never forgive you." Ronnoco brought his face right next to Ray's ear and added: "Isn't that right?"

Ray shook violently and wept. He protested and said he never planned the apparition, that it had been an accident.

"Liar!" said Ronnoco loudly.

Mr. Miltedew confessed that Louie forgot the projector at the house after they argued and when Louie left, Ray was so despondent he wrecked the house and tried to kill himself.

"Obviously, you failed."

"I knocked myself out," said Ray between sobs.

"Liar!"

Ray said that because it was so dark when the children got home, they must have stepped on the projector and it went off by itself.

"You're lying, Ray!"

"No, I swear I'm not!"

"Did you tell your wife you tried to kill yourself?"

"No."

"And you never told her about the projector?"

"No," answered Ray. He knew that if found out, the disgrace would be such that they would have to move, and Harriet would take the children and leave him. He might as well be dead.

"I'll tell you what I'm going to do," said Ronnoco. "What you did is pathetic but, it's done. Listen carefully, because I have decided to help you. What you said just now never happened. As of this moment, the miracle, the apparition—I don't care what you call it—it is now out of your hands. Where is the machine, the projector and the film of the Blessed Mother, Ray? What did you do with them?"

Ray was overcome with fear, as if he was about to be murdered. "I—I—it's b-buried."

Ronnoco grabbed him by the shirt and pulled him from the stool. "Listen to me, you fool, find them and bring them to me or I'll call the police. Now, where is this—Louie? Have you seen him lately? Do you know where he lives?"

"He's—by the tracks, about three miles south—in a shack he built himself. I'll fetch him."

"No, Ray, you will not. You will let me handle everything from now on. If you're good, if you're very good, you'll come out of this a better person. Your children will be taken care of for the rest of their lives and you and Mrs. Miltedew can reap the benefits of being the parents of the children who saw the Mother of Christ. Of course, you never wanted much, did you? Just enough to get by."

Ray returned an hour later, lugging a green plastic garbage bag with everything that Louie had delivered to his house that fateful night when Teddy and Alice saw Mary.

"Is this everything?" asked the bishop.

"Yeah."

Ronnoco took the bag, waited for Ray to leave, burnt the film and put away the projector.

And Louie Peps? Well, everyone knew Mr. Peps was a liar and a thief.

20

"The evidence speaks for itself," said Pope Leo to the Four Horsemen, as Bishop Ronnoco called the pope's top advisors. Leo pointed to a stack of papers and photographs on top of a small table at his side. "We have lie detector tests that prove the children are telling the truth. Their mother and father were also questioned. The results are conclusive."

If Cardinals Pino and Bailey on the left, and Cardinals Numa and Tomaso on the right of the papal throne had taken the time to examine said results, or risk offending the Holy Father with a few questions, they would have realized that far from conclusive, the Miltedews had never been strapped to a polygraph and the pontiff was lying.

"But, Holiness, that doesn't mean the Blessed Mother was there. At best it means that these people believe she was," observed Cardinal Bailey, the only American of the group. Tall as the pope, Bailey was a handsome, aristocratic looking man, with a good head of gray-streaked hair, dark eyes and a deep, resonant voice.

"That makes sense, Holiness," joined Cardinal Pino, smiling. He was short, fat, amiable and a little too sharp.

The pope got up, and rebuked the four red hats: "We will tell you what makes sense. It makes sense that we travel to America and meet with the two children. It makes sense for the Church to recognize the apparition as a miracle because that's what it is! Must we remind you that one of the tenets on which our Church is founded is the miracle of the resurrection? Christ died on the cross and a few days later walked out of his tomb and rose to heaven. And why did Christ rise to heaven? Why?" Leo waited and looked at the four men. "He had to! Man was condemning himself to hell and His Father, God Almighty, in His magnificent wisdom, sent His only Son to intercede for us. Now, as fantastic as it seems, an apparition by the Blessed Mother is nothing compared to that. So, we put it to you, are we going to allow the technocrats, the skeptics and the atheists to shake our faith? Because if we do, we might as well become lawyers and forget that the existence of our glorious institution is based on something that is not tangible, that cannot be measured with instruments and computers but is as real as the blood Christ shed for us, as real as the love in our hearts and the faith in our souls!" The pope paused to gather breath, but though his strength faltered, he was firm. "After two thousand years," he continued, "man is again slaughtering children by the tens of thousands, hunger and famine are rampant, crime, perversion, drugs—where will it end?" Leo pointed his finger at the cardinals. "This apparition is not a hoax. It is a warning!"

"Holiness, do we know what the Blessed Mother said to the children?" asked Cardinal Tomaso. At seventy-four, he was the senior member of the group as well as a staunch conservative and ally of the pope. A plain looking man, he had wispy white hair and a flat nose he kept as far away from politics as possible.

Leo looked him squarely in the eyes. "That is a sacred confidence between the children and Mary to be revealed exactly thirty-three days from now."

"Holiness, I take the—little ones—they are American?" continued Tomaso.

"They are," confirmed the pope.

"And Mary spoke to them in English?"

The pope approached his friend, and said: "The Blessed Mother relayed her message in the language of universal love."

"Holy Father, as you know, in the last several hundred years there have been many apparitions; apparitions that have surfaced all over the world. From Japan to Rome, from Ireland to Greece; from Mexico to your own homeland of Croatia. The latest apparition was to a seer called Yolandita, and before that, there were reports in early December 1996, of an image appearing on the windows of the Seminole Finance Company of Clearwater, Florida, in the United States. It resembled the Blessed Virgin Mary as Our Lady of Guadalupe. It is extraordinary that a building owned by a finance company should become a shrine, but so it has. Nevertheless, the Holy See has kept its distance from all these apparitions because as you know none of them, including that of Yolandita, stands up to scrutiny."

"What is your point, brother?" asked the impatient pope.

"Who met with the children, Holiness? Who is making sure that the information we get is correct?" asked Numa.

The pope returned to his throne. "His Excellency Bishop Ronnoco."

"Ahhh!" The eminent exclamation was accompanied by nods and smiles.

"Tomaso, please arrange for our travel to America. Bailey, this must be the religious event of the century! For once we are going to legitimize a contemporary miracle. Pino, make sure that the American president is in on this. He is Catholic and should be proud of what will take place in his country." The pope beckoned Cardinal Numa aside. "We will not tolerate meddling of any kind, do you understand?"

"Yes, Holiness."

"Holy Father, I want to be clear about everything." Tomaso walked up to the pontiff. "You want the miracle to be authenticated by the Church?"

"Yes. Any objections?" Since there were none, the pope asked everyone to leave the room. "Let's get to work!"

Meanwhile, in New Orleans, Bishop Ronnoco invited Father O'Malley to dinner at La Colombina. The restaurant had sparkling white tile floors, white stucco walls, big, indolent fans, round potted plants and watercolors of the French Quarter, rendered with dazzling originality by a host of local artists.

The two dressed in civilian clothes, Ronnoco in blue jeans and a peppermint-green striped shirt, Father O'Malley in a pair of black trousers and a white shirt. Both ordered the same dish, grilled rack of lamb with wild rice, accompanied by an excellent bottle of California Barbera (a new experience for the bishop), coffee, fresh raspberries with cream, flan and brandy. At one point, O'Malley remarked that Bishop Ronnoco was unlike any other high-ranking Church official he had ever met. "Where are you from?"

"Croatia."

"Like His Holiness," observed the priest.

"Like His Holiness," agreed the bishop.

"What do you do, Excellency, at the Holy See?"

"What do I do?" Ronnoco sipped his wine.

"Yes, if I may ask—what do you do for the Holy Father—besides making sure that miracles happen?"

"You know, Father, I like men who speak their minds."

"Oh, I do that."

"I know. I read your file. You're tagged as a troublemaker. Did you ever wonder why you're stuck in this place?"

"Punishment for being a big mouth, I guess." Father O'Malley shrugged.

"I don't think it is meant as punishment, though it is certainly a way to keep you from getting in trouble. They thought of sending you to an even more insignificant outpost in New Mexico—to teach Native Americans about Jesus and Mary. The only reason you are here, and not there, is because the bishop who had your life in his hands, thought, rightly, I might add, that you would have less opportunity to do mischief in this heat and humidity, which has a tendency to smother initiative." Ronnoco smiled.

"Ha! And you've been here less than a month!" Father O'Malley stuck his spoon in the flan. Both men shifted their attention to the coffee before the priest asked the bishop where he went to school.

"The Gregorian Institute. And you?"

"Saint Joseph's," returned O'Malley.

"Let me ask you—you've been the priest at La Place for twenty years and in that time the congregation diminished by a fourth. Why?"

"People are disillusioned and disappointed," answered O'Malley.

"With your guidance, your leadership or with something else?"

"With a Church that doesn't have a clue, a Church that has lost its sense of purpose and became a bureaucracy selling mysticism to perpetuate its existence."

"That is a strong condemnation, Father."

"But it doesn't surprise you. I'll be frank, Excellency. I've remained at the parish because I find it impossible to abandon the poor souls that faithfully attend mass in search of spiritual comfort. I advise and offer guidance. If not for them, I would have left long ago and done something else—teach tennis, for instance."

"You lost your faith," observed Ronnoco.

"Long ago," returned O'Malley.

"Why?" asked the bishop.

"To begin with, I'm convinced that Jesus Christ, that wonderful character that is the foundation of the Christian church, is fiction. He never existed," answered the priest.

"What makes you say that?" inquired Ronnoco, matter-of-factly.

"Read Eusebius and the minutes taken during the First Ecumenical Council and you'll conclude, as I did, that it's all a fraud." O'Malley noticed the look of concern on Bishop Ronnoco and paused. "I'm sorry, but—"

"No, not at all," returned Ronnoco. "Go on."

"Are you sure?" asked O'Malley sipping his brandy.

"Please," added Ronnoco.

The priest sighed, leaned forward and added: "Unfortunately I discovered this too late. That's why I'm loyal to the Church, not because I believe in what it represents but because I too became a bureaucrat in a multinational corporation selling salvation as others sell toothpaste. Of course, if our Church—"

"Our Church?" interrupted Ronnoco.

"Oh yes—very much. What I mean is that if our Church suffers from so many problems, the Protestant church is rotten beyond anything we have seen so far because it has become an industry run by swindlers and charlatans. Islam, of course, is another fraud with Muslims the unhappiest people on earth, always blaming others for their misery and shortcomings, with leaders that lie and corrupt the teachings of their holy book. And, of course, there's the Jewish State and the horrible things it's done to the Palestinians. The Israelis are nothing but opportunists that took advantage of the tragedy of the Holocaust and use the imbecilities mentioned in the Old Testament to justify an immoral and completely illegal land-grab. What I find outrageously funny is that those people are violating the eighth commandment of their own Law of Moses. People are slowly calling them on it. Folks are beginning to think for themselves and the communications revolution going on in the world is helping wipe out injustice founded on ignorance and superstition, leading to a new era of enlightenment. At least, that is my opinion on the matter, Excellency."

Ronnoco laughed and offered the priest another brandy. "So, tell me, Father, what I should do with you?"

"Do? With me? I didn't know you were supposed to do anything with me." Father O'Malley laughed.

"Things are going to get pretty busy around here in a few days."

"You're not afraid I'll spoil the miracle for you?"

"You wouldn't do that." Ronnoco smiled.

"No, I wouldn't." O'Malley returned the smile. "What do you want from me, Excellency? Tell me what to do and I'll do it. Despite what people say, and despite my big mouth, I've never disobeyed my superiors."

"I am sure. But I would rather you don't get involved in what's going to happen. Look, you're a good man and I like you. I'll talk to His Holiness and maybe rescue you from the swamp. Why don't you take a few weeks off, go to Rome, maybe it will help you regain the faith?"

"Rome?" It was the first time since Bishop Ronnoco met Father O'Malley that the priest seemed interested in something. "I'm afraid I can't afford it."

"Leave that to me. What do you say?"

A week and a half later, on orders from Pope Leo XIV, a contingent of Franciscan friars arrived in La Place to be secretaries, messengers and watchmen. They slept in cots inside the little church and Brother George, a tall, muscular man with small eyes, a long nose and not much hair, became Bishop Ronnoco's lieutenant.

The bishop assigned three of the brothers to be with the Miltedews day and night. The men helped Harriet with the groceries, took out the garbage, kept out the tourists, the curious, most friends and most relatives and screened all calls.

The fence was reinforced and electronic sensors and surveillance cameras were added. A dozen devices that discharged "white noise" (an acoustical or electrical interference used to mask conversations and make them unintelligible to someone trying to listen in from a distance) were aimed at the gate from the roof of the house. Also, Bishop Ronnoco warned the family not to talk about the apparition with anyone outside the house.

It was during one of those frantic afternoons that Ray stood outside his door, a beer in one hand, and watched mesmerized as a hundred men built the white and yellow canopied stage from

which Pope Leo would address Catholics around the world
(with Teddy and Alice at his side, of course). Ray felt a short-
ness of breath and staggered into a rocking chair. He pressed the
cold can to his forehead as his stomach tightened and his body
quivered. Mr. Miltedew had finally realized that his family was
being held hostage by the Catholic Church.

The local paper carried a headline that was repeated around
the world: "Leo XIV Travels to Meet with Blessed Children."

Cardinal Bailey's press kits helped the propaganda machine
of Vatican Radio and its web of confederates throughout Europe,
the United States and South America. Some in the commercial
media (controlled by Jews and Protestants, according to insiders
at the Vatican) wondered why the Holy See had decided to place
its considerable prestige behind such an unbelievable story. In
the end, the press resolved not to express its opinion, fearful they
might be labeled intolerant by disgruntled Catholics. Instead, the
media sent dozens of trucks and vans equipped with long-lens
cameras and high-power microphones, parked them outside the
gate and waited. Bishop Ronnoco smiled; he was ready for them.

While New Orleans hummed with news of the papal visit, a
brown Ford stopped at a gas station on its way to Destrehan. It
was one o'clock in the morning. The driver bought a two-gallon
plastic container and quickly filled it with high octane gasoline. He was the sort of fellow who, even in the light of day, and
regardless where he stood, looked like his own shadow, gray and
flat; a silhouette without features or color, that allowed him to
move in and out of crowds with no one taking notice.

Wearing black pants, a black windbreaker and matching
leather gloves, it took the specter less than half an hour to reach
the overpass, then parked next to the railroad crossing, opened
the trunk and took out the gasoline. Annoyed at the insistence
of numberless flying pests that buzzed about his head in the

dead of night and in a rainstorm, including colorful love-bugs copulating in the air, and swarms of determined mosquitoes, several of whom could have been drowned by a single raindrop, his heart stuck in his throat when the biggest rat he had ever seen dashed from a bush less than a meter away and disappeared into the swamp. "Shit!" he said, spitting out a few bugs he had inadvertently inhaled. "Good evening. Hello!" he added, shining a tiny flashlight upon Louie Peps, who lay under a thick blanket covered by green garbage bags.

"Eh! What, what?" Louie blinked at the weak but persistent beam shining in his face.

"Excuse me, is your name Louie?"

"Who the fuck are you?" Louie was not in a good mood, but who would be? It was very late and it was pouring buckets, not to mention the inconsiderateness of whoever the fuck this asshole was, waking him up.

"Are you Louie Peps?"

"Who wants to know?"

"I'm from the Red Cross and have some money for you—if you are a—" and the fellow read from a piece of paper, "Mr. Louie Peps."

"Ya fuckin' out of your pissing mother-fuckin' brain!"

"Sorry I disturbed you, then. Goodnight."

"Wait! Ya said you got somethin' for me?"

"If you are Mr. Louie Peps."

"How much?"

"Twenty dollars."

Well, twenty bucks was twenty bucks in any weather, and it allowed Louie to eat for a few days, and even to pay for a pint of moonshine from the Dooley brothers. "Yeah, I'm Louie."

"I'll need to see some form of identification," said the representative from the Red Cross.

"What kind of 'dent'fication?" The Fox showed his toothless grin.

"Driver's license?"

Louie did not have one, of course, because he never learned to drive, and so produced his welfare card, which was good enough.

"Excellent. Here you are, Mr. Peps," said the man from the Red Cross holding out a wilted twenty dollar bill, before stabbing the Fox several times in the heart with a switchblade, dousing him with gasoline, and setting him on fire.

About the same time Louie Peps lit the dismal night-skies of Louisiana, Father O'Malley arrived in Rome, left the airport terminal and was immediately whisked into a waiting black Mercedes-Benz with tinted windows and Vatican plates. There were two priests inside; the one who sat in the back with Father O'Malley was thirty-something, big and fat, with short hair, a long nose, thin lips and buck teeth. The other, who was driving, had hard features, a rough beard, a complexion that had seen its share of inclement weather, a broken nose, long oily hair that reached his shoulders and eyes that said nothing.

"Welcome to Rome, Father," said the first priest in fair English as they left the airport. "I am Father Humberto," he added. "I am personally to see to your comfort."

Father O'Malley engaged in some light conversation as he looked out the window and recognized the sights of the Eternal City. He remembered the time that, as a young man ambitious to be a shepherd for Christ, he toured the Holy See. Yes, thought Father O'Malley, Bishop Ronnoco, had kept his word.

The car never stopped at a traffic light and almost never stopped for pedestrians, either.

Thirty-five minutes later, it entered an alleyway, turned sharply several times and pulled up to the back of a building.

"Follow me, if you please, Father," said Father Humberto to O'Malley. The driver opened the door for O'Malley at the same time another young man appeared from the building. "Please," he said. It was the only word he knew in English and he said it with such grace that Father O'Malley thought it should have been accompanied with a smile.

The priest, flanked by the two men, walked quickly into the Institute of Saint Jerome, which had changed very little since Ante Pavelić had been a guest there. Since Father O'Malley was not a VIP, he was lodged in one of the smaller rooms and told to wait.

The room had four cement walls, a desk with a lamp and a Bible on top; at one end of the room was a toilet and sink, and at the other a stained mattress on the floor. As the door closed and the lock was secured, Father O'Malley realized he had traveled all the way to Italy to end up in a dungeon.

Father Humberto returned three hours later and by then Father O'Malley was understandably upset. "Excuse me, but I think there has been a mistake. I was told by Bishop Ronnoco to—"

Those were the last words from Father O'Malley because he was shot in the head, bringing to a close the American priest's well deserved Roman holiday.

The rectory of the small church in La Place was transformed into the command center for the pope's visit to the United States, equipped with monitors, computers, burn baskets, paper shredders, special electronic gear to prevent bugging and secured telephone lines.

Bishop Ronnoco was on his laptop writing an email to the pope, when Brother George walked in the room.

"Excellency?" said Brother George, "Thomas—Brother Thomas says Mr. Miltedew is acting strange."

"Strange?" Ronnoco looked up from the screen. The pope was due in New Orleans in a few days and they could not afford second thoughts, guilty consciences or instability on the part of the players. "Well, let's find out what ails Mr. Miltedew today," he added, hitting "send" and logging off.

A short and stumpy friar opened the gate the moment he

recognized Ronnoco. "Good afternoon, Excellency!" The bishop waved at the brother and drove the car slowly through the mass of reporters and paparazzi camped outside.

"Hello, Harriet. Where is your husband?" asked Ronnoco.

"In the back. I'll call him. Ray!"

Mr. Miltedew had not shaved in several days and looked exhausted.

"What is the matter?" Ronnoco and Mr. Miltedew stood in the backyard beside the clothesline that stretched from one side of the white fence to the other, and which, at that moment, had nothing hanging out to dry.

The matter was, according to Ray, that he was a prisoner in his own house. "These men are not friars. They are gangsters!"

"That's no way to talk. They are here to help you, Ray. Listen to me," said His Excellency softly. "You brought this upon yourself. You wanted comfort, you have it. You wanted your family looked after, you have that too. Unfortunately, this type of enterprise—and that's all it is, Ray, a business deal, you know—in this type of enterprise the parties have to be extremely careful and make sure nothing is said or done to invalidate the agreement. I don't think that is too much to ask. The brothers are here to protect our interests. Take a little time, if you will, and think what would happen to us—to the Church, to the reputation of the Holy Father—if something went wrong. That just cannot be allowed to happen and I am here to make sure it does not. Now, what else? Speak up; I've had a busy day and if you don't mind—"

Ray pulled out a newspaper clipping from his shirt pocket and handed it to Ronnoco. It was a short notice from the police blotter. It said that a Louie Peps, a resident of La Place, had been found murdered underneath an overpass. It added that the deceased was stabbed before he was burnt to death. The inquiry continued although the police didn't have any leads in the case. Ronnoco carefully refolded the clipping and gave it back. "Poor man, God have mercy on his soul." The bishop noticed that Ray was lighting a cigarette. He had not been aware that Ray

Miltedew smoked. "Is that why you are upset, Ray? Look, as sad and tragic as it is, men like that often meet with misfortune."

"What happens after the pope leaves?"

"What do you want to happen, Ray? Do you and Mrs. Miltedew—with the children, of course—do you want to go on vacation?"

"Vacation?"

"Yes."

"Where?"

"Europe. You can fly back with us, in the pope's plane. First Italy—you'll stay in a palace."

Ray's eyes widened. "A palace!"

"Would you like that, Ray? Do you think Harriet would enjoy living like a queen, if only for a few weeks?"

"Yeah! Sure!"

"You see, Ray, all I want is to make you happy. You keep your side of the bargain and I'll keep mine. Relax. Everything will be fine."

21

Leo XIV's unprecedented travel to legitimize the miracle of the apparition in Louisiana was such a spectacle that the international media pre-empted its programming to cover live, not only the pageantry of the pope's arrival to the United States, but also his mass for an expected half-million faithful from a stage built in front of the Miltedews' veranda.

The temperamental climate that has managed to disrupt every outdoor activity in Louisiana since time began—from jazz concerts and funerals to political rallies and barbecues—was on its best behavior, and aerial spraying on the marshy state-owned fields adjacent to the property was ordered to control the colorful variety of vermin that otherwise would have feasted on the brethren.

Even as they prepared to welcome the Holy Father to their home, Ray and Harriet Miltedew followed the event like everyone else, on television, spending the time running errands and looking after their children who, surprisingly, were the only ones unperturbed by the surreal activity going on around them.

Bobbie Black, a hair stylist from Baton Rouge—rumored to have done Jimmy Swaggart—did the children's hair and makeup, while a friend of Harriet's by the name of Jenny Tarr, who ran a boutique from her mobile-home kitchen in Destrehan, designed the outfits for their meeting with the pope.

For Teddy, a celestial blue suit and tie with a shiny white belt and matching shoes, and for Alice an understated, yet beautiful white chiffon dress adorned with tiny yellow sunflowers and pink ruffles.

Being very young, sweet Alice was not required to do much except meet the pope, wait for the Holy Father to bless her, then step aside. Teddy, however, expected to be introduced to the world right after Leo celebrated his first American mass.

Bishop Ronnoco helped the young boy rehearse the few lines he was expected to say and Teddy showed a remarkable talent for sounding sincere and truthful, while looking like a little angel.

What nobody was aware of—including Harriet—was that since meeting the Blessed Mary, Teddy had acquired a taste for the morning evangelists who crowded the airwaves of local television. Sometimes he stood in front of a mirror and imitated his idol, a man who, though not Catholic, could storm and rage on stage and even make his nose turn bright red and tears flow in an instant.

Teddy could not sing very well yet, and he had never learned to play the piano. Still, he knew he could beseech the faithful with offers of salvation or scold them and threaten them with damnation. He could also beckon them with a grateful glance, seeming sadness, grief, remorse or joy; it depended on the sentiment required at the moment.

Two days before the glorious event, around noon to be exact, Ray and Brother Thomas drove to the local supermarket. On the way back they stopped to buy five pounds of fresh oysters from a stand by the side of the road. Ray and Teddy loved raw oysters, especially when swimming in Tabasco, horseradish and lemon.

"You think His Holiness likes oysters?" Ray asked Brother Thomas.

Back at the house, Ray dropped the oysters in ice, took out the Tabasco, the horseradish, five lemons, a beer for himself and a soda for his boy, then took the lot and joined Teddy in front of the TV.

"What are you watching, son?" asked Ray.

"Movie," said Teddy dipping his first oyster in hot sauce.

"What's it about?" asked his father, when he noticed Teddy turning green.

"Daddy—" said the boy, softly.

"What's the matter?"

"I—" That was all Teddy Miltedew was able to get out, in the way of words anyway. He threw up violently and then fainted because tainted oysters do not take long to do their nasty bit of work.

The large white jet with the golden papal seal prominently displayed on the fuselage touched down as delicately as if it had been carried aloft by a legion of angels with silken wings.

A passenger ladder immediately appeared at the front of the plane and the TV cameras zoomed-in to witness the receiving line of VIPs, including the American Secretary of State and his wife, the governor of Louisiana and his First Lady, the mayor of New Orleans with his son and three daughters and half a dozen children bearing flowers.

The high-ranking clergy from the local archdiocese was accompanied by dozens of priests and nuns, as well as His Excellency Bishop Felix Ronnoco who made his slow and dignified ascent up the ladder—his purple cope fluttering in the wind—and vanished inside the plane.

Leo XIV sat in the forward section, on a supple, white velvet papal throne with a seatbelt.

Cardinal Tomaso and his secretary, an Ethiopian priest, tall and black as an American basketball player who answered to the name of Father Ricco, stood next to His Holiness. Cardinal Bailey was there as well with his own aide, a languid and pale young priest by the name of Rostentini, as well as Cardinals Pino and Numa (traveling without their secretaries).

In addition there were the pope's personal bodyguards (who numbered about twenty and answered to Bishop Ronnoco), the pope's chef, his physician and his secretary, Brother Serafio.

"Excellency!" called Leo from his seat when Ronnoco entered the plane. "How is the child?"

Ronnoco, who had spent the night at the hospital and looked very tired, replied: "Not well, Holiness. He is in a coma."

"What!" Leo took Ronnoco aside. "How can this happen? Who did this? We want him found! Are you telling me no one tasted his food?" For some reason, His Holiness thought that the little boy was the victim of a premeditated attempt on his life.

"Tata," replied Ronnoco, aside, "we're not in the Middle Ages. The oysters were bad. His father was also taken ill."

The pontiff grabbed the bishop by the elbow. "We can't afford to go home until this child recovers!"

"I'm afraid there is very little we can do." Ronnoco spread his hands in a gesture of resignation.

Leo summoned Tomaso, Pino, Numa and Bailey, and what began as a private conversation between the pope and Bishop Ronnoco now turned into a mini conference.

"I beg your pardon, Holiness," said Cardinal Bailey. "I believe we should consider the alternatives."

"Explain what you mean, Eminence," said the pope.

"It is not complicated," added the American prelate. "An apparition is a wonderful miracle, no doubt about it." The cardinal addressed everyone in turn. "But, if the child succumbs without delivering Mary's message, we will have wasted a tremendous amount of time and money, not to mention that our detractors will have a field day. The Holy See will become the butt of every joke for the next five hundred years." Cardinal Bailey clasped his hands and fixed his eyes on the pope. "On the other hand, if we use this unfortunate accident to our advantage, and present to the world, not as an apparition, but as an ascension, now that would be a formidable event."

Cardinals Tomaso, Pino and Numa stood like a wall of red behind the pope and listened—carefully. "Think about it," Bailey went on. "What is more impressive, an apparition without a message and possibly without a witness, or an ascension where the party in question is raised to heaven in body and soul?"

"Begging your pardon, Eminence," interrupted Ronnoco, indignant, "the boy is plugged to a respirator. He has tubes in his mouth and nose and has needles feeding him antibiotics. Ascensions may be melodramatic but I doubt very much if this little boy will float!"

"Felix!" Leo was peeved. He could not afford dissent or, worse, discord among his advisers. There were a great many people waiting outside. He had to act quickly. And so, he decided: he would visit Teddy in the hospital. He would be in the room alone with the child, and if the boy died, then announce his ascension to the world; the miracle, as always, a matter of faith, of course.

Bishop Ronnoco protested and was immediately overruled by the Holy Father. Ronnoco bowed, nodded and was about to leave the airplane when the pope called him back. He made sure they were alone, and said: "We want the boy to get well, Felix! Now, please, don't be angry. We have a lot to do. The world is watching, Felix, keep that in mind!"

Leo XIV stood at the top of the ramp, his perfectly white cassock and matching zucchetto beautifully set off by the azure of the Louisiana sky, a sky so bright and pure it was as if the Almighty had cleared away the clouds. His Holiness than extended his arms toward the citizens of the world and, a moment later, stepped onto the red carpet that had been rolled out to receive him.

Leo acknowledged the flowers from the children, blessed each and every one, shook hands with some of the men and women on the welcoming committee, then climbed into his white, custom-made Mercedes-Benz and led the way to New Orleans.

At the head of the convoy was a police motorcycle escort, followed by two vans with a well-armed security contingent that included members of the US Secret Service.

Bishop Ronnoco, Cardinals Tomaso, Pino, Numa and Bailey rode in an SUV behind the pope and were trailed by two ambulances and the press.

Both sides of the interstate were closed to traffic. Hundreds of thousands of spectators—Catholics and non-Catholics—lined the streets. They mingled with thousands more who were hawking everything from the oysters that sent little boys to the hospital to ceramic figurines of the Blessed Mother, little Teddy and sweet Alice.

Police and media helicopters buzzed overhead, supplying an exciting, airborne accent to a spectacle that was bigger and more outrageous than Mardi Gras.

Learning that the pope was on his way to Saint Paul's Hospital, the throng in front of the Miltedews' immediately followed, creating a traffic snarl the likes of which had never been seen below the Mason-Dixon line, at the same time confusion, anger and frustration replaced the goodwill that had lingered in those who had waited for days for a glimpse of Leo, Teddy and Alice.

Monsignor Stevens, the chubby and agreeable hospital administrator, welcomed the Holy Father and his retinue of high-ranking clerics and personal staff to Saint Paul's, then led the group to the ICU where Teddy Miltedew was kept in a private room.

Accompanying the Holy Father was Dr. Franko Gotovać, his personal physician, a tall, thin man with small, round wire-rimmed glasses and a hooked nose who dressed in black and, in proper lighting, could have been mistaken for the angel of death.

Given the seriousness of the situation, and, in a way, the change of strategy brought about by Teddy's encounter with tainted oysters, Bishop Ronnoco planned to secretly bury the child—once he passed away, of course—in a plot behind the church in La Place that dated back to 1875, and whose occupant was unlikely to protest. With that out of the way, the pope would announce the miracle of—the ascension.

"Teddy," whispered Bishop Ronnoco in the boy's ear, "the Holy Father is here to see you."

The pope took the boy's hand and nodded for Dr. Gotovać to examine the child as the machines tracking his vital signs slowed to a crawl and their "beep, beep, beep" took on a frightening, elongated rhythm.

Suddenly, the child opened his eyes, took one look at Dr. Gotovać, and said: "Hi."

With the energy and resilience of youth, Teddy Miltedew sat up in bed and before long was declared out of danger by Dr. Gotovać.

"A miracle!" claimed Leo.

As luck would have it, the window in Teddy's room faced the front of the hospital where at least a million people, including the media, were now stationed. Half the world watched when the blue curtains were pulled back, observed a microphone appear at the window, and witnessed Leo XIV in his sacred vestments step up to say mass, spread a little smoke, sprinkle a little water and raise a large silver cross above the mass of humanity assembled below (many of whom fainted when sunlight, reflecting from the cross, struck their eyes like a bolt from the heavens).

Whatever half the world thought was going on, Leo hoped it would be over soon because his miter was too hot for comfort.

Finally, the moment everybody had waited for was at hand. Little Teddy's bed was rolled beside the pontiff, the Holy Father blessed the child, turned to the microphone and, in a heavily accented but clear English, announced: "My children! We have witnessed another miracle!"

"Amen!"

"This child who until a few minutes ago was thought to have succumbed, has been brought back to life! This is no accident! The Blessed Mother of our Lord Jesus Christ, in Her loving

heart and wisdom deems it an absolute imperative that he, along
with his sister—" And the world saw that sweet Alice now sat
beside her loving brother on the bed, as Leo XIV feebly pointed
at them—"convey what Mary, in Her glorious sanctity, demands!"

"Amen!"

Leo XIV turned his head and fixed his eyes on Teddy. The
Catholic world held its breath.

There was a moment of silence—only a few seconds, but it
was enough for suspense and anxiety to build to such a point
that when the faint and sickly little boy uttered the first word,
everyone watching, regardless of religious affiliation, became
convinced he was special indeed.

In that brief pause, Teddy himself thought of crying out
"Hallelujah!" He considered taking the microphone off the
stand, so as to have the freedom to jump and prance about on the
bed. He even thought of going into "Good Golly Miss Molly,"
which had nothing to do with the purpose at hand but had a
hell-raising chorus. But since Teddy still did not feel perfectly
well, and since he did not know if it was proper to raise hell in
front of the pope, the little boy stuck to his lines, and in his soft,
sweet child's voice, said at long last: "Hail Mary, Mother of God!
She did weep. She was sad. Begs Her children to come back.
With Her Son She returns in the year 2020. To bring love, reign
in peace. Everlasting glory be!"

22

"*Jesus Returns!*" read the headlines.

To Catholics from every corner of the world, especially zealots like the leader of the Catholic League, and even those in far-off lands where they lived in hiding or in isolation, His Holiness' official announcement of the Second Coming of Jesus Christ was wonderful news. The rest, well, some said the pope was senile and others that the Vatican had overplayed its hand, as Protestants, Muslims and Jews laughed and ridiculed the Holy See, and everyone, including many followers of the Roman Church, scratched their heads, wondering what would happen if Jesus and Mary did not show up as planned in 2020.

The press, eager to cover the pope's trip to America, issued a few unflattering editorials, but jotted the year 2020 in their calendars anyway, before moving on.

It is worth pointing out that Pope Leo's travel to Louisiana and his Mary's Crusade of 2020, as the event became known, exceeded the Vatican's expectations. In less than three months Mary's Crusade was responsible for a 50 percent surge in church attendance and a 75 percent increase in donations and contributions, especially to local parishes. But, as Bishop Ronnoco had warned, those same parishes suddenly found themselves stretched to a breaking point, and as the growing numbers of urgent calls for help reached the Holy See, its lumbering bureaucracy was caught unprepared and did not offer much except countless apologies. To complicate matters, as soon as Leo returned from the United States, he took to his bed with the sniffles. Since no one dared to make a decision without his consent, Mary's Crusade of 2020 spun out of control.

Of the Miltedews, Teddy recovered, but even before the pope had left Louisiana, Ray fell in a coma, died and was buried in the same plot that had been reserved for his son. Given the turn of events, and with financial help from Bishop Ronnoco, Harriet decided not to go on vacation. Instead, she sold the house at an unreasonably high price because it had been blessed by the pope and was considered a shrine, moved with the children to California, enrolled the boy in a professional children's school, and dedicated her time to his promising acting career in a land where apparitions, annunciations and even resurrections are the rule, not the exception.

Exceptions or not, it is a fact of life that as soon as someone becomes entangled in controversy, loyalties split, factions are formed and conspiracies are hatched, especially in the politically charged environment of the Holy See.

Early one Thursday morning, Cardinal Tomaso was in his office when Father Ricci announced that Bishop Ronnoco was outside and needed to have a word.

"Ronnoco?" Tomaso looked up from the letter he was writing. "What does he want? No, never mind. Tell him to come in, of course."

The secretary fetched the bishop while Tomaso put away his pen, placed the unfinished correspondence in a drawer, got up, and walked around his desk to receive His Excellency.

Cardinal Tomaso's office was, by far, the largest and most lavish in the Holy See, conforming precisely to the needs of the most influential member of the Curia. Not even the papal apartments dared display the conspicuous affluence that adorned the walls of his bureau with masterpieces from the Renaissance (paintings as well as tapestries), Napoleon's traveling desk, and furniture that Louis XV himself had made for the Marquise de

Pompadour. Since the cardinal liked a well-lit space, one wall was nothing but tall windows...now open to the morning air...framed with delicate off-white curtains that waved ever so gently in the breeze. On top of the Napoleonic desk were the usual inkpads, inkwells, lamps, and telephones... all rather ostentatious... and two photographs in silver frames that showed Cardinal Tomaso as a priest in the company of Pope John XXIII and later, as a bishop in the company of Pope Paul VI. A third photograph of Tomaso as a full prince of the Church in the company of Leo XIV was framed in gold and stood slightly in front of the other two.

"Excellency, this is a surprise. Would you care for something to drink? Coffee—tea?" Ronnoco shook his head and smiled in such a way that Tomaso instructed Father Ricci not to interrupt the meeting, then joined the bishop at a wide sofa underneath an enormous Titian.

"Eminence, we have a problem," began Ronnoco, looking quite concerned. "I am taking the liberty of coming to you because I know the Holy Father does not have a more loyal servant. He also treasures your counsel, as, in my humble opinion, he should."

Mary's Crusade was unraveling, said the bishop, and had to be stopped. The Holy See was under fire; it was being attacked by its own leaders, bishops and cardinals who did not believe Leo had been in full control of his faculties when he traveled to New Orleans. Several bishops were speaking openly against the pope, and some had even demanded in writing that he abdicate. Added Ronnoco: "Eminence, Hannibal ad portas!"

Whether Hannibal was knocking at the gates or somewhere else was of no consequence to Cardinal Tomaso, who could not imagine why, in the first place, the pope's closest confidant would seek his advice.

"That is true, Eminence," replied Ronnoco. "But we both know that when the Holy Father sets himself on a course it is very difficult to make him switch lanes. You understand what I'm saying?"

"Yes, of course, but you are at the vanguard of this movement, are you not? You know the dangers faced by the Holy See better than anyone." It had begun to rain and Cardinal Tomaso got up and shut the windows halfway.

"I understand, but I have not been able to convince His Holiness to yield to reason and it is my duty to inform the Curia. We must act before the damage becomes irreversible. We are alienating our members to the point that not even a miracle will bring them back. In Mexico, fifteen churches shut down after the congregation rioted for lack of priests. In Canada, six; in Spain three, in Argentina four—and the list goes on."

Cardinal Tomaso extended his hand to Bishop Ronnoco, led him to the door, and said: "Let me think about it. I'll get back to you no later than tomorrow morning."

No sooner had Ronnoco arrived back at his office that he received a call from the pope, to come at once.

He found Leo in bed, covered to the neck in white silk sheets and a comforter, and in the company of Dr. Gotovać, who took his pulse.

"Franko, we have to talk to His Excellency now," said Leo XIV, sitting up in bed with the doctor's help.

"Holiness, you cannot exert yourself," warned Gotovać, before turning to the bishop. "He can't!" The doctor left his bag of instruments behind and stepped outside the room.

"What's going on? It's bloody depressing in here. Can't you open the windows a bit?"

"Stop swearing, Felix," said Leo, with a cough that shook every inch of his ailing frame. "We should never have gone to America. God, what a mess!" The Holy Father smiled ruefully, but the pain soon wiped the smile off his face.

"Here." Leo took a white envelope from under his pillow and gave it to Ronnoco. "Traitors! They want me to step down!" Leo coughed again and had to close his eyes and breathe deeply to regain his strength.

"I know about the letter," said Ronnoco, giving it back to the pope. "They're feeling the pressure."

"They're like a bunch of —"

"They are what they are, Tata," Ronnoco interrupted. "You can't expect anything else from them. They are complacent, happy bureaucrats, always were, always will be. They are enamored of their elevated ranks and their lofty opinions of themselves. Why should they risk everything for an ideal? You don't think they believe that Christ will descend from heaven surrounded by angels, against a backdrop of a starry heaven, accompanied by Mary and Handel's hallelujah?"

"We'll deal with them soon enough. Call Serafio."

Ronnoco popped his head out the door and was about to call for the secretary when he noticed Cardinals Tomaso, Pino, Numa and Bailey waiting in the vestibule. He acknowledged their presence with a nod, summoned Brother Serafio, and stepped back inside.

"What are the Four Horsemen doing outside?" asked Ronnoco.

"Yes, Holiness?" said the secretary entering the room.

"Tell them to come in, and get the red hat."

The members of the Curia entered and inquired about the pope's health, while Serafio opened a drawer in Leo's desk, took out a white velvet cushion with a red zucchetto on top, placed it beside His Holiness, took half a step back, and left the room.

"I beg your pardon, Holiness, what are you doing?" asked Ronnoco. He realized that, aside from himself, there was no one in the room who could be created cardinal.

"What does it look like we are doing?" The pope smiled.

"You can't!" protested Ronnoco.

"We can't?" The pope's smile disappeared and he seemed annoyed.

"I—don't do this to me, please!"

"This is not your decision, Felix."

"Please, Holiness—I can't accept it. I am not worthy!"

Tomaso, Numa, Bailey, and Pino each took turns trying to persuade His Excellency that once the Holy Father decided to confer the title, to become a prince of the Church was not so much an honor as an obligation. Ronnoco listened, walked up and down... his arms alternately at his sides and waving in the air... all the time looking at the red hat as if it were a dead animal in the middle of the road.

"Brothers," began Leo, "many years ago, our late dear Pope Paul blessed us with his favor. The only witnesses on that occasion were two other brothers much like yourselves, close friends of His Holiness, and a boy, young Felix Ronnoco." Leo described the afternoon he was made cardinal and young Ronnoco's reaction to that event, so important in the life of the former priest Draganović. "Felix Ronnoco has been at our side through the best, and he has been at our side through the worst. He risked his life to serve our Church as legate to Vietnam and Cambodia, as well as in Jerusalem, Iraq, behind the Iron Curtain and most recently in Bosnia. His love for Christ and his dedication to the Holy See are unquestionable! No one else could have undertaken the delicate assignment in America, or cleared the way for that most glorious event. We do not know of anyone who is more worthy—" and with a nod, Leo XIV beckoned Ronnoco to kneel.

"Papa!" the little boy cried out again. He heard the dark man ask him his name.

"A-lek-s-sandar," he answered in a soft voice.

"Aleksandar, your name is Aleksandar?"

The boy nodded.

"And—" the dark man looked at the priest, "tell me, Aleksandar, they call you Saša, eh? Is that what your papa calls you? Saša?"

More silence. Saša tried to look up, but the sun positioned itself behind the dark man, and he could only nod and blink a few times at the towering silhouette asking questions.

"Of course they do, of course they do," said the dark man. He looked at the little boy next to him, again looked at the priest, and finally at the soldiers, before turning his attention once again to Saša. "Do you know how to cross yourself, boy?"

The little shepherd looked at his father wringing his hands, unable to hold back the tears of dread and impotence.

"Come, boy, cross yourself."

Time at the Holy See is, for the most part, not important and it is a fact that no one can do anything about. Yes, the pope was ill but everyone knew that he would eventually get better, and if he did not, it was God's will and the only thing to do was choose a new leader of the Universal Church.

The Vatican State bureaucracy, naturally, continued to move along as Ronnoco and the Four Horsemen finally agreed to present their concerns to Pope Leo.

The meeting was scheduled for ten o'clock at the Apostolic Palace, where they found Leo sitting behind his desk, wearing a long and heavy white robe and red velvet slippers, and looking frail. "This better be important. We should be resting. What is it, can't you decide on anything anymore? Do we have to tell you everything you have to do?" said Leo, annoyed.

"Holiness," said Cardinal Pino, approaching the Holy Father, "your brothers in Christ have respectfully written a letter—" and he put out his hand to Bailey, who handed the envelope to Numa, who passed it to Pino, who presented it to the pope, and after the expected obeisance, returned to his seat.

The official document was signed by every member of the Curia. The pope took a quick glance and tossed it aside. "Denied. What else?"

Tomaso took back the letter and began to protest, but Leo turned sharply and said: "That is nothing but a childish attempt at a palace coup! We won't have it!"

"But, Holiness!" began Pino, though he did not get very far.

"No!" thundered the pope, pointing from one cardinal to another, including Ronnoco. "What kind of men are you? You are supposed to be the leaders of the Church! So what if hundreds mobbed a church because there was no room for them inside! Mary's call was a call to arms! There is no turning back, and we must get ready for 2020! We are ashamed of you! We won't stand for it!"

With the exception of Ronnoco, none of the cardinals present. . . they were, after all, men whose careers depended on the goodwill of the pope. . . thought to challenge Leo. Doing so placed everything they had ever worked for at risk. Ronnoco, however, left his chair, clasped his hands in front of him, and in a voice that was firm, direct and determined, spoke for the rest. "Holiness, we have to slow down. People are getting hurt, and worse, they are being disappointed. What for? For an ideal that, although magnificent, is flawed and untrue."

"Silence!" ordered the pope.

"I beseech Your Holiness, I can't be silent while so much confusion is going on. We are to blame! It is not right, it is not just and it is not Christian!"

Tomaso, Pino, Numa and Bailey looked like four sticks of wax dressed in red; their blood drained from their faces and plunged to their heels.

"How dare you!" bellowed Leo. "How dare you!"

"As God is my witness, I dare because it is my duty! I love and revere Your Holiness, but your actions are pernicious and the Holy See is suffering! Not since the Middle Ages have we been more vulnerable, not to attacks from our enemies but from within! It is a situation that cannot—must not—continue!"

Leo XIV got up and walked to Ronnoco. The sick old man trembled as he took his friend by the arm and shook him with all his might. "You think wearing red gives you the right to question our authority!?" roared the pope.

"As a true servant of the Church, as a true servant of Christ, and your true servant as well—yes, I do!"

Tomaso put out his hand and tried to interject an "Eminence!" It was inaudible and his arm remained outstretched; no one paid attention to him.

"This is treason!" said the pope, standing now in the middle of the room.

Pino and Numa were unable to contain themselves and spoke in unison. "No, no, Holiness, how can you even think we're—" while Cardinal Bailey shook his head so forcefully it seemed in danger of dropping off.

"Our word is that of the Church. To stand against us is to stand against the Church! To stand against the Church is sedition, heresy! We thank God He unmasked your treachery!"

"Holiness, I beg you—this is unfair!" said Ronnoco, helping the pontiff return to his chair. "You are a man known for justice and charity, how can you—"

"Stop!" screamed the pope. "Serafio! Paper and pen, now!"

The secretary entered quickly and found those in the room pleading with the Holy Father to calm down. Serafio immediately handed Leo a notebook and a Mont Blanc fountain pen, helped the pontiff to a chair and stood beside him, fearing what would happen next.

The pen swept across the paper with a flourish of emphatic strokes. "You think you know better?" Leo paused an instant and stretched out his arm, calling for the wrath of God to strike the red hats. "You want to be the new Bishop of Rome? The Vicar of Rome?" he said to Tomaso, in a hollowed, firm voice.

"No, no, Holiness! How can you think that?" Tomaso had no choice but to throw himself on his knees and beg forgiveness.

The pope then turned to his right and with the same accusing finger aimed the next volley at Pino. "What about you? Does the title Vicar of Christ and Successor to the Prince of the Apostles make you proud?"

Pino was just as eloquent as his colleague, crying out: "No, no, no! Oh, Holy Father, show a little mercy!" He too ended on his knees, then raised his hands and requested divine assistance.

Leo then addressed Numa. "You look like you could be Supreme Pontiff of the Universal Church, Patriarch of the West and Primate of Italy! You would like that, yes? Tell me! Coward! I can make it possible for you!"

The pontiff's uncompromising stare forced Numa to kneel beside his brothers. He did not say anything, but prayed to Mary.

"Ah, my American friend!" Leo turned to Bailey. "Your country has enslaved half of humanity and exploited the rest. Now you want to conquer the Holy See. It's so like you Americans to want to buy into power—and to let yourselves be bought by it! Imagine, a cowboy as Archbishop and Metropolitan of the Roman province!"

Bailey fell on his knees and cried: "Oh, Holy Father, have pity!"

"Let it be, then!" Leo stumbled to his seat and with one last stroke signed the document. "Wax!" Then he stamped his seal, gave the paper to Serafio, and said: "Read!"

"M-me?" stuttered Serafio, his hand shaking.

"Oh, give it here, you fool!" yelled the pontiff, snatching the paper back from Serafio.

"Of all the base, deceitful recreants in this room!" he yelled at Ronnoco. "You are the worst! To think—" Leo straightened his infirm body, so used to the debilitating burden of arthritis, and for the first time in years stood to his full height, towering above the others like an ancient gray specter, "—to think that you would attach your name—a name we gave you—to betray us! Judas!"

"Holiness, please calm down! We only—" said Ronnoco in a broken voice as tears rolled down his face.

Tomaso, Pino, Numa and Bailey crossed themselves and repented, but it was too late.

"You!" screamed Leo, shaking his finger at Ronnoco. "You shall rue the day! You will suffer worse than any!" Leo stood before the papal throne and read the document he had signed in a voice that seemed accompanied by thunder and lightning. "It is our wish and command that we, Leo XIV, Bishop of Rome, Vicar of Rome, Vicar of Christ, Successor to the Prince of the Apostles, Supreme Pontiff of the Universal Church, Patriarch of the West, Primate of Italy, Archbishop and Metropolitan of the Roman province, Sovereign of the state of Vatican City, Servant of the servants of God, choose as our successor Felix Cardinal Ronnoco! To make the succession immediate and irrevocable, we, Leo XIV, hereby renounce our titles and our obligations! That is our last command as Supreme Pontiff of the Universal Church!"

THE CONFESSION

23

While the abdication of Leo XIV raised more than a set of brows, it was not a unique event in the history of the Church, nor did it come about as a result of a political struggle or a bloody Byzantine palace coup.

As John XIII decided that Pope Paul VI should be his successor, Leo XIV chose Felix Ronnoco because he trusted no one else to follow his radical, grand vision for the Roman Church in the years ahead.

In the end, a relatively young man was chosen as supreme pontiff, and when asked what name he would take as pope, Felix Cardinal Ronnoco, pondered and said: "Felix," followed by the Roman numeral V.

With the coronation scheduled to give the leaders of the Church around the world time to assemble at the Vatican, the former Leo XIV returned to Trastevere in an ambulance, where he convalesced from a persistent case of influenza. "Popes come and go, but the curtains remain the same," he said, laughing, as Felix, dressed in a simple black cassock, accompanied him to their old apartment.

If the Four Horsemen had been present in the room, they would have been surprised at how the old and the new pope got along, without a trace of bad blood or antagonism. Furthermore, they would have been shocked to learn that the explosive theatrics displayed by Leo XIV the day he resigned had been carefully orchestrated with Ronnoco, after both recognized that Leo's age and frailty was putting the Roman Church at risk, as evidenced by the fiasco of Mary's Crusade. By then, the most influential members of the Catholic Church's governing body were on their knees, in tears, too stunned to interfere, and too horrified to realize they had been duped.

Two days after that meeting, Pope Felix received an urgent call from Brother Serafio and, arriving in Trastevere, found his mentor in bed, attended by medics and Dr. Gotovać, who slowly and sadly shook his head. "He was going to the kitchen and stubbed his toe against the table. The pain triggered a heart attack," said Dr. Gotovać, outside in the hall.

"Holiness—" said a red-eyed Serafio.

Felix went back in the bedroom, and pulled a chair next to the bed.

"Tell them to get out," whispered the old man. "My time— my time is here," he added, when alone with Felix. "I wish—need to confess."

Felix V took the old and bony hand of his dear friend in his, and leaned forward in his chair, the tears rolling down his face. How could it be otherwise? He had never known a sadder day in his life; he was losing his mentor, his guardian—his Tata. "Confess and be absolved," he began in a tremulous voice, before he continued with the ritual they knew so well: "In nomine Patris, et Filii, et Spiritus Sancti. Amen."

The old man took a deep breath and with great difficulty, said: "I confess to Almighty God, to the Blessed Mary ever Virgin, to Blessed Michael the Archangel, to the Blessed John the Baptist, to the Holy Apostles Peter and Paul, to all the angels and saints, and to you, Father, that I have sinned exceedingly in thought, word, deed through my fault, through my fault, through my most grievous fault, and I ask Blessed Mary ever Virgin, Blessed Michael the Archangel, Blessed John the Baptist, the Holy Apostles Peter and Paul, all the angels and you, my brother, to pray for me to the Lord our God, I confess—I confess—"

The baby was brought back to the farm a week later and he spent his days sitting by the road looking out for Damir. "Damir? Nana, Damir soon?"

As winter covered the mountains, the child confined himself to a side window in the parlor, his small chin cupped in his hands, ever vigilant, waiting for Damir. "Nana, where Damir? Damir soon?"

The old woman put away the yarn, sat the baby on her lap, kissed and caressed him and said the only words she knew would soothe him: "Soon, Damir will be back soon."

Damir's love, his smile, playfulness, tenderness, hugs and loving nature were sealed forever in the child's fondest recollections, there to remain in the unpredictable maze of his unfolding life.

Ana Draganović, of course, was not aware of this nor did she wonder about the importance of one little boy's fate set against the hundreds of thousands who died in the war, victims of a bizarre melodrama in which, for centuries, outside interests incited a nation to fratricide.

After Pero died suddenly, Rostas and his wife, Olga, abandoned their small apartment in town and moved to the comfortable house on the mountain to help Ana care for the baby and the farm.

Yes, they would have to put up with the old woman, but they did not expect the inconvenience to last long. And yes, Rostas was forced to assume the chores of a shepherd, but that too was a fleeting trouble because most babies grow up and some even learn to tend sheep. All in all, it was a worthwhile compromise, one that in the end the couple hoped would prove to their advantage.

They were right. The boy grew up, took over caring for the animals and Ana Draganović died in her sleep on a sparkling summer night. She was laid to eternal rest a day later at the top of the incline behind the house, among the flowers and the fruit trees she loved so dearly.

After commending his mother to Christ, Draganović changed to a black suit, and walked outside where Olga waited with a twig basket lined in white cloth, and full of dried meats, fruit, cheese, wine and a thermos of Puerto Rican coffee for the long trip.

"Where's the boy?" asked the priest.

"Saying good-bye to the cat," sighed Olga. She was thirty-three, rather plain, but with a healthy, youthful look, although her hair was beginning to show traces of gray. She had small black eyes that became slits when her temper got the best of her, as her husband had discovered more than once during their eight-year marriage.

"Felix!" Draganović walked to the car.

"The luggage is in the trunk," said Rostas.

Felix ran out of the barn with a kitten of infamous lineage called Tito. The boy dressed in a dark gray wool suit at least one size too big, one that thirty-six years earlier had belonged to young Krunoslav Draganović.

"Don't run, you'll get all sweaty. Come here." Olga did not wait for the little boy to go to her, but cut him off as he approached the automobile. "Put him down," she said, taking out a handkerchief and wiping the boy's face.

"You have black circles under your eyes, like an old man. Give me a kiss." Olga pushed back the light brown curls from the boy's face. Felix gave Olga not one but several kisses and embraced her longer than she thought was necessary.

"We have to go," called Draganović, holding the door for the boy.

"Promise you'll take good care of Tito," said little Felix to Olga.

"I promise, I promise." She let go of the boy, turned him around and pushed him gently toward the car.

Rostas shifted gears and released the brakes. Slowly, the

car began its long journey down the mountain. Felix waved at Olga from the back seat and she waved back until the Citroën vanished behind a turn. Then, she went back into the house— her house now, in a way, since Ana was dead and Draganović was taking the boy to Rome.

"Tell me, Felix, are you excited you are going to Rome?" asked Draganović. It was Felix's first trip outside Travnik.

"I don't know."

Rostas kept an eye on both through the rearview mirror.

"You are going to make many friends," added Draganović, smiling. Up until then, Felix had counted Tito the cat, the sheep and the other animals at the farm as his only friends.

"But I don't speak Italian."

"Ah, you—you'll learn soon enough," said Rostas from the front.

They reached the town of Split seven hours later. The waterfront, which had been destroyed in the war, was still being rebuilt. The cranes, the trucks laden with lumber, cement, sand and rock, all were hidden in the shadows, resting like giants for the time being, waiting for daybreak so they could begin anew the reconstruction.

Rostas stopped the car next to the ferry that would take Draganović and Felix across the sea.

"Look, Felix, do you see the water?" asked the priest. "That's the Adriatic Sea; on the other side is Italy."

"Why is the water black?" The only bodies of water Felix had ever seen were the small rivers running down the mountainside in Travnik.

"The water is black," explained Draganović, "because it is night. During the day the water is as blue as the sky."

"Well, look who's here. Hello, Draganović," said the burly customs officer sitting at the end of the pier, stamping the papers of those boarding the ferry.

"Good evening." Draganović stepped up to the platform and handed over his Vatican passport and Felix's traveling papers.

The officer turned his gaze on Felix. "Who is that?"

"My cousin. He will be traveling with me. Those are his papers." Draganović pointed to the official-looking document beside his passport.

"Ronnoco? Italian, eh?" The man stamped Felix's papers, gave everything back to Draganović, and looked down again, hoping the priest would go away.

Two loud toots alerted everyone within two kilometers that the ferry was shoving off.

Rostas had brought the two small suitcases and the basket of food (some of it already consumed), and said: "Well, Felix, I will not see you for a long time, now, will I? And when I do, you won't remember me."

"I won't forget you," said the boy, hugging Rostas. There was a time when Felix thought Rostas was his father and Draganović his uncle, only to have a change of heart believing that the priest Draganović was his father and Rostas his uncle; the reason Felix began to call Draganović Tata, although he learned the truth from Ana, three weeks before she died. Felix was an orphan and he did not have an uncle.

"You take care, you understand?" returned Rostas.

As the man in the suit and the little boy boarded the ferry, the boat's lights framed their silhouettes to show one tall, black and wide, the other short, black and thin.

Rostas looked after them until the plank was removed from the dock and the ship glided silently into the dark sea, on the way to the Italian port of Pescara. Then, he got back in the car and, feeling a heavy sense of loss, drove back to the farm.

"It's moving!" said Felix, feeling the swaying of the old red and white boat. "Ooohhh!"

"You'll get used to it." Draganović pulled Felix closer to him.

"What if it sinks?"

"Then we get in one of those, over there." Draganović pointed to the lifeboats.

"They can sink too," observed Felix.

"They certainly can," agreed Draganović.

"And what if they do?"

"We swim."

"I don't know how to swim," Felix reminded Draganović.

"Then I hope you have been a good boy."

The ten hour trip to Italy was as tedious and uneventful as anyone crossing a large body of water in an old boat might be thankful for. There, they were met by Draganović's driver, a man called Marco, who loaded the luggage in the American limousine, for the final leg of the trip to Rome.

"Buon giorno, Eccellenza," said Marco. He was in his fifties, had a long nose, dark complexion, cropped gray hair, a stout body and the quiet, impeccable manners of a professional servant.

"Marco, this is Felix," said Draganović.

"*Buon giorno,* Felix." Marco merely glanced at the boy.

Felix looked up at Draganović.

"He said 'good morning,'" translated the bishop, helping Felix get in the car, where the boy quickly fell asleep, waking up only when they reached the outskirts of the eternal city.

That's when Felix took notice of the mass of automobiles zipping past at any speed, the thousands of pedestrians, the tall office buildings, and the dozen monuments and ruins including that of King Emmanuel II, the Coliseum, and the *Circo Massimo*. "This is incredible!" said Felix. "There are so—many—and they are big!"

At a quarter to ten in the morning, twenty hours after they had left Travnik, the limousine crossed the Ponte Palatino and entered the district of Trastevere, where it maneuvered through a series of back streets, and arrived at Via Penitenza 26, and the uncommonly plain and inconspicuous entrance to the bishop's residence.

It was a four-story building that had not been painted since the war, and therefore, looked older than its four hundred years, with a balcony on the top floor, filled with flowerpots and plants.

Marco held the door for Draganović and Felix, then took the suitcases out of the trunk and set them on the sidewalk.

"Grazie, Marco," said Draganović. "A domani."

Marco nodded, bowed, got back in the car and drove away without saying another word.

The priest took out a set of keys and unlocked the entrance. "Are you hungry?"

Felix nodded. He had not eaten since the night before when the food in the basket ran out.

"Are you tired?" Draganović clicked on a light switch on the wall behind the door, turning on a bare light bulb on the high ceiling.

Felix nodded again.

"Are you more tired than hungry, or more hungry than tired?" Draganović bolted the door from inside.

"More hungry than tired," replied Felix with a grin. He found himself in a cramped hall with a door to the left leading to the cellar and a staircase to the right going to the apartments.

"Well, if I know Sister Ornella, she'll have a plate of pasta with meatballs and sausage waiting for us." And Draganović took to the stairs.

No sooner was the nun mentioned that she opened the sliding doors to the receiving room. "*Buon giorno, Eccellenza. Ma, che bel ragazzo! Benvenuto a Roma, Felix.*"

"Felix, this is Sister Ornella."

Felix smiled, but because he could not reply in Italian, decided not to say anything.

"Did you have a comfortable trip?" inquired the nun in passing Serbo-Croatian. Sister Ornella was not beautiful, thought Felix. She was a broad-shouldered woman with high cheekbones, a wide forehead creased with wrinkles, big hands, a long nose, short dark-brown hair she kept tucked under her coif, a very tight smile that never revealed itself unless her head was leaning forward, a set of yellow teeth (one of them chipped), a firm tone of voice and a tendency to be kind that ran contrary to her nature and had taken years of penance to mold. "I am sure Felix is hungry, yes?" The nun lowered slightly her head and led the way into the apartments.

"Before we eat," Draganović nodded to Sister Ornella, who was busy setting the food on the kitchen table, "I want to show Felix his room." The priest beckoned the boy to follow. They crossed into the living room where Felix stopped when he saw three photographs on top of a slender mahogany end table by the sofa. One of the pictures was in a white ceramic frame and showed Ivo and Ana Draganović sitting in front of their farm.

"Nana!" said Felix pointing at the picture.

"Yes, that's Nana," said Draganović.

Felix then turned to the other photographs, encased in plain silver frames. The one on the left was taken years earlier on the steps of Saint Peter's and showed Draganović next to a tall young man with a thoughtful, unsmiling face. "Who's that?"

"Your namesake," answered the priest smiling.

Felix did not understand what that meant nor did he get a chance to ask because the moment he looked at the picture on the right, he recoiled, threw his arms around Draganović, shut his eyes and held on tightly.

"What's the matter?"

The boy did not answer, shook his head and refused to look at the photograph of Draganović and Aloysius Stepinac standing on a street in Banja Luka.

"It's just a silly old picture. Come now." Draganović led Felix out of the living room, and across the hall. "This is my bedroom," said the priest pointing to a door on his left. "And that is your room," he said pointing to the door at the end of the hall. "Go ahead," he said moving aside so Felix could walk ahead.

Little Felix Ronnoco slowly opened the door and found a bedroom five times the size of the attic at the farm. It had big windows and clean white walls that reflected the sunlight, keeping the room bright and fresh. There was a portrait of Baby Jesus and his Mother, but what caught his eye was the collection of toys such as he had never seen in his life, all neatly on the floor and on his wide, comfortable-looking bed. There were balls, balloons, several armadas of toy soldiers, toy airplanes and trains, building blocks and coloring books; as many toys as any boy Felix's age might dream of playing with.

Felix put down his suitcase, looked up at Draganović with eyes that said, "For me!?" The boy walked around slowly picking up a ball and putting that down to pick up a train and putting that down to pick up a soldier and putting that down to pick up a coloring book—

Said the priest: "Things will be different here, Felix. This is your home now. This is your bedroom. These are your toys. Tomorrow, you'll see your school; then, we'll get you some clothes, the kind worn by kids in Rome, not shepherds. You're going to be here a long time and you will grow up and learn everything you can and become a wise, wise old man."

Whereas the children who, on occasion, roamed the halls of the residences of high-ranking Church officials were typically those of the staff, Draganović had adopted Felix as his own. And while he was strict and sometimes inflexible with most people, to this little boy Draganović showed understanding and love.

After his meal, Felix took a short nap and spent the rest of the day playing in his room. At sundown he stood at the window and saw clotheslines crisscrossing an inner yard. Across that, in the building next door, Felix saw an old man sitting in a large chair reading the newspaper, in a room that was otherwise bare except for the one light bulb shining down on him. He saw a family of five—three children, all of them older than him—sitting with their mama and papa having dinner in the kitchen. In another apartment, Felix saw a gray cat looking out a window, maybe waiting for the rising moon. And—there she was, bright, big and yellow, just like at home.

"Felix, Felix, Felix, come and stay,
Not in there but out to play!
Felix, Felix, Felix, come and stay—"

"She remembers me! The moon did not forget!" The boy smiled, jumped in his new bed and in a few minutes was fast asleep.

Draganović entered Felix's room at six o'clock the next morning and found the boy holding a yellow locomotive in one hand, and the little flute he liked to keep under his pillow, in the other. "Wake up," said Draganović softly. He put his hand on the boy's wet cheek, and little Ronnoco at last opened his eyes, and smiled. "Another bad dream?"

Felix nodded, yawned and stretched his limbs.

Draganović sat quietly for a moment, stroking gently the boy's face, then kissed the child on the forehead and said: "Brush your teeth and take a bath. Sister Ornella is making breakfast—though you ate enough yesterday for a week."

Forty-five minutes later, as the city began another Roman day, Draganović, dressed in a dark gray suit and tie, and took Felix by the hand in and out of a noisy, talkative crowd, through the tight alleys and narrow streets of Trastevere.

Because he was distracted, fascinated and bewildered by his surroundings—for instance, he had never seen a life-sized mannequin like those in Antonia's dress shop, nor the haberdasher across the street, had never seen a counting house with a dozen young, beautiful girls punching the keys of strange-looking machines, nor a tailor shop where a bald little man with a chalk in one hand, a measuring tape around his neck and needles in his mouth, knelt beside a client standing on a wooden box. He also never imagined a flower shop that specialized in wedding and funeral arrangements at the same time, with examples displayed on the pavement side by side as if to advise passers-by that the inevitable outcome of marriage was death, and he most certainly never visited a barbershop with a waiting line of six men, every one of them at least eighty-five years old ...

"Stop bumping into people," said Draganović, after the boy almost knocked over an old woman on her way to mass. "It's embarrassing."

"But, Tata," said Felix shading his eyes with his right hand, "there are so many of them!"

Madame Berini's Scuola Inglesa was only a few blocks from the house, at the corner of Via delle Scala 22. It was a plain two-story building with Romanesque windows and eight marble steps leading to the large arched bronze door with square reliefs. The strains of Jerome Kern's "They Didn't Believe Me" could be heard from a faltering trombone, mingling with the voices of children on the school grounds.

Draganović rapped on the door several times and waited.

At last, a large woman who seemed as wide as she was tall, with red hair, brown eyes and a little too much rouge showed herself at the entrance, standing sideways to grab any child thinking of escape. "*Eccellenza, che piacere!*" said Madame Berini, for it was the educator herself. "And who is this?" she continued in fluent Serbo-Croatian, something hardly surprising, because Madame Berini had been born in Zagreb and lived all her young life there before escaping to Rome during the war, after which she married a trombonist named Berini. "Is this little Felix whom we've heard so much about?" She was not surprised to see Draganović dressed in a suit; in fact, she had rarely seen him wearing anything else. Draganović and Madame Berini had met on several occasions at the Institute of Saint Jerome, where, on her arrival to Rome, she had gone for assistance and advice.

"Please, come in, come!" Madame Berini opened the door a little and stepped aside. The school was located in a large, two-story machine depot abandoned after the war. In the center of this unusual structure was an open, unpaved area that had been used as a dumping ground, and which Madame Berini, after ingratiating herself to local officials, converted into what she described as "a playground." Five small compartments on the first floor were classified as classrooms, each equipped with a clutter of tiny desks, a map of the world and a blackboard, while the second story was appropriated by the Berinis as living quarters.

The institution had been established to teach the young children of wealthy Roman families to speak what Madame Berini, a language instructor by profession, thought was the lingua franca of the future, English. Of course, if the Germans had won the war, Madame Berini would have been teaching German instead. Though she might have been an opportunist, Madame Berini was also an excellent teacher, and the school was an instant success, both because of its academic excellence and because many of the children at the school were, in fact, the children of staff members from the United States and United Kingdom embassies, who wanted their offspring to learn not English but Italian. "I am sure Felix is going to like it here," declared the educator.

Madame Berini's office was painted a light blue. Piles of papers and stacks of books were everywhere, including on a small table by her desk and the walls were decorated with photographs of many of the children who had excelled in her school.

"Felix knows how to read and write," said Draganović.

"He does? Well, that's wonderful!" said Madame Berini leaning forward. It hardly mattered, she thought, whether the little peasant knew how to read and write because even if he did, and Madame Berini had no reason to doubt the bishop, the boy could only read and write Serbo-Croatian. He could not speak Italian, and certainly knew no English, the reason he had been enrolled in the school to begin with.

"Nana taught me," said Felix, speaking for the first time.

"Nana?"

"My mother," clarified Draganović.

Madame Berini leaned back in her chair, clasped her hands, and said: "Of course."

At that moment the bell sounded and the hundred or so boys and girls playing in the courtyard suddenly became very quiet. The children scrambled like little soldiers and formed three lines in the center of the yard.

They waited patiently and quietly until four young women of very serious academic mien marched them inside.

"Yes, I know Felix will flourish here," said the educator.

After Draganović and Felix were finished with their tour of the school, accompanied by a trombone rendition of "Ain't Misbehavin', " Felix found himself once again colliding with strangers, as Draganović took him to Bambini, not far from the school. Because Draganović had never bought clothes for a child, he allowed the pretty young woman behind the counter to recommend, measure, collect payment for and deliver to the house ten shirts, five pairs of shorts and five pairs of slacks, ten pairs of socks, two suits, two pairs of sandals and three pairs of shoes, ten pairs of underwear, three belts and two pairs of suspenders. All in all Draganović bought Felix enough clothes to last the boy...well, at least until he outgrew them, or until Sister Ornella could not alter them anymore.

Back home, Draganović and little Felix lunched polenta and sausages with onions, before the priest retired to his room, only to resurface forty-five minutes later in the living room. "Felix," he called.

The boy found Draganović wearing a cassock, a purple sash, a cape and a little cap.

"Come, sit here, please." His Excellency pointed to a foot-stool in front of his chair. "Do you know what I'm wearing?"

"No."

"This is what I put on most of the time when I go outside. In here, of course, I like to change into something more comfortable because these robes are hot and heavy." Draganović brushed Felix's hair from his face, thinking the boy needed a haircut, and continued. "You know I am a bishop?"

"Y-yes," answered Felix. He remembered that Olga and Rostas always addressed him with deference, and had seen pictures of him in Rome, dressed in his clerical vestments. But knowing and understanding however, are two different things.

"Do you know what a bishop is, Felix?"

"N-no."

"Well, a bishop is a priest, but an important priest, one that other priests look up to and one who is always treated with great respect. If I had worn this outfit when I took you to the school or to buy your clothes, people would have been bowing to me and greeting me all the time and that is the reason I did not put on my bishop's clothes. In most cities of the world, but especially in Rome, a bishop is a very, very important person. Do you understand what I'm saying?"

"I think so," answered the boy.

"I am going to ask you to do something that will be very difficult for you at first, but, as with most things, I'm sure you will get used to it."

"What?"

"Whenever we are with other people, including Marco and Sister Ornella, it is important that you call me 'Excellency' and not 'Tata.'"

"Why?" Felix's first thought was that Draganović did not love him anymore.

"Because that is the way to address someone of my rank, that is the correct way to address a bishop." Draganović noticed that Felix had acquired a worried look. "That's not to say I don't care for you, or that I don't love you. It's not that at all. Of course, when we are alone, I want you to call me what you've always called me—"

"Tata!"

"Yes, but only when we are alone."

"I understand," said Felix smiling.

"Above everything else, you must know that my feelings for you do not change regardless of how I'm dressed. But, there are traditions and rules that must be observed." Draganović looked at Felix for a moment, then added: "Another thing. It is important that you do not tell anyone at school or anywhere else that I am your father, because I am not and could never be. Remember I am a priest, and priests do not have children—in the traditional sense. If someone asks who I am, tell them I am your cousin. Believe me, Felix, some day, when you are older, you will know why we've had this conversation." Draganović kissed the boy on both cheeks. "Now, look out the window and tell me if the car is here."

Felix rushed to the window, put out his head, walked back to Draganović, looked to his left, looked to his right and said with a big grin: "Yes, Tata, the car is downstairs."

Half an hour later, Draganović arrived in his office at the Government Palace, from where he directed the Commissione d'Assistenza Pontifica and the Holy See's alliance to Intermarion, an obscure federation of European states first established in the 1920s by the French and English Secret Services to inflame Catholic sympathies and spark a holy war against international communism. Unfortunately, by the end of the Second World War many of the nations that comprised the federation fell to the Soviet Union.

In 1946 Intermarion was reorganized, revitalized and newly funded by Britain's MI-6 and the CIA to recruit, train and run anticommunist insurgents in a campaign of sabotage, disinformation and assassination against the Soviet Union and its satellites, as well as against left-wing labor unions and regional communist parties.

Pope Pius XII was so impressed with Draganović's efforts that he rewarded the priest with much praise and a bishop's title. Archbishop Montini, by then pro-secretary of state at the Vatican and Pius XII's confidant, saw the bishop as the only man in the Apostolic See with the expertise required to deal with the cloak and dagger functions of Intermarion.

"Anything happen since I've been away?" asked Draganović.

"These arrived yesterday, Excellency." Brother Serafio stood just inside the heavy doors with a pile of telegrams and a writing pad. He approached the desk and placed all the telegrams on the desk except for one. "This came in today, from Buenos Aires."

Draganović read the Argentinian telegram, opened the right-hand drawer of the desk, placed the telegram inside, then closed and locked the drawer. "What else?"

"His Eminence Roncalli called to offer condolences on the loss of your mother, and would like for you to call him at your convenience. His Excellency Montini has also been coming around asking when you were coming back."

"You did give him a copy of my itinerary?"

"Of course, Excellency," said Serafio looking at his notes.

"Thank you."

"Call Roncalli. Ask him if I can come over at four."

"Yes, Excellency," said Serafio, then returned to his cubicle.

With the secretary out of the room, Draganović took Saint Jerome off the wall, opened the safe, removed enough bundles of Argentinian currency tied up with rubber bands to finance a small army, took out a brown diplomatic pouch with the Vatican seal, placed the money and the pouch on his desk, locked the safe, put Saint Jerome back in place, returned to the desk, placed the money inside the diplomatic pouch, and called Serafio through the intercom.

"Excellency?"

"Here." Draganović tossed the pouch to Serafio. "For Brother Martín." Brother Martín was Draganović's go-between with Ante Pavelić. The pouch was sent from the Holy See by special courier to the Alitalia office at the Rome airport. It would then be put aboard the next flight to Argentina, where Brother Martín would pick it up and deliver it to the Poglavnik.

"Yes, Excellency. Oh, His Eminence will be waiting for you at four."

"Thank you."

Serafio left the room. For a moment the bishop stared into space and thought of Felix. Then, he opened the drawer, took out the telegram from Buenos Aires, read it again and stopped at the word "wedding." Draganović walked to the other side of the office, tore up the telegram and tossed it in the burn basket. "Good."

24

Next morning, Sister Ornella insisted that little Felix not be left to wander the streets of Trastevere by himself, and volunteered to walk the boy to and from school every day if necessary. His Excellency reminded the good sister that the Scuola Inglesa was but a few blocks away, and that Felix was used to taking care of himself plus a flock of sheep and goats besides, in a wooded valley infested with predators. His assurances notwithstanding, the nun prevailed and escorted Felix to his first day of school.

The boy looked positively Roman in a new pair of brown shorts held up by suspenders, a cream-colored checkered shirt, matching socks and sandals, and his hair combed back with brilliantine.

Still distracted by the novelty of everything, he managed to crash into a little girl, an old man and a priest before Madame Berini—with "Putting on the Ritz"playing in the background—greeted him at the door.

His dress and bearing aside, Felix soon learned that it would take a while for him to adapt to academic life because he could not remember the last time he had to sit still for hours and pay attention to an unattractive matron speaking in a foreign tongue, or when he needed permission to go to the bathroom, a simple and very natural function that, due to the difference in languages, required the intervention of Madame Berini.

In addition, although some classmates made an effort to befriend Felix, they too were frustrated by his inability to speak

Italian, leaving the poor boy sitting on the sidelines, watching the other children enjoying themselves at play.

Le petit Croat, as the French teacher called him, soon became frustrated, though he was never one for giving up. He pondered for three days the question of "communications" when he remembered that he never had any trouble telling the sheep and the goats back home what to do, and they did not speak Serbo-Croatian, either.

That is why it made perfect sense, then, to treat his classmates like a herd: whistling and waving, running after the boys, chasing after the girls, knocking them on the head, shaking them by the arm, and poking their sides to nudge them along.

Before long, a group of indignant parents descended upon the headmistress to complain about the mad little Croat. One mother, the wife of a secretary at the English embassy demanded that Felix be expelled because he lacked the refined upbringing necessary in civilized society.

Madame Berini immediately summoned Felix to her office and delivered an awful scolding with assistance from her index finger. The tongue lashing would have gone on for days had the boy not looked up at the headmistress, as she took a breath, and said: "You are beautiful."

The compliment caused the headmistress to pause for a moment. She slowly retrieved her finger, and placed her arms to her side. "What was that?" asked Madame Berini, convinced that Felix had been coached to flatter his way out of trouble.

"I think you are beautiful," insisted the little boy, smiling. After all, when compared to Ana Draganović, who was dead, Olga, who was young and spent and Sister Ornella, who did not matter whether she was old, young, spent or dead, Madame Berini was as beautiful as a rose.

"Mmm—" mumbled the educator, who, after a long pause, added: "Would you care for some milk and cookies?"

It took Felix six months to learn enough Italian from Madame Berini to communicate with his classmates, without herding. He made many friends among the little girls of his class and was admired by the boys for his physical agility and endurance.

For their part, the teachers were enchanted with his wide-eyed innocence and endearing charm. They never suspected that, as young Ronnoco had demonstrated with Madame Berini, he possessed shrewd diplomatic skills acquired and developed early on; a result of having lived his entire young life among adults.

At home, Felix liked to run errands for Sister Ornella. She made things easy for him by telling him exactly what to ask for from the butcher, the baker, the fishmonger and the wine seller.

The "bishop's boy," as he was known, would go into the baker's shop and call out: *"Ciao, Carlino! Bisogno pane!"* Then, he would cross the alley and burst into the wine shop with *"Ciao, Roberto! Bisogno vino!"* All of them, the baker, the wine seller, the butcher and others, tried to find out about his relationship to the bishop. "Oh, he's my uncle," said Felix to the butcher. "He's my cousin," he told the baker. "He's my neighbor," was the story he fed the fishmonger. "He's just my friend," explained the boy to the florist, and "He's my brother," was the account given to the wine seller. It was enough to keep inquiring minds perplexed, off balance and thirsting for more.

The nights when Draganović was home, Felix sat at his side, on the floor, spending hours describing what happened in school that day, about a new friend he had met, or simply telling about something interesting he had witnessed in town. The experience was enlightening as much for the bishop as it was for the boy.

One night Draganović arrived home later than usual and found Felix playing in his room.

"Tata!" cried Felix, rushing to give His Excellency a hug.

"What on earth happened to you?" said the bishop, holding the boy at arms' length.

"I lost a tooth!" said Felix with a grin that showed a large gap in the middle of his mouth.

That's when Draganović realized that there was a world of difference between spending a few hours with Felix at the farm—where Ana and Olga always cared for the child—and then, where every day-to-day event in the little boy's life was intertwined with his own.

A week later, Felix and Draganović were having dinner when the boy asked if he could visit a friend after school.

"After school?"

"Tomorrow," explained Felix.

"What is your friend's name?" asked Draganović.

"Robert."

"Robert?" pondered the priest. "Where is he from?"

Felix thought about it for a moment, then answered: "I don't know. He's English."

His Excellency laughed, and said: "Then, he's from England."

"Is he?" asked Felix, surprised.

Draganović smiled. "Yes, he is. And you can visit with your friend. Just make sure you're home by six and don't forget to tell Sister Ornella you're coming home late."

Two weeks went by and Felix asked Draganović if Robert, his English friend, could come to the house after school.

This time the bishop pondered the situation more carefully. "What for?"

"To play."

"Ah—" said Draganović, under his breath. It seemed that raising a little boy was full of unpredictability. "Tell Sister Ornella when you plan to bring your friend."

"Yes, Tata." And he did just that, two days later, as he left for school. Then, at four-fifteen, Sister Ornella heard the door slam, followed by a noisy dash up the stairs. "Why can't that boy walk like normal people?" thought the nun, when Felix and his friend appeared in the room, their cheeks flushed and their happy faces wet with perspiration.

"This is my best friend Robert—" said Felix.

"Goldsmith," offered the boy. Robert was a little taller and a little fatter than Felix. He had an oval face, curly sandy hair, two little brown holes for eyes beneath two copper-colored brows, an elf's nose, an extremely pale complexion and a set of very small teeth. He was dressed the way any boy his age might have been dressed in London, with a pair of brown slacks, socks and sandals, a white T-shirt with a dark blue knitted sweater on top.

Sister Ornella did not reply but dropped her head slightly, which meant Felix had permission to leave the room.

"*La tua mama?*" Robert chased Felix down the hall.

"*Sorella,*" Felix answered, throwing open the door to his bedroom.

Sorella, of course, means "sister" in Italian, which is what many people call a nun. Italian not being his first language, however, Robert did not grasp the ambiguity between "sister," meaning "nun," and "sister," meaning "daughter to your father and mother," and the thought of Felix having such an odd-looking woman for his sister, mystified the English boy.

That evening, Draganović arrived at the house about eight o'clock and no sooner did His Excellency walk in the door, Sister Ornella described the events of the afternoon, before returning to the kitchen to fix his supper.

Felix was in his room looking over a coloring book when he heard the door open. "Tata!"

Draganović kissed Felix and sat on the bed while the boy related everything he had done with his friend. "He likes movies, Tata, and asked if I could go to the movies with him next Saturday! Can I, please? I've never seen a movie!" Felix stopped and frowned, then looked at Draganović. "What's a cowboy?"

"My boy," said Draganović with a sigh and in a way that required little Ronnoco to pay attention. "I would prefer if you did not bring that boy here again."

"Not bring him here? Why? You don't like Robert?" asked Felix. The happiness that had been so evident in his face vanished.

"Why don't you like Robert? He's not a Serb." Felix knew of Draganović's special dislike for Serbs.

"No, he's a Jew." To think that Madame Berini allowed Jews in her school! But the bishop understood that the Americans and the English had the money to pay her high fees and everybody knew the Americans and the English were a strange mix.

"A Jew?" Felix remembered on many occasions Draganović and others saying the Jews betrayed Jesus, that they turned against Christ and had him crucified. "I'll beat him up!"

"No, you will not."

"But, the Jews—they killed Jesus!" cried Felix getting angrier and angrier.

"Stop it, Felix. I mean it," said Draganović holding the boy by the shoulders. "Just don't bring him here, that's all. I am a high-ranking member of the Catholic clergy. I can't have little Jews, big Jews or Jews of any size running up and down my halls. It's not right."

Felix was not sure what all of this meant or what it had to do with Robert, but he wanted to cry. To think that he had brought home a Jew. "I hate Jews!"

"You must not hate Jews, Felix. Pray for their salvation and for their repentance, but don't hate them. It's not Christian to hate."

Felix cast his eyes to the floor. "I'm sorry."

Draganović kissed the boy goodnight, and the moment he stepped out in the hall, he heard Felix call out: "I didn't know he was a Jew!"

The melody heard the following morning was Gershwin in disguise since the lazy undulations of the trombone that tried to interpret "I Got Rhythm" had everything but.

Felix, tired after a difficult night's sleep, filed into the schoolyard with the rest of the children when he saw Robert, who was clearly waiting for him.

"Hey, Felix!"

Young Ronnoco felt his cheeks burn, but remembered his Tata's warnings to forgive, something he found difficult to do because he did not understand what forgiveness was about, therefore, he decided to simply ignore Robert altogether.

"Felix!" insisted the English boy, this time rushing over and slapping his pal playfully on the back, which earned him such an awful contemptuous look that he stepped back.

Jews, like Serbs and balijas, thought Felix, fooled people with alarming simplicity, disguising themselves to make others think they are something, when in truth, they are not.

The duplicity of human nature troubled Felix so much that when an American kid approached to show him some cards with pictures of men in funny uniforms, holding wooden clubs, he asked: "Are you a Jew?"

"I'm American—from Washington, D.C. Why?"

Felix did not know about Washington D.C., whether it was possible for Jews to live there or in fact, if Jews lived there at all. He assumed that because Freddy—that was the American boy's name—looked so different to Robert in every way—that he could not be a Jew, so, they became pals, chums and plain best friends.

Like Felix, Freddy kept mostly to himself because for all his charm and friendly nature he did not care, or even understood football, or as Americans call it, soccer. He, however, was passionate about one sport that no one in Rome knew anything about, baseball.

His love for the sport was contagious and he spent every free minute talking about the game, telling Felix about its heroes, the incredible money they made, and late one morning, grabbed a broomstick and a tennis ball to show him how it was played.

With the rest of his classmates looking on from the sidelines, Freddy asked Felix to throw him the ball, then whacked it as hard as he could, sending it soaring as high as the eye could see.

"Catch it!" yelled Freddy.

Confused, young Ronnoco looked up, but instead of the tennis ball, he saw a white dove against the bright sun, spiraling lazily downward, landing softly at his feet and turning into a pool of blood.

"Get the ball!" called Freddy, from across the yard.

Felix did not. He covered his eyes with his left hand, crossed himself twice with his right, said a quick prayer, peeked between his fingers, and saw that the bloody specter had vanished.

"Felix, the ball! Throw it back!"

"What for?" asked Felix.

"So I can hit it again!" answered Freddy.

The demonstration continued for a few minutes until young Ronnoco became tired of chasing balls, at which time, he asked: "Freddy, is that all there is?"

Obviously, it was important that the yank teach his Croatian friend the subtleties of the sport of baseball, although he would have to do so after the Easter holidays, when Christian love and goodwill prevailed during the religious observance that culminates on Easter Sunday, commemorating the resurrection of Jesus Christ after his crucifixion.

Because Felix had never been to Vatican City, Draganović secured excellent seats for him and Sister Ornella in a roped-off section reserved for the important bureaucrats of the Vatican. The bishop thought that they would enjoy sitting in a packed and stifling St. Peter's Basilica while Pius XII offered the traditional mass of Easter Sunday.

Felix being Felix, however, Felix would not sit still. No sooner the choir began to sing and the Holy Father made his spectacular entrance sitting in full regalia on his throne, as it was carried to the altar atop the shoulders of a dozen men, Draganović, who along with other high ranking clerics accompanied the papal procession, became alarmed when he saw Felix asking a Swiss Guard to let him get a closer look of il papa; a request courteously but firmly denied.

The ceremony lasted close to an hour and a half, after which Felix and the nun filed out of the church and joined the thousands upon thousands of followers crowding the Roman streets, on the way home.

About eight o'clock next morning, Felix and His Excellency Draganović—in his clerical best—reached the walled domain of the Holy See by way of the Viale Vaticano.

"Where are we going?" asked Felix, who was impeccably dressed in a brand-new gray suit, white shirt and a bright yellow bow tie.

Replied Draganović: "It's a surprise."

The limousine drove past Saint John's Tower, entered the Vatican and stopped at the Government Palace.

The boy looked up at the five-story building resting in a manicured garden with a topiary rendering of the Vatican's coat-of-arms and a small, columned bell tower capped with a statue of Jesus. "What is this place?"

"It's where I work," replied the bishop.

"You mean this is all yours?" asked Felix.

Draganović laughed. "No. I work here. I have an office."

"Are we going to your office? Please!"

"No, we are not. It is not a place for children. But, I am going to take you to see the most wonderful treasures in the world. Would you like that?"

"Oh, yes, very much!"

"Well, let's go!" said Draganović, taking Felix by the hand, when he heard someone calling his name.

The bishop turned around and saw Archbishop Montini walking quickly in their direction.

"Good morning, Excellency!" greeted Draganović.

"And a good morning to you, too. What are you doing here this early?" asked Montini.

"I thought it was time to show Felix around," answered Draganović, nodding toward the boy.

Montini looked carefully at the child, and said: "Is this the little cousin we've heard so much about, Excellency?"

"Yes, he is." Draganović moved to the side. "Felix, say hello to His Excellency, Archbishop Montini."

On cue, Felix bowed, took Montini's hand and kissed it.

"How old are you, young man?" asked Montini.

"I think I am—about eight years old, Excellency," replied Felix with a firm voice and an ingratiating smile.

Montini laughed. "Charming."

"Thank you, Excellency." Felix bowed again to the archbishop, then smiled at Draganović.

"Going anywhere in particular?" Montini started walking and Draganović and Felix followed.

"The Academy of Science."

"It is so inspiring," said Felix in a calm, meditative voice.

Montini stopped, took Felix's chin in his hand, looked the boy in the eye, but addressed Draganović. "Why don't you do that later—the Academy, I mean—and come with me, Excellency—you and Felix. I'm on my way to meet with his Holiness."

"But—Excellency, I can't very well—" Draganović meant he could not take a little boy to visit the pope as if they were visiting an old uncle.

"Nothing to worry about, Excellency. Besides, I'm sure Felix would not mind meeting the Blessed Father."

Minutes later, the archbishop, the bishop and a very nervous Felix Ronnoco entered the Apostolic Palace from a side door, walked past a couple of Swiss Guards, climbed the wide marble stairs to the third floor and reached the antechamber to the pope's study.

Two cardinals and three bishops lounged about, waiting for a word or a command from the pontiff. Although they did not recognize Draganović, the Vatican's man to Intermarion had compiled dossiers on them, secret papers that were hidden away behind Saint Jerome.

Of course, the unfamiliar sight of a small boy raised the prelatic brows to higher concerns, especially after Montini, His Excellency Draganović and his young cousin entered the papal apartments without having to be shown in.

"Excellency!" beckoned a feeble Pius XII. "Come, come!"

Draganović walked quickly to Pius XII, took his skeletal hand and kissed the sacred ring. Felix remained at the far end of the room after a quick glance and a sudden squeeze of the hand from his Tata warned him not to move, talk and if possible not breathe until he was called—and, if he was not, to imagine he was a potted plant.

The room was not as grand as the Sistine Chapel but it was grand enough. The Blessed Mother watched over the proceedings and eight scarlet chairs, four on each side of the white throne, remained empty atop a thick rug with the papal seal.

"Kruno, what a pleasant surprise," said the pope in the faintest of voices.

His Excellency Bishop Draganović and Pius XII whispered to each other for a moment, while Felix focused on the white, shimmering vision of the illuminated throne because it seemed, at least to him, that an aura of blessedness, goodness and love radiated from the small figure talking to his Tata, while a chorus—it must have been angels—raised their voices in praise.

In that time, Felix did not blink once for fear that Pius XII would vanish in a puff of magic smoke and ascend to heaven, to take his place next to Christ. The boy certainly did not expect Pius XII to move his head ever so slightly, touch his glasses with his right hand and cast his eyes on him.

The Holy Father said nothing, of course, and he did not have to. Felix knew the pope was calling, and there he was, aware that he was walking toward Pope Pius XII and he could not stop himself.

Gently, His Holiness reached out and touched the boy's face. That confused Felix. He had intended to kiss the papal ring but was never given the chance.

The pope looked Felix in the eye, then the very complex man asked a simple question: "Tell me, Felix, what do you want to be when you grow up?"

Felix paused, blinked a few times, and said: "A baseball player."

The pope frowned and looked at Draganović.

"I think, Holiness," whispered Draganović, leaning forward, "it has something to do with sports." He then darted a look at Montini as if to say: "This was your idea!"

Pius XII left the chair and laughed. "I know about baseball, Excellency, I do!" He then led Felix by the hand to a tall, hand-carved cabinet, flung open its doors and pointed to a cobalt-blue lead crystal ball, hand blown, hand cut, polished and engraved with stripes and "NY." "Take it," added the pope.

The boy looked at Pius XII, then, with both hands, carefully lifted the beautiful and mysterious orb from its solid mahogany base, and noticed that it split in two.

"Lift the top, go ahead," said the pope, smiling.

Felix did, and found another ball covered in white leather, with seams stitched in red and a blue ink autograph.

The pope took the ball in his hand, and said: "Do you know what this is?"

Felix hesitated, then shook his head, afraid he'd be sent to hell for being ignorant.

"That, Felix, is a baseball."

The boy turned very red. He was stunned and angry with himself because Freddy never showed him a real baseball!

"You know, Excellencies," Pius XII turned to Draganović and Montini. "This is the first time I've asked a boy what he wants to be when he grows up, and he says something other than 'priest!' Good for you, Felix!" The pope laughed again, and tossed the baseball in the air once or twice. "Can you read the autograph?"

Try as he did, Felix was unable to decipher the scribble.

"He's a great baseball player—a star. His name is DiMaggio. He dropped by last year," added Pius XII, returning to his chair. "Keep it. We certainly—" and the pope laughed again, "we certainly have no use for a baseball. A bat, maybe—to bang a few red hats—But a baseball? No. Take it my boy, with my blessings!" It was the last time Pius XII had any fun.

Back home, Felix could not wait. He paced his room anxiously, because he wanted to tell the world, but particularly Freddy, about his gift—and what a gift, straight from the hands of the Holy Father himself!

"You're not to take it out of the house," said Draganović.

"Why? I want to show Freddy!" pouted little Ronnoco.

"It is too valuable. I don't want you getting hit over the head and robbed. This is Rome, Felix, not the mountains. We have to be extra careful. If you want to show it to your friend, he'll just have to come here."

Good idea!

With Easter break over and school restarting the following day, Felix placed the sacred baseball on a shelf, next to his svirala and spent most of the night staring at the moonlight glow off the blue crystal.

Even though he was very tired, young Ronnoco was up and out of the house before the clock struck 7, but found that Freddy had gone back to the United States for two weeks, so in the end, he would have to wait to show off his prized and blessed baseball.

Draganović, on the other hand, was enjoying his cup of Puerto Rican coffee when a telephone call forced him to stop off at the Scuola Inglesa, before heading to Vatican City.

"Excellency, thank you so much for coming on such short notice," said Berini, greeting him at the door. "Please, this way—" she said. "I apologize—I know how busy you are, but—we have a problem."

"Felix?"

Obviously, thought the educator.

"What has he done?"

"Well, I don't know how long it's been going on, but I understand he keeps asking the other children in school if they are Jews."

Late that afternoon, Draganović joined Felix at the dinner table, and said: "I was at your school today."

Felix did not ask why Draganović had been to his school and guessed there had to be a reason for His Excellency to have gone there and that reason was, in all likelihood, himself.

Added Draganović: "Will you please tell me why on earth you are going around asking the other kids if they are Jews?"

It was, thought Felix, the sort of question that made children despair of grown-ups. Draganović knew why—and Felix knew that Draganović knew he knew—and yet, there it was, an inquiry into the most obvious, presented at the dinner table next to the salt and pepper shakers.

"Well?" Draganović waited for an answer while Sister Ornella placed a plate of cannelloni in front of him.

Felix darted looks from His Excellency to the nun, hoping that she would intervene so he did not have to give Draganović an answer that would make him feel silly.

"Felix, I asked you—"

Another pause. Felix tilted his head to the side and opened his eyes wide. "Because!" He left it at that.

"Because? Because what?"

"You don't want me to play with Jews."

"I told you not to bring them here. I did not tell you not to play with them, and I certainly did not tell you to find out who is a Jew and who is not!"

"But if you don't want me to bring them here it is because you don't like Jews and I shouldn't either! So I won't play with them. But how am I to know who is a Jew and who isn't if I don't ask them first?" The whole point made so much sense to Felix that his voice took on a slightly irritated tone.

"Finish your meal—" added Draganović matter-of-factly, "and don't ask anyone else if they are Jews."

Freddy finally returned to school, where he was greeted with the most sensational news he ever heard, and an invitation to see for himself the amazing sacred baseball. "DiMaggio!?"

At four-thirty sharp the boys stormed into the apartment and were scolded by Sister Ornella, for running in the hall.

"Ah, yes, sister. This is my friend Freddy Benton!"

"Hello," said Freddy with his engaging smile.

The nun inclined her head, and Felix pulled his friend into the toy warehouse he called his room.

A minute later *"Holy Yogi!"* rang in the hall as the American boy paid homage to the consecrated trophy.

That night, His Excellency Draganović arrived home very tired, hungry and disappointed because he had learned that MI-6's Kim Philby had been a KGB mole, and every agent recruited by Intermarion since the end of the war was compromised to the Soviets, and executed.

"Are you serious?" said the bishop when Sister Ornella met him at the door. "Felix!"

Felix ran to Draganović, when he caught sight of Sister Ornella standing in the doorway. "Yes—Excellency?"

"Madonna! First you bring home a Jew, now you bring home a colored boy? What's the matter with you?" yelled the bishop, ready to pull his hair.

"But he's Catholic," said Felix, calmly.

25

It took several years. Nevertheless, little Felix applied himself and did surprisingly well in school, becoming fluent in Italian and acquiring a solid grasp of Latin, English and French. By then young Ronnoco was about eleven years old and ready for St. Pius.

Housed behind a Vatican office building and its south wall perched high above Via Stazione Vaticana, St. Pius X was Vatican City's preparatory boarding school for altar boys. Sterile and lacking warmth of any kind, its mustard-colored walls were stuffy and hot in the summer and frigid as a penguin's breath in winter.

Most of its thirty-odd eleven to sixteen-year-olds sought the high academic standards of the preseminario that later helped them join the priesthood. Felix, on the other hand, had never displayed evidence of religious devotion nor did he possess the serious and meditative turn of his comrades. By the time he arrived at St. Pius, he had already stated an interest in baseball and had declared to Sister Ornella his intention to become a Roman emperor in the tradition of Marcus Aurelius. Still, His Excellency Draganović thought that even if their home was less than fifteen minutes walking distance from Vatican City, the discipline and the sense of sacrifice the school inspired would help the child grow into a responsible, ethical and spiritual young man.

Naturally, everyone at St. Pius, including the rector, Father Uncelli, the other boys and the four Sisters of Jesus Crucified, in charge of housekeeping, expected Felix to take advantage that his mentor was a powerful and influential member of the Vatican elite.

On the contrary, his day began at dawn, and after a quick breakfast of bread, cheese and coffee, young Ronnoco filed out of St. Pius with the other altar boys to spend the next two and half hours helping the priests at St. Peter's get dress, and prepare the underground chapels for mass.

If a boy got sick or was unavailable, Felix always volunteered to take his place, like he did so often to help the few priests that the other altar boys shunned like the plague, for example, Father Catalini, a fat little man with a cassock that reeked of boiled onions, forcing Felix to sprinkle his surplice with cologne and the holy water with perfume. Eventually, the little Croatian shepherd grew into a lean, healthy and graceful young man, winning the admiration of his classmates and the trust of Father Uncelli, with his charming smile and obliging disposition.

One benefit to living within Vatican City was that it allowed Felix to explore the libraries, treasure rooms, warehouses, catacombs, secret archives and the tunnels of the holy city, where he got to know on a first name basis the groundskeepers, the clerks and the men in charge of security, who, unbeknownst to him, answered to His Excellency Draganović.

As he strolled the grounds behind St. Peter's—he must have been about sixteen years old—Felix noticed a flurry of activity at the Government Palace, with priests, bishops, archbishops and cardinals running in and out. "He was such a good man!" they said, meaning that Pope John XXIII was dead and the Catholic Church, again, found itself without a leader.

Later, at home for the weekend, Felix found Draganović in the bathroom, shaving. His Excellency had just enough time to shower and change his clothes before returning to the Holy See. His hair had turned gray but, other than that, he looked the same as the day Felix arrived in Rome. Of course, every one of his views concerning raising children—a little boy, now an adolescent—had been revised or discarded long ago.

Felix leaned against the door, and, with the haughty smirk that typified his age group, asked: "Do you know who will be pope?"

His Excellency did not halt the careful glide of the blade, did not turn and did not lose a second. "It is my business to know."

"Who?"

The bishop put down the blade, pour water on his face, picked up a towel, and said: "Your friend, Montini."

Felix smiled and let out a slow whistle because, without so much as a warning, His Excellency had revealed the greatest secret in the Catholic world, the name of the next Vicar of Rome.

A few weeks later, after the new pope was properly crowned and life in the Holy See returned to normal, Draganović called Felix into the living room, sat back in his favorite chair, crossed his legs, looked at the boy, and said: "Have you thought about what you'll do when you leave St. Pius?"

Felix, who dressed in blue jeans and a black sweater, replied: "Yes."

"And?"

"I want to be like you."

If the bishop's chest did not swell with paternal pride it was because he was unsure if Felix clearly understood what he said. "Felix, I am a priest."

"I know," said Felix. His Excellency was a priest, and a rather important one at that.

Draganović left the chair and kissed the boy on the cheek. "You make me very proud. But, you can change your mind. You don't have to do or be anything unless you want to. The world is full of possibilities. I've made my choice and you have a right to make your own."

A few months later Felix was at St. Pius when Father Uncelli sent for him. He was a wiry little man with a wicked sense of humor Felix enjoyed very much. Bald, with large brown eyes, a wide mouth, a long face and a very long nose, the priest ordered Felix to put on a clean cassock and surplice and immediately report to the papal apartments.

Thinking that His Holiness had requested Felix as his altar boy during mass—a great privilege, because to serve the pope on the altar was an honor usually granted to young seminarians— he arrived five minutes later at the apostolic palace, where he found Brother Serafio waiting for him.

"Quick, quick! Follow me!" called out the secretary, from the staircase.

"What's going on?" asked Felix, chasing Serafio, who did not answer, but led him into the same room where Pius XII had given him the fabulous baseball so many years before.

Nervous, Felix saw His Excellency Draganović standing next to Pope Paul VI, two bishops and a cardinal, and noticed a white velvet cushion with gold stitching and a red biretta on top, resting on the pope's desk. "Surely," thought the boy in a panic, "I'm too young to be a cardinal! Yes, boys had become princes of the Church before—in the Middle Ages and the Renaissance, but—"

"My dear Felix! My goodness, how you've grown!" greeted Pope Paul. The pope put out his hand and Felix kissed it. Then His Holiness turned to his guests, smiled, and said: "When Felix was a small boy—in this very room—" And he related the story of the meeting between Pius XII and little Felix Ronnoco. Everyone laughed and thought it was a splendid story, including Draganović, who grinned, as any proud father. "Well?" asked Pope Paul, patting Felix on the cheek. "Do you still want to be a baseball player?"

What a silly question, he preferred to be a prince of the Church, anytime. "It's not practical, Holiness," answered Felix with a sheepish smile.

The answer caused the Blessed Father to laugh aloud. "Felix, please—bring that here," said the pope, pointing to the velvet cushion.

For an infinitesimal half a millisecond, Felix thought of turning down the nomination because he did not have any idea what cardinals did!

"Dear Felix, I called you here this afternoon because as the only living relative of—" Felix felt his knees shake, much like they did when Pius XII called to him "—our dear brother in the faith, Krunoslav Draganović, you will be proud to know that from now on he will be Krunoslav Cardinal Draganović."

"Tata!"

Well, it took Felix several days to recover from that brief and moving ceremony, often smiling at himself when he remembered his silly expectations. Nevertheless, as his dull, consistent and predictable daily rounds of school and church resumed, God, who is known to have a sense of humor, decided that young Ronnoco had become complacent, and threw a pie in his face.

One day, Felix returned from mass at St. Peter's and found that his roommate of almost a year had gone home and another boy by the name of Benny Lubri, had taken his place.

Lubri was from Florence and was younger and smaller than Felix. He had sandy blond hair, large blue eyes, a sensuous mouth, a fine, narrow nose, a sweet voice and androgynous features.

This beautiful "angel" who could have modeled for Michelangelo or Raphael, was a natural seducer and it was not long before he insinuated himself into the affections of the Sisters of Jesus Crucified and one priest, at the same time he was despised by some of his schoolmates and enjoyed by others.

Perhaps it was Benny's apparent worldliness and unconcerned cool that attracted Felix. He, of course, did not remember the other sweet-natured boy—though far more chaste—who had loved and nurtured the first years of his life and who left an indelible yearning for love in a baby known by another name.

Now, because of the strict morality at home and in school, despite his innate curiosity and in great measure because most of his peers shared a similar isolation from the world outside Vatican City, Felix had managed to remain indifferent to that singular preoccupation of youth that turns sweet innocent little boys and girls into fiendish, insatiable ghouls; that adolescent obsession that transforms the introverted and quiet child into a tormentor, daddy's girl into a vixen and a childhood buddy into a rival; the one fixation that dominates the senses of almost every teenager since Adam looked at Eve and realized there was something behind the fig leaf.

In fact, part of Felix's disarming innocence that struck others as delightful was due, in part, to his complete ignorance and disinterest in carnal pleasure.

Three months after moving in with Felix, late one cold November evening, Benny asked if they could share the bed.

"Why?" asked Felix.

"It's freezing in here," replied Benny.

Felix agreed because Benny was a boy who bathed regularly and did not smell. "Bring your blankets—and don't kick," he said. "You don't snore, do you?"

Benny chuckled, leaned over and whispered in Felix's ear: "I want to eat you."

Felix felt Benny's warm breath on his cheek, and his pulse quickened. "W-what?"

"I want to eat you," repeated Benny, softly.

Confused, Felix did not answer right away. Things were happening that he did not understand and it made him very uneasy. "W-what do you mean?"

Benny chuckled, slipped under the covers and before Felix could offer the slightest resistance, an overwhelming, mounting excitement seized every nerve in his body. "Are you—are you eating me?" he moaned.

But Benny was taught never to talk with his mouth full. "Uh-huh."

"Oh God—Jesus!" gasped Felix, feeling in the dark that he and Benny were naked, and that for the first time in his life his bed was as wet as his pillow.

"How do you feel?" asked Benny, sitting up in bed, without a stitch of clothes. It was almost time for breakfast and neither boy had gotten any sleep.

"Why?" asked Felix, with a frown.

Benny laughed. "It's guilt. Don't worry. It goes away."

What did not go away were the minutes and the hours that Felix thought went by so slowly it seemed the sun and the clouds refused to move. He was so anxious and tired that he almost dropped the chalice at mass and would not sit still in class because he could not think of anything but Benny, who he had not seen since breakfast.

There were a million questions and twice the doubts. He had heard that priests were obligated to abstain from carnal love; spilling the seed was a sin and physical love between boys was an aberration. He did not care. He was not a priest, not yet, anyway. As far as his other doubts, he prayed very hard that Benny could provide the answers.

It was almost six that afternoon, when they ran into each other in the dining hall.

"How do you feel?" asked Benny, sitting next to Felix.

Felix darted a quick look around, and said, a little alarmed: "Why—why do you keep asking me how I feel?"

Benny shrugged and smiled.

Father Leoni entered their room around 9:30 and found Benny beside his bed, praying and Felix already asleep. "Lights out, Lubri, come on." The priest waited until Benny climbed in his bed, turned off the lights and left.

It was at least an hour and a half, after the last sounds of the evening had died out that Felix turned from the wall, and asked: "Did you do it before?"

"Yes," whispered Benny.

"Who—who taught you?"

"Nobody." Benny tried not to laugh.

"It's my first time," said Felix.

"I know."

"Benny, is it right? I mean—"

"Don't you read the Bible?" asked Benny. "We're going to hell—"

"Oh, God!"

"—and so is the rest of the world," added Benny, laughing, before he climbed in with Felix. In an instant, guilt and doubt gave way to desire.

"Does—does this mean you love me?" asked Felix.

"Do you want me to?" asked Benny, slipping under the sheets.

Father Uncelli rushed down the hall and if anyone had come upon the rector, just then, they would have heard him mutter "Felix" repeatedly. Uncelli had been at St. Pius for almost twenty-five years and he knew the signs, had seen them often enough. Two boys would start ignoring their classmates and everyone else; they would become inseparable; sit together, play together, study together, work together, do everything together—even go as far as to ask to serve mass together.

It was expected, yes, because it was a matter of numbers and probabilities. In every barrel there is likely to be one or two rotten apples. Still, he was disappointed. Felix Ronnoco of all people, a boy admired by his fellow students, a hard-working, honest kid with a good heart. It was not, however, up to Father Uncelli to judge, but to protect the other boys from immorality and, above all, from a scandal. As confessor to Felix and Benny, Father

Uncelli drew a blank: "Bless me, Father, for I have sinned—" followed by trivia and lies. The priest searched their room, went through both trunks and all four drawers in the small desk and found—nothing.

Back in his office he had decided to confront Felix and Benny and see if he could finesse the truth out of one of them. He reached for the phone when young Ronnoco burst in, looking flushed.

"Why are you running?" asked Father Uncelli. He put down the receiver and placed his hands on the desk. His office was sedate and comfortable with furniture inherited from several Vatican warehouses. It had two tall bookcases accessible by a ladder on rollers, several potted plants, a large figurine of the pope and saint the school was named after, a picture of Jesus Christ that according to myth was six hundred years old, and four windows with a view of Piazza Santa Marta.

"I'm sorry, father," apologized Felix. He was going to take a seat when—

"Don't sit down. You have work to do. I called you because we have a new boy and I want him to move in with you. Benny will go to another room."

"Father—" said Felix after a pause, "that is not a good idea."

"Not that I care what you think, but—why not?" asked Uncelli.

Felix stepped forward, and said: "We study together, Father. I-I help Benny with his Latin, he—he helps me with algebra. If Benny moves—if he moves out our grades will suffer."

Father Uncelli reminded Felix that if he was interested in studying with Benny they could do so in the peace and quiet of the library. "Benny's to room with Marcello."

"But Father, Benny hates Marcello!" Marcello was a bully, and Father Uncelli had obviously not considered that fact well enough.

The priest walked to Felix, who was confused. "Fine. If you think Benny will not get along with Marcello, then you move in with Marcello and Benny can share the room with the new boy."

"But I hate Marcello, too!"

"Felix, you're trying my patience. I told you what I want. Now, carry out my orders."

Young Ronnoco did not understand why Father Uncelli was being difficult. He thought they were friends; after all, they spent hours playing chess and talking about airplanes because the priest had a passion for flying things. Felix also knew that the more he argued with the priest, the less chance Uncelli would change his mind. "Please," he pleaded, "Benny is my best friend. He's used to my nightmares in the middle of the night—he's used to all that!" Felix looked away so the priest would not see his tears.

It was too late. Uncelli picked up the phone and called for Benny. Then, he turned to Felix. "Now—sit."

"No."

"Is there something I should know, something you're not telling me?" asked the priest softly.

A knock on the door broke the momentary lull that found Father Uncelli return to his desk. Felix knew Benny was in the room, but he did not dare turn to look at him. If he had, Felix would have seen that Benny was not the least frightened.

"Lubri, our friend Ronnoco is upset because I told him that you are moving out. Perhaps you can shed some light why Felix is acting so—unlike Felix?"

Benny looked from the priest to his friend and back to the priest. "I think Felix has become a glutton, Father." Felix felt the hairs on his neck bristle. "Yes," continued Benny, "Felix loves to snack in the middle of the night. You didn't know that, Father? Well, it's true."

Though Felix felt wretched and sad, and a little angry with his friend, he had to bite his tongue to keep from laughing.

"I keep a little this and that in the room. When Felix gets hungry he just—takes it. What can I do?" asked Benny, innocently. "He's my friend. I give him what I have."

Father Uncelli glared at Benny and ordered him to move in with Marcello.

"W-when, Father?" Benny's voice took the higher end of the scale.

"Now!" screamed the priest, and Benny quickly left the room. "As for you, Ronnoco—"

Felix wiped off the tears and walked into a trap. "I will call my cousin, Father. I'm sorry, but I have no choice."

"No, Felix, you are wrong!" yelled Uncelli. "I will call His Eminence. Get out!" Felix had played his hand, and, as the saying goes, the priest called his bluff and raised the stakes.

Back in his room, Felix found Benny packing. "You bastard! You were trying to make me laugh in front of the priest!"

"Well, I thought you needed cheering up! Wasn't it cute?"

Felix shut the door to the room and said he was going to complain to his cousin. He would not allow Benny to move in with someone else.

"Don't," said Benny. "It'll only make things worse. I don't want you to get in trouble. Besides, I'm not going anywhere. I'm moving across the hall, that's all."

"No!"

"We'll see each other every day—"

Felix cursed in Serbo-Croatian and smacked a pillow against the wall.

"Everything's going to work out, you'll see," said Benny.

Just then, Marcello, the same Marcello Felix and Benny despised, threw open the door and said in that whiny voice of his: "Well, girls, I understand one of you whores is moving in with me. La-di-da! Won't we have fun!" Marcello was not ugly, he was plain. Nor was he unkempt, though he was not particularly concerned about whether or not his very small, tight black curls received their proper ablutions once a week. Marcello was, on the other hand, tall—much taller than Felix or Benny—and dull. He never smiled, no, not unless someone else was in pain. No one liked Marcello; not even Marcello liked Marcello.

"Listen to me, fuck-face," began Felix in a voice too soft for anyone except Marcello to hear, "you touch my friend and I'll rip out your heart and stick it up your ass, got it?"

"You Slav piece of shit!" Marcello curled his upper lip into the beginning of a sneer, and his right hand closed into a fist. But he was not fast enough for the shepherd boy. Felix kicked him in the groin so hard that the only thing Marcello could do was grab his crotch and double over in pain. As Felix readied to punch him in the back of the head, someone grabbed his fist.

"Father," said Draganović, in his scarlet cope and zucchetto, standing next to the rector, "take the boy and see that he's all right."

Father Uncelli led Marcello between the students, priests and nuns that gathered in the hall while the towering presence of Cardinal Draganović was enough to chill the eternal memory of St. Pius.

"Get your things, Felix," said His Eminence. "We are leaving."

Felix and Benny looked at each other, and never said good-bye.

26

Felix arrived in Split on a perfectly sunny day that, unfortunately, did not brighten his mood.

"Come here!" yelled Rostas, taking Felix in his arms. "I almost didn't make it! His Eminence should have called before!"

Felix hugged his friend, and began to cry.

"What's this? Oh, shit. Don't tell me you've been exiled! And I thought you were coming to see your old friends. You can tell me about it in the car."

And Felix did—well, almost. He relayed only the prejudice against him and his friend by a stupid priest (Father Uncelli) and a Neanderthal altar boy (Marcello).

Rostas listened, shook his head, and said: "Terrible, awful. I tell you, Felix, priests can be so arrogant. That's what I admire about His Eminence, he's never been like that. He's so—down to earth."

Felix opened the window and filled his lungs once again with the clean, fresh air of his country.

"Don't worry. If I know His Eminence, he will take care of the priest," said Rostas, with prophetic reserve, because, shortly thereafter, Cardinal Draganović received a call from the rector of St. Pius, expelling—regrettably, of course—Felix from school.

Less than an hour later, Cardinal Draganović, imposingly attired with a red cope sweeping the floor, dropped by St. Pius for a one-on-one with Father Uncelli.

"Your Grace, please—" the priest pointed to a comfortable chair across his desk, before inquiring half-heartedly after Felix.

Cardinal Draganović did not sit down. He said: "This won't take long. I just need something explained."

"And what is that?" Uncelli leaned forward in his chair.

"Did you decide to expel Felix because he was insolent, or because of something else?"

The priest stared at the red hat, and replied: "Felix challenged my authority, Eminence. He was disrespectful. Frankly, I was disappointed."

Continued Draganović: "What happened? It is not like Felix to be impertinent."

Uncelli raised his hands, and said: "He was upset because I ordered his roommate to move to another room."

"Why?" asked the inquisitor in the scarlet hat.

"It was—necessary," replied the rector, clearing his throat.

Draganović tilted his head to the right and placed the priest in his sights.

"Necessary?"

Uncelli tiptoed around the unpleasant subject and explained that St. Pius had to be uncompromising about discipline and the moral excellence of its boys.

Said Draganović: "Yes, yes, I know—but did Felix quarrel with his roommate, lacked discipline and perhaps made a mess of things? Did he not get along with his classmates, or was disrespectful to teachers or members of your staff? Was he disruptive doing—doing whatever it is that boys do these days?"

For a moment Father Uncelli imagined the cardinal as a woodpecker, hammering him with question after question. But the priest was a stolid man and only the slight twitch of his right eyelid signaled his irritation. Replied the priest: "I have no such complaints. Nevertheless, I must be vigilant. It is my responsibility to the other boys."

Draganović leafed through a small volume on the Stuka that lay on the rector's desk. "Why did you feel it was necessary to separate Felix and his roommate?"

A trace of moisture became evident on Father Uncelli's upper lip. "As a precaution."

"Precaution? Who was Felix's confessor?" asked His Eminence.

"I was, Your Grace."

"And the other boy?"

"Him too—yes, Eminence."

"So, you take confessions from the older students?"

"I do, Eminence."

Asked Draganović: "I know that the intimacies entrusted to us during the rite are sacred, but did Felix or his friend ever intimate anything that made you wary of their friendship?"

"They did not, Your Grace."

"Then, I must be frank. Felix should be reprimanded, but to expel him from school is unjustified. It casts him in an unfavorable light."

"Eminence, he also struck a boy."

"Yes, he did that, did he not?" returned Draganović, almost as an aside.

A half grin slowly appeared on the rector's face—he liked having bishops and cardinals asking favors—when Draganović approached, took out a large envelope from inside his cope, tossed it on the desk and stood back with clasped hands in his most practiced, devotional stance.

There were seven large black and white photographs. Two were taken from a distance and showed Father Uncelli sporting a raincoat, a large hat and sunglasses. Another revealed the priest knocking at the door of a building found in a neighborhood of dark alleys and streets teeming with garbage and pimps; a tenement that, because of its proximity to the Holy See, stood close to the gates of heaven, yet had a foot caught in hell.

The most arresting photographs, however, were taken inside a bedroom. They were of excellent quality and offered a pictorial account of the naked priest with his nose stuck between the legs of a similarly undressed female, wearing a blond wig.

Father Uncelli gasped, feeling faint and nauseous. "This—this is blackmail!"

"It's more than that," said His Eminence. "You are a sinful, wicked, lecherous hypocrite; a disgrace to your brothers, and to this institution. You are also an embarrassment to the Holy Father. Felix will be back at St. Pius. You, on the other hand, are moving on."

It was past midnight when Felix and Rostas reached the farm where Olga waited in the kitchen with a pot of peasant soup hearty enough to raise the lowest spirit.

Felix kissed and embraced her affectionately, but noticed that the strain of the farm was finally taking its toll on Rostas' wife. She looked much older than her husband; her face had become drawn, wrinkled and pale, and her hair was completely gray; her once compact body was flaccid and her bones brittle. They talked for an hour, then Felix excused himself, kissed Rostas and Olga goodnight and went up to his old room, where he banged his head on the low beam.

It was a first because Felix had never stood so tall in the little room. He rubbed his head and saw that everything was as he remembered from his last visit, two years before. He opened the window, noticed the full moon, and said: "I'm not happy and you know why." Then, he lay on the bed, threw off his shoes and cried himself to sleep.

Next morning, Felix slept later than usual before the sweet smell of fresh-baked bread and coffee beckoned to the kitchen, where he breakfasted alone because Olga and Rostas had gone into town. After devouring an entire loaf smeared with home-made butter and downing three cups of coffee, the boy took a bath, changed clothes—all black to match his mood—and wandered into the living room. There, on a dark, blue cushion on top of a chair, he found a copy of the Bible with a note from Olga, that read: "Felix."

He picked up the book, sat by the window and saw a young man he did not recognize taking the sheep and goats to graze. Rostas, it seemed, had hired a new farmhand.

Felix watched the animals trot down the hill and remembered the happy, carefree days of his childhood, chasing after sheep and goats and playing with his dog. That, in turn, reminded him of the day he left to live in Rome, which brought back memories of Madame Berini's, St. Pius—and Benny.

Misery cast itself again upon the boy and he wept. He blindly opened Olga's Bible and found himself reading The Song of Solomon:

—*His banner over me was love. Stay me with flagons, comfort me with apples for I am sick with love*—

He tossed the book aside, went up to his room, picked up his jacket and went out for a walk, like he used to before he was sick with love.

Curious to meet the shepherd, Felix walked down the hill and after ten minutes, saw the sheep and scraggy goats grazing on the side of the mountain. The dog picked up his scent at once and pricked his ears. The boy then approached slowly when, thirty meters from the herd, someone jumped him from behind, and knocked him to the ground.

"What the—! Get off me, you shit!" yelled Felix looking up at a boy, a bit older than himself, with green eyes, a mass of red hair, freckles and thick eyebrows so blond they were almost white. Dressed in a wool and leather jacket with colorful embroidering, a pair of dark, and coarse baggy pants and boots, he would not stop laughing as he punched Felix in the shoulders.

Suddenly, the shepherd's expression changed and he quickly scrambled to his feet, apologizing over and over. "I'm sorry! Oh, God, I'm sorry, I—I thought you were my—oh, I beg your forgiveness!"

"Take your filthy hands off me! Fucking balija! Attacking people from behind!" Felix considered beating him up. "I live here, you know!" He turned and walked back to the house, cursing all the way up the hill.

Later that day, Rostas demanded an explanation from the shepherd who was extremely contrite and embarrassed.

"He's a witless fool," observed Olga, sitting with Felix at the kitchen table.

"He's afraid I'll let him go," said her husband, taking a chair. "Said he mistook Felix for his cousin."

"His cousin! What, he goes about pouncing on his kin, does he?" Olga had opposed hiring a Muslim to work at the farm. "That boy is a fool—a balija with red hair, thank you! I don't trust him, not a bit!"

"Well, we'll see," said Rostas grabbing his jacket, then playfully lifting Felix from the chair. "Let's go."

"Where?" asked Felix.

"To Paradise."

Paradise was a large house on the outskirts of Travnik, with white stucco walls, a red tile roof, an attractive well-kept garden, and a gravel driveway. Inside, it was satin and frills from end to end, lace window curtains, a large parlor with an enormous and extremely cozy fireplace, garish replicas of Victorian chairs, sofas and divans, imitation Tiffany lamps, a grand piano, and hardwood floors so polished that many visitors slipped and hurt themselves.

A Jew who had run the printing press in town, owned the house before the war. One day the man and his family disappeared and the property fell into disrepair until a Croat from up north saw it, bought it for almost nothing from the authorities, fixed it up and sold it to a lady friend who quickly became known throughout the province.

Her name was Esmeralda, which was not her real name, of course, but it sounded better and more interesting than, say, Helga.

Esmeralda, who was Swabian, arrived in Travnik with her husband and four very beautiful girls between fourteen and twenty-two. The young ladies, naturally, were not Esmralditas but Magdalena, Esperanza, Caridad and Voluntaria; each named after legendary eighteenth century Spanish madams. Why Spanish and not Danish? No one ever found out.

"What is this place?" asked Felix, standing in the foyer.

"Rostas!"

From the end of the hall, a voluptuous white-haired matron ran the whole six meters, flung herself into Rostas' arms and showered him with kisses. She was tall and strong-looking, had perfect teeth, too much rouge on her face and seemed the very embodiment of sensuality and delight. This was a woman who liked giving pleasure, whether for money or not, a philanthropist de rigueur who spent most of her life in the arms of men and women, sharing their most intimate secrets.

"Esmeralda, you look ravishing—as always!"

Ravishing! Felix had never heard Rostas speak that way before; more to the point, he had never heard his friend express any such sentiment, not even to Olga.

"How's your dear, lovely girl?" said Esmeralda. "Tell her I miss her. She should come down and have a drink with me, like in the old days."

"She might. I think she's bored. The farm is a lot of work," said Rostas, before pointing to Felix. "But I did not come here to talk about the old days, my love. I came because we have to look after the future, and here he is in the flesh!"

Rostas pulled Felix by his jacket and set him in the middle of the conversation.

Esmeralda put her hands to her face. "Oh, he's beautiful, Rostas. Your own?"

"Almost."

"And he looks so—sad!" There was not one fake note in Esmeralda; every phrase, every gesture and every expression was as true and sincere as a heartfelt love song.

"He is. I need you to make him happy." Rostas put both hands on Felix to make sure he would not run out of the house.

"Oh, to be fifteen, again," sighed Esmeralda.

"To be dead!" thought Felix, wishing to be struck by lightning, when Sofisticada, struck him instead.

The gorgeous girl with silky black hair, striking blue eyes beneath copper-colored eyebrows and rosy-soft, flawless features dressed in a pair of loose men's pants, a white blouse and no shoes. She could have been twelve or eighteen years old, but, according to Esmeralda, was nevertheless, untouched, untainted—and just arrived.

"What! No! I—don't want to! I—can't! I—" protested Felix.

It was no use. With the introductions out of the way, Rostas and Esmeralda retired to sip brandy by the fire, and Sofisticada took over. "Shhh—I don't want them to hear me!" she said, putting her finger to her lips.

"What?" said Felix.

"I don't want to do this any more than you do, but I have to make a living. I have my mother, my old grandpapa, two little brothers and my uncle depending on the money I make. Let's go to my room. I'll close the door, we'll talk for a while, you'll come out buttoning your fly, say everything was great, smack your lips a few times, I get paid, you go home and everybody's happy. Please, Felix. Be nice, please!" Her eyes were moist and Felix thought Sofisticada was going to cry.

He pondered a moment, and could not help feeling sorry for the young girl, and so allowed her to lead him to a neat and clean bedroom in the back of the house, with a good-sized and comfortable bed, perfectly white and fresh linen, one chair, a small table with a bottle of brandy with several glasses, and a mirrored ceiling.

"Sit down," said Sofisticada, laying on the bed. "Where are you from?"

"Here," answered Felix, mortified, when he looked up at the mirror on the ceiling and saw the beautiful girl's reflection as she spread her legs and slid her hand inside her pants.

She then expressed her admiration for his eyes, his nose—his mouth, and begged to see the rest of him. She asked if Felix had a girl, although she was sure he did not.

Felix did not listen, not really; he kept looking at the ceiling, watching how Sofisticada loosened her blouse and caressed her breasts, how she removed her pants and parted her legs some more. "Don't be scared. You're not the first who's never done it before. There's nothing to be ashamed of."

"I don't know you," he replied, thinking of Benny, and tears rolled down his face.

"What's wrong?" she asked, pouring him a brandy. "Take it, it's not going to make you feel better, but it will keep you from shaking."

The brandy set his throat on fire.

"Why are you so sad?"

"I love someone," confessed the boy.

"Oh, Felix, this has nothing to do with love."

Well, by the time young Ronnoco left the bedroom, his feet hurt. He also did not want to go home. He wanted to stay with Sofisticada for at least—at least until he was sent back to Rome. But, as Rostas reminded him on the return to the farm, Paradise was expensive.

Next day, Felix slept till noon and awoke to another beautiful day in the mountain. He heard the chickens outside, and the shepherd yelling at the dog, before dragging himself downstairs, his thoughts divided between St. Pius and Paradise—where he would have to pay to get in.

"Good morning."

Draganović sat in the living room, reading a magazine and sipping coffee. Said His Eminence: "You have an interesting smell. Musk, I think. You look exhausted. Take a bath and come down. We have to talk."

It took Felix one an hour to regain a semblance of his former self, then, with Draganović, set out for a long walk.

"Are you going to tell me about Paradise?" inquired His Eminence.

Oh, God! How was he going to explain the whorehouse? "It was not my idea."

"No, it was mine." They had come upon a small brook surrounded by poplars and Draganović sat on a boulder by the stream.

The sound of the water soothed Felix. He leaned against a tree, and asked: "Why?"

Draganović did not reply. Instead, he picked up a twig, and said: "I tell you—when a man has a child, it is usually not by choice. As often as some men love their children, others do not. I could have put you up for adoption, or left you to live your life on the farm. I did not. I baptized you—I made you my own." His Eminence got up and paced back and forth.

"So, why Ronnoco, and not Draganović, like you?" asked Felix.

"I would have been proud for you to have my name, but you can't." Draganović lowered his voice. "I have made many enemies and it was not fair or practical to put you in such disadvantage. So, I made up a name for you. Ronnoco—O'Connor spelled backwards."

"O'Connor?" asked Felix, very surprised.

"It's Irish."

"Irish?"

"My closest friend was from Ireland. His name was O'Connor—a real Catholic, and a patriot. He was murdered in Belfast in '46. He's the one in the picture—on the steps of St. Peter's. Remember? Anyway, it doesn't matter. What matters is that you speak several languages. That you're getting—or were getting—the best education possible, and that you will continue to excel, to grow, and become a man to carry on my legacy."

Asked Felix: "Were you ever in love?"

"Like you, I grew up on this mountain. It was, however, another time. I had but three people in my life—my mother, my father and the old shepherd. I almost never went to town, but spent my time working on the farm and reading the Bible and my father's books about the heroes of Croatia, the empire—things like that. At fifteen, they sent me to the Franciscans and there's nothing much I can add." Draganović allowed a smile that hinted regret. "God and country, Felix, I've been in love with God and country as far back as I can remember."

"You never made love to another person?"

Draganović shook his head, and said: "I took my vows at seventeen. Maybe—I was too young?"

"What if you'd fallen in love—before you took your vows?"

"Like you think happened to you?" asked His Excellency.

Felix nodded.

Draganović shrugged, and said: "Who knows? Fact is, I didn't." He opened his arms and his gesture encompassed the world around them. That was his passion, that was the air that sustained him, that gave him life, nothing else. His goal was to see his land and his Christ united again; a Catholic Croatia as in those few, terrible years during the war—before Felix was born—when people suffered and died only to see their vision of a great nation turn to rubble. "Croatia will once again be independent and Catholic, I swear." And he tossed the twig into the brook. "Maybe I should have been a politician—"

Felix had never heard Draganović talk so freely before, so relaxed.

"Which brings us to why we are out here, instead of you being in school and me tending to the pope. You can't afford to lie to me, Felix, just as I can't afford to lie to you. Nothing you say or do will ever make me love you less, not now, not ever—unless I find out that you've lied. Look at me!"

Felix tried not to cry but the tears were already running down his face.

"I had the most awful time convincing Father Uncelli to let you stay at St. Pius. So what is it with you? Do you like boys or do you like girls?"

Felix did not hesitate; he relished Sofisticada, but he loved Benny.

Said His Eminence: "Do you know that the Church holds your type of affection for this—Benny, a great sin?" Draganović paused, shook his head and smiled. "You are a boy. In twenty years—no, in ten—you will look back on your so-called love for your friend, and laugh—perhaps shudder at the silliness of it all. If, as you said once, you want to be like me, God will absolve you of your sins through the loving grace of the Son. But you must renounce your infatuation with Benny. Boys, men, girls, women—you will serve them, you will not take pleasure from them." He took the boy's face in his hands, bringing it so close to his own that their noses touched. "You will find comfort through Christ the Redeemer. Without Christ, Felix, you do not have a chance. It is up to you."

27

Enes the shepherd borrowed the only horse at the Draganović farm, and rode for hours to the housing complex where his people lived, three kilometers south of Komar. It was past eleven o'clock when he knocked on the door, guessing that everyone inside was sleeping or sitting around the sheet-metal stove, in the back room, complaining about life and doing nothing about it.

"I knew it!" said Enes, quickly stepping inside, when Adnan—or Ady, as he was called—a good-looking boy about fourteen years old, with wavy sandy-colored hair, big, brown eyes and a lovely smile, answered the door.

"What are you doing here? It's almost midnight!" complained Ady.

The front room was small and plain and lit by a single bulb dangling from the ceiling. Some walls were missing stucco, exposing the bricks underneath. Two brown curtains fashioned out of a rough fabric and decorated with green leafy patterns, hung from warped wooden slide bars that never allowed the curtains to open and close all the way. Several old photographs of ancestors and an outdated calendar decorated the room.

"Enes?" said Hamdai, coming out from the back room. He was a thin man about forty years old, had a distinguished nose, a rough and weather-beaten complexion, intelligent eyes, full lips, curly brown hair and a wide mustache that curled up at the ends.

"He's drunk, papa," said his son.

"Oh, really? Well, what if I tell you that I found Nermin?" said Enes, excited.

"What?" said Elma, joining her husband. She was still dressed in her work clothes. "What do you mean? Nermin? My Nermin?" A stout woman with pale skin, long brown hair and a mouth that showed a gold tooth in front, Elma had been beautiful and proud. However, her face had since recorded every day of her difficult life on her forehead and her blue eyes were tired and sad.

"It's Nermin—has to be! He looks just like you!" added Enes, pointing at Ady. "Rostas calls him Felix!"

"Felix?" said Hamdai.

"He supposed to be the priest's cousin, from Banja Luka. Rostas mentioned him before, said he was an orphan or something—brought to live at the farm before moving to Rome with the priest. I don't believe it. It's Nermin!"

A meteor crashing through the roof would not have caused as much commotion as news that maybe, just maybe, Nermin had been found. Everybody in town knew what happened to their grandmother, but the baby she carried with her that day long ago, was never found. It was a family tragedy retold a thousand times.

Hamdai had sought help from the authorities, of course, but it all happened right after the war, and in those days the police was the militia, and the militia was undisciplined, uncaring and unwilling to search for a missing child, especially when it belonged to an impoverished Muslim clan.

"Nermin is dead! He is dead!" screamed Elma.

"No, he's not! He's not dead and he's living in Rome! Oh, it's Nermin—has to be!" countered Enes.

"How did you get here?" asked Hamdai.

"I borrowed the—"

"Get back before they say you stole that animal and have you arrested," ordered his uncle.

"Nermin is dead! Dead! Dead!" screamed Elma.

"Don't say that! He's alive and doing very well for himself!"

Chief Inspector Durković arrived at police headquarters at ten o'clock in the morning. He was tired, with red, bleary eyes and blocked sinuses. Time had left its mark on the Chief Inspector and he rarely ventured out on the field, anymore. Travnik was a poor town and most people had nothing worth stealing, so most crimes were a result of passion, revenge or misadventure.

"Comrade!" called the man sitting on a bench under Tito's picture. Since the fellow did not call the inspector by name and Durković was a busy man, he did not feel that a reply was in order, thus he ignored the Muhammadan who, along with his wife and kid, had arrived in a horsecart.

"Inspector Durković!"

"Damn!" He had made it all the way to the green door of his bureau when he heard his name. He slowly turned around, acknowledged the fez, and said: "What is it?"

"You don't remember me," began Hamdai.

"Why should I?"

"I didn't say you should remember me, I said you don't," corrected Hamdai.

Durković sighed, looked at Hamdai for a moment, closed his eyes, and said: "What do you want?"

"My name is Hamdai Hadzimulić."

"What do you want?" repeated the Chief Inspector.

"I need help and the man at the front desk said that I should talk to you."

"What do you want?" said Durković a third time.

The Chief Inspector would not open his eyes and Hamdai could not tell if the police officer was thinking, taking a nap on his feet, or was suffering from abdominal pain.

"What is your problem? You lose a goat? Someone took your sheep?" asked the Chief Inspector.

"No," answered Hamdai, "someone took my son."

The morning began with Olga making breakfast, Rostas fixing a leak on the roof, Draganović still in his room and Felix going out for a walk.

No one saw him step into the thick fog and wander like a ghost between the real and the netherworld. He heard the shepherd's call and guessed the flock was no more than fifty meters out in front. Felix knew that he could not get any closer without the dog getting wind of his scent, and yet, he wanted to do just that. Or did he?

He was curious and fearful. Why was he following the shepherd? Many people remind others of someone else; it is commonplace. To Felix, however, that routine coincidence meant, perhaps, a clue to his past. Who were his parents? Were they living? How did he end up at the farm? Did he really want to find out? Did he want to risk giving up a privileged lifestyle in the greatest city in the world to live in a shack with heaven knows how many brothers, sisters, uncles and aunts, grandfathers and grandmothers, and share what others called "family?" If so, there was no need to have ambition or aspire to great things. Speaking Italian or French was useless, and so was meeting popes, cardinals and bishops when you were just a shepherd or a farmer's son. And what about Tata? How would Draganović feel if Felix left? Abandoned and betrayed. Could Felix do that, trade so much for so little?

Young Ronnoco walked along the edge of the woods, keeping an eye out for the small herd grazing in a clearing, below. Like a wolf watching its prey, he saw the shepherd in the distance, lying down on a thick blanket spread out on the grass. Why not? The dog did most of the work, anyway.

He remembered that he had done the same thing as a child; before St. Pius, Benny, Paradise and Sofisticada.

Felix chuckled and turned to walk away. They would be returning to Rome in a few hours and the confounding and unanswered questions of his life would have to wait, to be considered at length when the need to know overrode the desire to be happy.

That is when two words entrusted years before to the brown bark, caught his eye: Damir and Saša.

Transfixed, he felt his heart pounding as he gently outlined each letter with his fingers. Damir? "Who was Damir?" he asked himself, when he heard the mysterious whisper of long ago: "Didi!" And who was Saša? he wondered, sinking to his knees.

"Where have you been? His Eminence is asking for you," said Rostas, now working on the Citroën, when Felix walked up the hill.

"We're leaving soon. Get ready and—better eat something before we go," said Draganović when the boy joined him at the kitchen table.

His Eminence noticed that Felix was very pale and looked sad. "It's time you got back to Rome."

"Who's Damir?" asked Felix.

Draganović slowly pushed away his plate and said: "I don't know where you heard that name, Felix, but don't repeat it, please."

"Who is he?" Felix asked again, making sure not to say the name aloud.

The priest knew Felix would not give up trying to get an answer. He said: "He was the boy who found you and brought you here—to the farm."

"Found me? Where? How come you never talk about him?"

"There are things," began Draganović slowly, "that are better left unsaid. It's just not safe to talk about those people."

"What people? Why?"

"Felix!"

"Did he kidnap me? Did he kill my parents and—"

"Stop it," said Draganović. "No, he did not kidnap you and he did not kill your parents."

"How—how did he find me? Where?" asked Felix.

"We don't have time for this now," said Draganović, getting up.

"Tata, I want to know! I—I need to know the truth," said Felix, almost in tears.

His Eminence took a deep breath, and said: "He was the Poglavnik's son. After the war, he, along with his mother, his sister and their driver left Zagreb, to come here. They traveled all night—they said the weather was terrible, and they had an accident that forced them to stop in the middle of nowhere. That's when they found you, abandoned by the side of the road and brought you to the farm. They stayed three years, until I got them safely out of the country. He was a brooding and morose young man. He always called you Saša—"

"Why?" asked Felix.

"He never said why."

"Saša," muttered Felix, under his breath, before acquiring a worried expression. "That's Serbian! Am I a Serb?"

"You are not," returned His Eminence.

"Would you hate me—if I'm a Serb?"

"Hate you? How can you think that?" asked Draganović.

"You hate Serbs. So does Rostas—he was Ustaša!"

"Oh, for God's sake, I don't care if you're a long lost Obrenović, a Jew or a—Chinaman!"

"What became of—" began Felix.

"He's dead, was killed in Argentina during an attempt against his father." Draganović noticed that Felix was biting his nails. "Enough. I've said too much already. Get your things. We're leaving."

"Eminence!"

Draganović walked outside and saw a police car heading their way, stop, and those inside get out. "Who are those people?" he asked Rostas.

"That looks like Durković, remember? He was here when—"

"Yes, yes," replied Draganović, with a dismissive frown.

"—and that other fellow—I think it's Enes' uncle," added Rostas.

"What do they want?" asked Draganović.

Rostas shrugged.

"Well, well!" called out Draganović. "Is that you, Inspector?"

"Your Grace," replied Durković, approaching the priest. "I didn't know you were back." He then scolded the uniformed recruit at his side: "Why didn't you tell me His Eminence was home—" before turning his attention to the priest. "I am sorry to disturb you, Eminence, but I need to ask you a few questions. Do you mind? Are you very busy? Would you like for us to come back some other time, perhaps?"

Draganović laughed, and said: "Those were your exact words last time you dropped by. Talk about consistency in the constabulary. Still hunting for treasures, Inspector? I heard you are a full Chief Inspector now, are you not? I'm glad to see life treating you well after so many years of devoted service to your community. It's nice when a dedicated civil servant gets his just rewards."

"Thank you, Your Grace," said Durković.

"And what can I do for you today, Inspector?" asked Draganović.

"This man is Hamdai Hadzimulić and that is his wife. It appears they have a complaint," added Durković.

"What about?"

"They say you have their son living here," said the Chief Inspector, matter-of-factly.

"Her son?" Draganović turned to Rostas. "I thought he was their nephew. He's not living here, Inspector, the boy works here. He tends the farm."

"No, not Enes," interjected Hamdai. "Nermin."

"Nermin? I'm sorry, but I do not know anyone by that name." Again, His Eminence turned to Rostas, who shook his head.

"You call him Felix," said the Muslim woman.

The smile on Draganović vanished.

"Are you mad?" yelled Rostas.

"No, I'm not!" added Elma, then grabbed Ady and brought him forward. "Look at this boy!" she yelled. "Look at him! Does he look like your Felix? Like my Nermin?"

"Inspector, may I have a word with you?" His Eminence and Inspector Durković stepped to one side. "You know, you have an uncanny ability for coming up with the most tortuous but, I must add, original plots I've ever heard of. First, the—episcopal treasure as I like to call it. Comrade Tito was quite amused."

"Tito?"

"Yes, we met by chance at La Scala—that's an opera house in Milan. Josip Broz was there on a state visit—I think he was going out with a soprano singing that night. He loves opera, did you know that? Anyway—" and Draganović smiled—"I was on official business and we were introduced by the Egyptian ambassador. Well, we talked during intermission, and when I told him about your treasure hunt, he actually held his sides and laughed! I put in a good word for you, mind you. But Inspector, I would hate to think you have a personal vendetta against me."

"Why do you say that?" calmly answered the Chief Inspector.

"Felix is my cousin. He was born in Banja Luka. You must remember him from the last time you were here. He was the baby my mother held in her arms."

"Ah, yes—"

"And now you come to my house and accuse me of—"

"Cardinal Draganović, no one is accusing you of anything," interrupted Inspector Durković.

"You certainly are. Look, I have Felix's birth certificate, his record of baptism, his identity papers issued by the central government, and photographs of him as a newborn with his parents before they were killed in an automobile accident. I will get them for you immediately. Mind you, I thought Belgrade had made it official policy to promote religious tolerance in Yugoslavia."

"With all due respect, this has nothing to do with tolerance, but with a missing child, who, I'm told, disappeared in 1947."

"Really, Inspector, you have other means available to investigate this sort of thing. It was unnecessary for you to bring them here. You know how many people disappeared after the war? Is this woman going to run to the police every time she sees a boy that reminds her of her son? It doesn't make sense."

Inspector Durković was unmoved. "You said you have proof that the boy is your nephew?"

"No nephew. He is my cousin," corrected His Eminence.

"Nermin!" screamed Elma, when she saw Felix walk outside.

Felix recoiled and slammed against the side of the house because he found the woman disgusting; from her gold tooth to her stench of poverty.

Hamdai held his wife back as she screamed, "Nermin!"

"Silence!" commanded Draganović in a loud, forceful voice that immediately restored order.

Elma fell on her knees, threw up her arms and wailed.

Everybody thought that, except for a slight difference in height, Felix and Ady were almost identical. Nevertheless, the priest immediately produced overwhelming and irrefutable evidence that established the boy's identity, including at least a dozen photographs of Felix as a baby in his mother's arms, as a toddler playing with his father, and later, standing beside Ana Draganović and her son, the priest. "I admit," added His Eminence, "that there is a resemblance to this young man," he said, pointing at Ady, "but we are all children of God."

"Nermin! I am your mama! Your grandmother—" Elma gasped, "she died for you! They found her—" and was unable to continue.

"Help me with your mother," said Hamdai, to his son, taking Elma in his arms, and leading the way to the car.

Draganović approached them, and in a voice full of Christian compassion and understanding said: "You have suffered a great loss and I'll pray for you, but please believe Felix is not your son."

"His papers are in order," said Durković to Hamdai. "He's not your boy. Let's go. We have inconvenienced these people enough." Case closed.

A moment after the police car disappeared down the road, Draganović found Felix throwing up in the bathroom. "Are you all right?" he asked.

"I hate them!" answered Felix.

"No, you don't," said Draganović, embracing him. "Those people have suffered a lot."

"I don't care!" said Felix, crying.

"Listen," said Draganović softly, "it's no use denying the obvious. You were abandoned."

"Which means I could be one of them!" interjected Felix.

"If by them you mean a Muslim, sure, anything is possible. However, that boy—the one that found you always called you Saša," added Draganović. "Also, the night they arrived, I had their driver take us back to the scene of the accident. It was about an hour from town, and we found the mangled bodies of two men. Although they did not have papers on them, I can tell you they weren't Muslims."

"Are you sure?" asked Felix.

"Oh, please, don't do this—not now. We have a long trip ahead," said an exasperated Draganović, before adding: "They wore some kind of religious habit. I didn't get a good look because it was dark and raining hard. And—as I said, they were in pretty bad shape. Listen, none of that matters anymore. What matters is that you are Catholic. I baptized you in the name of Jesus Christ and no one can take that from you. You have gone through confirmation. Even if you had been born to a Muslim or a Serbian tribe, you can never be one of them." Draganović paused long enough to give Felix time to ponder. "There were millions of refugees after the war wandering up and down the country looking for food, shelter—hoping not to starve to death. It was an awful time—awful—and I don't think we'll ever find out who were those men killed on the road that night, or how or why you ended up with them—if in fact you were."

"Where did you get the pictures, the ones you showed those people?"

"I had them made—years ago," said Draganović.

"Why?"

The priest stepped back and took the boy's face in his hands. "Because there are thousands, and thousands of families who can't, and will never forget the children they lost in the war. This—just now—was sad, and unfortunate, but I'm not surprised."

True, and even if Inspector Durković had been a good police-man, and he was not; even if Inspector Durković had had a sharp investigative nose, and he did not; even if Inspector Durković had taken the time to write down the information provided by His Eminence Draganović, then follow up with a couple of tele-phone calls, he would only have confirmed that in fact, a young couple named Ronnoco was killed in an accident, right after the war, that they had been parents to a little boy named Felix, and that all that information was available in several dusty files found in more than one government bureaucracy, besides having been chiseled on a humble and forsaken gravestone in a cemetery outside Banja Luka.

"Do you think I'll ever find out—about my parents, I mean?" asked Felix.

"I—I hope you do," returned Draganović, after a pause.

Felix sighed. "I've been such an ass. I let you down, but I swear it will never happen again!"

THE SAINT

28

"You are my legacy. You cannot allow distractions, can't allow anything, not even people to get in the way," said the old man in a raspy voice that was almost inaudible. "I—" Draganović gasped. The tubes supplying oxygen made it difficult for him to talk. In a last desperate attempt, he let go of Felix and ripped them off.

"What are you doing!?" Felix reached over and tried to stop him.

"Listen—oh, listen to me!" cried out Draganović.

"Tata, you can't take that off, you will—"

"I—I did what had to be done to protect the Church! Holy Father, I confess—Pero—" blurted Draganović.

"Pero?"

"The old shepherd. My only friend from childhood. He found the treasure, and I couldn't take the chance! I killed him with my own hands."

Felix stared incredulously at the old man. "Treasure? What are you talking about?"

"Pavelić."

"What?"

"The thief—" continued Draganović.

"What thief?"

"—in America—"

Felix wondered if the old man meant Louie Peps.

"—the priest, and the little boy's father, they were killed on my orders."

The struggle for the final breath began and Draganović barely held his own.

"To shield our Church!" He stopped talking for a minute and Felix heard the heavy, hollow sound as Draganović's chest heaved, fighting the conclusion of his extraordinary life. "My Church—our sacred, holy Church, and the land of my fathers, Croatia—" The words hung in the air then dropped and seeped quickly through the cracks of the hardwood floors. "I did it for Christ—for my country!" Draganović seized Felix's hand as tight as he could and closed his eyes. He was not dead, no, he was waiting to hear the words that would absolve him of his earthly transgressions. "You must do the same!"

"You are a priest!" cried Felix. "Life is sacred!"

"The Church is sacred!" croaked Draganović.

Felix was horrified. He had considered his Tata the most honest, just and loving human being on earth, only to find out he was no more than a common fanatic, and a sociopath. "You used me," he said, with tears in his eyes, as he felt his indomitable faith crushed. There was nothing else to do, but entrust his mentor to eternity. "Misereatur tui omnipotens Deus, et dimissis peccatis tuis, perducat te ad vitam aeternam. Amen."

Late that night, outside the inviolable papal apartments, the Swiss Guards had expected the calm and serene silence of the sacrosanct marble halls. Who, they wondered, was playing a flute?

Days later, after the quiet and unassuming funeral for the late priest Krunoslav Draganović, Felix met with his advisers. "Holiness," began Cardinal Bailey, "we're being bombarded with requests for your photograph. Father d'Stesi found one but it is at least ten years old. I'm afraid it won't do."

"Everything in good time, Brother. Please, send a news release at once saying that after a careful investigation, the Holy

See realized that the predictions of a Second Coming of Christ were inaccurate. Also, mention that we apologize for any suffering or confusion caused by the announcement from America and will do everything possible to prevent anything like it happening ever again."

Bailey nodded as d'Stesi entered the room, and whispered in the pope's ear: "Holiness—Zagreb is on the line."

Pope Felix begged to be left alone, waited for the red hats to leave, and picked up the phone: "Mr. President—Milo, my friend—well?"

President Milo Babić had known Draganović since the end of World War II. When, in 1991, Croatia seceded from the Federal Republic of Yugoslavia, Babić emerged as a political force thanks to his coalition of ex-fascists, most of whom had worked closely with the Ustaša. "Yes, that's good, yes." The pope wrote down the information. "Thank you, Milo. God bless you."

Next morning, Pope Felix informed the Curia that he was taking a trip.

"But Holiness," said Tomaso, "the investiture is less than a week away."

"I'll be back in a couple of days. I have a pressing family matter that I need to settle."

It was late that same morning when Pope Felix V boarded a small private jet, on his way to Madrid. He traveled alone and dressed in dark gray slacks, a matching turtle-neck, a dark-brown leather jacket, and black loafers. The man behind the shades could have been a movie star instead of the Vicar of Rome.

A black limousine drove up to the tarmac to receive the VIP and Felix directed the young man behind the wheel where he wanted to go. "Is it far?"

"No, sir, it's in the center of town," said the driver, looking at Felix through the rearview mirror.

Half-hour later, the car pulled up to a luxury high-rise with extravagant chandeliers, dark wood paneling, marble floors and large mirrors in ornate gold frames.

"I won't be long," said Felix, getting out of the car and walking in the building. "Contessa Folinari, please," he said to the doorman.

"Your name?"

"Felix Ronnoco."

A butler dressed in a white bolero and black trousers met him in the foyer of the fifteenth floor penthouse. He led Felix to a large study at the far end of a hall where the Contessa stood by the fireplace. She was a slim and beautiful woman in her mid-sixties, and wore a black dress adorned by pearl earrings and a necklace.

Behind the Contessa, hanging above the fireplace, Felix could not miss the large portrait of Ante Pavelić in full military regalia.

"Contessa Folinari," announced the servant, showing Felix in the room.

"Excellency." The Contessa walked up to Felix and kissed his ring, though, in the moment of introduction, she did not notice it suggested a higher rank in the Church. "Have you had dinner? Would you care for something to eat?"

Felix smiled and shook his head.

"Something to drink, then?"

"No, thank you. I don't have much time," returned Felix.

"Our friend in Zagreb said you have something important to ask me." And the Contessa took a chair across the room.

Felix looked at her for a moment, and said: "Contessa, I understand you are the daughter of Ante Pavelić. Is that correct?"

Contessa Folinari did not reply, but acknowledged as much with a slight nod.

"Sometime in 1947, your family—and I mean your mother, your brother and yourself—stayed for a time in the mountains, above Travnik, in a farm belonging to Ana Draganović, the mother of our late Pope Leo. I don't expect you to remember me, of course, it's been a very long time and—well, I was a baby—" added Felix, when he saw Katarina's eyes open wide and a slow smile brightened her expression.

She placed both hands on her mouth and her eyes welled up, trying to recognize a trace of the baby she remembered. "Oh, my God! Saša?" She left her seat and gently placed her hand on his face. "It is you! Oh, Lord—!" she cried.

"Contessa—"

"We—we were devastated!" she said, crying.

"Contessa," Felix tried again. "I need to ask you something."

"My poor, poor brother! He was heartbroken!"

"Why—why do you call me Saša? I need to know this, it's important," said Felix.

"That was your name. That's what he always called you."

"Who? Who are you talking about?"

"Didi."

"Why?" asked Felix.

"I don't know," said Katarina. "He never said. At least—at least I don't recall if he did."

"Are you sure? Never? He didn't give you a reason?" Felix saw his hopes dashed and realized that the search for his identity would end in a luxury flat, in Madrid.

"Damir was quite strange and moody. I do remember we were on our way to the mountains; it was the middle of the night and we were terrified of getting caught by the reds. We had an accident and had to stop. That's when Damir found you by the road and said your name was Saša. That's it, period. He also got upset when Father Draganović suggested you should be baptized. We'd been at the farm, oh—a year maybe. Damir wouldn't hear of it."

"Why not?" asked Felix.

"He said no, and that was that. But—Excellency, I thought your name was Felix Ronnoco?"

"It is."

"Not Saša?"

Felix shook his head.

"Who said you were called Saša?" asked Katarina. "As you pointed out, it's been a long time and, forgive me, but people have a tendency to—"

"His Holiness, Pope Leo, years ago," said Felix. "He was a priest then, and I was in my teens. He told me about Damir, about you and your mother, and the time you spent at the farm."

Katarina looked carefully at Felix, and in a tone measured by the sudden unraveling of an age-old mystery, simply said: "He changed your name. Why?"

Felix shrugged.

"And he had you baptized, isn't that right, Excellency?" said Katarina, wryly. "Now, you've come looking for answers."

They sat quietly for a moment, each searching for a familiar trace in the other.

"You should write to him," she said, at last. "I'm sure he'd love to."

"Write? To whom?"

"Damir. I can—"

"Damir? You mean Didi is—alive?" That time it was Felix who jumped from his seat.

"Why, yes. Well, at least I hope he is—haven't heard from him in months, and, as you know, that whole area is still dangerous."

"Where, where is he?" blurted Felix, his hands shaking.

Back at the Holy See, Father Marcello popped his head in the door, and said: "Eminence, your three o'clock has arrived."

Cardinal Carelli nodded and Inspector Nestor Picol followed in.

The policeman, with his full head of tossled hair, dressed, thought Carelli, like every policeman he had ever known, and carried a thin briefcase.

"Good morning, Inspector," said Carelli.

"To you too, Eminence," returned Picol.

Cardinal Carelli languidly put out his hand and waited in vain for Picol to kiss his ring.

"What brings you to our precious corner of the world, Inspector?" began Carelli.

Picol took a chair across the wide desk, and said: "Your Grace, three days ago Interpol arrested a man called Humberto Venavić, who, at one time was a priest assigned to the Institute of St. Jerome."

"Arrested? On what grounds?" asked Carelli.

"Arms smuggling," answered Picol. "Because the arrest happened in our jurisdiction, I questioned Mr. Venavić, and he confessed."

"The word you should use is admitted," interposed Carelli.

"Admitted, then. Among his many indiscretions, he murdered a priest," added the policeman.

"Really?" asked Carelli, indifferently. "When?"

"When is not as important as why, Your Eminence," returned Picol, taking out a document from his briefcase and handing it to Carelli. "It's a copy of the deposition. If you would be so kind—I highlighted the relevant paragraphs. It is true we have not found the body—"

Carelli glanced at the paper, slid it back across the desk to Picol, and said: "Most of the people in that list are no longer with us."

"But that leaves one or two that I very much would like to interview," said Picol.

"Inspector, you know you have no jurisdiction inside these walls and although we do what we can to cooperate with your department, your request is inconvenient at the moment. The Holy See is again—in transition. You understand," said Carelli.

"I do, Eminence, but I wanted to bring the matter to your attention now, and we can talk again—say in a week. Does that suit you, Eminence?"

"I will see if that is possible," added Carelli.

"Thank you," said Picol.

"You are welcome," said Carelli, stifling a yawn. "Oh, Inspector—"

Picol was halfway out the door, when he turned, and said: "Yes, Your Grace?"

"You will let me know if you find out anything else, won't you?" said Carelli.

"What, for instance?" asked Picol.

"Well—the body," added Carelli.

Things were moving too fast. After spending less than three hours in Madrid, Felix returned to the Holy See, and because it was only seven o'clock in the evening, he immediately summoned his secretary to the Apostolic Palace.

He was changing to a frock when d'Stesi walked in the room, and said: "You're back early."

"Briefly," returned Felix V. "I need you to arrange for a helicopter right away and I also want to talk to the pilot."

"When?" asked d'Stesi.

"Now."

"On the telephone?" inquired the secretary.

"In person. Isn't his name Dumi—"

"Dumitrana, Colonel Dumitrana," interjected the secretary.

"He's usually assigned. Tell him I want to leave at dawn," said the pope.

"May I ask where you're going—in case he wants to know?"

"Who?" said Felix.

"Dumitrana," said d'Stesi.

"I'll tell him when I meet with him. This must be handled with utmost secrecy. Do not tell anyone else about the helicopter, in fact, don't let anyone know I'm back."

"Holiness," observed d'Stesi, "we can keep your return quiet for now, but I doubt if the Four Horsemen won't look out the window when the helicopter comes to town."

"By then, it will be too late," said Felix, waving the secretary out of the room.

At nine-thirty in the evening Colonel Dumitrana, dressed in a dark suit, entered the private quarters of the pope, who was having cookies and milk. "Ah—Colonel," greeted Felix, extending his hand, "so glad you could make it."

"Of course, Holiness," returned the officer, kissing the papal ring. He was a tall, handsome and gracious man with graying hair who carried himself with the authority of a military professional.

"Colonel, I have something to ask you. You'll think it unusual, and it is. I am putting a request for a helicopter for early tomorrow morning—please, take a chair—would you like some wine?"

Dumitrana sat across the desk, leaned forward and accepted a glass of Chianti.

Felix knew that as an officer in the Italian Air Force, Dumitrana was not accountable to the pope. On the other hand, servicing the Head of State of the Holy See was never an issue for the Italian military.

"We need an aircraft that can travel about 950 kilometers and carry—oh, about two dozen people. Is that possible, Colonel?" asked Felix.

Dumitrana paused, sipped his wine, and said: "It depends, Holiness. Is that 950 one way or—?"

"Round trip," said the pope.

"The HH-3E can do the job. It's expensive to operate and we would need to refuel along the way, but it's a large ship and it's equipped with GPS, so I can punch in the coordinates and it will take us there—wherever 'there' happens to be. Do you want the helicopter to show your colors, or do you prefer no identifying marks?"

Felix looked away for a moment, then said: "This is a humanitarian mission sponsored by the Holy See."

"So the craft will be identified as such. May I know where we are going, Holiness?"

The helicopter then climbed to 5,000 meters and headed northeast.

Felix, dressed in jeans, his dark-brown leather jacket and hiker boots, said: "Please, watch out for mountains and very tall people."

Colonel Dumitrana laughed and Felix V retreated to the passenger section where he placed a sleeping bag on the floor and lay down thinking of the many times he had taken that same route to his homeland, although by more conventional means.

What would his Tata have done in his place? His Tata, the same man who betrayed his trust, who lied to him to further an immoral, improbable quest. Felix felt overwhelmed by profound sadness because he realized that his life had been a well-crafted piece of fiction shrouded in secrecy and distrust.

"Holiness—"

Felix got up, looked out the window and saw that they were touching down at a secluded corner of the airport, in Split, where a fuel truck and two men in suits and dark glasses waited on the tarmac.

"Good morning, Your Grace," said one of the fellows, flashing his ID from the Croatian Security Services, before kissing Felix's hand. His Holiness thought that the agent looked no more than twenty-five.

"Good morning," returned Felix. "Were you able to get a picture of the area?" he added, not wasting time.

The other government man, who was taller and redder than his companion, immediately pulled out several 8x10 satellite color photographs, and said: "Yes. We should thank the Americans."

"Looks like barracks, a large one story building—about 1,200 square meters, built deep in a valley surrounded by wooded hills and mountains. There's a stream running behind it and you can see people outside, but there's no sign of military hardware," said the young man, pointing to a particular picture.

"There is a van—it's the white dot, on the right—" observed his companion. "What is that place?"

"Orphanage," said Felix, carefully studying the photographs.

"Bad news. We have intelligence of a Serbian paramilitary group operating in the area, and—they're up to no good," said the young-looking agent.

"I don't understand. That place is so remote," said Felix. "What are they after?"

"Same thing as you, perhaps?" returned the taller agent. "You really don't want to run into them. Here, better take this, Your Grace," he added, giving Felix a satellite phone, "in case you get shot down—although we have no one in the area and once you cross into Bosnia, you're on your own."

"Thank you," said Felix, dryly, and tucked the phone in his jacket. "Colonel!" he called, then handed the pictures to the pilot. "How long will it take us to get there?"

"One hour—more or less," answered Dumitrana.

"Let's go," said Felix, boarding the helicopter. "Thank you very much for everything," he called out to the Croatian agents, "and please, convey my gratitude to President Babić."

Ten minutes later, the helicopter climbed to 4500 meters, headed north along the border with Bosnia at 150 kmph. Then, 13 kilometers east of the Croatian town of Kijevo, Dumitrana turned to Felix, and said: "Please, secure your seatbelt, Holiness, and hold on," before banking suddenly to the right and sending the large helicopter into a steep dive.

It was a dangerous maneuver followed by an incursion into foreign—and probably hostile—air space at tree-top level to avoid detection by radar. Colonel Dumitrana had traced a route that avoided towns and small villages as a precaution against small arms fire and the large white helicopter adorned with the papal seal, skirted mountains and hills with the nimbleness of a smaller, lighter craft.

Below, the lush green valleys of Bosnia Herzegovina and the pastoral setting of sheep, goats and shepherds belied the ugly, terrible truth of a land reverting back to ancient tribal conflict, a story Felix knew first hand.

Twenty minutes later, south of Ždrimci, Colonel Dumitrana pulled back on the stick, increased power and flew less than 40 meters above a densely packed forest that turned into a wide valley of fertile, hilly grassland that gradually narrowed, until it reached an elevated expanse of land surrounded by a canopy of large trees, plants and underbrush.

It was 10:45 a.m.

So far, the weather had cooperated and it was a perfect, clear day for taking to the skies, observed Colonel Dumitrana, before calling out: "There it is!" He pointed to a bright yellow speck in the horizon, slowly gained altitude and speed, did a flyby and found a safe, flat spot to set down the helicopter, thirty meters from the front door.

The moment he cut the engines, two dozen children from 4 to 18; boys and girls—Bosnians, Serbs, Croats, Muslims and Gypsies of all color and size—ran from the building and rushed the aircraft.

Dumitrana dropped the loading ramp and Felix quickly walked out, making his way among the children.

He approached a girl, about sixteen years old with dark-blonde hair and large blue eyes, dressed in dungarees, a red sweater and sneakers, who tried in vain to get the kids back in the building. "I am looking for Miguel Bianchi," said Felix, when he saw the sign above the entrance: Saša.

"He's inside," replied the girl, grabbing a little boy tugging at Felix. "He's very sick—can't see anyone."

"What's wrong with him?" asked Felix.

The girl shrugged and was going to chase another child when Felix took her by the arm and forced her to pay attention. "Listen! This is urgent," he said, "I don't care what condition he's in. I need to see him—now!"

The girl summoned a ten-year-old boy with freckles and long brown hair wearing jeans and a hand-me-down Brooklyn sweatshirt, and said: "Take him to don Miguel."

"Who are you?" asked the boy, leading Felix in the building.

"A friend," answered Felix.

The boy stopped before a door marked Director, and said: "He had a headache, began to mumble and fell on the floor. It took six of us to carry him here. I think he's dying."

Felix walked quietly in the room that served as office and living quarters. The desk was topped with papers, an old record player and a rotary telephone. Several bookshelves covered the walls behind the desk and heavy curtains draped the windows. At the far end, he saw the white-haired man on a canvas cot, lying down on his back, fully dressed.

Felix felt Damir's pulse, turned to the boy, and said: "Run outside and tell the pilot to bring the first-aid kit. Run!"

The boy rushed out while Felix pulled aside the drapes, and opened the windows to let in fresh air and the morning sun.

"We have to get him to a hospital. I think he had a stroke," said Felix, when Dumitrana entered the room.

The Colonel took Damir's blood pressure, waited a moment, and said: "198 over 130. He's critical. I suggest we go back to Split. I'll call ahead."

Felix turned to the boy standing beside him, and said: "Who is second in command, here? Who tells you what to do when—other than don Miguel?"

"Misha," said the boy.

"Get Misha in here."

A minute later, the girl Felix met earlier, walked in, carrying a toddler in her arms.

"Call the children, you are all leaving with us—now," ordered Felix.

"But—we can't leave. What about don Miguel?" asked Misha, sounding scared.

"We have to get him to a hospital and you can't stay behind because some really bad men are on the way here, and trust me when I tell you, they will kill every one of you," said Felix. "Now please, we can't waste time. Take the kids outside and leave everything—and I mean everything behind."

Felix and Dumitrana then carried Damir—in his cot—to the helicopter, and placed him down gently, as the children took their seats on the floor.

The extra weight meant the HH-3E did not handle as graciously as before. Even so, it was a smooth and uneventful return trip to Croatia, and no sooner did they cross the border, Felix called his contacts in the Croatian government to make sure that an ambulance was waiting on the tarmac.

As they landed, Felix recognized the agents from before standing next to three paramedics, an ambulance and two policemen on motorcycles who would escort it into town.

As soon as Dumitrana dropped the loading ramp, the medics boarded the helicopter, took charge of Damir and transferred him to the ambulance.

Felix ordered the children to a private lounge in the airport so they could have something to eat, while he looked after his friend. "I'll be back as soon as I can," he told Dumitrana, "then, we'll decide what to do."

"Holiness—" said Colonel Dumitrana, aside to Felix, "you do know that everything we've done so far is illegal?"

"Like what?" asked Felix, slightly distracted.

"Like—kidnap children across the border and secretly transferred them to another country. I'm an officer of the Italian Air Force. I'll be sacked."

"You won't. Remember I'm infallible," said Felix, smiling. "Stay with the helicopter. Those kind gentlemen will look after the children."

And before Dumitrana could raise another objection, Felix climbed aboard the ambulance, where Damir was hooked to a respirator and an intravenous drip to stabilize his blood pressure.

> *"Damir, Damir, Damir, come and stay,*
> *Not in bed but out to play!"*

The beautiful flowers of a forgotten time called his name, but again, the child held fast. As the ambulance raced through busy streets clogged with traffic and the mist of that lovely recollection gradually faded into the noisy confines of his surroundings, Damir at last opened his eyes and recognized the face at once. "Saša?" he whispered, forcing a smile. "You're back."

"Yes, dear friend," said Felix, holding back the tears, "I'm back."

29

Only two days after he declared his love for Isabella at the Teatro Colón, the Giglis sailed home. The Pavelićs, without the Poglavnik, enjoyed Beniamino's hospitality for the last time in his cabin on board the Queen Mary. The compartment suited the discriminating affluence of the great tenor better than its counterpart on the Afortunato. Damir and Isabella spent their last moments together holding hands by the railing and looking out to sea. They said little and tried not to cry because they knew too well how much they would miss each other.

When it came time to say good-bye, Marija and Katarina had to drag the boy off the boat, but not before he announced to the world—with a rare display of bravado and a sudden flight of inspiration—that there was no person more beloved than his beloved Isabella. In return, she threw kisses at him from above, laughed, waved and, in the end, broke down and cried.

Damir waited on the pier until the ocean liner vanished in the distance and Isabella did not leave the railing until the coast of Argentina faded into the blue-green mist of the horizon.

The only Pavelić not saddened because the Giglis had left the city, the country, the continent—and who would not have minded if they had been cast off the earth itself and banished from the solar system—was the patriarch of the family. The Poglavnik had had about enough of brooding adolescents, infantile tantrums and insolent wives and perhaps without the interference of a brazen, meddling troubadour and his over-solicitous daughter, life in his household could assume the quiet, dignified pace he had planned for the family all along.

At long last and for the first time in their lives, his children attended a regular school. They did so under their counterfeit identities and, at first, the other children at the Academia Americana thought that Miguel and Sara Bianchi were slightly distracted, perhaps snobs, possibly deaf, or simply stupid, because Miguel and Sara never seemed to notice when someone called them by name. It would be weeks before Damir and Kati got used to being called Miguel and Sara.

Marija was thankful that, when Isabella left for Rome, Didi did not surrender again to melancholy, but instead spent his time catching up on his studies, listening to music and writing long letters to Isabella, letters that crossed the Atlantic laden with sighs and plans for a future life together.

He learned the hybrid of Spanish, Italian and local inventions that made up the vernacular spoken in Argentina, and longed for spring, when Isabella would return to Buenos Aires.

So, Marija stopped worrying about Didi and began to worry about Kati, who delighted with the company of the other children in school (particularly the boys), amassed half a dozen admirers and developed a fondness for debutante balls and polo that led her mother to distraction. Life was not perfect, but then, it had never been.

Ante also kept himself busier than usual. Although he had been in Argentina for years, he continued living in fear of reprisals from the Yugoslav government. That, however, did not keep him from coming out of his deep freeze, establishing a social club for Croats whose members were, for the most part, fellow expatriates, though none as notorious. For a while, things began to look like the old days except that, while it was true some faces in those secret gatherings in Buenos Aires reminded Pavelić of the backroom plots and conspiracies hatched in Milan and Zagreb before the war, it was also true that, among the Poglavnik's confederates, Death was counting heads.

When the Soviet Union exploded its first atomic bomb in 1949, the news transformed many fascist autocrats around the globe almost overnight from murderous tyrants into anticommunist prophets and patriots. In the late 1940s and early 50s South America had an impressive list of strongmen, among them Trujillo, Somoza, Dornelles, Pérez Jiménez, Batista and Perón. Still, Ante Pavelić's legacy outscored the collective Latin American contingent by hundreds of thousands of victims, putting the Poglavnik in a league of his own.

One morning, while Rubén was driving Miguel and Sara to school, Ante informed his wife that he had agreed to an interview by the Italian publication Epoca, supposed to detail his lifelong struggle against communism, and show him at home in the company of his wife and children, as they planned to return one day to an independent and Catholic Croatia. The banished Croat community around the world could take hope.

A few things came to mind as Marija listened to her husband. First, how the publication contacted Ante, since he kept his identity and whereabouts a secret. Second, was it necessary to take pictures?

With his inimitable laconic charm, the Poglavnik explained that the magazine had not contacted him but it was he who contacted the magazine. Ante, it appeared, was tired of being and anonymous outcast while others (less deserving) basked in the struggle against international communism. Egotism, that half-brother of inferiority, still thrived in Ante Pavelić.

Marija turned from the door and, in a casual way, said that she would ask Damir and Katarina if they had any objections being photographed.

"The matter is not up for debate," said her husband.

"I will ask them anyway," returned the wife.

Katarina loved the idea. Damir, on the other hand, found the thought of standing next to Ante Pavelić in a portrait of family bliss revolting.

The relationship between father and son had not worsened since Damir had recovered from his bout with depression, but it had not improved, either. Marija kept her son's opinion to herself, hoping that the interview would not take place and that the matter would quietly go away.

Not likely. Several weeks later, on a clear warm Saturday morning, Ante announced that the family should be ready that same afternoon to receive the interviewer. Upon hearing the news, Damir asked the Fritz for a plate of meat pies and a pitcher of grapefruit juice, carried the food to his room, shut the door and turned on his music, with no intention of leaving the sanctuary the rest of the day. Marija knocked on his door, but received no answer beyond the opening bars of Tosca. At precisely two forty-five, the Fritz, wearing a maid's uniform that included a white cap and matching apron, served coffee, tea and sandwiches in the library. Marija, who had changed from her ordinary housecoat into a dark-green cotton blouse and skirt, arranged her hair, added a little makeup and returned to the study with a bouncing Katarina—wearing a blue and yellow polka dot dress and black patent leather shoes, but—no Damir. The Poglavnik, in a dark gray suit and black tie—sure to impress the interviewer with its sobriety—urged his wife to go back upstairs and demand that Damir present himself to the study without delay. Again, Marija tried to persuade her son to join the family. Her second attempt took a bit longer, but the outcome was the same—no Damir.

Time for Damir to change his mind ran out at three o'clock, when Rubén helped Rodolfo Cracci, the journalist out of the car and led him to the library where he was greeted by the exiled President of the Independent Nation of Croatia, and by his wife and daughter.

Cracci was in his forties, not too tall, with curly gray hair and the look of someone who enjoyed not knowing what came next. He was a simple, friendly chap sent to ask the right questions and get the right answers. He took pictures of Ante, Marija and

Katarina with their incredibly big and dangerous dogs walking beside them in the backyard and never noticed the boy looking out the window from above.

The scene reminded Damir of the times when such men always followed his father around the courtyards of Florence, Milan, Zagreb and Banja Luka. They snapped pictures, wrote praiseworthy articles and disseminated lies.

"I was told you have a son," asked Cracci, at one point in the interview.

"Yes," answered the Poglavnik, turning red, and left the matter at that. Once Signor Cracci left, he sent for Damir. "If you don't mind," Ante said to his wife, "I need to talk to Damir."

Marija hesitated for a moment before she took Kati by the hand and went into the kitchen to watch the Fritz prepare the Argentinian version of Mexican chimichanga.

"You better understand something," said Ante softly to his son. "This is my house. If you wish to live in my house, you will respect my wishes and obey my orders. I don't think that is too much to ask, is it?"

As always when he met with his father, Damir stood in front of the desk looking sullen and bored. "Anything else, sir?"

"Answer my question, Damir. Do you think it is too much to ask?"

Said Damir: "Sir, I cannot respect your wishes because I do not respect you. I cannot obey your orders because I will not yield to your standards. If, to live in this house with my mother and sister I have to do as you fancy, I will move out at once." Didi looked at his father with the same scrutinizing stare that made many other people uncomfortable. "Anything else, sir?"

Ante stood up suddenly, planted both hands on the desk and leaned forward. "You are a spoiled brat—a useless, spineless, soft-bellied disappointment of a son!"

"And you, sir, have never been a good judge of character." Damir turned and left. Now, instead of going up to his room to start packing, he went into the kitchen. Instead of addressing his mother or his sister, who were sitting, as they say, "on pins and needles," Didi asked the Fritz if she knew someone who could put him up for a few days. The question surprised not only Juana but Marija and Kati as well. Because they did not know what he was talking about, they followed him upstairs, where he explained in a sad but determined voice that he was moving out.

Kati cried and tried to convince Damir to change his mind. Marija rushed downstairs and confronted her husband. "Damir is not, I repeat, is not moving out!"

"Madame," said Ante with self-righteous dignity, "Damir is free to do as he sees fit!"

Damir, in fact, did not move out, at least not right away. Even after the Fritz volunteered to give him shelter in her mother's home in Córdoba, or suggested that he stay with an old flame who ran a tango bar on the other side of Buenos Aires, the boy had several practical reasons why he thought better of it, and did not go anywhere.

Reason number one: money. He had no money of his own and would not think of asking his mother for money because she would only ask his father. Reason number two: his music collection. Moving more than twenty thousand records required planning and a big room. Didi was eighteen years old, but sensible for his age.

Once, Didi woke up in a sweat at two in the morning. He stared at the ceiling and tried to work in his mind how he could go look for Saša and how he could marry Isabella, or marry Isabella and then go find Saša. He needed a lot of money to travel and even more to get married, especially to someone like Isabella. He did not want to study law, medicine or work in anything else except opera. As a singer? No, he was too shy. So, do what in opera?

Didi tossed and turned until he sat up in bed and decided to ask Isabella. In a long letter drafted at four in the morning, he explained his concerns and received a reply a month later, in a postscript to her regular dispatch. It was short and to the point: *"Go see Don Fulgencio de Jesús, at the Teatro Colón."*

Don Fulgencio received Didi in a white shirt with the sleeves rolled up to the elbows, a red bow tie, dark pants and reading glasses. "No, no, no—no bowing, please. I would have to bow in return and I'm too short as it is. It puts me at a disadvantage. A handshake will do. Come in, come in—" the Artistic Director waved him into his office, pointed to a chair, closed the door and went behind a little table that served as his desk.

The office had wooden floors, tall ceilings, a large window with red drapes that at one time must have been part of a theater curtain, redbrick walls and three bookshelves replete with countless musical scores. "Your face is familiar."

Damir explained that they had met on opening night of—

"Of course!" And Don Fulgencio chastised Didi for almost ruining the opening night with his calling and screaming backstage for Isabella, before he waved a telegram. "From the Great Gigli. It is about you." At that point the interrogation began in earnest. Damir was asked, first of all, if Damir was his real name, how old he was, where he was from—

"Cr—Yugoslavia."

"Cr—Yugoslavia. Is that like Yugoslavia?"

"I'm sorry, yes, Yugoslavia."

And why did he want to work in opera. Was he a singer?

Didi shook his head and smiled.

"Why do you smile?"

"Because I imagine that most people who come here looking for work, are singers."

"Wrong," replied Don Fulgencio. "The people who walk through that door already have work. I'm not running an employment agency. The fact that you're sitting there, young man, is because Beniamino Gigli—who is a dear man but a pain in the rear—asked me to see you. I am—seeing you, that is—and I do not like what I see."

Didi blinked several times. He didn't know what he was doing to make the Artistic Director dislike him. Perhaps the fellow had found out about his father.

"First, you're too good-looking and my experience with good-looking people is that their brains are full of chimichurri." And without pausing for breath, Don Fulgencio asked Damir what he could do, and could he work full time. Did Damir mind not making much money, because he was not going to make a lot at the Teatro Colón? Could he work nights? What did Damir's family have to say about his taking a job at the Teatro Colón? And, did Damir understand that by getting hired by don Fulgencio, Beniamino Gigli would be compromised? Beniamino, of course, was aware of that because the Great Gigli was not a fool. Beniamino must have liked Damir a lot, which was lucky for Damir, and he should accordingly report next Monday afternoon at four o'clock, ready to work.

"Y-y-yes sir," stammered Damir, "but sir—"

"What?" Don Fulgencio was holding the door for Damir.

"What am I supposed to do?"

"Well, you don't sing. Do you conduct?" inquired the artistic director.

"No, sir."

"Of course not, you seem like a nice young man. Can you direct?"

"No, sir."

"I didn't think so. Stage directors have a flair for the impossible and small brains. So, what can you do?"

"I—I don't know, sir."

"Well, if you don't, how do you expect me to? But don't worry, I'll think of something." Don Fulgencio smiled, closed the door and left Damir staring at the grain in the wood.

It took Beniamino six years to consent to the marriage of Isabella and Damir because he wanted to make sure that in spite of everything that was said, of the despondent tears that were shed and in the many scenes reminiscent of the best of Puccini, Verdi and Bellini, the young couple's love was not a transient infatuation, but a passion that would endure the harsh realities of married life. He also wanted to give Damir time to settle down in a vocation that promised advancement. For the two young people, six years was already nearly half a lifetime; because they were in love, it was an eternity.

They saw each other once a year when the Great Gigli arrived in Argentina with his usual fanfare for another series of performances. It was during those greatly anticipated, nerve-racking get-togethers lasting a couple of weeks, that Damir and Isabella learned more than to love each other.

She took it upon herself to show Didi the world he had missed while hiding from his father's enemies. She taught him to play tennis, to dance (Didi could cha-cha and rumba but would not tango), and—thinking that Didi perhaps needed a little gaiety in his life—she introduced him to American film comedies and young Pavelić became an ardent fan of the Marx brothers' Duck Soup.

For Isabella, she could not have turned out more beautiful, with a noble bearing and a slender, statuesque figure. Her hair was a little darker than when she was a young girl, the blond waves of childhood shading into amber, but her eyes—her eyes retained the joy, the excitement and the hope of a child's spirit.

At the same time, Damir grew tall and his once ungraceful, gangling ways smoothed out to an elegant deportment. He also became an independent young man, finished secondary school, withdrew his savings and moved out of his father's house to a one-room flat in a six-story walk-up in a working class neighborhood of little shops and tenements, he decorated with pictures of Isabella, his mother and sister.

Shortly after, he enrolled at the University of Buenos Aires and divided his time between school and the Teatro Colón. His passion for opera, in addition to the skills he learned at the

university, allowed him to be promoted often; faster, in fact, than
most. He amazed everyone with his knowledge of and respect
for the craft and gained almost universal admiration among the
artists and staff who worked and struggled at the opera house.
Many were so impressed with the good-looking young Croat
they offered both their hearts and other, more succulent parts
of themselves—regularly. As a result, Didi spent many nights
anxiously debating with himself whether he should acquire a
measure of sexual expertise before joining Isabella in marriage,
but in the end decided that it would be unfair to expect from
his bride that which he could not deliver himself. It was difficult at times, even excruciating, but Didi harnessed his libido,
tempering it with long hours of work, study, music and lots of—
meditation. And so Damir reached the age of twenty-two and at
twenty-two and a half, graduated from the university, and three
days later was promoted to Assistant Artistic Director of the
Teatro Colón.

That same week, he received an offer from the Teatro
dell'Opera in Rome. The position of Production Supervisor
paid three times what he was earning in Argentina. Things
were looking up for Damir. The Teatro dell'Opera was but three
blocks from the apartment that Beniamino had bequeathed his
daughter as a wedding gift; a few hours' drive from Yugoslavia—
and hopefully—Saša.

Lepanto was the finest, most exclusive and most expensive
restaurant in Buenos Aires, maybe in all of Argentina. Said the
Great Gigli: "Ladies and gentlemen, I wish to invite everyone
here tonight to join our celebration. My daughter—this beautiful princess to my right—is getting married to this handsome
prince sitting at her side!" And with typical Gigli flair, and as he
had done many times in *Traviata*, he added: Libiam!"

Isabella was radiant in a long-sleeved, blue silk dress adorned
with yellow gemstones in the shape of half-moons. Next to the

Giglis, Didi was positively a pillar of conservatism in his dark gray suit, resplendent white shirt and red silk tie.

Of course, the entire room expressed their congratulations, embarrassing Damir and Isabella with applause, followed by a call for the groom to kiss the bride. The wish was granted. Immediately, the pops from the champagne bottles turned into a fusillade. The Great Gigli, wearing a maroon jacket, white silk shirt and ascot, and looking a little more plump, a bit more gray but a great deal happier, kissed his daughter, turned to his future son-in-law and said: "Now, Didi, what's this I hear you don't want your father at the wedding?"

Damir had been expecting the question since he sat to dinner. The Poglavnik had never been consulted, told about, and was not expected to attend the wedding; that was Damir's wish.

"Oh, oh, I think I'd better go powder—whatever I have that needs powdering," said Isabella, getting up.

"No, no, stay." Damir took Isabella's hand to keep her from leaving the table.

Isabella shrugged. She rarely talked about Ante Pavelić with his son, but had learned about the Poglavnik from Croatian dissidents and Serbian exiles whom she met in Rome. The repugnance she felt for Ante Pavelić only increased the love she felt for Damir.

"Maestro," said Didi, "I want the wedding to be a celebration of life. Having Ante Pavelić there would deny that." Beniamino looked at the glass of wine in front of him and listened to the quiet words spoken without hate or anger, just regret. "I wanted to get married in Rome," continued Damir, "but my mother and sister are still afraid to go to Europe. I don't have to explain why."

A momentary and uncharacteristic silence crept over the shrimps in garlic. Said Beniamino: "There was a time when your father was considered a great man."

"There was a time," observed Damir, "when people thought the world was flat."

Isabella chuckled and Beniamino tweaked her nose playfully, then turned to her betrothed. "It is your wedding and your decision. I promised your mother that I would talk to you about it, and I did. Now—Scarfino!" Scarfino was the Maître d', a spindly man with a wide forehead, a snub nose, curly brown hair, a thin mustache, bulging eyes and perfect poise who, right on cue, led three waiters from the kitchen with trays of lobster and veal prepared with special care by the chef for Damir and Isabella.

Ante Pavelić, of course, was not mentioned again that evening. He was dismissed for the time being to those cracks of the subconscious where the human spirit stows its unpleasantness. Unfortunately, the Poglavnik was like a pogo stick; the moment he hit the ground, he bounced right back.

With two days before the wedding, Damir was summoned by his mother to the house and she requested that he go alone. Marija was in charge of planning the event because Isabella lived in Italy and Damir did not have a clue what to do.

Marija chose the church, booked the ballroom at the Alvear Palace Hotel, hired a theatrical set designer to decorate and imbue it with the proper wedding mood, chose the menu, collected names and addresses for the exclusive guest list of close friends and government ministers, had the invitations printed and sent out by courier, hired the musical group that was to provide entertainment, offered counsel on the wedding gown and asked Beniamino to pay for everything.

A whole year planning and buying, making changes to the plans and the buying, and then changing the changes; Marija even procured an Argentinean passport for Damir, so he could travel to New York for his honeymoon, before going to Rome. Finally, she went out of her way to calm and reassure the sweethearts who, as the date of their wedding approached, became more and more relaxed.

30

"Good morning, Juana. I must say, I hope you are as happy as you look today," said Damir, walking in the house.

"Didi!" The Fritz threw her arms around Damir, and kissed him on both cheeks. "Señora, llegó Didi!"

"I think I can find my way." Damir walked through the kitchen and into the study where his mother and sister waited. The window curtains were open, a sign of the family's lessening apprehension that someone might take aim at them from outside.

Marija embraced and kissed him affectionately. The years had been kind to her, although she had gained some weight, a few lines, and more than her share of gray hair; after all, she was closing in on sixty. "I'm so glad you could make it," she said with a dash of sarcasm preceding her smile.

"I don't know if I share your enthusiasm," answered Damir.

Katarina kissed her brother. She was dressed in a peculiar American fashion that was just beginning to take hold among upper-class Argentinos: blue jeans, a white polo shirt and tennis shoes. "I love the apartment!" Kati meant the one in the photographs her brother had shown her, where he and Isabella would live, after their honeymoon. "I hope Papa is that generous when I get married." Katarina stepped back, looked at her brother and added: "I see you're acquiring a sense of—adventure in your dress, Didi." Damir wore a pair of khaki slacks, a navy blazer over a white cotton tennis shirt and chocolate colored, suede shoes.

"Isabella picked them out for you, right?" Katarina smiled and turned to her mother. "Wait until they're married!"

"Enough, please," said Marija.

"Oh, dear!" cried Kati.

"What is it?" asked her mother.

"I don't know if Cedric knows the mambo." Cedric, whose last name was Fogstrand, was the son of the British ambassador and Kati's most fervent admirer.

"He's English, dear, they don't dance," replied Marija, sitting next to Damir. She took his hand, and said: "We have to talk about your father."

They did not talk; they argued for two hours and Katarina was his most formidable adversary. Damir still loved his sister dearly, but before he moved out, Pavelić and son had quarreled constantly, with the Poglavnik never raising his voice or threatening Damir—merely stating his position, one that was inevitably based on common sense, a call for discipline, and obedience—and Damir turning aggressive and confrontational.

Kati was convinced that Isabella had instilled Damir with a bit too much self-confidence, and began thinking of her brother's fiancé as an instigator. Soon, lines of loyalty were drawn, and Kati ended up on the side of the Poglavnik.

"Didi," said Marija, "to have your father not attend the wedding is unacceptable, and humiliating. What do you think people will say when they find out the bridegroom's father has been banned from the wedding by his son?"

"I don't care what people think."

"You've become a boor. You have no regard for anyone except your precious Isabella," declared Katarina, louder than necessary. "You're not being fair, not to Mama, who's busted her ass for this wedding—I mean, your father-in-law has done nothing but tell us to spend his money, thank you—and you're not being fair to Papa, either. All he's ever done—since we arrived in this country—is go out of his way for us. But you—you hate him. Why? Is it that bullshit—?"

"Katarina!"

"But that's all it is, Mama! The show trials and the rest of Belgrade's propaganda—it's bullshit! Is that what's bothering you, Didi? Grow up!"

Damir looked at his mother. He seemed irritated but not surprised because their meeting was turning out as expected.

Continued Kati: "Papa was a great leader who unfortunately was caught on the losing end of a hopeless war! I'm telling you now, Papa stays home, I stay home."

"Didi, meet with him, do it for me, I beg you!" said his mother.

Damir sighed. The Poglavnik would have his say after all.

That afternoon, Damir and Isabella could be seen from outside, sitting by the window of El Cuchillo, a hangout for beatniks and starving artists. Isabella rested her elbows on the narrow marble square that stood for a table, and kept her eyes on Damir. Nothing in the dark, smoke-filled bohemian café distracted her—not the imitation Renaissance portraits of princes and dukes peering down from the massive, ornate and very old (but not, properly speaking, antique) frames; not the loud political debate going on two tables away; not the rhythm of jazz from the loudspeakers; not the espresso machine hissing incessantly above the babel and the music; not even the short, round waiter with an attitude who bounced up and down the room like a beach ball with a mustache, and who was told to bring two coffees, two glasses of water, one piece of chocolate cake and two forks.

"You have time to change your mind," said Damir at long last.

"Do I?" returned Isabella, feigning indifference, as she brought the cup to her lips.

"Be warned, if you do, me caso con Juana." Damir imitated Isabella's coolness by taking a piece of the chocolate frosting and dipping it in his coffee.

Isabella quickly put the cup down on the table, took a napkin and covered her mouth to avoid spitting out her drink. Her eyes filled with tears and she held her breath. As soon as she swallowed, she laughed and coughed until Damir got out of his chair and slapped her a couple of times on the back. The thought of Damir marrying the Fritz was as outrageous as Animal Crackers.

"She's older, but Juana is a great cook!" said Isabella with great difficulty, unable to stop laughing. When she regained her composure, Isabella leaned forward, took Damir's face in her hands and gave him one of those kisses that are almost never seen except on the silver screen—in close-up, with the music of a thousand strings filling the air, bursting every living cell with sensation.

In a different establishment the shameless display of affection might have raised an eyebrow or two, it might have even brought out a smile between the older gentlemen and ladies who still had fond memories of when they were young and in love. But in a dive where Argentinean beatniks debated what it meant for a third-rate cabaret singer to lead one of the most male oriented chauvinistic nations in the world, then to die and become a martyr, nothing was sacred, certainly not love.

"I adore you," said Damir.

As Beniamino had observed one night aboard a steamship called Afortunato, they indeed made a handsome couple.

"I better go. It's a quarter to." Isabella grabbed her purse and got up, but Didi took her hand.

"He's never on time. He likes to make people wait."

"Well, I don't want to risk it. I'll be at the hotel." She could not visualize a man like Ante Pavelić sitting among radicals, some intellectuals, and some with secret leftist leanings.

Sitting alone, Damir saw the street lights come alive. It also began to rain, not hard but enough to make people quicken their steps. The drops on the window diffused the headlights and turned the street lamps into miniature, haloed suns against the darkening skies. Slowly, the drizzle turned to heavy rain. Cars splashed the sidewalk, and people covered their heads and scurried. Didi was looking out into the street when he noticed a little boy getting wet on the sidewalk, his back to the window.

Suddenly, the boy turned, fixed his eyes on Didi, cupped his hands and yelled: "Are you a Jew?"

"What?" said Didi, when, from the corner of his eye, he saw the black limousine turn the corner. By the time he looked again, the boy was gone. "What's he doing asking people if they are Jews?"

The limousine went around the block once. Finally, it stopped in front of the café, attracting its share of attention from a neighborhood not used to limousines driving by. Rubén—who had grown a comfortable paunch—went around with an umbrella for el Jefe, and Ante Pavelić carefully left the car.

He wore a black suit, a hat, dark glasses and a mustache and looked like any other Argentinean businessman or member of the Junta. "You come here often?" He looked down at his son while Rubén waited at another table nearby.

"Yes," said Damir.

Ante pulled up a chair and sat down, placing his hat on the table. He had lived in Argentina almost eight years and his appearance had not changed much except that his flesh had taken on an ashen, pasty look, though his hair remained as black as his soul.

"Mother said you wanted to see me."

Ante looked around, inspecting the room, then brought his eyes back to his son. "They tell me you're getting married." It was the same indifferent monotone, seasoned with arrogance that Damir remembered.

Damir did not answer.

Ante reached inside his breast pocket and took out a thick brown envelope. He put it on the table and without a word passed it across to his son. Damir pushed it back toward his father. "Why don't you at least see what's inside?"

"I know what's inside, and I thank you, but I cannot accept it."

"That is your choice, but have the courtesy to at least open the envelope." Ante pushed the envelope back toward his son.

The exchange did not go unnoticed by the debaters a little distance away. Although they could not hear the conversation between the handsome young man and the stately older gentleman—with all the music and the hissing contraptions—they speculated that either, the older gentleman was propositioning the young man and the price had not been met, or the latter was a hired thug, assassin, or police informant haggling for the same reason.

"It's a lot of money," said Ante.

"I'm sure it is," said Damir.

"You're going to need it."

"No, I won't," Damir replied without hesitation. "And even if I did, I still would not take it."

"Why?" Ante asked matter-of-factly, his hands clasped in priestly fashion. "What is the difference between the money in that envelope and other money? It's worth the same, buys the same, costs the same—"

Damir knew Ante was trying to keep him from leaving. "May I ask you, sir," Damir leaned forward and looked at his father sternly, "how much the fascist government of this country pays you for whatever it is you do for them?"

Ante smiled.

"Let me guess," said Damir. "It is not enough for you to live the way you do, for my mother and sister to wear the fancy dresses and expensive jewels they wear, and for you to be this generous." Damir pointed at the envelope still in the center of the table. "That tells me that you have another source of income, a vast source, a treasure. Like the one I found in a cave in the mountains above Travnik—six chests all together, full of gold teeth from your victims at Jasenovac. The war booty you left in care of Stepinac and that is being looked after and kept for you with Catholic efficiency by Draganović." If Ante Pavelić's complexion had turned a sickly gray in the last years, his son's words made him turn as white as the foam on a cup of cappuccino—without the cinnamon flakes—that was making its way to another table.

"I've never told anyone. I love my mother, my sister and Isabella far too much to burden them further with your—indecency." Father and son looked at each other. "Do you remember the little boy you murdered in front of me? Do you remember his name?" Damir did not wait for a reply. "Aleksandar—he was called Saša." Ante looked away and stared at the white marble tiles dark with grime. "Why did you do it? I never figured it out. He was pathetically poor, starving—in rags. Did you feel good afterwards? Did it make you a better leader, a better soldier, a better Croat, a better Catholic—a better man to kill the child? Did you think that killing little Saša would help realize your grand vision of Croatia?" Damir's voice was soft, monotone and spellbinding. "You have caused great suffering." Damir stopped and stared at his father for a moment. "Why?" Damir thought he caught a glimpse of a tear forming in the Poglavnik's left eye, a mere wisp of a glint. He turned to look out the window. "I had a friend years ago—"

"Damir—"

"—back in Travnik. His name was Pero. He was an old Serb who worked for Draganović—a shepherd. I'm sure he's dead now." Damir paused, remembering the sad, sad look on the old man before they said good-bye. "Pero told me that people are not evil, that it is in our nature to do good, and it is ignorance that makes us do evil things. I've often wondered about that. If little Saša had not been a stranger, if you had known him like you knew Katarina and me, would you have put a bullet in his head?" Damir pushed back his chair, and placed two bills under the sugar bowl. "I don't hate you, and you should thank Pero for that. I just find it impossible to forget." Damir paused. "The wedding ceremony will be simple enough," he added. "The church, I believe, is open to the public."

It was a perfect afternoon for two to become one. The May sun could not have been more radiant if Botticelli had graced it with his singular magic. Crowds gathered on the sidewalk, and a small crew of attendants did their best to keep it away from the notables pulling up in front of the Iglesia de San Andrés. The small church where Damir and Isabella were to be married was, as churches go, an attractive, though not imposing building, standing in front of a park full of fountains, iron lamps and marble statuettes. The church had been built a hundred years before and had a narrow campanile, and a conspicuously plain façade because the local bishop, at the time the little church was built, decided to devote the diocese's money to a magnificent altar, an altar that, being much higher than those in most other houses of worship, forced the faithful to look upwards at all times during the service, stressing the point that the priest was closer to God than those sitting in the pews.

The groom arrived first. Damir, Marija, Kati and the Fritz stepped out of the limousine and stood outside the church, welcoming the guests. Minutes later, the British ambassador and his family arrived. Sir Malcolm and Lady Fogstrand, along with their son Cedric, guests of the groom's family, were extremely charming and all smiles as they congratulated Damir on his wedding day. Sir Malcolm and young Cedric were perfect examples of British propriety and dress, although Lady Fogstrand might have lost points for her tepid red gown and dead mink stole (not that a live mink would have been any better). The Fogstrands waved at a few people in the crowd, who clapped for some unknown reason. Finally, Kati escorted the Fogstrands inside San Andrés, and an usher showed them to their seats.

An official government limousine pulled up containing Don Anastasio Gómez, the Minister of Culture and his wife Belinda, good friends of the father of the bride. The minister—his chest full of medals and ribbons—was in formal attire. His wife wore a dress much better suited for the occasion than that of the British ambassador's wife. In a gesture that would be repeated throughout the afternoon, Don Anastasio and Doña Belinda congratulated the groom and kissed the groom's mother; then they waited outside for Don Fulgencio de Jesús, Artistic Director of the Teatro Colón and Best Man, who arrived in his long black American car.

And so, after the wedding party had assembled, after countless repetitions of "Hello!" and "So nice to see you again!" and "My, you've put on weight!" Damir went into the church, took his place and waited for his bride. The young groom, who not long before had been a nervous, shy, insecure, bewildered and sometimes stuttering Damir, remained nervous, shy and somewhat bewildered, but was less insecure, no longer stuttered and was indeed quite a happy Damir. It was in his eyes, thought his mother, in his smile and in his gracious and gentle ways. He was talking to the priest who would marry him to Isabella when a loud cheer was heard outside.

"Gigli! Gigli! Gigli!"

Beniamino waved and threw kisses at the crowd at the same time as he helped Isabella get out of the car. If someone had asked Beniamino how he felt at that moment, the great tenor would have raised his arms to the heavens and praised God, for he was the happiest, proudest father on the face of the earth.

Isabella was the spirit of light. Six beautiful little girls in white dresses with gold lace, and three pretty little boys dressed in blue and gold, each child the essence of innocence, appeared from the church. The little girls scattered rose petals before the bride and the little boys carried Isabella's train.

"Gigli! Gigli! Gigli!"

The dazzling sunlight cast its radiant halo upon Isabella, and the congregation stood while Verdi's exultant march from Aida filled the chamber. Finally, Isabella and Damir stood side by side, waiting for the moment when they would vow their love for one another.

While the wedding ceremony was going on inside, another limousine pulled up to the curb quietly, without anyone taking notice. El Jefe arrived with his bodyguard. They made their way through the crowd and into San Andrés, where they were forced to remain standing in the back.

In the front pew, Marija was visibly affected; so was Kati, although every so often she would glance at Cedric Fogstrand, hoping that one day, before too long, another wedding would take place. The Fritz was dabbing her eyes with a handkerchief. Elvira, on the other hand, who had known many dramatic moments in life, never allowed herself to display undue sentimentality—never, that is, until Father Macero Roca, a placid little man with big eyes, a small mouth and arms that seemed too big for the rest of his body, introduced Beniamino Gigli.

The Great Gigli was more nervous than he had ever been in his life. This was the most important moment in the life of his daughter, the daughter who was his reason for living. The Great Gigli walked to the altar, cleared his throat, and with a smile that betrayed his nerves said: "To my daughter Isabella and my new son, Damir." No sooner did he stop talking than the Great Gigli transported the assembly to the gates of heaven with "Ave Maria."

"Bravo Gigli!" came the shouts from outside. After three other musical selections, which included operatic favorites of the bride and groom, Beniamino stepped down from the altar, embraced Isabella and Damir, and the ceremony continued.

Father Roca beckoned the bride and groom, and said: "We are here today to witness Damir and Isabella join in holy matrimony."

Katarina finally broke down. She had tried to maintain a cool, detached demeanor, but now, as she saw Damir hold Isabella's hand, she remembered all the wonderful as well as the horrible moments they shared. The big brother she worshipped, now belonged to someone else. She was happy for Damir, yes, but she was also aware of her own most profound loss.

Marija held her hand tightly, as if to assert their unique bond. She also felt sorry for her husband, and wondered if Ante had made it to the church, after all. If she had been able to see him just then, she would have felt even greater pity for the Poglavnik. Completely disconnected from the love that imbued the ceremony, Ante Pavelić felt as wretched as when—ten years before, in another life—he had boarded a freighter en route to Argentina.

Damir could not take his eyes off Isabella, not even to look at the priest, who, at one point, called his name three times before giving up and calling the page to bring forth the red velvet cushion with the rings.

"Do you Damir take Isabella as your wife in sickness and in health, for better or worse?"

"Yes, of course I do," he said, earning an admonishing look from the priest.

"And do you Isabella, take Damir—"

"Yes."

The priest stopped, cleared his throat, decided it was useless to go on, ran through the essentials needed to make the wedding legitimate, and pronounced Damir and Isabella man and wife. "You may—do whatever you want to do, such as—why don't you kiss her now?" Father Roca shrugged and moved to one side.

Damir did, except, that to everyone's surprise, he did not kiss his new wife on the lips, or make any other such dramatic gesture. Instead, he held Isabella's face in his hands and gave her—on the cheek—the sweetest, purest kiss ever seen, then took her in his arms and lovingly embraced her. In one remarkable moment, he showed the world just how much, and in how many ways, he loved Isabella. She was not only his spouse, she was his closest friend. Later, they would exchange the passion of lovers, of husband and wife.

A chorus of children sang hallelujah or something like it, and friends and family gathered about to congratulate and kiss the bride and groom. Marija had to go and sit with Beniamino for a minute because the tenor would not stop laughing, singing and crying, and she was afraid that the strain of the wedding had finally taken its toll on the great tenor.

It was about ten minutes before Damir could pull Isabella away from the well-wishers, leading a procession of friends and family out of the church amidst applause, cheers and showers of rice. He did not see his father standing against the wall inside the door; the Poglavnik remained hidden in the shadows.

When the newly-weds at last exited the church, they found themselves going around shaking people's hands, embracing some, kissing a few and thanking everybody. The bells rang out and suddenly a thousand doves were released from behind the bell tower. White against the blue backdrop, they circled above the throng; a white winged swirl on its climb to happiness.

"Oh, Papa! Thank you!" Isabella and Damir lavished Beniamino with kisses and hugs. "Thank you for everything! Thank you for Isabella!" yelled Didi, in the commotion, when he saw his father leaving the church.

Ante hesitated, was about to step up to offer his congratulations, when, suddenly, from across the street, two men who had been standing behind a police barrier, slipped underneath, pulled out their revolvers, rushed forward, and attempted to assassinate the exiled President of the Independent Nation of Croatia.

Rubén returned fire, and, amid the terrifying fusillade, those that had come to witness the joyous celebration, ran hysterically for cover.

Caustic smoke and the stench of gunpowder underlined the horror. "No! No! No! God! Don't! No!" Damir darted frantic looks at his mother and sister; outraged, impotent to stop the carnage. Then, he screamed, fell to his knees, cradled Isabella in his arms for the last time, and allowed his tears to wash her blood from his lips.

PROPHECY

31

"Welcome, Eminence!" exclaimed Carelli, reaching out. "I always marvel when I visit you, my friend," said Pino getting out of the car, "how pure and sweet the air is out here."

"I know. The fresh air and the fragrance from my gardens, is why I would never consider moving to the city," said Carelli.

His Eminence Pino was followed by Cardinal Tomaso ("My dearest brother, it has been too long!"), who was followed by Cardinal Bailey ("My friend, how are you? It's been ages!"), who arrived just before Cardinal Numa ("You've lost weight, Eminence.").

Antonio Cardinal Carelli had invited his brothers to his villa forty-five minutes north of the city, a property that along with a substantial cache of gold, his family inherited from Maximilian Carelli, who in 1808, was rewarded by Napoleon, for helping to extinguish the insurrection against the invading French armies.

The two-story building with molded wood ceilings and pink marble floors stood in the midst of spacious gardens surrounded by woods teeming with forest creatures. The rustic interior was decorated not only with a sculpted frieze of garlands and an elaborate cornice, but with a splendid collection of Baroque art acquired by Maximilian's family that included works by Van Dyck, Caravaggio, Rubens, Vermeer and de La Tour.

For the last of the Carellis, maintaining a proper standard of comfort was not always easy and it was expensive. He employed a tall, dark, Spanish butler who answered to the name Rodrigo, a

Filipino valet, a French chef, three gardeners and four maids. The upkeep of the estate was paid for by the fortune his Eminence had inherited from his father, wealth that had made possible the red hat from Pope Leo XIV.

Dinner that evening was nothing short of magnificent. The poached salmon fillet was wonderful and the wine superb; the dessert was obscenely chocolaty and smooth, and the coffee was not to be believed. "You are a man who lives well, Eminence," said Numa, looking sideways at Carelli. "This brandy is wonderful," said Bailey.

"It is Duque de Alba," said Cardinal Carelli of the brandy.

Pino shrieked and giggled like a silly schoolgirl. "He was a horrible man!"

"But very Catholic," Tomaso pointed out.

"And they've named the best brandy in the world after him," observed Carelli.

At ten-thirty, the Eminences retired to the comfort of soft leather chairs—matching the rich paneling of the library—where they sat absorbing the heart-warming glow of the fireplace, every detail under the gracious supervision of an immense portrait of His Eminence (minus the hump) atop the mantelpiece.

Rodrigo the butler placed a large manila envelope on the ornate side table with a marble top, bowed, and left the room. The eminent host, then refilled the snifters, and said: "Dear brothers, have you ever met my secretary?"

The prelates exchanged looks and shook their heads.

"He was a student at St. Pius, you know, the school for altar boys," continued Carelli. "He was a classmate of our brother Ronnoco."

Pino took his nose out of the snifter and paid attention.

"According to Marcello, young Felix Ronnoco was kicked out of school by the rector—a Father Uncelli, I believe. A week later, Uncelli was transferred and Ronnoco was back in school." Carelli pulled several copies of a large black and white picture he shared with his guests. "Take a look at this," he added. "Marcello brought it to my attention. It is a group picture of his classmates at St. Pius X. The boy in the circle is our brother Ronnoco—in the back row. You notice that, unlike his classmates, he was not looking at the camera? Do you see? He is looking to the side—at the boy next to him. Is that a grin on young Ronnoco? It's clear he was elbowing his friend. Marcello does not remember the other boy's name, but he is sure it was the same kid that Father Uncelli ordered to move in with Marcello. Ah—there on the side, is the eagle-eyed rector himself. He is looking at young Ronnoco with distaste, don't you agree?"

"I take it you have a point to make?" said Tomaso, looking around for the brandy.

"I think that picture reveals more than it is supposed to. Oh, the precious, fleeting exuberance of altar boys," observed Carelli.

"You say the rector was transferred?" asked Numa.

"Relocated," offered Carelli.

"Dismissed," guessed Bailey.

Cardinal Carelli shrugged, and offered his guests Cuban cigars.

"What year was this?" asked Pino.

"Early sixties," returned Carelli. "I don't know about you, but I'd love to know what happened." He lit the long and pungent Havana that, along with the brandy, was as close to heaven as Cardinal Carelli would ever get.

"The rector stepped on the wrong toes, that's all. Our late brother Draganović was Ronnoco's—mentor," observed Pino placing a mischievous emphasis on mentor, "and Draganović was a man to be reckoned with."

"Even then?" Carelli's tone carried the inflection of naiveté.

"He was Pope Paul's man," said Numa.

"And he was arrogant, secretive, devious and had no regard for anyone except—Ronnoco, of course," added Bailey.

"Of course," echoed Carelli.

"And we know what that was about," added Pino.

"Hmm," this from Bailey.

"Leo was a tyrant and so is his successor," continued Pino.

"My dear brothers," said Tomaso, arching an eyebrow, "I am sure His Eminence did not invite us here to gossip about things we can't do anything about."

"No, I did not." Carelli puffed a few times on his cigar, sipped his brandy, and added: "I wanted to tell you of a curious visit I had the other day. A police Inspector—not very tall—called Picol." And his Eminence described in detail the full interview with the investigator.

"Oh, my! Can you imagine if the press gets wind of this? A priest murdered on orders from Pope Leo!" cried Numa. "It's a nightmare!"

"Worse!" asserted Pino.

"I think the question we should be asking ourselves is, is it true?" said Tomaso.

Carelli held his peace, admired the ethereal emanations from his mouth with distracted fascination, then said: "Do you remember the American children who professed the visit of the Blessed Mother, the little darlings that triggered Pope Leo's Crusade? Well, I called the archbishop of New Orleans and they confirmed that a Father O'Malley was the priest in La Place and he disappeared around the time of the pope's visit. It is possible that Father O'Malley knew the Apparition never happened and Leo would have none of it."

"He wanted his crusade," said Pino.

Carelli got up slowly and opened the French doors leading to the garden. "The worst thing about this awful mess is that I have no doubt it was Brother Ronnoco who put O'Malley on the plane to Rome." And Cardinal Carelli turned to face his guests.

"You're not suggesting—" began Numa, before his voice faltered.

"It is very possible, Brother, regardless of our personal feelings for those involved, that the man sitting on the apostolic throne is an accomplice to murder."

Tomaso put down his glass, stood up, and said: "We are committing a great injustice and I refuse to speculate on matters that can cause the Holy See irreparable harm. I know the Holy Father and what you suggest is simply not possible."

"Injustice?" Carelli was vehement. "Think about it! Murder, venality, corruption—it will destroy the Church!"

The ambulance arrived at the hospital run by the archdiocese, and Damir was placed in a private room, for observation.

"You can't go back to Bosnia. It's too dangerous—for you, and for the children," said Felix, standing bedside, as nuns and nurses cared for Damir.

"The children—" whispered Didi.

"I'll take care of them," said Felix. "Don't worry. You do need to get better. As soon as the doctors say you can leave, I'll send for you. I have a large apartment in Rome—where I grew up. I'd love for you to move in—we'll see each other every day. Would you like that?"

Didi smiled and nodded, as two nurses prepped him for tests. He took Felix's hand, and said: "You know who paid for the orphanage and everything in Bosnia? My sister. Do you know where she got the money?"

Felix shook his head.

"Draganović," said Damir. "I found the Poglavnik's hoard. Were you ever in the cave?"

Felix frowned, and said: "No, but I know about the gold."

"It was more than gold," said Damir, his eyes filling with tears.

"Please," said Felix, kissing Damir on the forehead. "Put that aside for the moment. I need you to get well. We have a lot to talk about."

Rostas looked out into the open. The dew glistened like drops of crystal beneath the thin layer of mist. The sun peered from the top of Mt. Vlašić and he felt the eternal tranquility of the mountains that made up his personal haven that not even war could disrupt, and made life bearable. For some reason, they—the people who sit in gray little rooms and decide the fate of others—forgot Rostas. He was not sure if anyone in town remembered that he had been a member of the Ustaša and a friend of the priest Draganović, and doubted anyone cared. The world, it seemed, had greater concerns and had left him alone, as Olga did, seven years earlier.

After becoming pope, Draganović never returned to Yugoslavia, and Felix had not visited the farm since Olga passed away. It was too long to be by yourself, too long to sit in a tavern until curfew.

He had the house to himself, of course, and the barn was empty now, the last sheep having died the year before. That was all right, though, he never liked tending sheep.

And so, there he was in a bright morning late in summer, just out of bed enjoying the view and wondering if he should boil water for tea, when he heard a strange rumbling from the other side of the range. The war that had brought so much suffering to Bosnia was still going on, but far away, and Rostas hoped the noise would do the same.

It did not. It became louder until the old man saw a tiny dot against the sun and it was a good five minutes before it turned into a helicopter, approaching slowly from the south, doing a quick fly over, before it disappeared for a moment behind the mountain, only to reappear suddenly, with every intention of landing twenty-five meters outside the front door.

"What the hell!" he yelled, running outside as fast as his legs allowed. That is when he saw the loading ramp open and the children, in the company of two dour looking women and Felix, leave the aircraft. "Kids!"

"Felix! Is that you? What is this?" cried Rostas.

"Time you had company," said Felix embracing his friend.

"Company?" said Rostas, alarmed.

The children had lined up in two rows next to the huge HH-3E.

"Colonel Dumitrana," said Felix, "this is Rostas. You landed in his front yard."

"Following orders, Holiness," replied Dumitrana, shaking hands with Rostas.

"Holiness!" said Rostas, catching his breath.

"Pope Leo is dead and—well, I'm afraid things have changed," returned Felix. "But don't worry, you call me what you've always called me, my dear friend. By the way, these are Sisters Anna and Sister Eunice—all the way from St. Pius."

"But—Felix, I mean—" blurted Rostas.

"Give me a second," urged Felix, turning to Sister Anna. "Please, have the children unload the clothes and food."

"Yes, Holiness," returned the nun.

"Things are going to get hectic around here, at least the first couple of days," said Felix, taking Rostas aside. "A construction crew from Travnik is coming in a few days. I'm turning the barn into a dorm and we're going to install solar panels so you can finally have electricity."

"Elec—! Felix, please—" began Rostas, following Felix into the house. "What—do you mean 'Holiness?' Who are these kids? What is going on?"

Pope Felix entered the living room and noticed that it was in awful shape. Rostas, he guessed, was too old to care. "Do you know that once I thought you were my father?" he added, facing his friend. "You were very kind to me—all those years before I went to Rome. I owe you the fond memories I have of this place. Don't worry. This is and will always be your home. But, in the same way that I came here long ago as an orphan, these children also need a place to call home. The sisters will look after them—and after you, if you allow it. They're not your typical nuns, so again, you have nothing to do but relax."

"You said Draganović—Pope Leo is dead?" asked Rostas, as if he could not believe the news.

Felix nodded.

Rostas dropped his arms to his side, and for a second Felix thought the old man was going to cry. He frowned, sadly cast his eyes to the ground then shook his head in disbelief.

"I am so disappointed," said Felix suddenly, the words spoken sadly. "I was nothing to Draganović."

"Why do you say that?"

"I was a tool, an instrument he used for his own gain, a puppet he manipulated to help him become pope and then to help him bully the Church to do his bidding. I loved him, Rostas, I was devoted to him. I never lied to him, never! I did everything he told me and I never betrayed my vows. But he—he lied to me." Felix shook his head. "I thought he loved me. He didn't. He used me, that's all." Felix sighed. "I was nothing to him. I was like another farm animal; one he branded with intolerance. He used me, Rostas, the same way he used everyone, including you and Olga."

"Me?"

"How many times did you risk your life for him? Do you have any idea what would have happened to you, to Olga, if the government had found out you were smuggling Pavelić's treasure out of the country?"

"Who told you that?" Rostas' color drained from his face.

"It must have taken you years to bring out of the cave and for Draganović to transfer it to Rome, piecemeal in his diplomatic pouch," added Felix.

"Are—are you sure he's dead?" asked a worried Rostas.

"Yes, Draganović is dead," answered Felix. "He was a sinful, wicked and despicable fanatic. You have no idea how evil he was," added the restless and very angry, disappointed Felix.

"That's not true," said Rostas.

Felix turned from the window and stared at his friend.

"I knew Draganović. I knew him better than most. We did a lot of things that were wrong, sure, and I'm not proud of that. I don't know if he was—proud, I mean—not that it makes a difference. The man is dead." Rostas paused, nodded slowly, and stared at his hands, resting on the table. "He was hard as nails, a fanatic, as you said. He was driven. You know he was tortured by the partisans, right? He was almost killed. I saw him when he got back from the hospital and let me tell you it was not pretty. I think—no, I'm sure he wanted to get even for what the Serbs did to him, but who wouldn't?" Rostas hesitated for a second before he continued. "I wouldn't be surprised if Draganović did some terrible things. I did, though I never killed anyone—at least I don't think I did. We were soldiers then, Felix, even Draganović. Oh, he might have worn a priest's collar, but he was a soldier, a soldier fighting everybody, the Reds, the Serbs, and the Muslims. Now, don't misunderstand me, I'm not saying we should justify murder because of what happened so long ago. No. But who is going to look after my family, my country, my Church if I don't—especially when I believe in my heart that unless we protect ourselves, we will be murdered? That's what Draganović felt would happen sooner or later. You say he was a liar? I guess—who knows? But he never lied to me. He always told me the truth, even—even when it was dangerous. A hypocrite? Never with me. Was he wicked and despicable? I am sure there are some who think so, with good reason, too." Rostas shook his head. "But I have news for you, Felix, no matter what you say, no matter what he was to others, and regardless of how you feel, Draganović loved you. He loved you more than anything or anyone in his life. You were the one person in the whole world who could make that man you call wicked and a hypocrite, smile because he was proud of you, of everything you did! You never heard him brag about you—of course not. I did. When he wrote to me, his letters were three pages long and only talked about you. You were his son, period. Before you went to Rome, those couple of years when you spent with us, he drove me crazy with telegrams and letters asking how you were. I had to go into town twice a week to call him just to let him know if there was anything you needed; if he could send you this or why I couldn't get you that, and did you have enough clothes, and to make sure I took you to see a dentist, and a doctor, and even—" Rostas laughed, and his eyes welled up, "—he even warned me never to spank you. That was not easy, you know. Look, you are a priest. You are supposed to forgive. Let it go—for your sake, and never again say he did not love you. That is just not true." Rostas seized Felix by the arm and led him to the cellar. "Come, I have something to show you."

There, Rostas removed a false brick from the wall behind a stack of firewood, then reached in and pulled out a stained paisley shawl. "You had this with you—that night when the Pavelićs brought you to the farm. We—Draganović and me—then had their driver take us back to the spot where you were found, by the road, not far from Komar. There were two dead bodies—"

Felix remembered Draganović telling him about the bodies.

"They had no papers on them—nothing. They were pretty mangled. We dug a deep hole—all three of us worked half the night—Draganović, the driver and me—and buried them in the woods," explained Rostas. "Draganović did not want to risk having them found, in case—"

"What?" interjected Felix, "—in case of what?"

Rostas sighed. "In case someone, by chance of course, made the connection between the men killed on the road and the Pavelićs; why he told me to get rid of that." Rostas pointed to the shawl. "It had nothing to do with you, Felix. You—you were an unexpected complication."

Felix stared at the stained shawl for a moment, and said: "Why keep it?"

Rostas shrugged. "I thought that you would want to know—sooner or later."

Felix returned upstairs and made sure Sisters Anna and Eunice had everything under control. Then, he went looking for

Colonel Dumitrana and found him in the helicopter, drinking coffee from a thermos bottle. "Why not go inside," he told the pilot. "Sister Anna will make you something to eat."

"Going somewhere, Holiness?" asked Dumitrana.

"I'll be back shortly," answered Felix.

"Before dark, I hope," returned Dumitrana.

"Colonel, you have no idea how grateful I am for everything you've done," added Felix.

"I'll remember that on my court-martial, Holiness," returned Dumitrana, smiling, as Felix V walked away.

Felix and Rostas reached Komar and found the compound where Enes' family had lived for generations. Hopefully they had survived the civil war. Noted Rostas: "Nothing has changed."

The Citroën slowly made its way down a dirt road leading to a group of cabins crudely built around a barren public square. It was, in its own way, a poor village whose half-naked children and livestock greeted strangers. "I think it's that one over there." Rostas pointed to a small shack with a thatched roof and a window on each side of the front door.

Two young boys about eight years old, had been kicking a ball back and forth when they saw the two men get out of the black car. One had light brown hair and a ruddy chubby face, while the other had very red, curly hair, was extremely pale and was full of freckles. Both boys were sweaty, barefoot and dressed in old clothes several sizes too large.

"Hey, kid," called Rostas, to the brown-hair boy. "Do you know Enes?"

"Maybe. Hey, Ady, what are you—? You're not Ady," said the boy, frowning.

"Who's Ady?" asked Felix.

"My uncle," interposed the red-head boy.

"You look just like him," said the other.

"Is he around? Do you know where he lives? Ady, I mean?" asked Felix.

"Or his family?" joined Rostas. "Find Enes—he'll know."

"Who are you?" asked the red-head.

Felix looked at Rostas, then turned to the boy, and said: "Father Felix Ronnoco."

"Uncle—there's a priest out here looking for you!" called out the red-head boy.

Hamdai Hadzimulić and his wife lived two doors down. Their son Adnan had come to visit when he heard someone outside calling his name. Ady, dressed in fatigues, grabbed his AK-47 and carefully looked out the window before daring to open the door. He saw his nephews with two men that looked familiar. "What do you want?" he asked, from inside.

Adnan had become a teacher before the war, had gotten married and moved to Sarajevo, when, in 1994 a mortar shell landed on a stall in a packed open-air market and killed sixty-eight people, including his wife. Traumatized, he barely escaped the siege of the capital, returned to Komar to look after his parents and shortly after, joined the militia.

"Young man," joined Rostas, "Your cousin Enes worked for me—up in the mountain some years back. Ask him!"

Ady did not have to ask anyone because he never forgot the humiliation suffered by his family at the hands of the priest Draganović. He still looked like Felix, except that the life of a poor peasant is full of scars and disappointments in ways that would never mark a pampered city boy.

Five minutes later, long enough for Ady to call his father and mother from the back room, Felix and Rostas walked in the house and saw Hamdai and Elma sitting across the room, with Ady standing behind them. The old couple looked remarkably well for their age, thought Felix, who apologized for arriving unannounced. He quickly alluded to their first encounter and without too much in ways of explanations or reasons, approached Elma, knelt at her side and placed the paisley shawl on her lap.

She looked at it for a moment and her eyes filled with tears. "My mother." Elma then took Felix's hand, and added: "Nermin, you came back."

Before soon, every cousin, nephew and niece—including Enes who had grown tall and fat—rushed to Hamdai's house to meet Nermin who, they were shocked to find out, was a priest.

Of course, the inevitable questions were asked and Rostas, recounted everything he knew about that day when Nermin vanished from a country road and a baby called Saša appeared at the Draganović farm.

"His name was—is Nermin," interrupted Ady. "Why Saša?"

Rostas shrugged, and said: "I think it is better if your Nermin—my Felix—explains that side of the story himself— later. However," and Rostas addressed Elma, "you say your late mother was found not far from here and that she apparently died of natural causes. My guess is—and I'm just speculating, of course—that the two fellows killed in the accident, came upon her after she died, found the baby, and because they were not from these parts, headed not to Komar, but in the opposite direction. That is when they were struck and killed by a car, in the middle of the night, in the middle of nowhere, outside Travnik."

"The priest—he knew," said Ady with a hint of bitterness.

Rostas shook his head. "I worked for Father Draganović, our late Pope Leo most of my life and it was as much a surprised to him when the baby showed up at his door, as it was for everyone else. Of course, Father Draganović could have placed him in an orphanage, in which case, well, I'm sure we would not be here today. Now, because of how Father Draganović—our late Pope Leo brought up the child—" and Rostas nodded towards Felix— "because our late Pope Leo instilled in him a sense of dignity and righteousness, your Nermin grew into a man of character who, immediately upon finding out what you've learned today, felt obligated to come to you, so that in some way that will certainly not satisfy anyone present, explain, make amends and perhaps re-establish the bond you shared many years ago. The rest is up to you."

Once, a little Serbian shepherd was murdered but returned to life as a child born to a Muslim couple. Fate, however, snatched the baby, placed him in Catholic hands, had him baptized in that faith and called him Felix Ronnoco; O'Connor spelled backwards. Serb-Muslim-Croat: a curious Balkan trinity.

32

Thick fog engulfed the Holy See and made landing a challenge for Colonel Dumitrana. Cardinal Tomaso and Father d'Stesi stood in the night air and watched the cumbersome helicopter gingerly touch down. Then, Pope Felix V climbed out, thanked the pilot one last time, and accompanied his advisor and secretary on a short,but brisk walk to the Apostolic Palace, while Tomaso described the mood of the Curia and the machinations playing behind closed doors, especially as it concerned the police investigation to the disappearance of an American priest.

Next morning, His Eminence Carelli arrived at the Apostolic Palace and found Pino and Tomaso waiting to meet the pope. "Ah—good morning, brothers."

Tomaso and Pino acknowledged his presence with a smile but did not say anything. If someone had taken Pino's blood pressure at that moment, His Eminence would have been hospitalized immediately.

Carelli, on the other hand, made himself comfortable and picked up a magazine when Father d'Stesi opened the door to the pope's study.

The red hats found His Holiness Felix V behind his desk. "Good morning, Holiness," said Tomaso, while the other two offered their obeisances.

The pope pushed back his chair, walked to the middle of the room, and said: "Brother Carelli—I understand you have something important to tell me?

Carelli, who had sat down the moment he entered the room, quickly got to his feet, and replied: "Indeed, Holiness, I do indeed."

"And what is that?" asked Felix.

Carelli glanced sideways to Pino and Tomaso, noticed that they were committed to self-reflection and not about to offer their blessings in any way, so he described how the Holy See was in danger of getting caught in a scandal that could cause irreparable harm to the Church.

"Contact our attorneys and tell them what you know. Of course, the Holy See will cooperate with the police inquiry, as long the investigation does not infringe on our sovereignty. Is that clear?" said Felix V.

Carelli frowned.

"Anything else?" asked the pope.

"But, Holiness—"

Felix stared impassively at Carelli and after a brief but uncomfortable pause, added: "Something else?"

Carelli, again appealed to his brothers (who seemed to hold their breaths), and with a degree of urgency in his voice and utmost humility revealed that the police, according to Inspector Picol, had found the body.

"And—?" said Felix V.

"What if it's true?" dared His Eminence.

Felix turned and was heading back to his desk, when he said: "What are you talking about?"

"What that man—Venavić claims?" returned Carelli.

"That is for the police to find out, isn't it? Now, I told you what I want done. Do it."

"But Holiness!" insisted Carelli.

"You have something to add, Brother?" shot back Felix V.

"I beg your pardon, Holiness, but how did Father O'Malley get to Rome?"

"Alitalia!" answered Felix V, annoyed. "You know, Brother, you have allowed your ambition to get the better of you. Tomaso, find another person—a more deserving servant of Christ, one that rose to his station by merit, not by the money spent buying our late Pope Leo's favor—a less impudent fellow to assume His Eminence's duties."

"Holiness!" protested Carelli, who had turned as red as his cap. "D'Stesi!"

Father d'Stesi appeared at the door and Cardinal Carelli was courteously escorted out of the study of the usurping, traitorous tyrant of the Holy See, while muttering nonsense between his teeth.

"Pino—" said Felix V, when Carelli had left the room.

Cardinal Pino looked up humbly, stood and faced the pope, expecting to be retired as well.

"The Institute of St. Jerome," said Felix, "shut it down. Kick everybody out and turn the building into a—into a library. Tomaso, please call that policeman—Inspector Picol—and tell him I would like a word with him."

"Yes, Holiness," replied Cardinal Tomaso.

"And I want you to be present at the meeting. And Tomaso—thank you."

Cardinal Tomaso nodded to the pope, who, with one look, let him understand he was grateful for his loyalty.

Finding himself alone again, Pope Felix V wrote a memo to the Curia, and included copies of the correspondence that, as bishop and representative of the Holy See in America, he had sent Pope Leo.

Early next morning, Cardinal Tomaso showed up in his study with Inspector Picol, who was surprised to meet a man so young destined for Peter's throne.

Said Felix V: "Thank you for coming, Inspector. Please, make yourself comfortable."

To which the policeman answered: "Holiness, it is my honor and a privilege to be in your presence and—I am grateful."

"Inspector," interposed Tomaso, "His Holiness has been informed of your inquest and is willing to answer and clarify any doubts—should you have any—regarding this very distasteful situation. Before he does, however, he would like you to read a memorandum he has prepared for the Curia that includes a detailed timeline of events that are pertinent to your inquiry. Since, the documents are confidential and cannot be copied, I suggest you follow Father d'Stesi to the next room, where you can sit and study them at leisure. Take your time. Rest assure that once you have had the chance to go over the papers, the Holy Father will be available to explain anything you don't understand."

Immediately, d'Stesi led Inspector Picol to the library, offered the detective coffee and almond cookies and left him alone. Less than thirty minutes later, Inspector Picol popped his head in the hall, called Father d'Stesi, and was returned to meet with Felix V.

"Any questions, Inspector?" asked Felix V.

"Is there anyone else at the Holy See you wish to talk to? Please have a seat," joined Cardinal Tomaso.

"No, Holiness—Your Grace," said Picol, looking from Pope Felix to Cardinal Tomaso. He followed with an obeisance, and said: "I do not wish to take more of your time. As you know, we found Father O'Malley's body—parts of it, anyway. The killer cut off the hands and the head. Given that many of the principal characters in this affair are no longer alive, I think it would be a waste of time and resources to pursue the matter further. Thank you very much for your cooperation. Have a nice day."

The princes of the Catholic Church arrived in twos and threes. Cardinal Carelli, although relieved of his obligations, arrived with Cardinal Pino. It was an occasion for all members of the Curia, many from around the world, to meet with Pope Felix V prior to the investiture. Most of the cardinals had never met the pontiff, although Cardinal Bailey's office had prepared a fine four-color brochure narrating the life and accomplishments of Felix V.

"Brother Pino, why don't we have an agenda? This is quite extraordinary." The complaint was issued by a thin red stick under a zucchetto at the very end of the line who was Archbishop of Pretoria.

"We don't have an agenda because His Holiness did not think it was appropriate. The Holy Father will arrive shortly and I'm sure he will explain everything." Pino wondered when.

"We should address the problems triggered by that ill-advised crusade of Pope Leo!" The suggestion was volunteered by a flat-faced prelate who did not bother to stand. His brothers reacted by making snide remarks and showing solemn frowns.

"That is important, yes," answered Pino, yawning.

"We are coming apart at the seams," said Eleuterio Cardinal Calderón, from Bogotá.

The cardinals mumbled, shuffled their feet and became restless. It was almost lunchtime.

Suddenly, the doors opened, and Pope Felix V walked in at a pace described by some as between a quickstep and a jog. He was followed closely by Father d'Stesi. Energy radiated from the pope, a vivacity of spirit, a sharpness of the senses that contrasted dramatically with the other men in the room. "Dear brothers," he began, after a quick look at the assembly, "it is time the Holy See use its resources to wage war against poverty, and illiteracy in a quest to eliminate ignorance and superstition. In that spirit, we must also engage with nations around the world, and do our share to help eradicate the illegal drug trade decimating our young, and the environmental damage created by man-made pollution that is destroying our planet." Felix took off his glasses, had a sip of water and continued. "These are lofty aims, many will feel threatened by our assertiveness, and will do anything to see that we fail. But we will not fail as we open our parochial schools to any child, free of charge and regardless of creed or ethnicity."

Jews, Protestants, Muslims, and—free! The emphasis was on "free." The word floated back and forth among the pope's audience like a soap bubble.

"We will contribute to the well-being of the communities where we live, and worship by paying property taxes, and, in keeping with our apostolic embrace, abrogate *Humanae Vitae,* except for abortion."

"Holiness! The sanctity of life!" cried half the men in red, leaving their chairs.

"We are not talking about the sanctity of life!" The pope raised his voice just enough to be heard over the protestations and cast a long and hard stare at the cardinals. "We are talking about contraception. Abortion is wrong, but contraception is not abortion. Contraception is the intentional prevention of impregnation. The key word is prevention. Who are we to tell a woman she should not avoid getting pregnant? It defies common sense. If we can do that, we might just as well argue that people should not inoculate themselves against disease, since inoculation is also a means of preventing a natural, and normal condition that affects everyone—getting sick." Pope Felix took a deep breath, one that Cardinal Pino thought was close to a sigh. "*Humanae Vitae* is flawed. You remember that our venerated Brother Pope Paul organized a group of experts to counsel him on the subject, only to end up discarding their advice. I think it is arrogant for men who have taken a vow of celibacy, men who know nothing or very little about bearing children, to tell a woman when she should or should not get pregnant. Let me ask you, dear brothers, who in this reverent group has ever seen a prophylactic?"

Well, the cardinals were not making snide remarks anymore, and they were not shuffling their feet or grumbling because they were hungry. They were stunned. Pope Felix V had just declared a revolution that would be felt by every man, woman and child on the face of the earth. The Church would turn away from Superstition, and embrace Reason.

☩

Hours later, feeling the jeweled, pointed miter on his head, Felix remembered one of the great minds of the Middle Ages, the Franciscan friar Roger Bacon, who, in the year 1271, wrote:

"The Holy See is torn by the deceit and fraud of unjust men. Pride reigns, covetousness burns, envy gnaws upon all; the Curia is disgraced. Let us see the prelates, how they run after money, neglect the care of souls, promote their nephews and other carnal friends, and crafty lawyers who ruin all by their counsel. The ancient philosophers, though without that quickening grace which makes men worthy of eternal life, lived beyond all comparison better than we, both in decency and in contempt of the world with all its delights and riches and honors, as all men may read in the works of Aristotle, Seneca, Tully, Avicenna, al-Farabi, Plato, Socrates and others; and so it was that they attained to the secrets of wisdom and found out all knowledge. But we Christians have discovered nothing worthy of those philosophers, nor can we even understand their wisdom; which ignorance of ours springs from this cause, that our morals are worse than theirs. There is no doubt whatever among wise men but that the Church must be purged ... "

Pope Felix V took longer than expected, although he managed to institute many of his reforms less than two years after his coronation. Many bishops complained, some protested. Felix allowed no dissent, and his opposition was quickly dealt with by expulsion, and early retirement.

At the dawn of a new millennia, with a little more gray at the temples and wearing reading glasses, Pope Felix V addressed the world from the loggia of Saint Peter's basilica. "In six days we begin another thousand years. We hope the new era becomes one of enlightenment, understanding and empathy, not of ignorance that leads to division, envy and mistrust. We beg forgiveness for the unprecedented bloodbaths of the Crusades, repent for the intolerant and murderous pursuits of the Holy Roman Inquisition, atone for our indifference to the suffering of millions of victims during the Second World War, and humbly, and without reservation lament the betrayal of our sacred trust and the violation of duty by reverend brothers. Amen."

Damir Pavelić never fully regained his health. He moved to the apartments at Via Penitenzia 26, in Trastevere, where his Saša, Pope Felix V, protected and cared for him until his death, in 1999.

As for the Holy Father, he found out from Elma that he had been born on the 14th of March, in 1947. That meant he would no longer have to explain that he was about eight, twelve, or fifty years old. Because he was almost twenty years younger than the youngest bishop or prince of the Church, His Holiness sat back, held fast to his reforms and allowed time to run its course. He never appointed another bishop, or created a cardinal. Spurred by universal education, science, and technology eroding the core of unfounded beliefs, some time at the end of the twenty-first century, the Italian government took over the Vatican City State, converted its territory to a national park, and its buildings to museums where they kept for posterity the treasures of one of the more colorful chapters in the history of the human race.

The End

www.ingramcontent.com/pod-product-compliance
Lightning Source LLC
Chambersburg PA
CBHW031332020726
47499CB00005B/1224